TOO SINFUL TO DENY

"You came back," she whispered.

"I couldn't stay away," was all he said in reply.

She stepped forward, then checked her progress. But her gaze was darkening and her breathing rapid, and Evan could no longer withstand this distance between them.

His lips covered hers and there was no more talking.

He expected resistance. There was none. Her mouth opened beneath his, kissing, biting, tasting. She seemed desperate for him, as he was for her. So he gave her what she wanted. Took what he wanted. And still he burned for more.

"We can't be caught kissing," she breathed against his cheek.

"I know."

But he didn't pull away.

And neither did she. . . .

Books by Erica Ridley

TOO WICKED TO KISS

TOO SINFUL TO DENY

Published by Kensington Publishing Corporation

Too Sinful to Deny

Erica Ridley

ZEBRA BOOKS
KENSINGTON PUBLISHING CORP.
http://www.kensingtonbooks.com

ACKNOWLEDGMENTS

A huge thank you goes to my editor John Scognamiglio for loving this book as much as I do, to my agent Lauren Abramo for being generally awesome, to my critique partners Darcy Burke, Lacey Kaye, and Janice Goodfellow for believing in this story right from the beginning.

Enormous hugs also go to several talented authors I'm proud to call my friends, who have provided support in uncountable ways: Diana Peterfreund, Karen Rose, C. L. Wilson, Elissa Wilds, Kimberly Llewellyn, and Eloisa James. I owe a huge debt of gratitude to my local RWA writing chapters as well—TARA, who put me on the path from "someday" to "today," and STAR, who allowed me to read the first draft's opening chapter at a critique session, way back when.

But the biggest thank you of all goes out to everyone who loves romance, who talks about their favorite authors, and who shares keeper-shelf books with friends or family. You are fabulous!

Prologue

February 4, 1814
London, England

Miss Susan Stanton muttered a most unladylike curse as yet more black snow slid down her ankle and into her already ruined boots. No matter. *Faster.* If Mother's watchdogs discovered her absence before she had gotten the merest glimpse of Freezeland Street, Susan's great escape would be for nothing.

It was unfair enough to be confined to one's quarters for months on end whilst living in the greatest city on earth, and quite another to be forced to do so during the most celebrated fête of the Season: the once-in-a-lifetime Frost Fair. (Technically twice in a lifetime, in her case, but as Susan was two years old the last time the Thames froze over, that occasion didn't signify.)

Dirty snowflakes streaked her spectacles, but Susan didn't bother to clean the lenses. Her gloves were too wet to do much good, and her muff would only leave bits of fur in its wake.

Susan glanced over her shoulder to make sure the driver waited for her as promised before she dashed across Blackfriars Bridge to what was left of the carnival below.

Running on snow-covered ice, however, involved a fair bit of sloshing and sliding, and Susan was forced to slow her pace or risk breaking her neck. Devil take it. How long before someone realized the caged bird had escaped? Thirty minutes? Twenty? Scarcely enough time to regain the town house before Mother arrived home, even if Susan gave up now and left posthaste.

But she was *so close.* Off-key music trilled from the gaudy tents. The elephants she'd read about were long gone, as well as the donkey rides and skittles, but the sharp wind still carried the garish laughter of the common folk and the pungent scent of fresh-brewed ale.

Five minutes. She could spare five quick minutes, just to see.

She paused at the foot of Blackfriars Bridge and gazed at the tattered tents still dotting the frozen river. Rot. There was no possibility of walking all the way to the designated Freezeland Street entrance in under half an hour, so she'd have to cut diagonally across the ice toward the tents. No more dallying.

But the instant Susan's boot touched the frozen river, her foot sank through the melting snow, touched the ice, and shot forward as if propelled by magnets, sending her lurching. After a few moments of windmilling her arms, she managed to transition from sliding on accident to sliding on purpose—that is, until the entire cacophony of color and sound tilted drunkenly before her eyes.

Cold, wet air scraped down Susan's throat as she gasped to see the ice breaking apart in jagged chunks. A terrible thunder filled the air. The river unfurled, rippling beneath the fragmented fair like a washwoman shaking crumbs from an old carpet. Far ahead, pie-men and toymakers alike abandoned their wagons in their mad scramble for the shore. The stench of the river's fetid breath blasted from its frozen cage. Susan whirled around to dash back to the safety of solid land.

The ice disintegrated beneath her feet.

Susan flailed her arms for purchase as her body plunged into the frigid Thames. A jagged hunk of thick ice intercepted her forearm with a sickening crack. Pain engulfed her. Susan's head went under. Hungry river water swept through her clothes, weighing her down, dragging her below.

She kicked with all her might and shot upward. The top of her head slammed against a floating sheet of ice with enough force to knock the spectacles from her face. Her thoughts turned sluggish. Her vision blurred.

Where was the churning slush she'd fallen through? Had the current swept her so far already? Fingernails bent backward as she clawed at the ice with one gloved hand. The other refused to respond to her commands, floating limp and heavy in the murk.

Her glove tore. Faster and faster, she scraped at the unforgiving ice until blood seeped from her raw fingers with every thudding heartbeat. Numbness, everywhere. Was she making progress? She couldn't see. Her boots were leaden; her luxurious fur a smothering blanket, her string of pearls a noose.

Where were the peddlers, the barmaids, the fiddlers? So dark underwater. So cold. She beat at the ice, tried to scream for help, gagged when her aching lungs filled with frigid river water. Strange faces peered at her from the darkest edges of her vision, then melted into shadow.

Her limbs began to fail. Even her fluttering heart beat slower and slower, until . . .

Nothing.

The tumultuous river no longer tugged at her useless arm. Her lungs no longer struggled against the waves of foul water. The unrelenting cold no longer permeated her every pore.

Strange lips sucked at Susan's mouth, drawing up putrid river water and forcing dry air into her lungs.

Her eyes flew open. People, everywhere. Not dozens, like before. Thousands. Many of them staring down at her from pale, misshapen faces. Some of them in the water, oblivious to her. And dry. How could they be dry underwater? Her vision greyed as they faded before her.

The lips returned, cold and clammy, and blew more foul air into her throat. Disgusting. She jerked her head to the side, stretched out her good arm, and reached for one of the strange dry people. Her hand floated through his chest and he blinked out of sight. Susan gasped, choked, vomited salt-water and algae. Her spinning head fell back hard, splintering a patch of ice.

Blackness again.

Chapter 1

March. The last of the plumed lords and ladies swooped into Town like crows feasting upon carrion. Susan had escaped both her splints and her bedchamber for the first time in six long, dark weeks—only to be bundled in the back of a black carriage and jettisoned into the vast void of nothingness beyond London borders.

To Bournemouth. *Bournemouth.* An infinitesimal "town" on a desolate stretch of coastline a million miles from home. Less than a hundred souls, the carriage driver had said. Spectacular. Thrice as many bodies had graced Susan's London come-out party four years ago, not counting the servants. Being banished from Town was the worst possible punishment Mother could've devised. Nothing could deaden the soul quite like the prospect of—

Moonseed Manor.

Susan's breath caught in her throat. Her mind emptied of its litany of complaints as her eyes struggled to equate the stark, colorless vista before her with "town of Bournemouth."

Dead, brown nothingness. Miles of it. A steep cliff jutted over black ocean. There, backlit with a smattering of fuzzy stars, a bone-white architectural monstrosity teetered impossibly close to the edge.

Moonseed Manor did not look like a place to live. Moonseed Manor looked like a place to die.

Not a single candle flickered in the windows. The carriage drew her ever closer, its wheels bouncing and slipping on sand and rocks. Susan's skin erupted in gooseflesh. She hugged herself, struck by an invasive chill much colder than the ocean breeze should cause.

The carriage stopped. The driver handed her out, then disappeared back into his perch, leaving her to make her presence known by herself. Very well. He could stay and mind the luggage while she summoned the help. Miss Susan Stanton was no shrinking violet. Although she wished for the hundredth time that her lady's maid (and frequent collaborator in the very schemes that had gotten Susan in trouble in the first place) hadn't been forbidden from accompanying her. She was well and truly exiled.

The back of her neck prickling with trepidation, Susan found herself curling trembling fingers around a thick brass knocker, the handle formed from the coil of a serpent about to strike. The resulting sound echoed in the eerie stillness, as if both the pale wood and the house itself were hollow and lifeless.

The door silently opened.

A scarecrow stood before her, all spindly limbs and jaundiced skin with a shock of straw-colored hair protruding at all angles above dark, cavernous eyes. The sharpness of his bones stretched his yellowed skin. His attire hung oddly on his frame, as though these clothes were not his own, but rather the castoffs of the true (and presumably human) butler.

"I . . . I . . ." Susan managed, before choking on an explanation she did not have.

She what? She was the twenty-year-old sole offspring of a loveless titled couple who had banished their ostracized disappointment of a daughter to the remotest corner of England rather than bear the sight of her? She nudged her spectacles up the bridge of her nose with the back of a gloved hand and forced what she hoped was a smile.

"My name is Miss Susan Stanton," she tried again, deciding to leave the explanation at that. Mother had written in advance, so what more need be said? "I'm afraid I was expected hours ago. Is Lady Beaune at home?"

"Always," the scarecrow rasped, after a brief pause. His sudden jagged-tooth smile unsettled Susan as surely as it must frighten the crows. "Come."

Susan slid a dozen hesitant steps into a long, narrow passage devoid of both portraiture and decoration before the oddity of his answer reverberated in her ears. *Always.* What did he mean by that, and why the secret smile? Once one entered Moonseed Manor, was one to be stuck there, entombed forevermore in a beachside crypt?

"P-perhaps I should alert my driver that your mistress is at home." She hastened forward to catch up to the scarecrow's long-limbed strides. "I have a shocking number of valises, and—"

"Don't worry," came the scarecrow's smoky rasp, once again accompanied by a grotesque slash of a smile. "He's being taken care of."

Normally, Susan would've bristled with outrage at the unprecedented effrontery of being interrupted by a servant. In this case, however, she was more concerned with the rented driver's continued well-being. She was not sure she wanted him "being taken care of." Shouldn't the butler have said her *trunks* would be taken care of? She glanced over her shoulder at the corridor now stretching endlessly behind them, and wondered whether she were safer inside these skeletal walls or out.

Susan didn't notice a narrow passageway intersecting the stark hall until the scarecrow disappeared within. She stood at the crossroads, hesitant to follow but even more nervous not to. After the briefest of pauses, she hurried to regain the scarecrow's side before losing him forever in the labyrinthine walls.

If he noticed her moment of indecision, he gave no sign. He made several quick turns, passing tall closed door after tall closed door, before finally making an abrupt stop at the dead end of an ill-lit corridor.

This door was open. Somewhat.

A candle flickered inside, but only succeeded in filling the room's interior with teeming shadows.

"Sir," the scarecrow rasped into the opening. "It's Miss Stanton. Your guest."

"Guest?" came a warm, smartly accented voice from somewhere within. The master of the house? No. "You were expecting guests at this hour, Ollie?"

Ollie? Susan echoed silently in her head. Lady Beaune's husband was named Jean-Louis. Perhaps she was about to meet a distant relation. A cousin would make a lovely ally.

"All guests arrive at this hour," a deep voice countered. "It's midnight."

Before Susan had a chance to parse that inexplicable response, the door swung fully open and a fairy-tale giant filled the entirety of the frame.

Her shoulders reached his hips. *His* shoulders reached the sides of the door frame and very nearly the top as well. His broad back hunched to allow his dark head to pass beneath the edge. Small black eyes glittered in an overlarge square face, his mouth hidden behind a beard the color of fresh tar. Arms that could crush tree trunks flexed at his sides. He did not offer his hand.

"Miss Stanton."

Although her name was more a statement than a question, Susan's well-trained spine dipped in an automatic curtsy as her mouth managed to stammer a simple "yes."

He did not bow in kind. Nor was it remotely possible he was a child of Lady Beaune. He was easily five-and-thirty. Had Papa's cousin remarried in the unknown years since

Mother had last spoken to this distant limb of the Stanton family tree? Did Mother *comprehend* where exactly she'd condemned her daughter? Or care?

"Move out of the way, oaf," came the cultured voice from before. "I must see this creature that travels alone and in dark of night to visit the likes of you."

Rather than move aside, the giant stepped forward, crowding Susan backward. Her shoulders scraped the wall opposite. Her hands clenched at her sides.

A new figure filled the door frame. Tall, but not impossibly so. Well-muscled, but not frighteningly so. As smartly tailored as any London dandy, but with an air of barely contained danger more suitable to the meanest streets where even footpads feared to tread. Alarmingly attractive despite the too-long chestnut hair and day's growth of dark stubble shadowing the line of his jaw.

"Mmm, I see." An amused grin toyed with his lips. "My pleasure."

He performed as perfect a bow as any Susan had ever encountered in a Town ballroom. Before her trembling legs could force an answering curtsy, the giant moved back into place, blocking the . . . gentleman? . . . from her view.

The giant's thick arms crossed over his barrel chest. "Carriage?"

"Gone," rasped the scarecrow.

Susan jumped. She'd forgotten his silent presence.

"Driver?"

The scarecrow's terrifying smile returned. "Taken care of."

Satisfaction glinted in the giant's eyes. Susan was positive panic was the only thing glinting in hers. Would she be "taken care of" next?

"Take her to the bone chamber."

Susan's heart stuttered to a stop until she realized the giant had said *Beaune* chamber, not *bone* chamber. Beaune, like Lady Beaune, her father's fourth cousin thrice removed, with whom her family clearly should have kept a much more detailed correspondence. Yet even with this correction firmly in mind, Susan couldn't help but doubt the Beaune chamber would remotely resemble the sumptuous Buckingham-quality guest quarters she'd hoped to find.

The scarecrow turned and headed down the hall without bothering to verify that Susan followed. He was wise not to worry. She had no intention of standing around under the giant's calculating gaze any longer than necessary.

Susan scrambled after the scarecrow without a single word of parting for her host—not that the giant seemed particularly concerned about adhering to social niceties—and rounded a corner just in time to see the scarecrow ascend a pale marble staircase she swore hadn't existed when they'd traveled this exact sequence of corridors moments before.

She hurried to his side before she got lost for good. "That . . . wasn't Lord Beaune."

A dry laugh crackled from his throat, accompanied by a sly glance from his dark, glittering eyes. "He seem dead? That's the new master of Moonseed Manor. It's to him you owe the roof over yer head tonight."

Dead. Her ears buzzed at the news. The news that Lady Beaune had been widowed and remarried was surprising enough. But the idea that Susan owed anything to anyone—much less her cousin's new husband—was intolerable. She had once been Society's princess! And would be again. Just as soon as she got back to London.

The wiry manservant led her through another complicated series of interconnected passageways. A lit sconce protruded from the middle of an otherwise unadorned passageway, as bleached and unremarkable as all the rest. Orange candlelight spilled from an open doorway, chasing their shadows behind them. Susan wished she could flee as easily.

"Your room," came the scarecrow's scratchy voice.

Susan nodded and stepped across the threshold. When

she turned to ask him directions to the dining areas and drawing rooms (and when she might hope to see the lady of the house), he was already gone.

She faced the cavernous chamber once more, doing her best to ignore the uneasy sensation of walking into a crypt. Although the room was as cold as any catacomb would be, a large canopied bed, not a casket, stood in the center. The shadowy figure next to the unlit fireplace had to be a maid provided to ensure Susan's comfort. Thank God. At least there was *some* hint of London sensibilities.

Susan stepped forward just as the cloaked figure swiveled without seeming to move her feet. Long white braids flanked a narrow face hollowed with hunger and despair. Age spots mottled her clawed hands and pale neck. An ornate crucifix hung from a long gold chain. Trembling fingers clutched the intricate charm to her thin chest. She did not appear to be starting a fire in the grate. She did not appear to be a maid at all.

"M-may I help you?" Susan asked.

The old woman did not answer.

Were there more sundry guests in this pharaoh's tomb of a manor? Was this one lost, confused, afraid? So was Susan, on all counts, but the least she could do was help this poor woman find her correct bedchamber.

Before she could so much as offer her hand, however, a sharp breeze rippled through the chamber. She shivered before she realized she could no longer feel the phantom breeze—although it continued to flutter the old woman's dark red cloak and unravel the braids from her hair.

In fact . . . the breeze began to unravel the old woman herself, ripping thread by red thread from her cloak like drops of blood disappearing in a pool of water. The wind tore long curling strands of white hair from her bowed head, then strips of flesh from her bones, until the only thing standing before Susan was the empty fire pit. The glittering crucifix fell onto the hardwood floor and disappeared from sight.

The chamber door slammed shut behind her with foundation-shaking force. Susan didn't have to try the handle to know she was trapped inside.

She wondered what else was locked inside with her.

Evan Bothwick swirled his untouched brandy, then tossed the liquid into the fire. He didn't jump backward as steam and sparks shot from the flames, giving the smoke a slightly sweeter air. For a moment, something akin to rancid fruit overpowered the more pungent peat. Neither odor, however, was what soured his stomach.

Empty glass dangling from his fingers, he faced his companion.

"I must know the truth."

Ollie's oversized frame hulked before the bar. "I don't know a damn thing. She's some London deb, here to repent the wickedness of her ways."

"Not about your houseguest, brute." Evan hurled his empty tumbler into the fire. The glass shattered on impact, but the smell of the smoke did not change. "I'm scarce interested in the blasted woman slamming doors abovestairs."

"Humph. You're always interested in women." Ollie poured a fresh glass of brandy and proffered it in one large paw.

Evan made a shooing motion to decline the offer, then watched in silent horror as his host downed the entirety in one swallow, like a shot of cheap whiskey. "I'm interested in wenches, not women, Ollie. Wenches are . . . perfect. Much easier to deal with."

Ollie swiped the back of his hand across his beard. "How could what's-her-name be any easier? She's upstairs. And no lock ever kept you out of somewhere you wished to be."

"Exactly. She's upstairs. Whereas if you pick the right wench, you never have to clap eyes on her again." Evan glanced at the fob in his waistcoat pocket. "Like I said . . . perfect."

Ollie's too-loud laughter filled the smoky room. "From what they're saying in town, you clapped more than your eyes on that scrumptious little Miss—"

"Let's just talk about Timothy, shall we? He and Red were meant to dock this time last week."

"Red ain't here, either."

"That's my *point*." Evan leaned back, his shoulder thudding against the mantel. "Timothy was the lead on that mission, and he's responsible enough to—"

Ollie shrugged. "Smugglers aren't responsible."

Evan's fingers twitched at his side. "Ollie, could you please be serious for a moment? If I had a pistol handy, I'd shoot you just for prevaricating."

"There you go. Now you're acting yourself again. Except for the 'please.'" Ollie turned back to the sideboard. "Sure you don't fancy another brandy?"

Evan glared at him. "Red's a useless corkbrain and always has been, but Timothy would've sent word if something went wrong."

"Then nothing went wrong. Just because you're a few years older doesn't mean you've got to mother the poor bastard. Perhaps the two of you are cut from the same cloth. Could be he's shacked up with a few bits o' fluff and is far too busy being naked to bother sending his brother love notes. He'll be home when he's had his fill."

Evan shook his head. "That doesn't sound like Timothy at all. He's irritatingly punctual, and you know it. Time's running out. Ship has to be seaworthy again by Friday, or heads will roll. Timothy does not need trouble with the captain."

"They'll be back." Ollie downed another shot of brandy. "Like you said—your brother's a responsible sort."

Evan's eyes narrowed. For a fellow water rat, Ollie was

far too cavalier about the disappearance of their ship and fellow crew. "If you know something, tell me. Now."

Ollie slammed his empty tumbler onto the sideboard. "I know you're becoming well annoying, that's what I know."

Their eyes locked for a long moment before Evan growled and turned toward the fire. He wished he'd taken that second brandy after all, just to have something to destroy. "We should've all gone together."

"It was a two-person job."

"Then I should've gone instead of that shit-for-brains Red."

"I believe Timothy asked you to do just that, but you were occupied with the bit o' muslin you met on the *last* job."

"Just for one night." Evan snatched his greatcoat from the arm of a wingback chair. He couldn't imagine what had possessed Ollie to wed. Or the type of woman that would want him. Evan himself couldn't handle the oaf's company for long stretches. The little blonde upstairs would soon regret whatever impulse had brought her so far from home . . . and wearing bejeweled Town finery into a den of smugglers. "That new guest of yours is certainly fancy. Hope she knows enough to lock her door."

"My house." Ollie lifted his empty brandy glass. "Nothin' locked to me."

At that, Evan stalked out of the study. Ollie could be so infuriating. Just because he'd been a member of the crew for several years—as opposed to Evan and Timothy's mere six months—Ollie took great delight in treating the two of them like imbeciles.

Irritatingly, the overgrown brute did have a point. Evan undoubtedly would've been late coming home if he'd been the one on the ship.

But it wasn't Evan on that ship. It was Timothy. Timothy, with the rule-following soul of a ledger-keeper. Timothy, who'd wanted to create charts and schedules for swabbing the deck and cleaning the privies, for Christ's sake. If the captain said to dock by Monday, Timothy would've docked on Sunday morning.

But he hadn't.

Evan let himself out of Moonseed Manor. Few stars lit the cloudy sky. He circled the perimeter of the house and crossed through the rock garden to the steep path plummeting down the sandy cliff to the beach below. Timothy would've—

Wait. What was that? There, smudged between the shore and the horizon. A ship, the hull rocking with black waves, the sails fluttering with the ocean's salty breath.

Evan scrambled down the narrow trail, his sure feet keeping him from tumbling to his death even as the sharp rocks and brambles scratched at his boots and clothes.

He leapt the last few feet and sprinted toward the ship. Running in boots on thick sand was never easy, but at least he wasn't doing so weighted down with large wooden crates. The craft shimmered in the distance, a mirage of sails and shadow. Why weren't the damn things helm-lashed? And why cast anchor so close to home? If Timothy didn't have the ship housed in the usual spot before day-break, half the town would see the flag from their breakfast windows.

Lungs burning from exertion, Evan slowed to a jog when he got close enough to realize there was no way to board the ship without swimming a fair bit out to it. The crew hadn't bothered to drop anchor within shouting distance.

Evan sighed and shucked his boots and greatcoat. Lucky that fashionable garments from illegal French silk were free for the taking—for him, anyway—or Evan might be a bit displeased about being forced to dive into frigid saltwater in his evening clothes.

Only one of his stockings remained by the time he reached the bower's cable. Soaking wet and shivering, he hauled himself up to the deck as quickly as possible. A ruined wardrobe he could forgive, but if he caught cold from dealing with his little brother's antics and became too ill to go on the next mission, Evan would have to seriously consider fratricide.

"Timothy!" he shouted as he leapt to the deck. His single stockinged foot shot forward every time the silk slid across puddles of water. Evan half-hopped, half-danced his way to a reasonably dry patch and jerked the offending garment free. "Timothy? Red? Where the devil are you two?"

And the rest of the crew, for that matter. A so-called two-person job still required the usual collection of riffraff in order to set sail—or return home. There was no cargo in sight, either. The anonymous local associate who sold their smuggled goods must have made short work of divesting the ship of its booty. The spoils were no doubt long gone, and the captain's share of the profits already in his pocket.

Damp footprints marked Evan's trajectory as he made his way through the empty ship, calling out crew-member names and pushing open doors. Timothy was no doubt at home before a fire. That straitlaced rotter would laugh himself silly if he knew his brother was dripping wet and clomping around deck barefoot.

Evan gave the wardroom door a halfhearted shove, convinced by now that he was the only one stupid enough to still be on board. He stepped inside the cramped quarters and jolted to a stop. *Damn* it.

For the second time that evening, his hands convulsed uselessly at his sides. He never had his pistols when he needed them. And neither, it seemed, did Timothy.

A pair of glassy eyes stared right through Evan. His brother's eyes. A trickle of dried blood seeped from the small black hole in Timothy's pale forehead, the thin red line separating his face into two ghostly halves. No point checking for a pulse. Evan crumpled to his knees. He lowered his head, no longer able to stare into the eyes that had once looked up to him as if he were a hero. He was no hero. He'd failed Timothy as a shipmate and as a brother. He should've been the one aboard the ship. The one to face whoever had attacked Timothy.

Evan forced himself to his feet. He would find whoever had stolen his brother's life. He'd catch the rotten son of a bitch, no matter who he was or where he'd slunk off to.

And then he'd kill him.

For the first time in her life, Susan Stanton did not sleep past noon. Witnessing a ghostly breeze rip an old woman into strips of nothing was not, as it turned out, conducive to a good night's rest. Although she considered herself a logical, fact-based, feet-firmly-on-the-ground sort, there was only one conclusion that could be drawn from such an event.

Moonseed Manor was haunted.

The only conclusion that could be drawn from *that* conclusion was that it was more imperative than ever that she return to London posthaste. She absolutely must be on the next carriage out of Bournemouth, even if she had to drive the horses herself.

Susan strode to the bell pull. Her hand had already curled around the cord when a chilling thought wriggled into her brain. Barely dawn. Would a *real* servant answer the call? Or a ghost? Her fingers dropped the cord as if the twine had branded her palm.

Perhaps—whilst she was having a steady series of firsts anyway—she should go ahead and dress herself.

Although she managed to remove her nightgown and don her shift with little incident, lacing stays and a morning gown proved quite impossible to do by oneself. Heart thudding, Susan gave the cursed bell pull a reluctant tug and sat down at a small escritoire in the corner to wait. After staring at a dusty pen-and-ink set for several moments, unlaced gown gaping open at her back, she decided to take this opportunity to inform her family of her impending return.

"Dear Mother," she scratched across the top of a yellowed sheet of parchment.

I was wrong. I do hate you more than you hate me.

"Moonseed Manor has proven to be an unacceptable choice for accommodation."

Not that I expect you care.

"While I have not spoken with Father's cousin—"

—because she's most likely DEAD—

"—I did meet the master of the house—"

—who could snap my neck as easily as a bird's—

"—and will inform him of my intent to return to London."

Unless I can manage to escape without him noticing.

"I have decided to leave at my earliest convenience, which happens to be within the hour. In fact, I shouldn't be surprised if I arrive on the heels of this very letter. In order to depart as expeditiously as possible, I shall leave my luggage behind and hire the first available—"

Bloody hell.

Susan stared at the ink drying before her. Mother hadn't exactly packed a purse full of money for her daughter's one-way trip to the edge of the world.

To be honest, the need for physical coin hadn't occurred to Susan either (not that she'd been given a voice in the let's-disown-our-daughter planning process), if only because credit was a given in London. Everyone knew her face and the Stanton name. If she wished for, say, an emerald necklace, she walked out of a store with an emerald necklace. Father would settle the accounts later. Well, he would've before the Incident that had gotten her locked in her bedchamber. Now what she needed was to marry a titled aristocrat with deep pockets and a generous soul. Not an easy feat, but at least *possible.* In London. Where her name meant something.

In Bournemouth, however . . .

Here, she had no limitless credit. Here she had nothing.

She could ask her parents for money, of course. But if they were aware she planned to use their funds in order to defy their wishes by returning home, the likelihood was high that no money would be forthcoming.

Bloody, bloody hell.

She would have to avoid all mention of just how disagreeable she found her exile. Best to act as normal as possible. She crumpled up her missive and began a new one.

"Dear Mother. Please send money. Yours, &c. Susan."

There. Her monthly allowance should arrive within the week. Assuming she chanced to survive that long in haunted Moonseed Manor.

The sound of the heavy door scratching across the hardwood floor sent gooseflesh rippling up Susan's arms. The figure that scampered inside made her gasp in horror. Was it terrible of her to *hope* this unfortunate creature wasn't among the living?

The—maid?—stood less than four feet tall. Her body was nothing more than a jumble of elbows and legs poking out from a shapeless brown sack of a dress. Her face (and neck and shoulders and chest) hid beneath a gravity-defying mass of tea-colored frizz. A cockeyed bonnet perched atop the whole.

How the tiny servant could locate the guest quarters with her face buried behind a waterfall of thick hair was beyond Susan's comprehension.

"Janey, mum." As if jerked by marionette strings, the entire collection of wild hair and bony limbs collapsed in an awkward curtsy. "At yer service."

Susan removed her spectacles, cleaned the lenses slowly and carefully in the folds of her skirt, then replaced her spectacles on her nose.

Janey was still there.

"Er, delightful," Susan said at last. Was this what became of those who stayed too long within these walls? No wonder Lady Beaune could no longer venture out-of-doors. "I was hoping you could post this letter and help me lace up my gown."

One of Janey's clawed hands shot out and snatched the folded parchment from the escritoire. The missive immediately disappeared into an unseen pocket.

"Quick as ye please, mum, and none the wiser."

What the dickens was that supposed to mean? Susan prepared to rise to her feet, but on second thought, remained seated. Although she wasn't much taller than the average Town deb, she towered over the spider-limbed lady's maid. Instead, she leaned forward in her chair to allow better access to the laces.

Despite being possessed of bones so thin they looked ready to snap at the slightest pressure, Janey's fingers made quick work of Susan's vestments. In fact, Susan could scarce breathe, so inhumanly tight were her stays. Mother would be beside herself to see her daughter exhibiting correct posture for once.

Thank God she wasn't here. Susan hated pleasing her mother.

She thanked Janey and sent her on her way before belatedly recalling she had no idea how to quit Moonseed Manor short of throwing herself from her second-floor window. No matter. She refused to sit in a cold, echoing bedchamber like a fairy-tale princess trapped atop a tower.

If she could escape her mother's watchdogs long enough to make her way to the Frost Fair (even if that particular incident resulted in being banished from the only city in which she'd ever lived), then surely she could find her way out of a lonely country house in the middle of nowhere.

Spine straight and shoulders thrust back with resolution— or possibly due to Janey's skill with laces—Susan pulled open the bedchamber door and stepped into the faded, lifeless hall.

Each passageway expanded endlessly before her. Myriad paths of pale nothingness.

Susan took a shallow breath. One of these identical corridors must lead to the spiral staircase. The spiral staircase led downstairs. And the downstairs antechamber led to freedom.

She just had to find it.

Several wrong turns later, Susan was forced to admit that at this point, she wouldn't be able to find her way back to the guest quarters. Nor had she stumbled upon the spiral staircase from the night before.

The upside, however, was that she now stood at the top of a very tall, very narrow, very non-spiral staircase that, while not being the precise staircase she'd hoped to encounter, still pointed in the desired direction. Down.

The only reason she was still hesitating at the top of said staircase instead of hurtling toward freedom was that at the bottom of the staircase, she could hear voices.

Male voices. Familiar voices. Angry voices.

Whenever Susan Stanton, undisputed queen of London gossip, found herself in a position where she could overhear conversation without being discovered herself—she didn't move a bloody muscle. Particularly when the first words to waft upstairs were:

"Dead, you say?"

That deep, disinterested voice belonged to the giant who'd married his way onto the Stanton family tree.

"Shot between the eyes."

And *that* rich, cultured voice had to belong to the dangerous "gentleman" from the night before. The one with the overlong chestnut hair, well-muscled figure, and devastating bow.

"Hm," came the giant's voice again. "That would do it."

"Don't provoke me, Ollie. I hate it when I have to kill friends."

"Have you got a weapon on you, then?"

"Never mind that." The smartly accented voice turned

low, suspicious. "A better question would be: Why don't you look surprised?"

"Of course I'm not surprised. You never have a weapon handy."

A growl ripped its way up the stairs. "As luck would have it, I do not require one in order to commit murder. Stop dancing around the subject. What do you know?"

"Nothing." Ice clinked, then sloshed. "Brandy?" Glass shattered against a wall. "I'll assume that's a no."

"*Dead,* Ollie. Dead."

"Right. My condolences."

"Your con—ah, will you look at that. I *do* have my pistol with me."

Dead silence.

If there was one thing Susan Stanton had learned as a result of the regrettable circumstance that had gotten her expelled from Polite Society the Season before, it was when to keep listening at keyholes and when to flee the premises.

This situation clearly called for the latter.

Unfortunately, as she could neither find her way to the original staircase nor back to her bedchamber, the stairs before her remained the only possibility of reaching the front door. They also provided the highest probability of passing madmen with loaded pistols.

"Easy, Bothwick. Killing me won't bring him back."

"But it'll damn well make me feel better."

A door slammed. Whatever the giant replied was too muffled to overhear. Good. She couldn't hear them; they couldn't see her.

The time to escape was now.

She hurried down the steps as fast as her booted feet could carry her and found herself in a spiderweb of colorless passageways identical to the unnavigable ones above-stairs. Now what?

A door banged open several feet ahead. The handsome gentleman she'd met the night before flew backward into the hall, crashed into the wall opposite, and landed in a crouched position. His pistol pointed straight ahead at the open doorway from whence he'd flown. The door immediately slammed shut behind him.

He didn't move for several long seconds, as if deciding whether to kick the door back open or to start shooting straight through it. To say his dress was in a state of disarray would be a gross understatement. But costume was a lesser concern than his propensity for indulging homicidal urges.

Just when Susan had come to the conclusion that she'd be better off sneaking back upstairs after all, the would-be murderer straightened, snapped seaweed-laden boots together with military precision, and marched down the hall in the opposite direction.

His sandy footprints had to be heading out. Which left her only two options: stay in—and hopelessly lost—on the other side of the giant's wall. Or follow the ill-clad, well-armed gentleman to freedom, and pray to the gods that he wouldn't discover her trailing behind.

She wavered.

Now that he was no longer in the company of someone he wished to kill, following someone this intriguing would be a close substitute to the rush of discovering juicy London scandal broth. Provided she stayed well hidden and far enough behind him that he not detect her presence.

The gentleman rounded a corner and disappeared from sight.

Decide, Susan. Decide right now.

She gathered up her skirts and dashed silently in his wake. After all, she'd been caught spying exactly once in the four fruitful years since her London come-out.

What were the chances lightning would strike twice?

Chapter 2

Damn it.

Bad enough the little blond houseguest's unexpected presence had thrown him enough off-kilter to miss taking a perfectly sound—if airborne—shot at Ollie's infuriating head. The chit was actually *following* him.

Bollocks the size of barges or incurably featherbrained? Possibly both.

Either way, she was now more than ever the exact sort of woman from which he should stay far, far away. He liked the freedom of leaving when he chose and going where he chose—without worrying about the possibility of anyone dogging his steps. Particularly a female.

Evan Bothwick tucked his pistol between his waistband and the small of his back before straightening his greatcoat and stepping outside into a brisk Bournemouth dawn. Usually the muted colors dancing in the waves' reflection brought him peace. Today the pale pink glow looked like so much blood seeping up from the dark horizon to stain the wounded sky.

Timothy, you jackass. If only you had *been in a brothel.*

The incongruous scent of jasmine clashed with the salty air. Unbelievable. Rather than stop when he quit the house, the chit had actually trailed him right out the door and into the Beaunes' rock garden.

Evan revised his initial opinion. Either Ollie's houseguest was a cloister-raised schoolgirl who'd somehow missed the significance of the pistol altercation, or she was looking for trouble. Why else would an attractive young woman follow an armed man into the half-lit outdoors?

Men could be dangerous. He should know. He was one of the bad ones.

Evan made his way down the steep, twisted path to the beach, jumping the final few feet, as was his custom. He glanced up in time to see the top of a blond head disappear from the edge.

Either she was smart enough to wait for him to walk away before continuing to pursue him, or she had enough common sense to give up altogether and go back inside the house.

He wasn't more than thirty yards farther down the beach when an avalanche of falling sand indicated a certain house-guest planned to break her neck tracking him to the shore. That answered the question, then. Smart . . . but without a lick of common sense. The deadliest combination of all. Just look at Timothy.

Evan sighed and turned back.

There was nobody else around to save her if she came tumbling headfirst off a fifty-foot cliff. He'd catch her, throttle her, and be on his way. Just a minor delay.

She was more than halfway down before she noticed his presence. Most likely because that particular path was a sui-cide risk even for those born and raised in the area, and her gaze had never strayed far from the next step. For some reason, however, she glanced at the beach . . . and saw him.

He hadn't moved. He was accustomed to holding per-fectly still for hours on end. Perhaps she'd caught *his* scent on the breeze, although Evan couldn't imagine he smelled like anything more the sea itself. Or perhaps it was his appearance that arrested her. His boots had stopped squishing, but he was still flecked with sand and seaweed.

In any case, the wide-eyed blonde had frozen on the jagged edge, arms outstretched for balance. If she stared at him instead of her feet for much longer, she really would hit the beach face-first. Of course, turning back around on a disintegrating sand path the width of a man's hand would prove its own unique challenge.

If her panicked expression was any indication, she was weighing those precise odds.

"Either go back or keep coming," Evan shouted at last, impatient to be on his way. "But it'd be much easier to catch you from twenty feet than fifty."

Her gaze never left his face, but she didn't respond.

She was a pretty thing, all right. Pretty annoying, yes, but also pretty attractive, if one's preference ran to slender blondes with high cheekbones and expensive taste in Parisian daywear. If it weren't for the bronze-rimmed spectacles and the rather precarious way she wobbled on the narrow path, she could easily pose for a fashion plate.

He hated that look.

Such women symbolized everything that was wrong with the world today. Shallow, pretentious, self-centered. Women whose thoughts—when they had them at all—were focused on the ensnaring of a husband and the spending of his money. Evan much preferred his bachelordom, thank you very much, and the ability to take his pleasure wherever he fancied, without fear of the parson's trap. The last thing he needed, at this or any moment, was to waste time with a London debutante.

Never mind that certain parts of his anatomy begged to differ.

"I probably won't bite," he called up, when it appeared she was willing to stand there all morning. The wind blew open her pelisse, molding her gown against her figure. He didn't bother pretending not to notice.

She stared back at him dubiously, arms still stretched wide for balance.

"Or shoot me?"

Evan paused to consider. Now that both options were on the table, he had to admit he was more enthusiastic about biting women than shooting them. Nibbling, rather. Why, there was one saucy wench he'd met one night off the coast of—

"If it takes *that* long to decide—"

"Oh, calm down." Evan held up his empty palms, to indicate peaceful intent. Not that he couldn't have a pistol aimed and fired in less than a second. Nibbling her, of course . . . now that would take some finesse. No. *Debutante,* he reminded himself. Hands off. "I promise neither to bite you nor to shoot you."

. . . Today. Unless she wanted it or deserved it. In that order.

She didn't move.

"I think," she said at last, "trusting you would be the height of naïveté."

Evan had to agree. He inclined his head. Perhaps she had a dose of common sense after all. Even he was starting not to trust himself. His mind was positive he should stay far, far away, but his body seemed to think a few minutes alone with hers would do them both quite nicely.

"Unfortunately," the dangerously comely blonde continued with a quick glance behind her, "at the moment, I seem to be without the luxury of choice."

"Pity." He held out his hand and flashed his most untrustworthy smile.

She scowled at him.

His smile widened.

"Scoundrel."

"You have no idea."

A frustrated sound escaped her lips. She glared at him,

wobbled, then cast her gaze skyward as if hoping for divine intervention.

Attractive as the untouchable debutante might be, Evan did not have time to waste. He debated walking off while she wasn't looking. Ungentlemanly, perhaps, but at least he could deliver himself from temptation.

"Look. I can't stand around waiting to see whether or not you fall to your death. Why don't you let me know if you're going to be heading one direction or the other, or if you're going to stand there all day? I've got things I really ought to be doing instead of—"

"What things? How can you have plans first thing in the morning? It's a wretched, ungodly hour. Where are you going? Are you meeting someone? On the *beach?*"

Evan stared at the blonde's suddenly animated face in disbelief. Here he was, undressing her in his mind, and she wanted to compose an interview? The only thing worse than a marriage-minded female was a *nosy* marriage-minded female. "I take it back. I hereby reserve the right to shoot you at will."

Her pink lips rounded. "But you promised—"

"Or nibble you." He flashed his hallmark can't-trust-me smile. "Whichever I prefer."

Her hands balled into fists. "I would never allow—Oh!"

A chunk of the sandy path dislodged beneath her feet, sending her arms flailing. She fell backward, still scrabbling for purchase on the crumbling slope. Instead of stabilizing, she slid down the side of the cliff on her rear, bringing most of the path with her.

"Christ," Evan muttered.

There went his shortcut. And here came his blonde.

Despite the torrent of sand raining into his eyes, he rushed forward, arms outstretched, and managed to intercept his erstwhile pursuer's rapid descent and swing her clear from the falling debris. He shook the sand from his hair. She clung to his neck, eyes squeezed shut. And she definitely smelled of jasmine.

"Next time," he murmured, "don't follow me."

Her eyes snapped open. Blue fire burned behind the spectacles.

Still holding her soft body tight in his arms, Evan backed up a few paces to scrutinize the beach. Empty. Thank God. He wouldn't want to be caught dead with a virginal London miss in his arms, regardless of the circumstances.

Even one who smelled like jasmine.

He glanced down at her. "At least you didn't scream."

"Why bother?" She relaxed her death grip. Slightly. "It never helps."

"Very true," he agreed. But why did Ms. Jasmine know it? When had screaming not helped a Society miss like her? This time, he gazed into her blue eyes looking for answers.

She wiggled in his arms. "You can put me down."

"I could," he agreed, irritated to realize he *was* still holding her. He was definitely going to put her down. Any second now. "But you've just gotten interesting."

"Oh, *now* I'm interesting? Arriving in the dead of night, secretly following you, sliding down a cliff on my sure-to-be-bruised derrière—all that is perfectly normal in your world? What the hell did I do in the past thirty seconds that's so bloody interesting?"

A mouth like that and the face of an angel. Evan held her a little closer. "This keeps getting better."

"Worse, you mean." She thrashed to break free from his hold. "Let me go."

His arms gripped her tighter. Woman had a death wish. "Flail around like that and you'll fall on your bruised arse again," he informed her. "You don't want that."

"You don't know what I want," she returned hotly, her entire body trembling.

He arched his brows and let his gaze travel down to her mouth. His body tightened. He should walk away. He should *run* away. He should at least stop staring at her lips. "I always know what women want."

She started thrashing again.

He let her fall.

"Ow!" She stared up at him, mouth agape.

"See?" He shoved his hands in his pockets so he wouldn't be tempted to pick her back up. "I knew you wanted down."

"You—you—*cretin*."

"And worse."

He turned and headed down the beach. He needed to get his mind off the softness of her body and back on the deadness of his brother's. The unbidden reminder caused a hitch in Evan's step. Fingers clenched, he strode faster. Despite their differences, his brother had always been his best friend. Evan would find whoever did this. And exact revenge.

"Wait. Wait! Where are you going?" The faint sound of footfalls on sand. "Can I come with you?"

No. Lord no. Not now, not ever. Why was she following him? He did not need this type of distraction, even on the blandest of days. No ties, no expectations, no *questions*.

She tugged at his sleeve. Unbelievable. All those warnings, and she still jogged at his side. What had he told Ollie just last night? Wenches were simple. Wenches were perfect. London ladies were an absolute mess.

Evan stopped. "Woman—"

"Stanton." She gave him a suspiciously sunny smile. "Miss Susan Stanton. So pleased to meet you. Oh, and thanks for saving me. Even if you were surly about it."

"It's my nature." He raked a long glance up and down her frame. Unfortunately, she hadn't gotten ugly in the past few minutes. If anything, the run gave her cheeks a healthy glow and the exertion made her breathing sound like she'd just been—No. He refused to let that image in his mind. For long. "Where are you from, Miss Stanton?"

"Mayfair. That is to say, London." She eyed him doubtfully. "Er . . . if you didn't know."

He chose not to respond to that comment. The only way to get rid of her would be to scare her off, once and for all. Because if she continued throwing herself in his arms . . . Well, what was a part-time smuggler to do? He couldn't be held responsible for the aftermath.

He let his gaze travel down her figure once more. Not quickly, surreptitiously, as he'd done before. Slowly. Enjoying the view. So she'd see him looking—and realize the danger she was in.

"In this 'Mayfair,'" he asked softly, "do unmarried young ladies trot off alone with respectable young gentlemen, much less conscienceless blackguards?"

Color leeched from her once-pink cheeks. Ah. His words made her as uncomfortable as his gaze. He smiled.

"N-not generally, no." She glanced behind them at the empty beach and sucked in a shaky breath.

"Know why that is, Miss Stanton?"

"I . . ." She retreated a step. Then two. Then three. "You weren't meant to notice me behind you."

He advanced. "Not notice a beautiful young lady all by her lonesome without a soul watching over her?" He allowed his meaning to sink in, then stepped forward, towering over her, and then lowered his mouth to her ear. "If I see you trailing me again, I promise to show you exactly what those conscienceless blackguards do when they catch unmarried young ladies unprotected and all alone."

He watched her.

She swallowed nervously, her eyes wide and her body frozen. Except for the pulse pounding wildly at her throat.

He framed her face with his hands, his ungloved fingers cradling her skull and sinking into the rich softness of her hair. He leaned back down until his mouth was a millimeter from her skin. The unshaven edge of his jawline brushed against the smooth curve of her cheek. She gasped.

"If that's what you fancy, Miss Stanton—to experience firsthand the despoiling of an innocent young lady caught very far from home—then I might have a little time to kill this morning after all."

She trembled. "I—I—"

"Shhh." He dragged his mouth to her ear. "I'm going to walk down the beach. If you'd like a taste of the kind of trouble I can provide, feel free to follow me again." He let his lips linger against her cheek. "If you don't, then I suggest you return to Moonseed Manor while I still find it amusing to allow you to do so."

In one fluid movement, he straightened, let go, and faced the opposite direction. Before his enflamed body could talk his brain out of behaving, he strode forward without a backward glance.

God help them both if she followed.

Susan turned and ran.

This was a nightmare. For the second time in her life, she'd been discovered whilst spying. Also for the second time in her life, a man's lips had touched her face. The first such occasion had been that return-to-life-from-drowning incident with the river water and the horrible algae. Since she'd been unconscious, the contact was unavoidable. What did she have to say for herself this time?

He'd caught her. Figuratively and then literally. But that was no excuse.

She could accept being an incompetent spy (although of course she wasn't). She could accept being stuck in Bournemouth a few more days until her money arrived. (Actually . . . no. That's why she'd kept following him—in the hopes he'd pass by a carriage she could rent or borrow or steal.)

But what she could not accept was the notion that Miss Susan Stanton, an accomplished young lady of unimpeachable marriageability, had behaved like a common slut.

Untenable. She would return to London, to a life of crowds and gaiety and comfort. She would marry a rich, titled aristocrat with a busy social schedule at the first available opportunity. To do so, she had to remain untouched and uncompromised. She knew this. She'd always known this. What the bloody hell had she been thinking, standing cheek-to-cheek with that—that—

She stopped dead.

There. Up ahead. An abandoned village.

Or, most likely, Bournemouth proper. But one could scarce tell the difference. Susan stared, eyes widening in horror. It was worse than she'd dreamed.

Boxlike structures sprang up along the pale curve of the shore like rotten teeth from a giant's jaw. Bone-white sand separated the ramshackle contraptions. The red of the rising sun gave the wooden exteriors a blood-tinted glow.

No posting-house in sight.

Even if she had a trunk full of gold, how the dickens was she supposed to get back to London with no posting-house from which to rent horses? How was one supposed to escape Bournemouth at all?

Is Miss Stanton at home? Always.

No.

She refused to be stuck here the rest of her life. She would not dally in this miserable hovel a moment longer than necessary. Her carriage driver (God rest his soul) had told her the closest town was Bath, some sixty miles northwest. No matter. She'd walk twice that far if that's what it took to hire a horse and get home.

Of course, with a sense of orientation as bad as hers, she probably *would* have to walk twice as far. At least she had new boots.

What was that, flickering up ahead? There, in the shadows between the giant's teeth. Another person! Thank God. Maybe he could direct her away from this macabre village and back to Moonseed Manor.

"Sir!" she shouted. "Sir, please!"

He glanced up as if as shocked to see her at the perimeter of the village. Or perhaps any inhabitant of this god-forsaken countryside would be startled to see a woman garbed in a proper morning dress. This simple creature had probably never even seen a mirror.

He was short, stocky, wide. Possessed of a bald pate and an unfortunate ginger-colored beard. He dressed in dull black boots spotted with muck. But he was human and a local, which meant he could help her get out of there.

"Sir!" she called again and sprinted in his direction. "Please!"

When he stepped into the sunlight, his dark form did not get any clearer. His bearded face was as smudged and indistinct as when still in shadow.

She really needed to take better care of her spectacles.

He darted toward her so rapidly his feet did not touch the sand. In fact—his legs did not seem to be moving at all. Yet he came ever closer, faster than should be possible.

Susan slowed down, worried they were about to collide.

He closed the distance between them.

She crossed her arms over her face and braced for impact. Her shadow trembled before her on the pink-hued sand.

He cast no shadow at all.

She glanced back up just in time for him to run right into her. Or rather . . . through her. Her lungs sucked in salty air as a cold, wet breeze blew straight through her bones. She whipped around to face the running man, her heart sputtering in her chest.

He was gone. The beach was empty. She was alone.

Susan swallowed and hugged herself tight, arms shaking. There was only one logical explanation for a man to vanish in the breeze after walking through her body. Moonseed Manor wasn't being haunted after all.

She was.

Chapter 3

Evan stared at the empty captain's chair in disbelief.

First, the pirate ship had mysteriously disappeared from shore and docked itself in the secret cave the crew used to load and unload cargo. Now that Evan had found the ship, Timothy's corpse had disappeared from the wardroom. How was he supposed to have a burial without a body? Evan made another slow round of the ship.

No little brother. No crew. No answers.

What the devil was he to do now? No sense going back to Ollie's. Whatever secrets that brute knew, he wasn't telling. Besides, he'd been standing right in front of Evan when the ship decided to mosey down the coast and anchor itself in the hidden cave.

Evan checked the current log. Empty. No—not empty. A missing page. *Damn* it.

He would have to talk to the captain. Except you didn't find the captain. The captain found you. And without his brother's body to back up his claims, what precisely was Evan going to say?

The boat was back. He was slated to sail this Friday. All four of them together—him, Timothy, Red, and Ollie. But they'd be missing one this time. Maybe even more than one, if Red and the rest of the crew weren't here either. Hell, *someone* had to have steered the damn thing and delivered all the cargo. Had to've been Red.

If that drunken sod had the slightest culpability in Timothy's death, Evan would kill him on sight. That'd leave just him and Ollie to do a four-person job . . . but vengeance would be well worth pulling a little extra weight. Even if the captain forced them to sail with a pair of scalawags from the other crew. Those cutthroat knaves took untrustworthiness to a hazardous level. Even for pirates.

First things first. Before he could take care of Timothy's killer, Evan had to discover the rotter's identity.

There was no chance of talking with the captain before midnight Friday when he arrived to give final orders to the crew. Red, however, was a more predictable sort. If he wasn't on the sea, he was in the nearest tavern. Evan headed to the gang-board sloping down to the rocky cave floor. After casting a final dark glance toward the frustratingly vacant wardroom, he disembarked the abandoned ship and strode back to Bournemouth.

At nine o'clock in the morning, the Shark's Tooth boasted half a dozen sundry customers in its rank, ill-lit interior.

Two of the town's drunkest inhabitants sat beside a barmaid who'd collapsed face-first onto a dirty round table. A flash of white at another man's throat indicated the town priest sipped his usual whiskey in the far corner.

The local magistrate leaned against the counter, murmuring to the barman. Probably trying to convince Sully not to open until noon from now on, so as to curb public drunkenness. God, how Evan hated self-righteous toadies who felt compelled to uphold the letter of the law. The magistrate was one of the worst.

Since Red wasn't part of this morning's mix, Evan would've turned around and left right then, had Sully not taken that moment to glance up and catch sight of him.

"Bothwick! Did you br—would you like a whiskey?"

Evan cringed inwardly. Drunken half-wit had been about

to ask if Evan had brought him a new supply of smuggled French brandy. Right in front of the magistrate. Christ. Sully'd get them both hung for treason.

"Got my own." Evan patted his chest where spare bullets, not a flask, filled his inside breast pocket.

The magistrate's focus remained on the bottles behind the bar.

"Good Lord." Sully leaned halfway over the counter. "What the hell happened to you?"

Sully's blurted words caused the magistrate to slowly turn around. Evan gritted his teeth but otherwise kept his expression impassive.

Gordon Forrester's holier-than-thou gaze took in Evan's sand-specked hair, salt-starched greatcoat, and stockingless legs. He was no doubt wracking his brain to think of a way to turn excessive dishabille into a gaol-worthy offense.

"Fell off a pier." Evan flashed Forrester a you-can't-touch-me smile and settled atop a barstool. "Seen Red lately?"

"Nah." Sully poured himself a whiskey. "Been about a week. Don't know where that good-for-nothing disappears to. Seems every time there's a new moon, he up and—"

"Maybe he's a werewolf," Evan interrupted. Lord have mercy. How had Sully not realized Red was part of Evan's crew, and therefore his actions ought to be secret from the magistrate? "Changed my mind. Give me one of those whiskeys." He turned toward Forrester. "How about you, Judge? Buy you a drink?"

The magistrate pushed away from the bar with a shake of his head. "Disgusting habit."

Of course it was. That's why Evan liked it. He downed his whiskey in one gulp.

Forrester stood and watched for one long, uncomfortable moment before tipping his hat at Sully and sauntering out the door.

"What bee's in his bonnet today?" Evan asked, shoving

his empty tumbler toward Sully. The smudged glass stuck to his fingers.

"Dunno. You're the one what chased him off."

Evan shrugged. "No bigger killjoy at a bar than a teetotaler. Why come in here if he's not going to drink?"

"Ain't the only one not drinking today." Sully jerked his head toward the rear of the tavern. "New gel's a peach to look at but hasn't spent a farthing."

Since when did any Bournemouth establishment have new customers?

Evan turned to take a closer look at what he'd thought was a barmaid passed out on a corner table. The light was too dim to make out much more than her silhouette, but he'd bet a barge full of French brandy he knew the identity of the mystery woman.

"Why have you been plying her with liquor if she's not paying?"

"Haven't. She came in all white-faced and trembling, and collapsed on the table herself. Been still as a corpse ever since."

If Evan hadn't already known London ladies were both incomprehensible and more trouble than they were worth, those words would've convinced him. Sure, he'd given her a hard time earlier today, but it hadn't been as bad as *that*.

"Two whiskeys."

Sully poured two healthy shots.

Evan carried them to the back table. The unsavories looming over the woman's slumped figure dispersed at the first glance at his expression. Good. He kicked a chair out from the table and plopped down beside her. Jasmine. Definitely his favorite houseguest.

"Thought I told you not to follow me."

Her head came up from the scarred table, but this time her eyes held no fire. They stared through him. As empty as Timothy's.

Evan hesitated. Something wasn't right. He snapped his gaze toward the drunks who'd just quit the table. There were women you could touch, and women you couldn't. They knew the difference as well as Evan did. If either of the fools had laid a finger on the misplaced debutante, he'd slice off their bollocks.

Both men's hands flew into the air, palms out. They shook their heads rapidly, as if reading his mind and disavowing all knowledge of Miss Stanton and her inexplicable condition. Fine.

"Drink."

He'd meant to share the whiskey with her—if he could goad her into trying it at all—but it now appeared a medical necessity. He pushed both glasses toward her.

Her hand shot forward and touched the back of his, then gripped it tight. Her fingertips were colder than the sea. At the contact, her lips trembled and her eyes filled with tears.

Damn it. He did not do crying females, but he especially did not do *publicly* crying females.

"Get up." He pulled her to her feet. "Let's get you out of here."

Despite his hand at her waist, she half-walked, half-stumbled to the door. Evan cast a murderous glare at the barman.

"I swear," Sully stammered nervously. "Nobody touched her and she didn't drink a bloody drop."

When she swayed on the single step and almost fell sideways into the sand, Evan sighed and swung her small body up and into his arms for the second time that morning. She clung to his neck and trembled. But this time, he doubted it was due to his touch. For now.

If he knew what was good for them both, he'd march her straight back to Moonseed Manor and lock her in her bedchamber himself.

Pale blue eyes watched him from behind tear-streaked spectacles. "Where are you taking me?"

Evan gave up. He never had been one for doing the right thing.

"My house."

* * *

Susan had never planned on being carried over a threshold by a man who by the light of day looked far more like a footpad than a gentleman.

Who knew how he'd managed to carry her a mile past the village and up a winding path to a surprisingly adequate two-story house perched in a hidden crevice in the side of the cliff. All right, perhaps his wide shoulders and strong arms and muscular frame accounted for that much. But as to why he'd bothered to help at all . . . the reasons for his altruism still remained a mystery.

She would be wise not to trust him. He'd concurred with that conclusion himself.

He deposited her on the softest-looking sofa in what could only be described as a sumptuous drawing room, and stepped back to give her a critical once-over.

"How's your arse?"

"Bruised." Susan rubbed at the gooseflesh covering her arms at the absence of his body heat. She'd actually forgotten the misadventure with the cliff . . . until he'd mentioned her backside. She chose not to be disagreeable. Much. "Thank you for inquiring."

Grains of sand speckled the carpet as he threw himself into an emerald-green wingback chair opposite her perch on the sofa. He stretched his legs out before him. Even in such unfathomable disarray, he cut an arresting figure. "You may be wondering why my stockings are missing and there's dried seaweed crumbling from my clothes."

"Er, not at all," Susan lied, intrigued despite herself. "One scarcely notices."

"Excellent." He gave her a satisfied smile. "Then I shan't bore you with the details."

Susan's jaw dropped to realize the insufferable man had just managed her. He *knew* she was dying to know the explanation, and purposefully broached the topic in such a way as to close it forever.

"Bore me," she tried anyway. She leaned forward, certain *here* was an excellent story.

His smile only broadened. "I couldn't possibly. I pride myself on my ability to not bore women. I prefer to keep them . . . entertained."

Her eyes narrowed. Once again, he had successfully changed the subject without overtly changing the subject. In fact, he was now expecting her to rejoin with something like, *Oh? And how do you plan to keep me entertained?* but she was too prudent to say something so leading. After four years of spying on the upper ten thousand, one got a fairly good idea of the sort of "entertainment" a couple alone might get up to.

She would only resort to such tomfoolery when she was back in London, safely ensconced in the arms of a titled gentleman about to find himself with a Stanton bride. Any flirtation, no matter how minor, with the man reclining in the chair opposite—devilishly handsome though he might be—could only get in the way of her goals. Susan *never* allowed anything to get in the way of her goals.

She tore her gaze from his and glanced about the drawing room. Frowning, she tried to reconcile the cozy nook awash in luxurious jewel tones and velvet-covered cushions with the unshaven reprobate lounging before her in wrinkled breeches and salt-hardened linen. She failed.

This had to be someone else's house. Someone well-bred and elegant. Someone who was going to come home, catch them inside, and kill them both.

Her gaze returned to the gentleman sprawled across from her. He was still watching her. One corner of his lips quirked up in a half-smile. The slight crinkle at the edge of his hazel eyes indicated he was laughing at her and trying not to show it.

Nobody laughed at Susan Stanton. Not the *ton* in their

fancy dress, and not this overgrown footpad in his water-shrunken breeches. If the proper owner of the house didn't show up and start shooting, she'd shove the blackguard off the cliff herself. Then again, he'd probably pull out his pistol and shoot her on the way down, and where would that leave her then?

Coming here was a very, very bad idea.

"Perhaps I should go," she suggested as brightly as possible, hoping to give the confident impression of a strong woman instead of a querulous victim-to-be. He'd made no bones about what he intended to do the next time they were alone. And she'd allowed herself to be carried to a location with a *bedchamber.* She sat up straight, ignoring the pain in her backside, and placed a firm palm on the arm of the sofa. "I do appreciate your hospitality."

He shrugged but made no move to ravish her. "I have no hospitality."

"Then why am I here?" she blurted, not trusting his intentions for a moment. Nor, truth be told, overly trusting her own. Susan gripped the arm of the sofa even tighter. Why wasn't she fleeing? She should escape while she still could. Yet for some reason, the sort of danger he exuded was more exciting than terrifying.

"I've been asking myself from the first." He rose and crossed the room to a small sideboard adorned with hand-blown glassware and a bottle of brandy. "You may leave whenever you like, Miss Stanton. But I won't be carrying you."

"Perfectly reasonable," she said, jerking her hands into her lap. "Once was enough for me, too."

"Twice," he corrected without turning around.

"Er . . . right."

To be honest, it had been a relief to melt into his arms, to relax in his strength and heat. He wasn't a ghost. He was real. Solid. A familiar face. That the face had belonged to a man capable of ruining her reputation just by being in the same room with her hadn't crossed her mind at that moment. Nothing had crossed her mind . . . but him. Warmth. Gratitude. Safety.

He reached into his vest pocket and laid a pistol atop the sideboard. Had she said *safety?* This was no doubt the very pistol with which he'd almost shot her host hours earlier! Susan had conveniently forgotten *that* little incident while she'd been busy being rescued.

He poured a glass of brandy. The golden liquid sparkled in a shaft of sunlight sneaking through the curtains. He sniffed the glass absently, swirled it, then held it in her direction.

She shook her head. She should go. Brandy was almost as boring as ratafia, and she had plenty of other concerns to attend to. Like removing herself from his company. And quitting Bournemouth altogether.

"Certain?" He sipped, closing his eyes in pleasure. "Delicious. It's French, you know. Quite expensive these days."

Quite illegal, if that were the case. Susan wavered. *Illicit* brandy wasn't boring. As tempted as she was to sample a bit, accepting drinks meant one ought to stay and drink them. And she was leaving. Now.

Brandy at his lips, he crossed the drawing room and retook his chair, looking for all the world relaxed and content. Despite the sand still dusting his muscled limbs.

The abandoned pistol was now closer to her than it was to him. That provided some measure of comfort, did it not? To be fair, she had no experience firing weapons of any kind. But at the very least, should he decide to go on a murderous rampage in his drawing room, traversing the length to fetch his pistol would give her advance notice as to his intention.

His clear gaze heated her face once more. "Not a drinker?"

"Not *staying,*" she countered primly. She sneaked a reassuring glance at the sideboard. The pistol was still there. As was the brandy.

"You didn't drink at the Shark's Tooth," he reminded her. "And you stayed there for a while."

"That was different. I was . . . having an unpleasant day." She choked on the understatement. She was being haunted. Good God. How was she supposed to ensnare a rich, titled gentleman whilst being *haunted?*

"Must be something in the water." He took another sip of brandy, but this time his eyes did not close in pleasure. He looked . . . anguished. But then he blinked, and the moment was gone. "I suppose you wish to talk about it?"

She snorted. (A habit she was truly endeavoring to break.) Talk about her inexplicable ability to see spirits? Never. Not to him. Not to anyone. The ghosts themselves were bad enough. Having others suspect such madness would ruin her life. She'd end up the subject of gossip instead of the one spreading it, and never make the kind of match she needed. "Absolutely not."

His eyebrows lifted. She'd surprised him, then, by not wishing to chat about her troubles. "Fair enough." He shrugged and returned his attention to his glass of brandy. "I'd have been feigning attention anyway."

Her mouth fell open. He was *so rude.* "Because I'm a woman?"

"Because whatever it is, I don't want to get involved."

Well, she scarce wished to be involved with him either. "Understandable. Well, I'm afraid I must be off. I do appreciate your many kindnesses this morning, Mr. . . . ."

Incredible. Twice in his arms and she didn't even know his name.

"Bothwick," he supplied helpfully. "Marquess of Gower, Earl of Huntington, Viscount Rockham."

"*What?*" There was no such—

"Just bamming you." His grin was infectious. "Evan Bothwick." He rose to his feet and held out his hand. "Plain old 'mister.'"

Right. Susan shook his hand without a word.

Now that he had a name and a personality—and no pistol—he was a little less frightening and a little more . . .

well, not *normal,* given the grains of sand caught in his hair
(although that was her fault) or the drinking habit (possibly
her fault as well) or the missing stockings (God only knew
whose fault that was). He seemed approachable. Uncouth,
but good-spirited. The sort who never had a problem
making friends.

What on earth was he doing in Bournemouth?

"Have you lived here long?" she found herself asking.

"Longer than you. What brings a proper London miss to
this great metropolis?"

Stalemate. Neither one of them was eager to discuss their
past. Susan leaned back in the sofa and regarded him beneath her lashes. She should go. She really should. But she
had never been able to resist a bit of gossip. Whenever
someone staunchly refused to elaborate more than three
words on a topic, something rife with scandal was surely
at its root. The best plan, she decided, was to keep him talking. He'd reveal himself naturally, during the course of conversation.

"I must admit," she said casually, "the 'city' ambience
here in Bournemouth isn't quite the same as back home."

"Oh?" He swirled his brandy glass and played along. "Is
something lacking?"

"It may be the case that I haven't explored the entire
shopping district yet," she allowed magnanimously, "but I
didn't seem to come across jewelers, frozen ices, modistes,
and the like. Nor did I notice any theaters, pleasure gardens,
racing tracks . . . not even a church."

"Which explains what our man of the cloth was doing in
Sully's tavern. Poor sap has nowhere else to be."

This gave Susan pause. "Does *anyone* here have somewhere to be?"

Something in her voice made him lean forward, elbows
on knees, and ask, "Truthfully?"

She nodded.

He appeared to ponder the question. "No."

That's what she was afraid of. She wasn't sure how long her parents expected her to remain here (they'd surely said "forever" out of anger) but Susan didn't intend to stay one more day.

"You may have noticed the beach," Mr. Bothwick continued slowly, appearing to give her question much thought. "But I wouldn't recommend bathing in it."

"Too cold?"

He plucked a piece of seaweed from his breeches. "I can assure you."

"And the neighboring cities?"

"We have neighboring cities?"

"Er . . . I was told Bath was somewhat nearby."

"A bit of a walk, wouldn't you say? In general, the locals stay local. About ten miles to the nearest posting-house."

Ten—Susan's lungs seized. When her parents' money finally arrived, she would have to beg a ride from one of the alleged persons with horses. *He* certainly didn't have any. The trail leading to his door scarcely allowed for a man on foot. And as he'd said, the locals preferred to stay local.

"Strong currents in the water." He gazed into his brandy. "Watch out for that if you do end up in the ocean for some reason. Cliffs are a bit dangerous around here, too. But I suppose you've figured that out for yourself."

"Er, yes." Susan shifted on the sofa cushion. "I did notice, thanks."

She had no wish to analyze whether her discomfort was due to her bruised derrière or the memory of wrapping her arms tight around his neck. Had she really clung to him in such abandon, chest to chest, her heart beating against his? And was her traitorous pulse truly speeding back up at the mere memory?

"—a few young ladies," he was saying now, obviously not plagued with memories of holding her in his arms. "Try the dress shop for that. You can talk fashion, I suppose, and see the new arrivals."

Susan doubted anything new had ever arrived in Bournemouth. "Where—"

"It's the only dress shop," he assured her, a wry smile at his lips. "You'll find it."

She doubted it. She still got lost in her Mayfair town house. "Would . . . would you walk me there now? I have a tendency to get turned around."

He rubbed his chin, looking at her as if he couldn't decide whether accompanying her would be a good idea or a ghastly one. Why? Was he afraid he would find her in his arms once again? Or that he wouldn't?

"All right," he said at last. "But I won't stay. I have to find a missing person."

"A missing person?" Susan leaned forward. How romantic! This explained his mercurial moods. And why he was equally averse to being sighted along with Susan. "Who is she? Where do you think she went? Why do you think she left?"

"Not a she." He drained his brandy. "And I doubt he had much choice in the matter. He's dead."

"You lost a dead person?" she echoed, fingers gripping her knees in horror.

His face hardened and his eyes sparked with simmering fury. "To be honest, I rather suspect somebody stole him from me."

"You . . ." Whatever she was going to say died on her tongue.

Susan leapt to her feet. What the bloody hell had she been *thinking,* whiling away the morning with this madman as if he'd invited her over for biscuits and tea? He carried a *pistol.* And misplaced *dead people.* (Of which she was seeing entirely too many as of late.) She fled from the elegant drawing room as if it had caught fire around her. How many times had gossip-seeking gotten her into trouble? How many times had she promised herself "never again"?

When did she plan to start keeping those promises—once she was dead?

Chapter 4

The dress shop was the last of the rotten wooden cubes jutting up along the bone-white shore. A long-ago fire had charred the lilting roof, adding the impression of a festering cavity to the illusion of giant's teeth. The faint smell of smoke still whispered beneath the salt of the frothing ocean. When the crooked door listed open on rusted hinges, Susan half-expected a nursery-tale witch to emerge from within, broomstick in hand.

She was not disappointed.

A pale young woman swung a spindly black parasol in place of a broom, its broken spines no doubt the cause of her tattered grey skirts' shredded appearance. Strands of flyaway red hair snaked across her face and neck. Wild eyes swept their gaze up and down the empty shoreline. Then she paused, ear to the cliff, as if anticipating an unwanted arrival. After a moment, she spun around, crimson pelisse rippling in the breeze, and closed the door behind her.

Susan shivered. Whatever sort of cabal gathered beneath the scorched rafters of the dress shop, Susan was certain she'd best not interrupt. Even if that meant spending the next eight hours trying to discover a usable path back to Moonseed Manor on her own.

She had just decided to brave the cliff's face alone when

she caught sight of someone skulking in the shadows behind one of the shuttered shops.

The scarecrow.

Were it not for his shock of straw hair catching the occasional ray of morning sun from the overcast sky, she might not have noticed his presence. As it was, she definitely did not wish for him to notice her. Although he undoubtedly knew how to return to Moonseed Manor, he did not appear to be en route to that locale. He appeared to be digging beneath the sand.

His jagged slash of a smile flashed grotesquely across his uneven face each time his shovel struck the earth. His eyes slid side to side in their sockets as he shot furtive glances over his shoulder as if expecting to see a Jolly Roger fluttering above the watery horizon. He raked his gaze around the entire perimeter of the village.

And saw her.

When his eyes locked with hers, Susan couldn't prevent a gasp from strangling in her throat.

The scarecrow's ragged-tooth smile disappeared into a thin line. His fingers flexed, then tightened around the shovel. Without bothering to refill the hole—no matter why he'd dug one to start with—he swung the sharp metal base over one bony shoulder like a deadly infantryman poising his bayonet. Then he stepped toward her.

She could run. But not fast and not far, and she hadn't the slightest clue where to run *to* that would possibly offer shelter from a homicidal butler who knew every grain of salt in this godforsaken village. Yet staying out in the open, alone, had ceased to be an option that ensured survival.

He crept closer. His jerky limbs gave his gait a disjointed rhythm, but the steel glinting behind his head lent him an air of imminent danger.

She needed to hide amongst people. Living people. *Now.* Before she had a chance to change her mind, Susan did the only thing she could.

She bolted into the dress shop.

Thick curtains blocked the sun. A flickering candelabrum illuminated the dank interior, casting a hellish orange glow over the two women hunched together between rows of dark, flowing silk. The witch stood mostly in shadow, the tip of her parasol digging into the floor next to her feet. She spoke in hushed tones to a porcelain doll of a woman with strawberry-blond locks and a beautiful lace-trimmed gown.

Both ceased talking at the hollow click of the door. They turned.

Two pairs of suspicious eyes glinted at Susan. The tiny flames from tarnished candelabra sent shadows scurrying across their faces. Susan hesitated, but could not flee. She knew what lurked, shovel in hand, on the other side of these walls.

"Will you look at that," the witch murmured without straightening her hunched spine. "A customer."

"Fresh blood." A terrible smile formed in the porcelain doll's perfect face.

They broke their tête-à-tête and advanced toward Susan. The porcelain doll's steps were as silent and sure as a prima ballerina flying across a London stage. The tip of the witch's closed parasol scraped across the hardwood floor like a sword hanging free from its scabbard.

The door creaked open behind Susan, sending a gust of salty air swirling through the room. Layers of silk fluttered with the chill. Neither the witch nor the porcelain doll halted their approach. Footsteps sounded in the doorway behind Susan. A shadow fell across the floor.

She turned to face the scarecrow.

He wasn't there.

Instead, a man of no more than thirty years stood silhouetted in the doorway, his body backlit by the morning sun and his features cast in shadow. He was nearly as tall as Mr. Bothwick, if a bit less muscular. Strands of golden hair danced between the sunlight and the breeze. He stepped forward. The door swung shut behind him.

"Mr. Forrester," the two women behind Susan breathed simultaneously.

"Ladies." He bowed. "Good morning."

Susan blinked. A *real* gentleman?

His gaze met hers. "I came to see the two prettiest young ladies in Bournemouth, and must say I'm delighted to discover a third in your midst."

Candlelight lit Mr. Forrester's face, exposing angel-blue eyes and a boyish smile beneath his head of golden curls. Blues and reds lent his attire the classic air of a Rubens portrait. He reached for Susan's trembling hand, dipped, and pressed a kiss against the back of her gloved fingers.

An awkward silence wafted amongst the shadows.

"M-Miss Susan Stanton," she stammered when she realized no one else would be able to make the introduction for her. Had she mentioned she *hated* not being in London?

"Gordon Forrester." He rose to his feet before releasing her hand. "Delighted to meet you." He inclined his head, then moved past her to buss the other ladies' cheeks without another word.

Dismissed so easily?

Susan stared after him in shock. That had to go on record as the shortest conversation she'd ever held with a gentleman. The sharks that swam up to her in London ballrooms smelled Stanton money in the water and scarcely let her have a moment alone to visit the retiring room. The ones who approached her outside the ballroom walls—well, those fancied an intimacy Susan had sworn never to grant any man unworthy of being her husband. But none had ever *dismissed* her.

And for women such as these!

She stared, arms crossed beneath her bodice, as the porcelain doll performed a perfect pirouette to show off her fashionable gown (and no doubt the ankles beneath). A blush as deep a red as her flyaway hair stole up the witch's pale cheeks as she curtsied behind her closed parasol. Neither one of *them* had bothered to introduce themselves.

Susan's jaw clenched. In London, she knew every face worth knowing and they all knew her. In London, hers were the cheeks being bussed by this viscount or that countess. In London, a thick ring of admirers stayed well within her orbit, eager to hear whatever words might fall next from her lips. But she was in Bournemouth.

Well, while she was stuck here, she'd show these "ladies" how quickly a Stanton could surpass their supposed popularity. Father's escape money should arrive within the week, but Susan doubted she required half that long to have the town salivating for her company. After all, she was queen of the world's one irresistible sweet: gossip.

First, however, she had to make her presence felt. She straightened her glasses and stepped forward. Mr. Forrester glanced up, but instead of smiling at her as all men did, his cherubic brow furrowed in a frown.

"I keep feeling we've met before, Miss Stanton. Have you been in Bournemouth long?"

"I'm afraid I arrived last night."

The witch leaned forward on her parasol, her pale white fingers gripping the ebony handle. "Do you drink, Miss Stanton?"

She shook her head. "I do not."

"What a relief," the porcelain doll cooed with false sweetness. "We were afraid you and an unfortunate blond girl who collapsed this morning in Sully's tavern might have been one and the same."

Susan's head swam. They'd been gossiping. About *her.* And it was true! (If not for the reasons they assumed.)

Mr. Forrester's lips rounded into an *O.* "*That's* where I saw you."

Her face flamed.

The two ladies tittered. They'd known precisely who she

was—most likely from the moment she'd stepped into the shop—and had chosen this method of revealing their knowledge so as to provide maximum humiliation before a handsome gentleman.

Susan knew this trick well. She had just never been on the receiving end of it.

No matter. She would rise above. So long as her name was never again linked to gossip-worthy behavior, talk would quickly die down. In the meantime, she would simply need to appear the veriest paragon of respectability and normalcy.

She opened her mouth to reply before she realized they'd moved on without bothering to wait for her response. They stood in a closed circle, heads bowed together. Short bursts of laughter punctuated their murmured conversation.

Susan stood off to the side. *Cut.*

Harrumph. The least these country bumpkins could do was provide a newcomer clear instructions on how best to return to her lodgings. Susan stepped forward again, piqued enough at their sophomoric behavior to interrupt their conversation, despite the rudeness of such an act.

Before she could do so, however, a fifth joined their midst. He entered by floating through the far wall.

The bearded ghost.

There was nowhere to run. The scarecrow could still be outside, waiting for her with his shovel poised behind his head. Even if the scarecrow had crept back home, mere walls would not prevent the bearded ghost from pursuing her.

Of course, whiling away the morning with *this* trio was no more palatable.

What she needed to do was get directions back to Moonseed Manor without letting the presence of a ghost in the room cause her to appear distracted (or insane).

"Ho there!" the bearded ghost exclaimed, catching sight of her. He ran a meaty hand over his bald pate and stared at her expectantly. "Don't you recognize me?"

She didn't answer.

He hopped up and down in front of her. Careful not to touch her, he waved his hands in front of her face.

Susan ignored him as best she could and tried to determine the best way to catch the others' attention without flat-out interrupting.

"When did you see him last?" Mr. Forrester was asking.

The porcelain doll rolled her eyes. "One doesn't keep tabs on one's grown brother."

"Especially a will-o'-the-wisp like Joshua." The witch picked at the spines of her umbrella. "He's here. He's gone. And then you wonder if he was ever here at all."

"Excuse me," Susan put in when they lapsed into thoughtful silence. "Could one of you direct me to Moonseed Manor?"

"It's at the top of the cliff," the witch said, pointing out the obvious.

"Yes, I know, but—"

"Didn't you *come* from there?" asked the porcelain doll with an equally amused expression.

"Yes, but I—"

"The easiest way," said Mr. Forrester in what he probably thought was a helpful tone, "might be to go back up along the same path you came down."

"And you know, I considered that," Susan said through clenched teeth. "But as the entire path slid down the cliff behind me, I suspect an alternate route back to the top might be in order."

The porcelain doll choked on a giggle. "You didn't take—"

"She did," crowed the witch. "She must have."

"Bothwick's the only one reckless enough to cut down that way." The porcelain doll shook her perfect head. "Next time I see him, I'll—"

"I thought you weren't seeing him anymore." The witch's eyes lit with mischief.

"That doesn't mean I won't *see* him," the porcelain doll

snapped. "It's not as though there's an overabundance of crowds to lose oneself in around here."

"So . . ." Susan prompted. "The path I *should* be taking is . . ."

The women ignored her and continued bickering.

She affixed her desperate gaze on the cherubic Mr. Forrester.

He smiled apologetically. "I'd take you myself if I knew the area."

The bearded ghost leapt between them and began gesticulating wildly, pointing at himself, then the others, then back to himself.

Susan pushed up her spectacles and tried to focus on Mr. Forrester. "You're not from around here, then?"

"I am from *around* here, but not from Bournemouth itself."

"Mr. Forrester is our local magistrate," said the porcelain doll, peering up at him from beneath lowered lashes.

"He serves several towns in the area," added the witch, looking very much as though she'd like to stab her fawning companion with her parasol. "He's not just ours."

Mr. Forrester appeared charmingly uncomfortable at the interplay beside him. "I live in Christchurch. I try to visit Bournemouth at least once or twice a month to see if my services are required."

The ghost was once again doing everything but handstands before her face, but Susan's mind was busy processing this new information.

One couldn't ask for a more upstanding citizen than a magistrate. And *she* couldn't ask for a better acquaintance than one with a horse. It was now more imperative than ever that Mr. Forrester think only the best of her. Although he didn't know it yet, he was her ticket to the nearest posting-house the moment her allowance arrived.

"I understand." Susan gave him her most gracious *ton* smile. "Don't worry—I'm sure I'll find my way back home."

He cocked his head, then turned away from the other ladies and proffered his arm. "Tell you what, Miss Stanton. If two heads are better than one, what do you say we give it a go together? If we can't find our way to Moonseed Manor, I'm sure I for one will at least have had the pleasure of enjoyable company."

If the porcelain doll's expression was any indication of her emotional state, her beautiful face was about to shatter into a thousand tiny pieces.

"Oh, bother," she pouted. "She can find it. It's not that hard."

The witch gestured toward the door with the handle of her parasol. "Behind the big pile of driftwood a dozen yards from the shop, there's a footpath leading up the cliff. It's flat and winding, so it often takes the better part of an hour, but it'll get you there."

Mr. Forrester beamed. "There you have it. Aren't these ladies too helpful?"

"Indeed," Susan said.

"Perhaps we will meet again, Miss Stanton?"

"Why, certainly. Next time you're in town, you'll know how to find me."

Next time you're in town, you can spirit me away from this madhouse.

"Thank you." He bowed. "I look forward to sharing your company for an hour or two."

Count on it. I promise to chatter your ear off all the way to the posting-house.

"It's a bargain." Susan curtsied to him and wiggled her fingers over her shoulder at the other two ladies. "Lovely to meet you. I'll come for a fitting another day. Au revoir."

She grinned to herself as she stepped out the door. Those two would rather fillet her in her sleep than sew her a new trousseau, regardless of the price. But at least now they knew Miss Susan Stanton was not as easily cowed as the limpid country misses they normally crushed beneath their heels. Miss Susan Stanton was never cowed at all.

The rough-hewn ghost materialized before her face.

Susan squeaked in surprise.

His bearded jaw dropped open, revealing half a collection of crooked yellow teeth. "You *can* see me."

She shot a nervous glance along the beach. The door to the shop had closed behind her and the scarecrow was long gone. Nonetheless . . .

"Go away," she hissed.

"You can *hear* me?" he sputtered. "Why weren't you paying any attention to me inside?"

"I was busy." She stepped around him and made for the landmark pile of driftwood. "Still am. Do leave me alone."

Please don't let him follow me. Please don't let him follow me.

He followed. "I'll go if you promise to do something for me."

"No."

A-ha! There was the pathway leading to the top. Susan grabbed the front of her skirt and began the tramp up the footpath.

"I just need you to relay a message," the ghost insisted, hovering over nothingness at her side. "How hard can that be?"

She sighed. "What's the message?"

"That I'm dead."

Susan walked faster. "Out of the question."

"That's it, I swear." He darted forward and floated a consistent two feet before her, flickering beneath the overcast sky. "Give my family news of my death and I'll leave you alone forever."

What rot.

"First of all, what gives me any reason to believe I can trust the word of a ghost? Secondly, are you *mad?* What am

I meant to do, walk around town saying, 'Oh, I ran into this dead chap the other day—'"

"Grey's my surname, but most call me—"

"All right, 'When I bumped into *Mister* Grey this morning, he asked me to let you know that he's *dead* . . .'"

He glared at her. "At least tell my sister."

"I won't tell anybody."

"It's the least you can do."

"It's not my business at all!" Susan ducked her head and strode faster, keeping her gaze locked on her boots rather than the shimmering ghost before her. "I didn't ask to start seeing dead people."

"I didn't ask to die."

"I'm truly sorry for your loss." She wavered for a moment, then sped up. "Did you not see the debacle that took place in that horrid dress shop merely because my encounter with you gave me such a start? Imagine what those two vipers would say if they knew I was speaking to you now."

"That's exactly who—"

"Forget it!" Susan swiped an arm through his misty form, expecting her angry gesture to do little more than annoy the persistent spirit.

Instead, he vanished.

She was so startled, she stopped in her tracks. What the dickens had just happened? Had she somehow killed a ghost? Dare she hope he was gone for good?

"What the devil are you about now, woman?" came a familiar voice below her feet.

Susan's gaze snapped down along the cliff's edge.

Mr. Bothwick. Delightful.

"Nothing."

"Didn't look like nothing." His smooth voice came closer. "Looked rather like talking to yourself and throwing punches at the wind."

Susan ground her teeth. This sort of reaction was precisely

why she would not be bringing Bournemouth inhabitants any ghostly messages from the grave. The only thing worse than being ignored was being mocked. Although she supposed fleeing his house at a dead run hadn't precisely been putting her best foot forward, as far as impressions went. Not that she cared about his opinion. Much.

"Just exercising," she said, turning around to wait for his inevitable reappearance on the serpentine path. "Latest London craze. You wouldn't understand."

Mr. Bothwick rounded another winding corner and appeared on the trail before her. He had bathed and groomed since the last time she saw him, and the change was breathtaking. He could have mingled in any ballroom to devastating effect. Out in the open air, however, with the wild ocean at his back . . . this was his element.

No tailor could hide the muscular lines of a body used to the out-of-doors (why would one try?) and the snowy whiteness of his perfectly creased cravat only served to accentuate the unfashionable bronze of his skin. A look, Susan admitted privately, that Mr. Bothwick wore very, very well. Particularly with the slight quirk to his lips that she'd come to recognize meant he was on the verge of saying something shocking.

"As it happens," he said with a slight incline to his head, "there's nothing I love more than . . . exercising . . . with a beautiful woman."

Susan reminded herself to be offended, not intrigued. Or at least feign as much. And stop ogling the fine fit of his breeches and perfect cut of his cheekbones above the creases of his cravat.

"Do you know how insufferable you are, Mr. Bothwick?"

He smiled. "I cultivate it. Shall I carry you up the cliff?"

"You shall not." Although, turned out in his present condition, the idea held a sinful allure. He looked so dashing, with the wind ruffling his chestnut hair and every other inch of him so perfectly put together. He was a gentleman on the

outside, and on the inside . . . something darker. A mystery.
A mirage. An enemy.

He studied her as if reading her thoughts. "Shall we 'exercise' together, then?"

Susan gasped indignantly. Well, somewhat indignantly.
The gasping might have detracted a bit from the indignation
and made her sound more . . . tempted. Knowing he was absolutely wrong for her just made him all the more intriguing.

She raised her chin and tried to appear aloof. "We most
certainly shall not."

"More's the pity."

He prowled closer. Bits of grass and dirt broke free with
each step and tumbled to the ground below. Suddenly they
were toe to toe on the sandy path. He didn't move. Neither
did she. She couldn't. His fresh-shaven cheeks looked sharp,
dangerous, yet touchably soft. He wore no perfume. His recently bathed skin smelled of sea salt and citrus. Ambrosial.
He was too close. Much too close. He lifted her chin with the
curve of a bare knuckle and gazed into her eyes.

"Anybody ever tell you it's dangerous to be out on the
cliffs alone?"

She jerked her chin out of his grasp, ignoring the rippling
shiver his touch had caused. Still caused. She should turn
around, right now, and walk away. She should definitely not
encourage him by responding. Or leaning closer. Or allowing the huskiness in her voice to give hint to her thoughts.
"I wouldn't be surprised to learn you're the sort of man who
makes it dangerous to be *anywhere* alone."

"Ahh. So you do get my meaning." His smile returned,
this time giving his eyes a predatory glint. "Not as innocent
as I imagined."

"A caryatid would get your meaning." Susan swayed, then
steadied herself with a palm to his arm. Her over-tight stays
must be making her breathless. It certainly had nothing to do
with the way he didn't bother to hide the blatant interest
darkening his gaze. Or the way her pulse quickened at every

touch. "I plan to remain innocent in the way you mean until the day I wed. So if you don't mind, please step aside and allow a lady to pass."

He tilted his head and considered her. "Would that be the gentlemanly thing to do?"

Yes. And that's what she desired. A gentleman. A rich, titled, *London* gentleman. Period.

"Of course."

"Then that's the first fallacy in your logic. You assume I'm a gentleman, when I am not. In fact, the only time I'm ever gentle is when I—"

"I don't want to hear it," Susan interrupted, desperate to cut him off lest she somehow be compromised by mere words alone. A proper young lady should have no interest in hearing any details regarding the style of his lovemaking. Yet her heartbeat tripled its speed.

"Discussion is pointless," the shameless reprobate agreed softly, "when actions speak so much more eloquently."

With that, he took her face in his hands and kissed her.

Chapter 5

Miss Stanton's fist connected with Evan's ribs.

Several stunned seconds passed before it occurred to him to let go of her face. The moment he regained his senses—which had tumbled from his head after suffering his first-ever setback by a woman—he jerked his hands away as if her pores exuded acid.

She had the audacity to look wounded.

"You hit me," he pointed out.

Miss Stanton crossed her arms beneath her breasts. "You *kissed* me."

"A mistake I shall strive not to make again, I assure you."

"Good," she snapped. But a slight wrinkle creased her brow, as if she weren't completely certain whether she were winning the argument or losing.

He, on the other hand, had no such uncertainty. If two people sharing as many sparks as they did were not occupied in the pleasurable task of lovemaking or the preparation thereof, they were both losing.

Evan hated to lose.

However, his primary mission—make that his sole mission—was to uncover Timothy's killer, not waste time dallying with fast-fisted blondes. Particularly one who now resided in the one house in Bournemouth he frequented nearly as often as his own. If she *would've* succumbed to temptation . . . Christ. The very thought of seeing the same lover's face on a daily basis set his skin to itching.

He would, of course, accompany the jasmine-scented beauty for the duration of the walk to Moonseed Manor, as her arse had demolished the only other viable route to the top. As she was still staring at him expectantly, one pale eyebrow arched higher than the other, he might as well give her what she wished and get this over with as fast as possible.

With an ungentlemanly sigh, he proffered his arm.

With an equally unladylike . . . huff? . . . she spun around without taking it and stalked up the trail with enough unnecessary stomping that Evan began to fear she was about to ruin this path, too.

"What is it you *want?*" he heard himself ask, as he hastened to her side while the walkway still existed. This was the main reason port wenches were better than Society women—he never had to ask what they wanted. The answer was always: him.

"I want you," the blond virago said without bothering to slow her steps, "to go away."

And right there was the second reason.

"Just to clear things up," he informed the irritatingly attractive sway of Miss Stanton's backside, "I am on my way to visit Ollie, not you."

Her step faltered, but she didn't respond.

Did she fancy his attentions or not? Then again, her wishes didn't signify. He had one goal, and one goal only. Avenge Timothy's murder. And revenge was best handled when not wasting time worrying over the illogic of the female mind.

Evan picked up his pace. Not only were his legs longer than Miss Stanton's, his feet knew this and every trail in Bournemouth by rote. Within the space of a heartbeat he was at her side, and within another, already beyond. He was almost to the next curve in the path when she gritted out, "*Wait.*"

He considered continuing on as if he hadn't heard her. After all, he was nine or ten feet ahead. Perhaps he was deaf in one ear. She wouldn't know. Yet some devil inside him made him slow. Or perhaps something in her voice beckoned him as irresistibly as a siren's.

Despite such warning bells, he turned to face her. "What now, woman?"

"Aren't you at least going to stay behind me?"

What did she expect of him? And why did she think he would grant it? Merely because *she* was a lady?

Her cheeks held a hint of pink, whether from pique or embarrassment, he didn't know. He had no idea why his body refused to obey his brain's directive to quit her presence for good. She seemed to be fighting a similar internal battle. He would solve the problem for both of them by making it easier for her to decide he was the last man a respectable young lady should be spending time with. He was no gentleman. Had never been. And had no desire to be.

"We're not promenading a ballroom," he reminded her. "I am not your suitor."

"Thank God for both of those facts," she muttered. He was *certain* that's what she'd just said. But then she met his eyes, her own blue and wide behind her spectacles, and gazed at him as if she'd said nothing. "What if I should fall?"

Evan stared at her. Was she expecting to fall? Did the woman plan such things? And when had he been enlisted as her personal net? The man so far below her lofty status that his only usefulness was that of impromptu carriage? His flesh steamed. He had left his past behind specifically to avoid class conflicts with the *ton*. This was Bournemouth, for the love of whiskey. He wouldn't let a comely little debutante play the superior.

"In that case," he replied icily, "you will have the satisfaction of knowing it was your own damn fault, given that I am too far ahead to give you a proper push."

Surprisingly, the London debutante did not gasp at his effrontery in highly dramatized outrage. In fact, if it weren't simply a trick of the sun's glare upon her spectacles, Miss Stanton's initial reaction had been to . . . roll her eyes?

"Walk with me," she gritted out in a voice even surlier than his own. ". . . Please."

He did. Primarily in surprise. She had not wanted to say please. He had not expected to hear it.

He did not offer his arm this time. He didn't have to. She slipped a gloved hand into the narrow gap between his elbow and his greatcoat and stared straight ahead as if wishing she were anywhere in the world but at his side. At this point, the feeling was mutual.

At least he wasn't expected to engage in small talk.

As they made their way up the cliff in silence, Evan turned his thoughts from his present companion to his late brother. How he missed Timothy. He'd had such a logical mind and strong sense of justice. Had their situations been reversed, Timothy would've solved Evan's murder with ease, Evan was certain. Timothy loved to use his brain, did so at every opportunity. To the exclusion of all else.

So why was he dead? Was it possible he *had* been doing something as trivial as adding sums when a miscreant chanced upon him? Evan let out a sigh. It was not only possible, but highly probable. There was no other explanation. How the devil was he going to track down a killer whose only complaint against his victim had been the happenstance of being in the wrong place at the wrong time?

The delicate fingers curving around his arm dug into his skin.

"What?" Miss Stanton's voice was interested. Too interested. He could *feel* her gaze boring into his skull.

"What's what?" he mumbled absently, trying to keep his mind focused on unraveling what few clues he had. He would show his brother that the elder Bothwick had as much ability to use his brain as his balls. Vengeance would be swift.

Provided he not lose time with jasmine-scented blond distractions.

"You sighed."

That warranted a complete set of nails puncturing his arm through three layers of fabric?

"I did not."

"You did," she insisted, staring at him as if the intensity of her blue eyes could force him to voice his darkest thoughts aloud.

"So I did," Evan agreed, so as to derail the current pattern before the conversation degenerated into the black tar of did-not, did-too as so many of his and Timothy's childhood arguments had gone. "If you must know, my sigh was because I suffer from horrible asthma. My physician says I should stop carrying women about, and the next time you fall . . . I should let you hit the ground."

As before, she failed to gasp in outrage. Her eyes were probing, not wounded. And her muttered response sounded almost like . . . "Bollocks."

"What was that?" he inquired politely. "I didn't quite hear you."

"I *said,*" she began, "I doubt you'd notice if I fell to my death. Something else is on your mind. What is it? The corpse you mislaid?"

Here he'd thought she'd been about to dispute his alleged lung condition.

He gave those alarmingly intelligent eyes his most careless smile and marched forward in renewed silence. He'd never have mentioned the missing-body situation had she—and the loss of his brother—not caught him utterly off guard. He was on guard now, however. He'd be watching his back around this little Londonite with big eyes, a dangerously round arse, and a grip like a deckhand. Matter of fact, he'd be keeping his eye on everyone.

Someone in town was a killer. And Evan would have revenge.

For best results, however, he would have to keep up appearances of his usual devil-may-care attitude and puss-on-the-prowl activities. In fact . . .

He slid Miss Stanton a sideways glance.

She noticed.

He couldn't prevent a slow, satisfied smile from curving his lips.

She noticed that, too.

"W-what?" she stammered, loosening her grip on his arm and edging away as much as the cliff's edge would allow.

Evan hid his smile and propelled them farther up the narrow path.

With no imagination at all, the entire town could be made to believe she was his newest conquest. Given the roguishness of his reputation and his well-documented lust for fresh blood, he probably would never have to be within shouting distance of the inquisitive blonde for the rumor to spread like pox at sea. The villain would believe Evan too wrapped up in a new skirt to be playing detective . . . and executioner. Then Evan would strike.

Blood for blood. Death for death.

Evan let himself into Ollie's library with the sneaking suspicion that Miss Stanton's exaggerated flight from his side upon entering the premises was more ruse than reality, and that she lurked nearby in the shadows. He waited a brief moment on the other side of the door before giving it a sudden wrench open and launching himself into the hallway.

He was alone.

The prickles on the back of his neck continued to plague him. He narrowed his eyes at the web of passageways trickling outward like so many rivulets of blood. He had no reason to believe she'd *meant* to spy on them earlier, particularly given the ghost-white terror in her expression when he'd flown into the hall, but something about the way she'd—

"Bothwick," came Ollie's coarse voice from across the room. "Get in or stay out."

With misgivings, Evan returned inside. He locked the library door before crossing to the half-circle of black leather chairs facing the fire, and threw himself into the one farthest from Ollie so he could keep an eye on any subtle changes in expression.

"I haven't come to kill you after all," Evan offered by way of greeting.

"Thank God, or I'd have to say you're not worth ship room anymore." Ollie glanced up from his ledgers. "If you fancy a brandy, get it yourself."

"I need your help. He's gone."

"Who? Timothy?" Ollie frowned, the deep lines that shadowed his face making his ugly face even uglier. "Didn't you say he was dead?"

Evan's stomach clenched at the memory. "The hole in his head gave that impression."

"Then how—"

"I obviously don't know. That's why I'm here."

"How the bloody hell would *I* know?" The surprise in Ollie's eyes was real. "Your brother was the least unsavory shipmate I've ever had. The only person I can imagine putting a bullet between his eyes is Timothy himself out of pure boredom."

"Suggest it again and I'll put a bullet between yours."

Ollie glanced away, by all appearances suddenly fascinated by the crackling of the fire.

That was as close to an apology as the brute had ever given, so Evan forced himself to stay on course. He needed answers. Ollie hadn't been present. But other hands *had* been on board. He just had to find them.

"Red wasn't at the Shark's Tooth this morning," he said aloud.

"Well, hallelujah." Ollie lowered his gaze to his ledger and ran a finger down one of the columns. "First time that sorry bastard hasn't drunk himself into a stupor since his mouth let go of his mama's pap."

"Don't you find that strange?" Evan insisted, leaning forward in his chair. Perhaps Red hadn't been in the tavern because Red had left town. Perhaps the sotted smuggler had turned on Timothy and fled Bournemouth forever.

"Red's a big enough imbecile to put a bullet in one of his own shipmates, but if you're suggesting he also managed to hush up the crew and escape by himself with the spoils, boat and all"—Ollie scratched at his beard—"I'm going to be a bit skeptical."

Hmmm. A valid point.

"Actually, the ship turned back up." Evan noted the surprise in Ollie's eyes at this bombshell. "But the last log page didn't. Who do you think might have taken it?"

Ollie blanched behind the midnight blackness of his beard. "A madman, that's who. Even Red's not that stupid. Taking a single word from any of the captain's log books is tantamount to signing a contract givin' away your balls." His big shoulders twitched in an involuntary shudder. "And before you ask, absolutely not. Timothy's sucket-fed. He would never have come within paw's reach of that book, much less ripped out an entire page." Lines creased his forehead. "Makes me wonder if I have any business hauling anchor come Friday. Ship could be cursed."

Evan turned his gaze to the fire and tried not to let Ollie's palpable discomfiture poison his own determination to set sail. This weekend's mission included a stop to the same port Timothy had been scheduled to visit before heading home. There was no way Evan could afford to miss an opportunity to look around, ask a few well-placed questions. He *had* to go. Despite the unnerving fact that he'd never seen Ollie look the slightest bit ruffled before.

For the record, Evan hadn't been about to ask if Timothy were foolish enough to rip a page from the captain's log. Everybody knew coming within touching distance of that book was the fastest way to walking the plank. If the captain had suspected Timothy capable of doing so, Timothy would've wound up dea—

Evan shot to his feet so fast Ollie fumbled with his ledgers and they spilled to the floor.

"What the deuce, Bothwick! You—"

"I have to go. I'll explain later."

He sprinted for the door, but the air stuck to his limbs like molasses, stretching the room out farther and farther as if he were trapped in a nightmare he could never escape.

Perhaps he was. At the very least, he was trapped in the library. Whose idea was it to lock the damn door, anyway? And what the hell had he done with the key? Ah—there.

"Bothwick?" came Ollie's clearly uneasy voice, but the molasses band had broken and Evan was already down the hall, through the maze, and bursting out of the front door.

Timothy would never be that stupid, he repeated to himself the entire way to his brother's house. His legs and lungs burned from running so fast, so far, but Evan couldn't stop, couldn't slow down. *Timothy would never be that stupid.*

Timothy's front door was locked. Of course the door was locked. All doors were locked today.

Evan kicked it in.

Sunlight filtered around him, sending his dust-flecked shadow spidering into the marbled receiving room—which was full to bursting. Crammed floor to ceiling with giant crates of brandy and silk and . . . What the hell was this? Hand-painted tea sets?

He staggered backward, collapsed against the splintered door frame, tried to make sense of what he was seeing.

Cargo. Specifically, the ship's stolen booty, which was always immediately dispatched to the captain's secret accomplice to peddle along the coast. *That* cargo.

Here. In Timothy's receiving room.

The next morning, Susan reached an important decision. If she were to succeed in her plan to win over the town's inhabitants with her unimpeachable deportment—and of course she would, given she succeeded in (almost) everything she set her mind to—she needed to stay far, far away from Mr. Evan Bothwick. And his kisses.

Especially his kisses.

Susan dragged herself out of bed and padded over to the washbasin. The freezing water she splashed on her face did little to alleviate her sluggishness . . . or to dilute the dream still swirling in the back of her mind. Him. His scent. His touch.

She bared her teeth at her dressing mirror before returning to the basin and scrubbing them again. She'd always had clean teeth and fresh breath. Her inability to leave the washbasin was in no way a new obsession. Truly.

Besides, it's not as if she'd done anything so vulgar as *enjoy* the reprobate's kisses. She was a proper lady. He was a rude, arrogant commoner who lost track of dead persons. And was, likely as not, the cause for them being in that state to begin with.

Susan rang for her lady's maid, then sat down at the escritoire, chin in hand.

Perhaps by now her parents had written, or at least decided to send money. Then all she would have to do was wait for the magistrate to reappear with his horse so she could make her escape back to London. Then life would be perfect.

She frowned. Usually that dream carried with it visions of Town bliss, as she swirled through ballrooms in the latest fashions and with the most important friends, admired by all. Today all her stupid brain could conjure was a stark emptiness, as if she'd missed an opportunity to experience—

The door slowly creaked open and Janey scampered inside.

As before, she was nothing more than a tiny jumble of elbows and knees poking out from a life-size ball of hair, as though she'd been swallowed whole by a carnivorous bird's nest on her way to Susan's bedchamber.

But also as before, her deft little fingers worked magic on the myriad ties and buttons that supported modern day-wear. Susan couldn't help the traitorous thought that Janey was significantly more efficient than her lady's maid back home, who knew all the latest gossip but hadn't the least clue what to do with a column of buttons.

Perhaps Janey was equally efficient in the art of gossiping.

Susan cleared her throat. "Are you familiar with the dress shop in town?"

The maid hopped around a bit like a startled grasshopper, but her stick-thin fingers never left Susan's hair. "I am, mum. That's Miss Devonshire what runs it, she does."

Information at last. "Would Miss Devonshire be the one who looks like a porcelain doll or the one that looks like"— Susan faltered for an alternate description and came up empty—"a nursery-tale witch?"

"Doll-baby, she is," Janey answered without hesitation. "Other one's Miss Grey."

"Are those two quite friends with Lady Beaune?"

Janey froze in place.

Startled, Susan tried to catch the maid's eye in the mirror, but her face was hidden as always behind a cascade of tea-colored frizz.

"Lady B-beaune," Janey stammered when she returned at last to the daunting task of Susan's hair, "never did have too many of what one might call . . . friends."

Susan all but purred at this bit of knowledge. Persons without friends were persons with Stories.

"And why is that, if I might ask?" She bit back a yelp as several strands of hair snapped from her scalp.

"Begging your pardon, mum. Pardon. It's just I—well, I can't rightly say why that is, mum. Imagine only Lady Beaune herself keeps the wherefores of all that past history."

Susan could scarce sit still in her chair. Unless her gossip senses were mistaken (and her gossip senses were never mistaken), her lady's maid had just delivered a bare-faced lie.

Janey knew the truth good and well but was clearly unwilling to part with that information. Susan would have to uncover the sordid details herself. Which, as it happened, was one of her favorite activities. The best source of information was always . . . well, the source itself.

"Where might I find Lady Beaune, would you say?"

"F-find Lady Beaune?" Janey echoed faintly.

Susan gave her most encouraging nod, which succeeded in divesting her of another strand of hair, but she no longer felt the sting. All she felt was the blood-warming allure of a scandal to be uncovered.

"I suppose . . . she might be found . . . out in the gravesite."

"Out in the—" A chill shivered along Susan's flesh. "What gravesite? Where?"

Janey swallowed audibly. "Out back."

"Out back? What do you mean, out back? By the rock garden?"

"In it, rather. That is to say, some of those rocks are more rightly called . . . *graves,* mum."

Susan shot to her window and jerked open the sash. A gravesite. Here, at Moonseed Manor. She herself had walked through that very "rock garden" when she'd followed Mr. Bothwick to the trail at the cliff's edge. Had she stepped on the final resting places of the dead? Was that who—and why—they plagued her? Perhaps if she apologized, begged them to stop . . .

"Shall I . . . shall I finish your hair, then, mum?"

Susan turned around as if in a trance, her mind moving too quickly for her eyes to process what they were seeing. "No, no, I don't think so. I think I'd best go right now and see these graves for myself. And speak to Lady Beaune, of course. Why does she tend the gravesite? Isn't there a gardener with that duty? Not that it's my business. I daresay—"

She caught sight of her reflection, and her limp mane of half-straight, half-curled hair. She twisted it to the nape of her neck and secured it with the first comb in hand's reach, never mind that the pearls didn't quite match the flowered sprigs embroidered on her morning dress. She tried to ignore the pang of guilt at Janey's strangled squeak as she watched her mistress undo all her hard labor with the single turn of a wrist.

"It's lovely, Janey, truly," Susan assured her. She'd have left the maid a sovereign if her parents hadn't left her penniless. Come to think of it . . . "Has a letter arrived for me, perchance? From London?"

If Janey blinked at this change in topic, it was impossible to tell beneath the mass of trembling hair. Her tone, however, could only be described as wounded. "No, mum. Nothing's come for you, or I'd have brought it with me."

"Oh. Of course you would've." Susan mentally chastised herself for her second gaffe in as many minutes. She needed to keep as many allies as possible, and it was probably still too soon for mail. "Pardon my distraction. I'm just eager to hear from my parents . . . and to speak with Lady Beaune at last."

"Family is important," Janey agreed after only the briefest of pauses. "There is that."

Susan had the impression her lady's maid had wanted to say something quite different. But Janey made a strangled sound, half-collapsed into an awkward curtsy, and fled the room without waiting to be dismissed.

What did she know? Something about Susan's parents? Or about Janey's own parents? But the maid hadn't said "parents," had she . . . ? She'd said "family." Whose family? Lady Beaune's? Or the unfortunate souls being trod upon between the rocks lining the backyard?

Susan marched through the still-gaping doorway. It was time to find out.

Chapter 6

By the time the clock on the mantel chimed noon, Evan was aware of three disturbing facts: He was exhausted to the marrow, his stomach had begun to consume itself from lack of sustenance, and the missing logbook page was definitely not in Timothy's house.

Evan hadn't left a stone unturned. Literally. Well, figuratively regarding the stone because the house was made of wood, but every single plank had been pulled up or back or to the side in order to peer beneath. Every stick of furniture had been removed, dismantled, and inspected. Every drawer had been opened, overturned, and searched. No logbook page lurked anywhere.

He slumped against a stack of still-mind-blowing stolen cargo. Was his rule-following brother the captain's secret link for selling stolen goods? Impossible. Timothy hadn't even *fancied* being a smuggler until Evan had joined the crew. And Timothy had never kept a secret from Evan in his life. There had to be an alternate explanation. A clue, no doubt, resided in the missing logbook page.

So where the devil was it?

Evan ran a finger along the rims of hand-painted teacups and catalogued the possibilities. One: The log page was never here in the first place, because Timothy wasn't stupid enough to have stolen it. This was a good theory because it gave his brother some brains, but bad because that meant any given brute could've taken the sheet anywhere on Earth, which made searching for it a tad more complicated.

Two: Timothy *was* stupid enough to steal the page, but not stupid enough to bring it home. Again, this theory gave his brother some credit, yet opened up the window to the world at large, as far as searching went.

Three: Timothy was stupid enough to take the page and whoever killed him had already taken it back. This was the worst theory of all because it slammed the door on the idea of Evan coming across the page himself, and he had the distinct suspicion he would never understand what had happened without knowing what was on that page worth killing—and dying—for.

There wasn't much he could do about that last scenario, and Timothy wasn't here to ask about the second situation, so he would have to consider possibility number one: Someone else took the sheet. Since Evan was convinced no one on his crew—including his brother—was suicidal enough to do such a thing, the only remaining suspects were . . . the other crew.

He glanced at the clock again. Still noon. Well, five past.

On the one hand, there was nothing he wanted more than to go home and sleep for a few hours. He would be wise to be in top form when entering the other crew's territory. Those soulless jackanapes made Evan's shipmates look like choirboys.

On the other hand, every day, every hour, every minute lost was another minute further from the truth, thereby increasing the villain's head start and diminishing Evan's chances of ever wreaking vengeance.

And *that* possibility was unbearable.

So he pulled himself together, shut his brother's front door as best he could what with the ruined hinges, and headed for enemy land. By the time he reached the hidden shore along the distant cliff, his clean clothes were laden with sand and the omnipresent spray of saltwater. This time, he didn't bother to hide his pistols. He kept them in his hands. Cocked. Ready.

The familiar rush of power and trepidation surged through his veins as he neared the crevice leading to a secret cavern that opened to the sea.

They wouldn't be happy to see him.

They resented sharing the captain's ship with another crew, despite the begrudging cooperation being a brilliant scheme of economics and alibis. If these water rats sensed any weakness, they'd have half a mind to make him disappear. To be honest, they only had half a mind among them anyway. That's what made them so dangerous.

Evan wished he could just speak to Timothy himself. Goddamn, Evan missed his brother. He glared at the waves raging against the shore. Best not to think too much about the hole in his heart, and keep his mind on unraveling the mystery surrounding his brother's death.

He approached the cave with caution.

This was the one place along the entire coast where his feet were unsure of their placement. Why smugglers sharing the same ship needed individual secret caves, he didn't know . . . unless that *was* the point. To keep Evan's crew unsure, off-balance, on an uneven keel. Easy pickings.

The faint stench of smoke tickled his nostrils. Disquieting, that. No one set something so obvious as a fire in a place they hoped to keep secret. Or maybe they'd seen his approach, set a trap, and were luring him in. Hard to say. Even fools were occasionally clever.

He tightened his grip on his pistols, then forced himself to relax. They wouldn't kill him on sight. Probably. But if he gave them the barest scrap of a reason . . . they wouldn't hesitate. He had to be on the ready.

He'd abandoned his boots at the shore—stockings too, this time, despite the icy water. Slip on one of these rocks, and he'd wind up killing himself in the fall. Which the other crew was probably hoping for, so they wouldn't have to explain themselves to the captain. He crept forward, his bare feet making no sound as he scaled the jagged boulders.

Evan glanced around at all angles, searching the shadows for movement. They were watching him. They had to be. *He* would be, in their shoes. The troubling stench of smoke slowly grew stronger. Were they planning to roast him alive? Or were they burning something else . . . a filched log sheet, perhaps?

He was through the crevice and into the blackness of the cave when the first gunshot rang out.

Behind him.

He grinned into the dark as delicious anticipation ruffled the hairs on his arms. A sentry outside had seen him, if belatedly. Which meant there was no going back now. Or possibly ever . . . but he'd deal with that on the way out. For now he had to keep moving forward.

Before long, he found himself at a point where the narrow passageway widened into a cavern more than spacious enough to hide a full-size ship and several missions' worth of cargo. The ship was still in its cave—he hoped—which meant this one was empty of everything but pirates. He double-checked his weapons.

There would be no way to hide his approach. So he didn't try.

He sauntered forward, straight down the center, a well-turned gentleman slightly spiced with dripping seaweed and a pair of loaded pistols.

They saw him. Of course they saw him. But instead of shooting him, a raspy chuckle scraped forth from the shadows. Then the pirate responsible for the chuckle stepped forth, gun in hand, barrel pointed at Evan's forehead.

"Bothwick," the scar-faced smuggler said, shaking his head as if he found Evan's attempt at infiltration wholly amusing. "Wot you doing here, you sneaky bastard?"

"Why, Poseidon," Evan returned conversationally, trying to keep one eye focused on the pirate and the other on the teeming shadows. "Good day to you, old chap."

"Is it, now? And you there, come a-calling with a pair of pistols. Why don't you put them away now, eh? We're a right friendly bunch."

Evan kept his pistols where they were. Poseidon's barrel didn't waver from Evan's face.

"Red's not about, is he?"

Poseidon let out a bark of laughter. "Bothwick's stumbled into the wrong cave, boys," he crowed over his shoulder. He lowered the weapon long enough to use it to gesture the other men forward. "He thinks he's at home."

A half-dozen burly smugglers spread out to surround him in a loose circle. Backing up would do no good, but that was all right because Evan wasn't ready to leave. He hadn't come this far to run off now—and lose the back of his skull for his efforts.

"I think it's pretty clear which cave I'm in," was what he did say. Idly, casually, as if he were remarking on something with even less importance than the crisp Bournemouth weather.

"Aye, I'd guess by now as it'd be obvious. Yellow's never been your color." Poseidon slid his gun into his waistband and stepped forward, hand outstretched.

Evan didn't think for a moment any of the barrels behind him had abandoned their precision. But he gave his hallmark devil-may-care grin, tucked one—but not both—of his pistols into his own waistband, and gave Poseidon's hand a hearty shake. And returned both pistols to his palms.

Poseidon leaned back and spit onto the rocks. "Peering about for Red, then, are you?"

"Timothy, as well." When Poseidon didn't immediately respond to this gambit, Evan cast about for inspiration. "I thought they might be together."

Gold flashed in Poseidon's gap-toothed smile. "That they might be, mate. One never knows about such things, does he?"

A chill crept down Evan's spine. He barely restrained himself from demanding, *What the devil is* that *supposed to mean?* Wherever he was, Timothy was dead. And if Red were with his dead shipmate . . .

He fought the urge to glance at the faces of the unseen men behind him. He might've taken a much bigger risk coming here than he'd realized.

"I never know much of anything," was all he said aloud, however. "And you? No clue where they might be?"

Poseidon snorted. "I'd have to see if they listed the port in the logbook, now, wouldn't I?"

Evan stared, completely forgetting he was supposed to look carefree, not gobsmacked. Poseidon thought Red and Timothy were together . . . at sea? Heading to an unknown destination? But how was that possible? Everybody already knew where they'd gone on the last mission. It was more or less the same route a few times a month, and both crews took turns. Not only that, but the ship should've docked on Sunday. Red should be at the tavern, and Timothy should be at home doing absolutely nothing, as usual. Poseidon wasn't making a lick of sense. Unless he was implying Red and Timothy had taken the ship *back* out.

Evan's pistols felt unnaturally heavy in his palms. "They went on a secret mission?"

"I try not to get involved." The pirate shrugged one big shoulder in studied unconcern. "Dangerous, you know."

If it were dangerous for Poseidon to poke his nose into secret missions, it was the height of stupidity for Timothy to set sail on one without the captain's blessing. Whose harebrained idea had that been? Red's? Unless the mission *hadn't* been a secret from the captain. After all, Poseidon's entire crew seemed reasonably informed. Did Ollie know, too? What did it mean if the captain were hiding mission details only from Evan?

God, how he wished he could ask those questions aloud. But he didn't dare weaken his already-undesirable position.

"Fire out, boys?" Poseidon asked suddenly.

A voice from behind them grunted in assent. Footfalls approached, but the grunter did not step into view.

Poseidon nodded. "Good." He returned his gaze to Evan. Another flash of gold between the crooked yellow teeth. "Anything else we can be doing for you, mate? Or were you just about done using up our fine hospitality?"

He should go. They were actually going to *let* him go. Probably. But he couldn't go yet, not like this, not with so many questions unanswered and so many more crowding his brain by the second.

If the captain were hiding missions from Evan, the only logical reason was that he didn't expect Evan to be a member of the crew for much longer. And the only—the *only*—way one ceased to be a member of a band of treasonous smugglers was the precise way Timothy had found himself retired from duty. If Evan was about to undertake his last mission come Friday, he had to know. Now.

"How did you know they'd gone?" he blurted unpiratically. Damn.

Derogatory laughter sounded from behind him. "Who you think sold 'im an extra night with the ship, ye lubber? We wouldn't be standing around this fool cave like ladies at a tea party if we wasn't waiting on those jacks to get back with the damn—"

A gunshot.

A yelp of pain.

It took a split second to realize that although it was Poseidon's pistol that had fired, it had not been Evan's cry. He risked a glance behind him. One of the water rats was doubled over, hand to his ample gut, blood seeping between his fingers.

"Ye shot me!" he choked out, then crumpled to his knees.

"If you'd shut yer carcass-hole now and again, I wouldn't have to." Poseidon gave the pistol handle an expert twirl but didn't return it to his waistband. No doubt the barrel was scalding hot. "Now, as I were saying. I'm getting right tired of all this chitchat. Anything else got your bonnet in a twist this fine day, Bothwick? Because one way or another, you're about to take your leave."

With a reasonably low number of wrong turns—and the discovery of yet another heretofore unseen staircase—Susan found herself shivering in the chill morning air beneath the arched entrance to the Beaunes' rock garden. Or grave garden, as it were. The serpentine rose vines twining the gate seemed lifeless and frozen, like the grounds of a bewitched castle awaiting the arrival of a handsome prince. Except there would be no waking up from this nightmare.

The dead would stay dead. (Well, perhaps. If she asked them nicely.)

Susan tiptoed out from beneath the thorn-encrusted archway, hyper-aware of each impression her booted feet made upon the cold soil. She did not see Lady Beaune. She didn't see a single soul. Perhaps that was for the better.

Now that she was looking for such things, she found the three flat stones with relative ease. The first two marble rectangles were unmarked. She might not have recognized them for what they were, had the third—otherwise identical—stone not been engraved, *Lord Jean-Louis Beaune, 1755–1813.*

He'd died last year. Last year! Susan's head swam with the implications. Not that there *were* overt implications.

Whom did the other two graves belong to, that their rotting corpses merited neither name nor date? Had they died last year as well? Or longer ago? Or—Susan's gaze jerked toward the skeletal manor looming over her shoulder—more recently yet? Did everyone who resided here meet an untimely death?

That's when she noticed the others. The (heaven help her!) dozens of freshly turned plots dotting the so-called garden. How could there be so many? And so recent? And so . . . small. Susan's stomach convulsed in revulsion as she realized that such spaces were only big enough for children.

She backed out of the garden in slow, uncoordinated motions, grappling behind her for a handhold and wincing when errant thorns drew blood from her fingertips.

The clouds broke overhead. A dull glow whitewashed the dead earth, giving the entire vista a bleached, colorless appearance more appropriate to a dream than reality. The marble slabs glinted. The pungent scent of the dark soil mixed with the too-sweet stench of dying roses. Or something else. Something darker. There *were* no roses this time of year. The garden itself tilted, uneven, impossible. Susan fled back inside, desperate for the sanctuary of her bedchamber.

But this time, all the stairs led down.

Down, down into the bowels of Moonseed Manor, down into a cellar she hadn't known existed. From those hellish depths came a plaintive whimper, like that of a lost cat . . . or a child, terrified of becoming companion to the unfortunates in the cold earth out-of-doors.

The last place she wanted to go was down into that darkness, from whence those horrible whimpers rose. But if a child needed help, how could she not?

Careful to keep her descent as soundless as possible—if a villain were there with the wounded child, she certainly had no wish to make her presence known—Susan crept down the steps one by one.

A dank chill emanated from the stone passageway. Tiny beads of moisture covered the smooth slabs, as if whatever misdeeds took place within these walls caused the house itself to break into a cold sweat.

Not for the first time, Susan wondered whether it would be smarter to just walk on back to London after all, with nothing more than the pelisse on her back. What were a hundred or so miles to the truly desperate? But then came another soft whimper. If she had within her power the opportunity to save an innocent from a terrible fate, she would never forgive herself for walking away.

She reached the bottom at last. There was only one room. And no way to miss what hunched inside.

The ghost from her bedchamber.

As before, a pair of long white plaits tumbled from beneath a hooded cloak. Age spots dotted ungloved hands. Dirty, ripped fingernails clawed at the cold stone walls, still damp with perspiration. Shadow obscured the rest.

Or did. Susan must have made a small sound. The figure turned around, hobbled forward, cocked her head . . . and the crimson hood fell away from her face.

A gasp fluttered from Susan's lips. Not a ghost at all. Not even *old*.

The elaborate crucifix was missing from the woman's thin neck. The braids—now that they caught the weak light from the candelabra in the corridor—were palest blond, not white. And the creature had just managed to brush off one of her age spots with the back of her hand. Dirt. From clawing at the walls. But why—

Then she saw it.

A chain. Thin. Delicately so. But strong enough to keep this poor woman's warped frame shackled to its cage. The slender chain stretched from an iron ring attached to the lowest corner stone to an invisible manacle beneath the hem of the crimson cloak.

The woman couldn't have been much older than four or five and twenty. She hobbled toward Susan. And whimpered when the chain checked her progress at her very first step. This time, its taut length revealed the iron clamp encircling a pale, bone-thin ankle.

Susan's lungs drew in a sudden, heaving breath as if she'd been underwater all this time and finally come up for air. It was not a feeling she liked to relive.

If this woman was locked, trapped, imprisoned . . . there must be a key to release her. Susan just had to find it. But the walls were empty. Consumed with urgency, she jerked her body around to search the corridor for a nail hanging a key in the shadows.

She came face-to-face with the giant.

The master of the manor did not look pleased. The scarecrow stood just behind him, grinning his horrible slash-faced smile. He still carried a shovel in one hand. From the other dangled a ring of keys. Which quickly disappeared into a pocket.

Susan tried to move, tried to smile and say she must've lost her way (dear Lord, why *hadn't* she lost her bloody way?), tried to squeeze through the half-inch of space not filled up by the giant and escape Moonseed Manor forever. But her limbs were frozen in place.

"There you are, Miss Stanton," drawled the giant's deep voice, as if he and the scarecrow had spent the entire morning looking for her.

Perhaps they had. The scarecrow's tiny eyes glittered at her above his evil smile.

The giant moved farther into the room. "I see you've met my wife."

His—Once again, Susan's lungs failed her. She turned to gape at the frail, hunchbacked creature chained to the wall. How could this be Lady Beaune? The woman whimpered, put both gnarled hands to her face, and cowered into the corner.

"Y-you keep my cousin chained up in the cellar?" Susan's voice was faint, tinny, a dim echo of herself.

"Got to," rasped the scarecrow, tapping the pole of the shovel into his free palm. "Else she'll run away from us again." His button eyes shifted their black gaze to the far corner. "Won't you, milady?"

Susan's horrified focus snapped back to the giant, who simply inclined his head in silent acknowledgment that yes, that's precisely how things were.

Is Lady Beaune at home? Always.

"I-I don't suppose you might unchain her," Susan ventured, determined not to flee (or faint dead away) without at least attempting to save her hostess from whatever these two blackguards had planned.

"I don't suppose I would." The giant strode over to where his wife trembled, face to the wall. "She's been a bit of a bad girl, and hidden something that I need. Haven't you, love?" His deep voice hardened. "Where did you put it? Show me. Now."

Lady Beaune whimpered, dropped to the dirt floor, curled into a ball.

A growl came from deep within the giant's barrel chest.

The scarecrow stood in the doorway, slapping the shovel into his palm, grinning and grinning.

Disgusted, the giant turned from his wife and loomed over Susan. His shadow cast her into darkness, making his expression impossible to read. "What are you doing down here, Miss Stanton?"

Somehow, she conjured the ability to speak. "I . . . got lost on the way to my bedchamber."

"Is that right?" He patently didn't believe her. Not that she blamed him. Shameful as her sense of orientation was, at a minimum she knew the difference between *down* and *up*. He turned toward the scarecrow. "Would you mind accompanying Miss Stanton to her . . . current . . . lodgings?"

The shovel dropped into the scarecrow's palm and stayed there. His straw-thin fingers flexed their grip around the hard wooden handle.

"My pleasure," came his scratchy reply.

"You know," Susan blurted, the words darting out so fast even she wasn't quite sure what she was saying, "now that I think of it, I was meant to go to the dress shop this morning and here it is afternoon already. Miss Devonshire is certainly wondering what on earth has become of that slugabed Susan Stanton, and I truly cannot have her and Miss Grey worried about my well-being. I'll just call over there now, whilst the errand is still fresh in mind, and do that fitting they promised me for the trousseau I ordered yesterday. I can find my way outside, no problem, although I thank you kindly for the offer of assistance." She cast her wild gaze toward the stairs. "Very well . . . I'll be off, then, I suppose. Er, now-ish."

The giant and the scarecrow met eyes above her head, reaching an unknown agreement in wordless communication. To her surprise, the scarecrow stepped aside, apparently instructed to let her pass, although he did so with unhidden ill humor.

Susan did not wait for her pardon to be rescinded, but tore up the steps as if the hounds of hell nipped at her heels. She doubted the comparison was very far off. Just ask Lady Beaune.

"Miss Stanton?"

At the giant's deep voice bouncing up the stairs behind her, Susan's joints froze up so suddenly that she nearly tumbled all the way back down from the top. She flailed for a nonexistent handrail and managed to right herself at the last second with each palm flattened against opposite stone walls.

"Yes?"

"It might be best for you not to become 'lost' in this area again."

"Er, right," she responded when she found her voice. "I can see where that could be sound advice."

"So long as we understand each other," was the giant's only reply. A chain rattled somewhere in the shadows.

"Yes, I . . . I'm certain we do."

The scarecrow poked his head around the corner, the slash across his face splitting his visage far wider than any human grin ever should.

"Don't worry, Miss Stanton," he rasped, once again toying with the shovel. "I'll be keeping an eye on you."

She ran.

* * *

By the time she reached Bournemouth proper, Susan's shift stuck to her back and her lungs were afire. She had never been so terrified in her life. She had to get out of this godforsaken village before escape ceased to be an option.

It was now more imperative than ever that she win the hearts of every breathing body within the town's borders. *Someone* had to help her escape before she stopped showing up one day. Otherwise, all the giant would have to do is say that she'd gone back to her parents, and her face would never cross their minds again.

Susan stumbled. Was that what was happening? Were all those tiny plots "visitors" who had "gone back home"? She forced her feet into motion. That would not happen to her. It would not.

As for Lady Beaune . . . She *would* rescue her, at the earliest opportunity. Whom should she tell first? Mr. Bothwick? No. He was a particular friend of the very fiend who had locked her in the cellar. Even if not complicit in the actual crime, Mr. Bothwick had already chosen his allegiance. But then whom could she go to? The townsfolk? How would she know who was or wasn't already in the giant's pocket? Risking her own freedom wouldn't help either of them. She needed an outsider. Someone guaranteed to be impartial.

The magistrate. Perfect. No one else could be expected to confront the woman's husband.

But until Mr. Forrester returned, Susan would continue attempting escape on her own. To do that she needed friends and horseflesh. Money, of course, could easily buy both people and beasts, but as she was stuck without coin, she would have to employ an alternate method.

She slowed to a stop when she reached the motley collection of ramshackle buildings rising from the jawbone of the sandy shore.

Where to? The only structures apparently open for business were the dressmaker's (where she really would need a heavy purse if she were to win over those cold fishes) and the tavern, which she supposed would have to do, given the lack of alternatives. At least there would be live persons.

She pushed open the swinging door and stepped inside.

The wild-haired barman looked all but terrified to find her within his walls again. The drunks who had crowded her before cleared a berth as wide as if she carried the plague. The priest was the one person who didn't leap back in horror upon her appearance in the tavern . . . and by the number of empty tumblers on his table, that might have been because he was no longer capable.

Nonetheless, the priest had to be the most upstanding citizen present. And when he was not in his cups, perhaps a key source of aid.

"I'm Miss Susan Stanton," she informed him when she reached his table. She bathed him in her sunniest smile.

He glanced up, blinking owlishly, then returned his focus to the glass in his hand, which he couldn't quite keep on a straight trajectory to his mouth.

She didn't bother to hide the slow death of her smile. All right . . . next plan. Her parents' money would get here soon enough. It had to.

"A round for everyone," she announced, opening an arm in a gesture wide enough to include the entire room.

The barman didn't move.

How Susan hated the loss of having the Stanton name be just as good as gold.

"That is," she continued as merrily as possible, given his lack of exuberance, "if you might extend me a spot of credit until my allowance arrives next week?"

"Aren't ye the new chit staying wit' Ollie?" piped up one of the drunks.

"Aye, she's one of *his* all right," put in the other, sotto voce.

In a flash, the barman burst into motion. "Your credit's just fine here, miss. Sit, sit. What can I get you? Name it. Anything. I'm Sully, by the way. At your service."

"Nothing for me, please." She climbed up onto a stool and recounted the patrons. Three. Just three. "But a round for the rest, if you would."

"A round for the rest," he echoed, pouring, "and a wee bit of French brandy for the lady."

"That's truly all right, I—"

"No, no, there's plenty, honestly, and more any moment, know what I mean? But of course you do. I've seen the company you keep. Truly, drink up. Drink, drink. There's a girl."

Susan found herself swallowing her first taste of French brandy. She was positive it was illegal to possess. Treasonous, even. But she supposed if an MP came to investigate her for a simple glass of brandy, he could rescue her from this hellhole. If not, she could always steal his horse and hie back to London that way. A hysterical giggle bubbled from her throat.

Sully frowned, concerned. "There, there, miss. Maybe not so fast, now. There's plenty, mind you, but I don't fancy—that is to say—"

"Don't worry," she assured him, returning the empty tumbler to the counter. "I don't drink spirits. It's just been a mite stressful today, one could say."

"Hear, hear," mumbled the priest.

Then her ghostly pursuer filtered in through the far wall.

"I know you can see me, so don't play otherwise," were his first words. He rubbed a hand from his ginger beard to his bald head. "Just tell my sister I won't be coming home, and I promise to go away."

"I want you to go away *now,*" Susan hissed between clenched teeth.

The barman recoiled in alarm from his task of wiping the counter beneath her glass.

"Begging your pardon, miss," he stammered. "It's just that there was a bit of brandy heading straight for the edge, and as I hadn't wanted it to muss your dress, I thought to myself, 'I ought to clean that spot, is what I ought to do,' but now I can see as I was overstepping myself and I surely wouldn't want—"

"No," she gritted out, torn between glaring at the ghost for causing this mess and patting the guilt-stricken barman in assurance. "Not you," she added lamely, but as the other living patrons were still keeping a fair distance, this explanation only earned wrinkles of confusion in Sully's brow.

"I told you, miss." The bearded ghost floated up to the stool next to Susan. "Just tell my sister I won't be coming home, and I'll leave this earth forever." A flash of doubt wrinkled his brow. "I think. I'm actually not rightly sure as to why I'm still here now, but we might as well make the most of it, wouldn't you say?"

She wouldn't say, actually. Not a bloody word. Not with the barman casting odd glances at her over his shoulders as he tidied up the far end of the bar.

The ghost materialized in the counter in front of her. "Come now, lass, don't be like that. Tell her I'm dead, and I'll be gone. How hard could it be?"

As it happened, Susan didn't want to think about the thousands of things that could go horribly wrong with that scenario. On the other glove, the ghost would obviously keep haunting her until she agreed to his scheme with some level of realism, so—

"What did you say your name was?" she murmured at last, pretending to be interested.

"Most call me Red," he replied promptly, at the same time the barman answered with a wary, "Sully, miss. Same as it was a moment ago."

Argh. Perhaps she should drink herself into unconsciousness, after all.

"Sully, darling." Susan leaned forward with what she hoped was a convincing no-really-I'm-utterly-sane expression. "How about pouring another—"

The tavern door burst open and a dozen fishermen spilled

inside, bringing with them a fair bit of the sea and the rancid stench of raw fish.

"Another what, miss?"

"Another round for everyone, she said!" called out one of the drunks in the back.

"Hear, hear," said the priest.

The fishermen cheered, and in seconds had crowded her from the counter so they could toss back the round of whiskeys she hadn't meant to order.

Susan leaned against the closest wall and closed her eyes. This was all that ghost—Red's—fault. She had to get rid of him.

"If you weren't dead, I'd kill you," she muttered.

"Ain't dead yet," came a jolly, fishy slur.

A sticky glass pressed into one of her hands, no doubt ruining her silk gloves. Uneven footsteps shuffled back toward the mix of fishermen. With misgivings, Susan opened her eyes.

The barman hadn't forgotten to include her illegal French brandy in the round of drinks. She tried to cast him a polite smile, but her face rebelled. It was *not* her plan to buy so many drinks that she'd need a year's allowance to settle the tab . . . particularly when her parents had given no sign of sending her so much as a farthing. An insurgence of more fishermen backed her into a far corner of the tavern.

"Well?" Red demanded, hovering above the teeming bodies.

Susan leaned her aching head backward until it settled against the wood-planked corner, and tried to approach the situation logically. "Perhaps you'd better start at the beginning."

"N-no," he stammered. If it were possible for a ghost to blanch, that was precisely what he was doing. "I can't be speaking of things such as those. Suicide talk, that is."

She was about to argue the point—him already being dead—but thought better of it. She was proud to be one of the most successful busybodies in all of England, but if there were something so dangerous to know that even ghosts trembled to speak the words . . . well, she had enough trouble at the moment. She'd have to make do with gossip about the living.

"You honestly believe if I tell this woman, 'Your brother isn't coming home again,' it won't cross her mind to ask me a few questions?"

Red scoffed. "Pah, Harriet knows better than to ask *questions*. Besides, we prepared for this . . . as much as anyone can. She knows what to do. And Dinah can help."

"Dinah?" Susan repeated. She couldn't recall hearing that name before.

"Dinah?" echoed one of the drunks behind her.

"Dinah! Dinah!" chorused the crowd.

"Sully's a little sweet on Miss Dinah, aren't you, ye randy bugger?" called out another. "Too bad there's no chance of that!"

The barman flamed red as a claret. He turned his back to the crowd and busied himself restacking already-stacked glassware.

"Sully and Dinah, Sully and Dinah," chortled the drunk as he staggered his way up to the counter to harass the barman at close range.

The door opened and yet more men stumbled in. The tavern was now standing-room only. She'd be stuck in this dusty corner for who knew how long, but at least the men weren't asking to add more drinks to her tab. When the barman discovered she couldn't pay, he'd have to turn to her host . . . and then the scarecrow would dig a new hole for her in the grave garden.

Or worse—he wouldn't. He'd just pull the ring of iron keys from his pocket and chain her to the damp cellar wall alongside Lady Beaune.

Red floated above the fishermen, distracted for the moment. "Heh, those lubbers don't think Sully has a chance with Dinah."

Susan's back straightened despite herself. Gossip! About the living!

"Sully and Dinah . . ."

"Don't know about Sully. He's a harmless sort. But Miss Dinah spent last night in her cousin's chicken shed with *somebody,* she did. That chit's not the angel these folk think she is. My sister, now . . ." Red gave a fond smile. "Well, Harriet Grey's no angel, either. Takes after me, she does."

"Harriet . . . Grey?" Susan repeated, brain clicking madly. The witch from the dress shop was Red's sister? And the porcelain doll had had a liaison in a *chicken shed?*

"Mark my words, she and Dinah are deadly when they get their heads together," he warned with a chuckle. "And they've always got their heads together."

That settled it. They could be none other than the cackling duo from the dress shop. Susan swallowed the rest of her brandy. She could scarce imagine dropping in to give the girls the good news from the Beyond.

"So, what do you say?" Red floated closer, voice eager. "Will you do it?"

Her teeth clenched in frustration, but she had no choice. If she said no, he would just keep coming back until she agreed.

"All right. Fine." She tried to look as though she meant it. "Yes."

"She said yes!" crowed one of the fishermen.

"Another round for everyone!"

"Pour me two!"

"Hear, hear," slurred the priest.

Susan's aching head thumped back against the wall. The tavern door swung open again. Who now? Miss Devonshire and Miss Grey?

The giant strode inside.

Chapter 7

If he couldn't find the missing log sheet, at least he ought to find his brother.

Evan stared sightlessly down the length of the beach, relieved to have escaped Poseidon's cave alive. If a bit bruised. He'd bathed, changed, stolen an hour or two's sleep—but none of that gave him the slightest clue where to begin. Timothy's dead body was just as lost as the missing log sheet. Possibly forever. A pirate's grave was usually a pirate's home: the vast nothingness of the sea. Which meant he'd never see his brother again, never have an opportunity to give him a proper good-bye.

Damn it. Evan hated feeling useless. Worse: powerless.

He continued along the rocky coastline anyway. Perhaps he would come across something, anything, to shed some light on this tangle of events.

And *Timothy*. On a secret mission! It defied all comprehension. Since when did his little brother hide things of that nature? Was this the first midnight venture? The first lie of omission? What else didn't Evan know? His brother was apparently a much better pirate than he'd ever dreamed. Possibly better than Evan himself, given *he'd* never thought to rent a secret outing aboard the boat. But what a brilliant scheme! Wenching and smuggling all the night long, and not the slightest need to turn any spoils over to the captain, because he wouldn't even know the ship had sailed!

True, you'd be shark bait within seconds if the captain ever found out, but who'd tell him? The other shipmates risked their necks by renting a night in the first place, and as long as you weren't fool enough to scribble down the co-ordinates of your secret mission right there in the captain's logbook—

Evan snatched up a rock and gave it a violent skip across the sea. That cursed logbook. Timothy would *not* have been stupid enough to advertise a folly guaranteed to cost him his life. But why had Poseidon intimated that the destination might've been listed?

Oh, this was pointless. He couldn't think. Not like this. He turned and headed into town.

What he needed was a distraction. Miss Stanton's angelic face and devilish tongue flashed in his mind. No. Not that particular distraction.

That is to say, he ought to keep interest in her as the public explanation for why he wouldn't be himself over the next days, weeks, months until he found Timothy's killer. But he wouldn't be able to *really* distract himself with her. Not in the sweaty way that left him limp and lifeless and brainless for several sweet moments of total relaxation. Delicious as that sounded.

He still couldn't believe she'd stopped a simple kiss. Well, her loss. She wouldn't know what it was like to have his mouth cover hers, to have his fingers in her hair, to have his tongue thrust deep inside—Evan's blood ran a little warmer. Trouble was, he was more than a bit curious to know what it would be like to feel her palm caress his body in passion, not strike him in outrage.

Assuming uppity high-society virgins could feel anything so base as passion.

But what if she could? What if with the right moment, the right words, the right touch, she would not only like it, but *want* it, beg him not to stop? What if beneath her haughty demeanor lurked a woman as wild and wanton as any tavern wench? A woman even *better.*

He couldn't prevent a quick glance at the facade of Moonseed Manor rising in stark censure atop the cliff overlooking the town. No. He would not tramp a mile uphill just on the chance he might see her. He wasn't a boy of fifteen anymore. Women came to him, or they weren't worth his trouble.

As if on cue, a too-high voice rang out, "Evan! Evan!"

He bit back a sigh. Unfortunately, most of the women who came to him these days were more trouble than they were worth.

"Miss Devonshire," he answered politely.

She came to a breathless stop before him, all flushed cheeks and bouncing curls and saccharine desperation. "I asked you to call me Dinah."

And he'd never asked her to call him Evan, but had that done any good?

"Shouldn't you be sewing clothes, Miss Devonshire?"

"Well, yes, but I saw you from the window—at least, I thought it was you. I couldn't be sure from such a distance, of course, but the shoulders were about right and the waistcoat looked awful familiar—so I left everything where it was and I ran all the way over here, and here you are, and here I am, and since it is you after all . . . Why haven't you been to the shop to see me?" Her eyelashes fluttered at him like hummingbird wings. "I wait by the window every day. I expected you to call, and you didn't. Or were you on your way to see me just now?"

Evan tried to keep his expression placid, but his balls shriveled a little more with every word tumbling from her lips. Miss Dinah Devonshire was a living, breathing reminder of why a man should never dally with a woman he would have to lay eyes on again the next day. Tenterhooks grew from her fingers. If he weren't careful, he'd wind up fastened among the cloth stretching to dry in her workroom.

"Actually," he said, "I was on my way to—" Where could he possibly be on his way to that she wouldn't follow him? Ah, yes. She'd avoid her least-favorite swain. "—Sully's."

"Oh."

She didn't bother to hide her disappointment. In fact, if his ability to discern a woman's manipulations weren't mistaken, she was batting her eyelids and biting her cheeks in the hopes of drumming up a pitiable expression of watery-eyed misery.

He took a step in the general direction of the tavern. With the way the barman had been making eyes at her lately, there was no way Dinah would follow.

She kept right to his heels.

"Did you know there's to be an assembly in Bath a fortnight from now? Mr. Forrester mentioned it to me. Next time he's in town, I think he's going to ask me to accompany him for the weekend. With chaperonage, of course. He's a dear soul, and a very good catch, but I'm not interested in going with him if you're going to ask me to go with you. Were you going to ask me?"

Why, oh, why had he ever allowed his cock to convince him to spend a few moments alone with this woman?

"I don't know anything about it."

"Oh! Good! Then you haven't asked anyone else. Not that you would've. I mean . . ." High-pitched, rapid-fire giggles shot from her mouth like the jabber of an over-excited squirrel. "We're more than just friends now, wouldn't you say? I know you said it wouldn't change anything and that I shouldn't get my hopes up or think you would be interested in a romantic relationship, but . . . you do fancy me, right? I don't just mean for another night of—well, you know—but I was thinking I could be your companion now to social functions, and we might start with riding together to Bath in your phaeton. Nobody else has a phaeton."

Ah. So she was equally enamored with his choice in carriages. Evan cursed the day he made that ill-advised purchase. He was probably the only one in Bournemouth who *could* take her to the stupid assembly.

"I'm afraid I'm out of town that weekend."

"Oh no, that's—that's—" Her eyes widened and her squirrelly voice rose even higher. "That's perfect! The next assembly won't be for yet another fortnight, which gives me plenty of time to sew myself a new trousseau in the latest fashions, using all the best materials. Oh, Evan. You fancy me looking as fine as any London lady, don't you? And since you don't lack for coin"—more near-hysterical laughter—"I'm sure you'd wish for the woman on your arm to look as stylish as any Ackermann sketch. I don't want you to be able to tear your eyes from me for a second. It's settled, then. Next time you stop by, just show me which colors you find the most fetching, and I'll do the rest."

That settled it, all right. The only way he'd enter her shop was in a casket.

"Do forgive me for taking up so much of your valuable time, Miss Devonshire. I know how busy you are. I'll let you get back to your dresses, and I'll go and pester Sully."

"Oh," she said again, the flash in her eyes indicating she'd hoped he would come pick out colors *now*—most likely for their wedding, too—or at least do the gentlemanly thing and offer her his arm and return her to her destination.

But Evan wasn't stupid enough to do either of those things. The moment she had him reasonably alone, that friend of hers would pop out of the shadows to claim she witnessed him taking untold liberties, and *Bam!* He'd be leg-shackled. No, thank you.

"I suppose I should head back. . . ." She glanced over her shoulder, clearly hoping to see someone, anyone, who might stumble across them and assume the worst if she threw herself into his arms at just the right moment.

One of the main reasons he wasn't already at the altar for

having ruined her—for anybody who would've clapped eyes on her disheveled condition would've known she'd just been tumbled—was because he *hadn't* ruined her.

She'd come to him pre-ruined, as far as that went, which had made him erroneously believe she wouldn't be trouble. What a mistake that had been.

He inclined his head. "Until next time, Miss Devonshire."

Hopefully never.

She wrung her hands in indecision but eventually made tiny hesitant-squirrel movements in the direction of her shop. She shot him hundreds of furtive glances over her shoulder as if expecting him to change his mind at any moment and tumble her right there in the sand. Christ.

Dropping in on the Shark's Tooth was sounding better and better. The best women within its walls would lie with him expectation-free, and if there weren't any such women today, well, at least he could have a drink. And look, there was Ollie just stepping inside. Perfect timing.

Evan jogged the last few yards. He pushed open the doors—or tried to, anyway. Ollie's overgrown form blocked one of them from swinging inward. Not that it was his fault. From the roaring noise and thick smell of liquor, Evan and Miss Devonshire must've been the only two souls *not* inside the tavern. What the devil was going on?

He elbowed Ollie's meaty ribs and tossed him a questioning look, since the cacophony prevented him from asking any discernible questions aloud.

Ollie gave a disgusted shrug and stepped back outside. His lackey-cum-butler trailed in his shadow. Evan wasn't surprised to see them cut in the direction of the path leading back up the cliff. Ollie hated crowds. And the lapdog always followed the master.

Evan, on the other hand, did not mind a good drinking crowd, particularly in the mood he was currently in. He pushed his way to the bar, ordered a glass of the brandy he'd sold Sully in the first place, and turned to face a neighboring group of drunken fishermen.

"Why the ruckus?" he shouted in the closest one's ear.

"Free drinks!" came the slurred reply.

Evan's brandy glass paused on the way to his lips. Free drinks? The only other man in town with enough money to buy rounds for everyone had just walked off without stepping more than a foot inside. He turned his questioning gaze to Sully.

The barman's head bobbed in acknowledgment.

Interesting. "Who's buying?"

"She is." Sully gestured toward the back corner of the tavern.

Evan turned around so slowly he couldn't be certain he was moving at all. Then he saw her. With her own brandy glass sloshing in her gloved hands. Having a rollicking time, by all appearances. Surrounded by fishermen singing sailing songs entirely inappropriate for a lady's ears. Even if that lady cursed almost as often as Evan himself.

Miss Stanton.

Although it was impossible for her to hear him breathe her name across all that noise, all that confusion, all that distance—right then, her gaze lifted. Through the glint of her spectacles, he could somehow see her eyes smile at him. She lifted her glass in silent invitation.

He made his way to her as if in a trance, barely registering the grunts of the fools too sotted to stumble out of his way. This was a sea at tempest. He was a ship. And she was his shore.

His sudden obsession was surely nothing more than temporary infatuation borne of lust and challenge. How many women had fascinated him over the years, however briefly? But none of that signified at the moment. Right now, there was only one woman on his mind. And he would have her.

"Miss Stanton," he said when he reached her. The crowd

jostled them together, flank to flank. Or perhaps he'd done that himself.

He didn't move away.

"Mr. Bothwick," she returned faintly, her back to the wall. "Good afternoon."

Yes. Afternoon. Right. He should be asking her what the devil she was doing drinking the day away like a common sailor—although, to be honest, the juxtaposition was putting him half-mast—but what he really wanted to know about was the little catch in her voice when she spoke his name, and the way her body trembled against his with each shallow breath. Was it the crowd? Too much brandy? Or perhaps the effect of having a man pressed against her so close that if it weren't for their vestments—and the witnesses—they could as easily be making love?

The sudden image was almost his undoing. He backed up slightly. There was now enough room between them for . . . well, maybe a feather. He fought the urge to press against her again.

"I—" The empty tumbler she clenched in one of her hands knocked against the corner wall. There you go. He could act normal, be a gentleman. Not that any of this was normal. "May I buy you a brandy?"

Stupid. He should have brought a bottle with him. As many as he could carry. Now that he was here, so close that her jasmine-scented skin set his blood to sizzling, he had no intention of leaving her side.

The rolling roar of the crowd masked her reply. It had almost sounded like, *please buy them all.* Evan frowned his confusion and took the drunken revelry as an excuse to lower his head and breathe in her scent more deeply.

When she opened her mouth, her lower lip scraped across his cheek. He was too close for propriety. He knew it. But he couldn't make himself care. Or give her space.

"I want out."

This time, he heard her clearly. And her wish dovetailed

nicely with his own, which was to remove them both to the nearest secluded area. Wherein he hoped they'd remove their clothes.

He took her hand. She let him.

He'd have carried her, if there'd been room to do so, just to feel her soft curves in his arms again. Instead, they forged their way together. He was the bow, parting the sea. She was—well, she was the sea he'd *rather* be parting. There was nothing he desired more than to feel her turbulent wetness on his—

"Thank you."

Evan blinked away the image. They were outside. He still held her hand.

"This way," he said, without letting it go. Without letting her go.

She hesitated, glanced back at the tavern, then allowed herself to be propelled forward. "Where are we going?"

Evan didn't rightly know himself. Until he saw it, pushed open the door, pulled her inside.

"The apothecary?" She glanced about. "Are you ill?"

Absolutely. Ill with desire. He dropped her hand, backed up to the counter, forced himself to think carefully about what he was doing. This had been a bad idea, from the moment she'd caught his eye. Yet he felt as powerless to change course as an iron ball firing from a cannon.

She gave up waiting on an answer and wandered around the tiny store, peering at this and that with an expression that indicated she wasn't truly registering any of the gewgaws. He propped his elbows on the counter behind him and watched her. To his surprise, he could've gladly done so all day. She was not at all his normal fare. Slender instead of voluptuous. Viper-tongued instead of saucy. Intelligent instead of—well, he normally didn't waste time with conversation at all. After all, it wasn't as if men and women were meant to be *friends*. They joined together for pleasure, and pleasure only. Or there was no point being together at all.

A cold worm of doubt wriggled along the edges of Evan's desire. She wasn't his usual pickings for a reason. Many, many sound reasons. There were wenches you tumbled, and women you didn't. If a female fell into the latter category, you stayed as far away from her as possible, because to do otherwise was nothing but folly.

But, oh, he yearned to kiss her anyway.

She glanced up as if reading his mind. No—that wasn't lust in her eyes. That was suspicion. For a moment, she might as well have been a figurehead afore a ship, frozen in position forever.

When she spoke, her tone was wary. "Where is the apothecary?"

Evan glanced over his shoulder. No one there. He turned back to face the empty little room behind her, but he'd already come to the same conclusion she had. They were alone.

"Shark's Tooth, I think." He belatedly recalled shoving the apothecary aside in his determination to reach Miss Stanton. The old fool had been too drunk to even grunt. "I imagine everyone in town is inside the tavern right now. Free drinks are always a lure."

She closed her eyes as if in pain. Probably to block out the impropriety of his words, to pretend she was not alone with him. To calculate the best moment to punch him in the ribs again. Or just to erase him from sight.

He, on the other hand, drank in every detail. Her soft eyelashes, dark brown against pale cheeks. The tendril of pale blond hair curled around the thin arm of her spectacles. Her breath, audible, coming faster.

Was this how she'd look when he kissed her? Eyes closed, lips parted, face tilted up for more? He could no longer take the suspense.

He closed the distance in one stride, held her face in his

hands before she'd have a chance to realize how imminent was her danger. His mouth was on hers before she could protest.

Just one kiss, he told himself. Just one kiss, one touch, one taste, and he would leave her alone forever, no harm done. They were alone. Nobody would have to know.

He brushed his lips against hers, slowly, softly, dragging the unhurried contact from one side to the other, trying to coax a response.

She sucked in a breath.

He kissed her.

No sloppy, brutish kisses, these. He knew better than to startle her with too much, too fast. Just slow, seductive, open-mouth kisses, where he could occasionally catch the edge of her lower lip gently between his teeth and taste the spicy flavor of Miss Susan Stanton.

Then she started to do the same.

Her lips parted, her mouth opened beneath his, she bit his lower lip—much harder than he'd nibbled hers—but followed the brief sting with more kisses. One of his hands slid to the back of her head, destroying her prim coiffure, locking her into place. Soft hair spilled across his hand, tangled in his fingers.

Something clinked against the wooden floor. Some useless frippery, fallen from her hair. He didn't pause. Neither did she. Her hands gripped his sides, his shoulders, his back. Pulled him closer.

Perhaps she wouldn't be *very* startled if he swept his tongue inside, just for a second. He tried it. Her breath caught, and for a moment he thought he'd gone too fast. Too far. He retreated into the safety of his own mouth.

Her tongue followed his. Sweetly. Tentatively.

Evan groaned, kissed her again, holding nothing back this time. He kept one hand cradling her head, slid the other down her spine to the curve of her arse, and pressed her to him.

The door swung open.

Chapter 8

Before the iron hinges on the apothecary door had time to finish creaking, Mr. Bothwick had scrambled backward as if jerked by a string, leapt over the impressively tall medicine counter, and disappeared through a window Susan was fairly certain wasn't meant to be an escape route. The capricious good-for-naught was leaving her on her own to deal with—

Red?!

The ghost floated inside, causing Susan's mind to boggle for the third time in as many seconds. How the dickens . . . ? But right on Red's (quite invisible) heels were the two women Susan was least hoping to see: the porcelain doll, Miss Devonshire, and the neighborhood sorceress, Miss Grey.

Spectacular. Susan lifted a hand to her swollen mouth, although whether she intended to wipe away the kiss or seal it there forever, she wasn't sure.

"Ho," cackled the witch, jabbing her spindly black umbrella in Susan's direction. "Look at her trying to hide the evidence!"

"Where is he?" the porcelain doll demanded, her voice as thin and frail as her delicate body. "Where did he go?"

That was a bloody good question, now, wasn't it? A flash of anger welded Susan's spine ramrod straight. Next time she saw that man, she'd push him off a cliff. She rubbed at her mouth, disgusted with herself for letting him maul her like that. Even if it hadn't felt precisely like mauling in the moment.

"He can't just disappear into thin air," announced the witch, whose magical talent appeared to be pointing out the obvious. The razor-thin tip of her umbrella thrust toward Susan again. "Ask *her*."

Red danced between them. "Tell her! Tell her now! Say 'Your brother Red—' Or Joshua Grey, if you like, but those who knew me best knew me as Red, and there ain't none that don't know a man as well as his own family, says I, so if I was you, right now I'd say, 'Your brother Red—'"

Susan's hands flew away from her lips in order to gesture him off. He jerked backward, eyes wide, hands in the air.

"No-ho, you troublesome bit of baggage. You're not doing that to me again. Not until you've kept your promise to tell my sister I'm now one of the dearly departed."

With her head still abuzz from Mr. Bothwick's kisses—and subsequent cowardly defection—it took Susan a moment to decipher what it was that the ghost didn't want her to do. Then it hit her. Rather, the first time, he'd hit her . . . and then promptly disappeared. The second time, she'd done the honors herself. Which meant if she could just . . . reach . . . him, she could get him out . . . of . . . here—

She missed her mark, lurched to an awkward stop, and realized both women were staring at her as if even bats would be too leery to reside in her belfry.

"I . . ." Susan was at a loss to explain her actions.

The porcelain doll rounded on her, perfect ringlets bouncing about her perfect face. "Don't think you're going to win him from me, *Miss Stanton,* because you're not."

Susan had never heard her name sound more like an epithet.

"I don't fancy him." No point pretending she didn't know of whom they spoke.

"That's not what it looked like." The witch's crimson coat fluttered behind her as she stalked closer to Susan. "That's not what *you* look like."

Bloody hell, how bad did she look? Susan's fingers returned involuntarily to her lips, then over to her hair, which was definitely not in its impromptu chignon. The blond mass now tumbled about her face in all its half-straight, half-curled glory. Spectacular.

"Do you realize that if anyone else had caught you two together, the next time you saw him would be at the altar?" The porcelain doll's voice rose to such a glass-shattering level, Susan half-expected cracks to spider across Miss Devonshire's china-perfect features.

Then the words sunk in. No. No, she hadn't thought of that. Why hadn't she thought of that? Because she was too busy kissing and being kissed? No wonder Mr. Bothwick disappeared through the closest window. He didn't want to be saddled with her any more than she wanted to have her life destroyed by being stuck here in hell with him.

"He's all yours." Susan knelt to pick up her fallen pearl comb. When she glanced up at the porcelain doll's continued pique, she couldn't help but add, "If you can find him."

Miss Devonshire's face went livid. "You think you're special just because he kissed you? Do you know how many women he's loved and left?"

No, Susan didn't think she was special because she'd let him kiss her. She was pretty certain her promiscuous behavior indicated an impending aneurysm. And yes, she had a fairly good idea as to how unremarkable she was compared with the legions of beautiful, moral-free women composing the colorful backdrop of Mr. Bothwick's personal life. Which was yet another indication she'd completely lost her mind.

"Who cares about Bothwick?" the ghost called from the

safety of the ceiling. "Just tell Harriet I'm dead and we can all get out of here."

Susan's teeth set. Sure, that'd cheer them up. Then maybe they could sing songs and bake pies.

"It's his money, isn't it," the witch said slowly, leaning on the curved handle of her umbrella. "Dinah, she's after his money!"

Susan rolled her eyes. She was not. Well, perhaps a little. Just enough to cover the bar tab. But she'd pay him back the moment her allowance arrived. She could buy the girls' entire dress shop when her allowance arrived.

If her allowance arrived.

"It's not fair for you to set your sights on the richest bachelor in Bournemouth," the porcelain doll shrilled. "Aren't there plenty of eligible dandies with buckets full of money for you to choose from back in London?"

Why, yes, there were. And Susan would capture one by fair means or foul. Once she made it to London alive. But— wait a minute.

She removed her spectacles and cleaned them in her skirts so as not to be distracted by the ghost's constant gesticulation. Mr. Bothwick had money? That meant . . . the gorgeous house with its tasteful, elegant interior . . . did belong to him after all. That man was getting curiouser by the second.

"Make that the only rich gentleman from here to Bath." The witch elbowed the porcelain doll, clearly trying to needle her into a murderous rage. "And she's trying to take him from you."

"Not the only rich gentleman," was all Susan could think to say to defuse the situation, since continuing to deny interest in Mr. Bothwick was obviously pointless.

"That right?" One of the witch's thin red brows lifted. "Who else is there?"

"Er . . ." Rot. Now she had to think of someone. "Mr. Forrester?"

"Is poor as a church mouse. And he's a *magistrate*."

The word was spoken with as much disdain as if she'd said "stable boy." Fair enough. Who else in this town had money? Well, her charming host, for one. "My cousin?"

The witch laughed. "He's plain old Oliver Hamilton, from nowhere."

"Not a connection to his name," the porcelain doll agreed with a little sniff. "He married the Beaune money."

"They all do," the witch added darkly.

They leaned in, as if waiting to see if Susan would take the bait of promised gossip. Since the two were thereby distracted from tearing her limb from limb, far be it from Susan to put the conversation back on track.

"What is that supposed to mean?" she asked, with genuine interest. "Who else married Lady Beaune for her money?"

"Not *her*. The *real* Lady Beaune. The first one. You're thinking of her daughter. Lady Emeline."

"The first one," Susan echoed faintly. The chill racing down her spine assured her she'd already met the lady in question. Haunting the Beaune chamber. And the terrified young woman in the cellar was the ghost's daughter. Lady Emeline. A cousin who must be very near Susan's age . . . yet had endured so much more.

"Who cares about that old history?" Red shouted, floating closer. "I'm the only dead person you should be talking about!"

She ignored him.

"Legend has it—" the witch began.

Susan frowned and interrupted. "What do you mean, legend? Didn't he die last year? Wouldn't that mean you *know* what happened to him?"

"They were both reclusive," the porcelain doll explained. "Nobody saw Lady Beaune. She was always cloistered inside Moonseed Manor. I almost didn't think she was real, until the day she—"

The redhead glared at her friend. "May I *tell* the story?"

"Please," Susan intervened before the ladies came to fisticuffs. "From the beginning."

"Legend has it," the witch repeated, stepping forward as if to edge the porcelain doll from Susan's view, "Lady Beaune's beauty and riches made her the fairest catch for miles, despite being a deaf-mute who—"

"She wasn't a deaf-mute yet, Harriet."

"Dinah, I swear, if you don't let me—"

"Then tell it right!"

"*Somebody* tell me," Susan begged. "Please."

"He married her for money," the porcelain doll blurted, casting a wary glance at the witch, who simply crossed her arms and hexed them both from narrowed eyes.

"Who did?"

"Lord Jean-Louis Beaune. He was in love with the Moonseed fortune and she was the sole heiress. Nobody knows what he was lord of—if he even was. But he was handsome and titled and penniless, and she was beautiful and rich and title-less, and they married within a fortnight."

"And *then* she became deaf-mute," the witch muttered.

"Yes." The porcelain doll nodded, as if this made perfect sense. "Exactly so."

Susan fought the urge to shake them both. "This unfortunate change occurred . . ."

"On the wedding night." The porcelain doll shivered delicately. "She was never seen again . . . alive. But Lord Beaune had the signed wedding contract, and with it came the land and the money."

"As far as I'm concerned, the contract could have been nullified," said the witch. "Think about it. Would you consummate marriage with a deaf-mute?"

"I'd consummate marriage with an *Irishman* if he were rich enough to whisk me out of here," the porcelain doll said, and tittered half-hysterically.

Susan considered throttling her.

"So," she said slowly, "this all took place . . ."

"Thirty years ago."

"Thirty—" Susan choked. "This woman became spontaneously deaf-mute the night her money-grubbing fiancé gained control of her funds and properties. She subsequently went missing for thirty years, and . . . nobody thought anything of it?"

"It was terribly romantic," the witch agreed absently.

"And tragic," the porcelain doll added. "What with the daughter and all."

Susan blinked. "But you said they might not have consummated—"

"On the *wedding* night," the witch corrected. "That's when her family could've annulled the marriage, had they known what had happened. Obviously the two consummated at some point. No doubt frequent . . . consummation. Men do want their heirs."

Susan stared at her, horrified. "And nobody thought her new husband might be a villain?"

"He was titled," the porcelain doll said with a careless wave, as if titles excused everything. "Besides, why would he have kept her alive for thirty years if he wished her dead?"

"Although . . . he did kill her eventually," the witch mused.

The porcelain doll's chin lifted. "He felt terrible about it, poor man."

Susan felt the bones in her skull slowly cracking apart. Somebody needed to teach these two how to gossip properly before their nonlinear, nonsensical storytelling made Susan's head explode.

Red popped in front of her, agitated. "If you would just—"

She slashed a hand through his face and he was gone.

"Who can tell me in twenty words or less," she articulated carefully, "how he killed her, why he killed her, and why nobody in this town did a bloody thing about it?"

"Pistol," the porcelain doll answered promptly. "And he did it out of love."

"She'd gone mad and thrown herself from her bedroom window." The witch's voice held a tremor of remembered terror. "It was a frightening sight. She didn't die on impact, but there was nothing to do. Being mute, Lady Beaune couldn't scream in agony from all the cuts, all the breaks. She could only lie there brokenly and whimper."

"Yes. She had the most terrible, heartrending whimper. . . ." The porcelain doll's eyes squeezed shut as if to block out the memory. "That's when Lord Beaune went for his pistol. Lady Beaune was dying, and he didn't wish for her to suffer. He said . . . He said . . ."

"He said it's a sad day when a man has to put his wife out of her misery like a common horse," the witch finished. "And then he shot her."

Susan's head reeled. Lord Beaune killed his wife like a common horse? *Nothing* about this story was common. Was that why the poor woman was haunting Susan? Because she was spending every night in the very chamber from which Lady Beaune had taken her own life in a desperate leap for freedom? Susan would never have another wink of sleep.

"Lord Beaune fell on his way down the cliff a few days later, leaving Lady Emeline the sole heir." The witch's eyes glittered. "But not for long. Ollie Hamilton married Lady Emeline before she was even fitted for mourning clothes. They've sequestered themselves up in Moonseed Manor ever since. If there's still money left, *she* doesn't come down to spend it."

Susan swallowed. Poor Lady Emeline had a macabre explanation for her lack of shopping excursions.

"Are—aren't you at all worried about her?" Susan asked hesitantly.

The witch scoffed. "Worried about what? She's married, isn't she? Her husband will provide anything she needs."

"And if he doesn't?" Susan insisted.

"He *owns* her." The witch flicked her red hair over a bony shoulder. "That's the point to every marriage contract. A bride becomes her husband's property. I, for one, do not choose to get mixed up in other people's personal lives. Particularly Ollie Hamilton's."

"Speaking of marriages," broke in the porcelain doll, her voice brittle. Susan realized Miss Devonshire had never once forgotten to whom she was speaking, or the circumstances thereof. "I've decided not to mention the impropriety we glimpsed here today, Miss Stanton. I suggest you do the same."

Susan nodded eagerly. There was no way she wished for rumors of her and Mr. Bothwick to circulate. The last thing she wanted was to find herself with a marriage contract tying her to Bournemouth. Particularly after *that* heartwarming tale. When Susan eventually staged a compromise for marriage, she'd do so on her own terms. And those terms were: Titled. London. Gentleman. Not mad-as-hatter country commoners.

The witch was staring at the porcelain doll as if she had grown yarn hair and button eyes. "You were never going to mention it, Dinah. A compromise between those two would've forced him to the altar with the wrong woman."

The porcelain doll looked perfectly happy to rip off her own arm just to club Miss Grey with it. "We didn't see precisely whom she was dallying with, did we?"

Susan started guiltily. "It wasn't exactly dall—"

"What?" The witch rounded on the china doll, ignoring Susan. "You haven't let him out of your sight in four years. I was right next to you all afternoon, remember? You watched every single step from the tavern to the apothecary through the back window!"

The porcelain doll's bone-white hands curved into perfect fists at her sides. "Well, he's not here to back that claim up, now, is he? In any case, I could easily say I caught Miss Stanton kissing some unknown gentleman. Anyone would take my word over hers. I'm the town angel, and she's . . . Well." Her little upturned nose gave a delicate sniff. "I can smell *tavern* on her from over here."

Susan's jaw dropped. Granted, during the few moments where she'd surely been possessed by the devil, she had in fact (eagerly) returned Mr. Bothwick's kisses, but come now. This was too much.

"If you're the town angel, I'm the Queen of England," she said hotly.

The witch snorted. "Then what were you doing kissing a libertine like Evan in the apothecary, Your Majesty?"

Susan smiled. "Better than lifting my skirts in a chicken shed, don't you think?"

The porcelain doll's perfect mouth dropped open.

And in that moment, Susan knew the truce was over. Curse her tongue!

The witch's umbrella clattered to the floor as she turned to stare at her friend, whose already-white face had blanched to an unhealthy hue.

"How do you know that, you little sneak?" she squeaked. "You were *spying* on us! That's the only way you could've known!"

"Why, that's a much better rumor to spread than 'Miss Stanton kissed Evan Bothwick.' After all, who hasn't?" the witch put in helpfully. She put her hand to her mouth and stage-whispered to her friend, "I think 'Miss Stanton spies through windows on people's private lovemaking' is far more damaging. That's the sort of juicy rumor that can follow a girl right back home to London. As long as she can't prove anything took place in any chicken sheds, it's our word against hers."

"Oh, I'll have plenty of words," the porcelain doll seethed, finding her voice at last. "Don't even think about breathing a single syllable of what you saw, Miss Stanton. After I walk out this door, you'll wish you had never laid eyes on me through those spectacles of yours. No one in this town will come within sight of you ever again."

She spun on her well-turned heel and marched out of the apothecary.

The witch snatched up her umbrella. She paused on her way out the door to turn back with a chillingly calm smile to add, "And if that doesn't do the trick . . . plenty of accidents happen to strangers here in Bournemouth, Miss Stanton. It'd be a shame if one happened to you."

Chapter 9

What the devil had he been *thinking?*

Evan hurled another rock into the ocean, not bothering to try and make it skip across the crashing waves, and faced the truth: He hadn't been thinking. Not one single second. The only idea he'd had in his brain from the moment he'd laid eyes on Miss Stanton back in the tavern had been, *Kiss her. Now.* End of story.

Except it almost wasn't the end of the story, now, was it? If he'd been caught like that, with her in his arms and their mouths locked together . . . A shiver deeper than the chill of the sea slithered between his shoulders. He'd be married, that's what he'd be. Leg-shackled. Good as dead.

He turned from the stormy waters and made his way to the narrow walkway winding up the steep cliff. He couldn't lose sight of his mission: vengeance for his brother's murder. The only intelligent thing to do was avoid Miss Stanton like the scurvy.

Naturally, when he hit the midpoint of the trail, there she was.

Evan cursed his damnable luck. Wasn't this why he had intended to avoid any intimacy with her in the first place? Because he wouldn't be able to help seeing her again . . .

and again . . . and again? And if that wasn't bad enough, she was a *lady.*

He paused to watch her wander along the path. Granted, the actual sight of her wasn't the problem. A backside that swayed that temptingly could never be a problem. Well, unless it was attached to a virgin, a lady, or a man-hunting debutante. Of which, she was likely all three.

Just then she turned, blinking in surprise. But didn't flee. Or offer a greeting.

Resigned, he trudged closer. "We meet again."

"Not on purpose." She backed up a small step, as if afraid the kissing could recommence at any moment. His blood warmed. The idea was sound.

No. No, it wasn't. Evan reined in his wayward thoughts and offered his elbow. Although, to do so was surely folly. If she touched him again, even as innocently as fingertips on his forearm . . .

She did not. She jerked her hands to her sides and glared at him from beneath her lashes, although her cheeks were now flushed and her breathing suspiciously shallow. "Don't touch me."

He held out his hands in silent surrender and sidestepped her in order to continue up the path. Would she follow, perhaps fall into step beside him? No. He heard nothing. Not even retreat. And then:

"I do not wish to be caught alone with you, Mr. Bothwick."

He stopped breathing. She didn't wish to be *caught,* did she? Interesting. If they weren't in plain view of pretty much every pair of eyes on the seashore, he'd have had half a mind to find out just what she didn't want to be caught doing.

As it was, however, he called backward without slowing down, "As you can see, madam, our goals are the same."

Problem was, he was a little worried that was true. The way she'd kissed him . . .

"Then do stop following me," her voice rang out.

He did stop. Moving forward, that was. He turned and stared at her in disbelief. How could he be following her if he were the one ahead and she the one behind? Was she just provoking him to prolong the interaction?

"It may surprise you to know that not only am I assuredly not following you, I also haven't the least desire to accompany you, wherever you might be going."

"Oh, really?" One of her thin eyebrows arched over the tops of her spectacles. "As if you're not headed to Moonseed Manor."

"As it happens," he informed her with complete honesty, "I am not."

Her jaw clicked shut. She seemed to war with herself for a moment, then jogged up to meet him. "You're . . . not? Why not? Where are you going?"

He shrugged a little to say *that's my business, isn't it,* and turned his attention back to the trail.

She hesitated again, perhaps debating whether it was too late to take the arm he no longer proffered, and then hurried to remain at his side.

"Then what are you doing on this path?" she demanded. "Why aren't you visiting—"

"Because," he interrupted, "I'm *busy.*"

"Busy?" she repeated doubtfully. Interest was replaced by skepticism. "How could you be busy?"

The question seemed innocent enough, but Evan couldn't help but feel Miss Stanton had just insulted him. He walked faster. "Why wouldn't I be busy?"

"For one, you're independently wealthy. The rich are never busy. I should know." She stumbled when a bit of sand gave way. He reached over and placed her palm on his arm. She let it rest there. "And for two"—she gestured with her free hand—"this is *Bournemouth.*"

Evan had to give her credit. Those were all valid points. Had he not started dabbling in high treason out of pure ennui? Even smugglers had to sail to another country in order to find some excitement. What kind of excitement did Miss Stanton seek?

He glanced down. Her eagerly upturned face appeared to be awaiting answers, not kisses. Pity.

"You'd normally be right." He let his gaze linger on her lips for the briefest of moments. "But I find myself unusually distracted."

She thought about that for a moment—and concluded the correct double entendre, given the deepening pink in her cheeks—then forged ahead, unswayed from her course. "So where are you going now?"

"To my brother's house." No harm in telling her that much.

"Your—" She gaped at him. "I didn't know you had a brother!"

Darkness settled into his bones, along with the now-familiar clenching in his gut.

"I don't . . . anymore."

Her fingers clutched his arm a little tighter. "I—You—Is he the one?"

He frowned. "The one what?"

"The one you lost!" She looked up at him, blue eyes wide and unblinking.

Damn it. This was another reason not to have conversations with intelligent females. They had the most annoying ability to *reason.* To pay attention. And to remember.

"The entire town lost a good man," he hedged carefully, "when we lost my brother."

Miss Stanton looked exasperated enough to push him off the cliff.

She scowled. "I'm not dense, you know."

He did know. That was the problem.

"It's best you not concern yourself with me or my brother."

From the sudden glint in her eye, those were the exact wrong words one spoke to Miss Susan Stanton. He began to think *he* should've been the one to run screaming when he'd first noticed her traversing the same trail.

"I'll come with you," she announced, the avid intrigue in her expression nothing short of dangerous.

"You'll do no such thing."

"Yes," she carried on, by all appearances attempting to drag him along even faster. "We'll just have to go together. You can explain everything on the way."

"I'll do no such thing!"

"Which house belongs to your brother? Is it quite a far walk from here?"

"Miss Stanton." They were nearing the end of the path, and if she didn't disappear immediately into the walls of Moonseed Manor, she'd be able to see precisely where he was headed. "Have you forgotten something? For example, that your most fervent wish is to *not* be alone with me?"

Her free hand fluttered as if shooing away a fly. "What could possibly happen?"

He almost laughed at the naïveté of that question.

"Oh, I don't know," he said slowly, softly, his voice deepening as he let the delicious images tumble forth from the dark corners of his dreams. "Once I have you alone, unprotected, you might find yourself in my arms once again. This time, I won't stop with a simple kiss. I will divest you of your pelisse, your gown, your shift . . . and *then* I will start the sort of kissing I've been desperate to do all along. The sort of kiss that begins at your mouth, and travels down your throat to your shoulders, all the way to your breasts. The sort of kiss where your nipple is caught between my teeth, where your back arches in pleasure, and—"

A choking gasp escaped her. She shoved herself away from him and up onto solid ground.

Had his ploy worked?

"You'd do no such thing," she whispered. Or possibly panted. Both her palms were pressed to her chest as if preventing her bodice from tumbling open of its own accord.

"I wouldn't?" he asked, not bothering to hide the amusement—and arousal—from his voice. He had half a mind to start right here at the edge of the cliff. "How can you be certain?"

"B-because you're *busy*. With something important." Her eyes were huge. But determined. "Remember?"

A more effective bucket of ice had never been thrown on his ardor.

"That's right. I'm busy."

He turned and stalked off, leaving her behind. Though truth be told, he was far angrier with himself than at her.

Even when he heard her little booted feet hurrying to catch up with him.

"Wait!"

He didn't wait. He imagined she'd follow him anyway.

He was right.

When they reached the porch leading to Timothy's door, he turned and put a finger to her soft mouth before she could start asking a barrage of unanswerable questions.

"Stay here," he ordered. "No matter what."

She nodded quickly. Too quickly.

"I mean it."

"All right." Her lips opened and closed against the pressure of his finger. "I won't move."

He paused to be sure, then leapt up the steps two at a time.

The door was unlocked. Technically, it was still off its hinges. He moved it aside and slid into the darkened entryway.

The cargo was missing. *The cargo was missing*. He turned around in a slow circle, half-expecting it to magically reappear.

It did not.

Timothy had—somewhat stupidly, as it turned out— deposited the first mission's spoils inside his entryway before heading out on his secret mission, and then . . . Somebody had stolen the stolen goods? Who the devil could've done such a corkbrained thing? This was Bournemouth! Evan was the one who did the stealing, and he did it from other people. He did not steal from people he knew, and he particularly avoided stealing from *pirates*.

Besides, who would bother risking their neck to steal stolen tea sets, anyway? The captain's secret buyer? To protect his anonymity—and to obfuscate the trail leading back to treason—the man had never stepped foot in Bournemouth. But *somebody* had carted the goods away. Someone with a large carriage.

"No wonder you look so shocked," came a soft female voice from just outside the doorway. Miss Stanton slipped inside, glancing around in awe. "What hit this place, a hurricane?"

His hands twitched. "I thought I told you to stay put."

"I did. At first. And then I came in to see what you were doing."

Evan stared at her. Such insubordinate behavior was precisely how a person found himself tied to the mast while at sea.

She stood in front of a portrait of a small boy. "Who's this? Your brother?"

"No." It was Evan at eight years old. Right around when Timothy, then six, had decided his older brother could do no wrong and should be emulated in all things. That had turned out to be one of the worst decisions Timothy had ever made. Whether holding on to such a portrait indicated blind faith or just plain blindness, Evan couldn't say. Yet a stabbing sense of loss throbbed beneath his ribs at the realization that he wished more than anything that he owned a painting of his innocent, impressionable brother at that young age. Or any likeness of Timothy. Something to gaze upon in those moments when he wanted nothing more than to talk to his brother one more time. "Wait for me outside. *Go.*"

Something in his tone startled her enough to check her from continuing her trajectory into Timothy's sitting room.

She turned around, bit her lip, nodded. "You're right. I'm sorry."

But she hadn't taken more than a few steps toward the door before dropping to her knees and sliding two slender fingers into a crack in the floorboard.

"Ooh," she exclaimed. "What's this?"

Evan ground his teeth. In this house, it could be anything— biscuit, bullet, chamber pot cleaning schedule. He almost didn't want to know.

"What's what?" he asked anyway, despite his better judgment.

"This." Miss Stanton rose to her feet and came toward him, her prize enclosed in her fist.

He held out his hand.

She placed the back of hers inside his larger palm and uncurled her fingers.

A skull-and-crossbones winked up from the center of a large gold coin.

"That's a Jolly Roger, isn't it?" she breathed, awestruck. "But why? What could it mean?"

It meant, Evan realized with another glance at the ruined decor and the cargo-free entryway, that things were far, far worse than he thought.

When dawn came, Susan was still staring into the blackness of the canopy.

She hadn't slept. She'd lain in bed, listening for the cries of the belated Lady Beaune and hearing what she feared were the faint whimpers of the present (no doubt soon-to-be-belated) mistress, Lady Emeline.

And, guiltily enough, reliving a certain kiss.

She still couldn't believe her instantaneous reaction to the illicit contact . . . and to the man himself. He was nothing but an unapologetic rake. Yet she could no longer look him in the eyes without remembering what he looked like with them closed in passion. And how he felt. How he tasted.

She suffered through the hourlong hair-curling process in uncharacteristic silence. If only because she scarce registered it happening. Her mind swirled with the memory of those heated kisses . . . and the humiliating realization that she'd *liked* it.

Despite her blue blood and her family money and her parents' titles and the years and years of proper upbringing and education and (mostly) impeccable deportment, when push came to shove . . .

The inner Susan was a common hussy.

Still in a bit of a daze from that undesirable conclusion, she eventually found her way downstairs and out the front door. She could not indulge such fantasies. She was a lady out to ensnare a lord. A plan not served by slumming with the commoners. If she was willing to stoop so far as to stage a compromise in order to capture the wealthy lordling of her dreams (and, yes, she was more than willing), the least she could do was provide said lordling with a worthy bride. A proper bride. A demure bride. A chaste bride. A woman who did *not* take pleasure in stolen kisses by men far beneath her station.

Worse than anything . . . she'd wanted more.

But she could not risk it. Her romantic reputation (or rather, lack thereof) was the one thing she had to offer her future husband. A compromise worked only if the man in question believed himself to be the one who had done the compromising. She needed to remain pure and untouched until the day she set foot back in London. In the middle of nowhere she might be, but she was still Miss Susan Stanton, sole heiress of a reasonably wealthy baron, eligible young lady soon to be re-immersed in the glory and gaiety of High Society.

The simple thing to do—the smart thing to do—would be to avoid Mr. Evan Bothwick at all costs.

However.

He had a secret.

She didn't know what it was, but she burned to find out. The tantalizing promise of gossip had always been her one weakness. The not knowing of Mr. Bothwick's secret was eating Susan from the inside out.

Last night, he'd all but thrown her over his shoulder and dumped her back in the Manor without another word. The reprobate. He could've at least helped speculate on what manner of ruffian might've ripped apart his brother's home.

Then again, seeing a coin like that in one's brother's sitting room would unsettle anyone. Even a libertine like Mr. Bothwick, with little more on his mind than finding a new maiden to deflower. Country folk might not realize the significance of the coin's insignia, but Susan Stanton certainly did. Gooseflesh rippled up her spine at the unquestionably dangerous raison d'être:

Pirates.

Now, it *was* possible that the coin was merely a collector's item and didn't mean much of anything other than Mr. Bothwick's brother being a bit of a pig, who ought to have invested a little money in a proper display case for his collection. And perhaps a housekeeper. Who was to say? She wasn't one to leap to conclusions.

But she'd bet her month's allowance (assuming it came— Janey had shaken her head *no* that morning before Susan could even ask) that the slovenly fool had gotten himself killed by the simple virtue of being at home when seafaring footpads came to ransack his house. They'd probably robbed him blind and then killed him. Or possibly the other way around. Or perhaps it had been simultaneous and he'd perished in the mêlée. She'd tried to speculate but, as before, Mr. Bothwick had been maddeningly unwilling to participate.

But she knew who might.

She reached the foot of the path and cut across the sand

and dirt toward the dress shop. Had she not hotheadedly alienated Miss Devonshire and Miss Grey yesterday afternoon, they would've made precisely the sort of diverting companions with whom Susan surrounded herself in London: gossip-minded women. She absolutely had to find a way to make up. Decision made, she pushed open the door and stepped inside enemy territory.

They were not alone.

Mr. Forrester, the local magistrate, rested a well-tailored elbow (he couldn't be *that* poor) against a ream of crimson silk. Excellent. She needed to speak with him anyway. His golden head was bent alongside the porcelain doll's in a cozy tête-à-tête. When they both glanced over upon hearing the hinges creak open, the magistrate's eyes crinkled into a welcoming smile. Miss Devonshire's, however, sparked with murderous rage.

Susan decided it would be best to just go ahead and give them a minute to finish their conversation. She turned her gaze toward the ginger-haired witch stitching a hem in the dim candlelight. When Miss Grey looked up from her handiwork, her eyes were not filled with hate, but with an intense, watchful craftiness. Susan had been told on many occasions that she wore that look quite often herself.

"Miss Grey," she murmured, treating her to a curtsy by way of apology.

"Miss Peeks-Through-Windows," the witch returned, without bothering to set down her needle.

Susan's eyes widened painfully as she jerked her gaze toward the magistrate. His head remained next to Miss Devonshire's, their eyes only for each other.

"Don't worry," drawled the witch, not bothering to hide the bitter sarcasm in her tone. "When Dinah captivates a man, he wouldn't notice the room catching fire."

Susan couldn't help but cast an involuntary glance at the charred rafters, still spicing the dank air with remembered smoke from long-ago flames. Was that what had happened here? She glanced at the couple again.

"I—" she began, then stopped, unusually tongue-tied. "That is to say, you—"

The needle stabbed through the cloth without pause. "We haven't mentioned your peculiar . . . proclivity . . . to anyone just yet, if that's what you're asking. Dinah says you've realized your mistake and won't compound it by making another one."

Susan took a fortifying breath. "And you?"

The witch's smile was slow and unforgiving. "I say, who cares?"

Well. So that's how it was. Susan swallowed. At least she knew where she stood.

"I must say," the witch continued, "you're the last one I expected to cross that threshold. What demon drove you to put your face back in our line of sight?"

"I . . ." The response died on Susan's lips. Her earlier hope now seemed far too silly to voice aloud. Her muscles itched to spring for the door.

The witch's skinny red brows rose to mock her. "You didn't think we'd make up and be *friends,* did you?"

Her cackle was loud enough to earn an annoyed glance from the couple in the corner.

"Of course not," Susan denied, her voice empty. Even her limbs felt hollow. "How foolish that would be."

"Indeed," agreed the witch, stabbing her needle through the folded cloth again. "Not that it would've mattered anyway."

"What wouldn't have mattered? Whether I sought friendship?"

"No." The witch tore a thread with her teeth and flipped over the fabric. "Whether I cared." She cast a disgusted glance at the quietly conversing twosome before turning her shrewd gaze back to Susan. "I'm leaving. Forever."

Susan raised her brows at the giggling porcelain doll entrancing the handsome magistrate.

"Miss Devonshire doesn't know . . . ?"

"Oh, she knows," said the witch with a derogatory chuckle. "You think I'd tell *you* something I hadn't told my best friend?" The needle resumed its attacks on the fabric. "She just doesn't believe me, that's all."

Miss Grey. Leaving. Forever. Hope blossomed anew in Susan's thumping chest. Her London connections were much better resources than a mere country magistrate. She could escape *and* rescue her cousin Emeline. Perhaps today!

"So . . . ," she began carefully, trying to mask her eagerness. "You have a horse? A carriage?"

From Miss Grey's incredulous expression, Susan might as well have inquired about dragons and magic carpets.

"I have my *brother*," the witch responded haughtily. "He's getting a ship."

A ship! Susan hadn't considered that possibility. Largely because the traditional path to London was by land. A ship could make an excellent vehicle of escape. But, unfortunately for them both . . .

"Your brother?" she repeated, unable to keep the disappointment from her voice. "Have you got more than one, by any chance?"

"No, I haven't got more than one." Miss Grey's tone dripped with condescension. "And he'll only have the one ship, if that's your next question. Luckily for me, that's all we need. No more needles in this lifetime! The moment he gets back, I'm gone."

"I see." A cold sweat began at the nape of Susan's neck, now that she'd been given a conversational opening she truly didn't wish to take. Miss Grey's brother was never coming back. And, viper though she might be, she deserved to know. Susan just didn't want to be the one to tell her.

"What if Red—er, Joshua—*weren't* coming back? For some reason. Ever."

Miss Grey stopped sewing. Unguarded fury replaced the scorn in her dark tone. "Why would you say that?"

"I just mean . . ." Susan wracked her brain, trying to recall exactly what the persistent ghost had told her to say. Where the bloody hell *was* Red, anyway? "He wouldn't have left you without instructions, right? That is . . . you'd know what to do if he weren't ever returning. Wouldn't you?"

"Who the hell do you think you are to suggest such atrocities?" The witch's eyes burned with brimstone and her handiwork fell to the floor. "My brother *is* coming back. We *are* leaving Bournemouth. He would *never* leave me behind."

"No. No." Susan floundered for the right words. If any existed. "I'm not saying he wouldn't *wish* to return. I'm just saying, what if he'd love to spirit you away forever but couldn't do so after all? Or get word to you to explain why? You would have an alternate plan, then, wouldn't you?"

The witch leapt to her feet, destroying the forgotten crumple of cloth with the heels of her boots. "Give me one good reason why *that* would be possible, Miss Peeping Tom. Did you *spy* on him planning not to come back? Ha! Impossible. You have no way of knowing what he's intending to do or not do. He'll be back as soon as he has the ship."

"Well, it might be possible to surmise he couldn't return, if he were . . . dead." The syllable floated from her mouth so faintly, Susan could scarce hear herself speak the word.

"He's not dead."

"Perhaps Red wished to come back, to send word—"

"*He's not dead.*"

"—but most of all, wished for you to take care of both yourself and the situation in whatever manner it was that you'd decided upon in case of emerg—"

"Get out! Get out! Get out!"

This time, even the lovebirds in the corner couldn't help but turn and gape at the spectacle unfolding before them.

Susan backed hastily toward the door. The razor-sharp tip of the witch's umbrella jabbed into Susan's chest, to ensure she did so as rapidly as possible.

She fled. But she didn't get far.

For a doll made of porcelain, Miss Devonshire could sprint across sand at exceptionally high speeds.

"You told Harriet her brother was *dead?*" she half-screeched, half-panted upon reaching Susan's side.

Susan stopped running. She'd already been caught.

"I said 'might' be," she mumbled defensively, but this only inflamed the tiny doll even more.

"That is the most despicable trick I could ever imagine someone playing on another human being!" Miss Devonshire's bow-shaped mouth gaped in both anger and shock. Her big blue eyes narrowed dangerously. "I was a fool to want to give you an opportunity to redeem yourself. You're obviously vermin without hope of redemption. But hear me now: I will get you for this, Susan Stanton. You *will* be sorry."

"Y-you're going to spread rumors about me?" Susan stammered, frantic.

The laugh that escaped Miss Devonshire's perfect teeth was nothing short of terrible.

"I'll do better than that, you horrible little tramp. Revenge so swift, you will never see it coming." Hatred soaked through each snarled word. "You predicted a death, Miss Stanton. *I'll* make sure it's yours."

Chapter 10

Susan searched the shore for the missing ghost until her legs gave out beneath her. She crumpled alongside the vastness of the ocean, her dry tongue tasting of sand and salt and hopelessness.

The problem with Miss Devonshire's threat was . . . Susan believed every word. She wouldn't have put a premeditated "mishap" past her *or* Miss Grey, even before today's interaction. From the sound of things, nobody in Bournemouth would bat an eye. Even the magistrate was blind to everything but Miss Devonshire's porcelain-perfect beauty.

The bigger problem, of course, was that she could do nothing to change their minds. Short of proving she saw ghosts. How could that happen when even *she* couldn't find Red, now that she was looking for him? Had she imagined him after all? Was he nothing but the product of a lonely, overactive mind?

If so, perhaps Miss Devonshire was right to take her revenge. Susan had seen the root of the terror in Miss Grey's eyes: Susan had voiced the very fear Miss Grey had refused to acknowledge to herself. How long *had* the woman been waiting for her brother's return? Susan sighed. She hadn't planted a suspicion. She'd salted an open wound.

And now there was no ghost to prove her words.

She'd tried the tavern, the apothecary, the endless trail curling its way up the cliff. No Red. No ghosts at all. With nowhere else to go, she'd ended up wandering along the beach.

When her heart rate returned to normal, she forced herself into motion. She *had* to find him. Talk to him. Demand answers. Or at least some help. Surely there was a way for Susan to "accidentally" stumble across Red's remains. For his sister to bury him. To have peace.

Because without a body to back up her words . . . Susan shivered in the damp ocean air. That was the only way. Proof or not, she could never admit she saw spirits. She needed her trip back to London to end in Stanton House, not Bedlam.

She clutched her pelisse about her a little tighter. She turned from the fury of the waves, intending to regroup back in her bedchamber, when she caught sight of a telltale flicker farther down the shore.

"Red?" she called out, her voice scratchy in the briny air.

No answer. The beach was empty.

She picked her way along the rocks in the direction of whatever shadow had caught her eye. A thick wall of rock rose from the sea, as high as the cliff on which Moonseed Manor stood.

When she neared, she realized the giant mass of rock was not as solid as it appeared. A man-size crevice gaped in its side. She crept closer. The narrow opening fell inward as far as the eye could see, swallowing the sun's meager rays in the thick soup of darkness.

"If you're in there—" She jumped back, shaken, to hear the distorted echo of her own voice bounce among the shadows. "You can just come out if you wish to talk to me," she whispered.

Something glimmered in the distance.

The darkness shifted.

A shape. A man. Red? No. Too tall, too slender. Not a ghost, then. Someone real. She should quit the premises posthaste before she found herself compromised after all. Except the incoming shadow belonged to—

"Mr. Bothwick?" she blurted out, simultaneously confused and relieved. "What on earth are you doing here? Don't you know caves are dangerous? I must admit, you gave me quite a start. You—" She broke off, gulping down a lump of rock-hard fear. "Y-you aren't moving your feet."

She fought a swoon. Mr. Bothwick was *dead?* How? When? Why?

"You can see me?" he said in wonder. Something in his voice was . . . off.

"Not well," she admitted, unnerved. She reminded herself that he couldn't hurt her, that if he touched her he'd simply disappear, harmless. "You're doing a fair bit of sputtering, like the flame of a candle. And the shadows aren't helping much."

"How did you know my name?"

She paused. Had he completely forgotten her, in death? She'd spent all morning in a pitiable frenzy because of his kisses, and the moment his heart stopped beating, the horrid man had put her out of his mind forever. Oh—God—*dead*. Her head swam. Suddenly too dizzy to keep herself upright, she slumped against the opening lip of the crevice.

"I'm Susan," she heard herself say through a thick mist. "Miss Stanton, rather, since we never did first-name ourselves. Don't you remember me at all?"

His voice was droll. And closer. "Trust me, I'd remember a face like yours."

Then she saw *his*. And he wasn't Mr. Bothwick.

Susan backed up, slipped on a slick rock, landed on her bruised arse.

The almost-Mr.-Bothwick didn't laugh. Didn't float closer. He cocked his shimmering head to one side and watched, silent.

The truth hit her.

"You're Mr. Bothwick's brother," she breathed. "The misplaced one."

"Timothy," he confirmed, then frowned. "Who, exactly, misplaced me?"

"Mr. Bothwick did," she answered promptly, then faltered when the Dead Mr. Bothwick's frown grew deeper. "Er, that is to say . . . I think he may have done."

What on earth had happened to the razor-sharp conversational skills she'd once been so proud of possessing? She'd sounded like a halfwit all day today. Exceptional circumstances notwithstanding.

"Might he now? Well, that changes things." Dead Mr. Bothwick's face cleared and he gave a short, wry laugh. "Or does it?"

She wasn't quite sure how to answer that question, so she said nothing at all.

"May I give you a hand up?" the ghost asked politely.

"Oh! No, it's all right." Susan scrambled to her feet. She dusted the sand from her skirts as best as she could. "Unfortunately, it doesn't work that way. I can only see you."

"And hear me," he pointed out.

"Er, right. I can only see you and hear you." There she went, sounding like a ninnyhammer again. When it seemed he might press the issue, she rushed to add, "What were you doing in that cave? Wouldn't it make more sense to haunt . . . people?"

The look he tossed her was irritatingly amused. "Is that why I'm still here? To haunt people?"

"Well, how would I know?" she snapped defensively. "Maybe you have a mission."

"A mission," he repeated, his expression thoughtful. "That I do."

In a burst of sudden lucidity, the morning's events clicked into place. Red had had a mission. He'd promised to disappear the moment she'd helped him break the news to his sister. She'd done so—however reluctantly and inelegantly—and now he was missing. But what if he wasn't missing? What if he was simply *done?*

"I'll help," she announced, willing to do almost anything for this new ghost to be gone from her increasingly complicated life. She gave him a sharp nod and tried not to be discomfited by his similarity in appearance to the (still living, she hoped) Other Mr. Bothwick. She'd quickly fulfill the Dead Mr. Bothwick's mission. Then he'd disappear forever.

He disagreed. "You can't help."

"How do you know I can't help? You haven't told me what the problem is."

A self-deprecating smile quirked his lips. "I have many."

Susan sighed. "Let's start with the first."

After a long pause, he admitted, "I'm looking for something."

"There you go! I'll help you find it." She beamed at him. "Er . . . what is it?"

"Look," he said, "I appreciate the offer. I do. But you can't help. I'm *invisible.* You're not. So don't worry. I'll take care of this. In fact . . ." He cast a startled look behind him as if half-expecting a herd of stampeding cattle to burst forth from the cavern. Susan shot a glance into the crevice herself, just to make sure. "In fact," he repeated, "this is not the best location for an unchaperoned young lady. What are you doing here all alone, might I ask? Don't *you* know caves are dangerous?"

Conceding the point, Susan followed his iridescent form away from the cavern, back toward Bournemouth.

"Caves don't frighten me," she said aloud with far more bravado than she felt. No way would she have trespassed within its walls.

"That one should." Dead Mr. Bothwick's voice floated back, casting a chill deep into her bones. "Promise me you won't come here again."

"Er, all right." Easy peasy. There wasn't enough gold to

tempt her. "But don't try to change the subject. I am determined to help you."

"Look, Miss . . ."

"Stanton."

"Right." He rubbed at his semitransparent face. "Look, Miss Stanton. You can't help. I can walk through walls and *I* haven't seen hide nor hair of it."

"Well, what if it's not within walls?"

His ghostly sigh was unsettlingly like his brother's. "I'm not just checking houses, lady. Did you not see me inside a cave?"

"Those are walls, too, even if they're not made of wood. What if whatever you're looking for isn't aboveground at all? What if someone put it in a box and buried it?"

Dead Mr. Bothwick appeared unimpressed with her reasoning. "It *is* a box."

"Well, there you go," she babbled anyway. "Anyone worth their salt knows you hide boxes by burying them, not by sticking them in some locked room where anybody could walk through the wall and find it."

She bit back a startled gasp when he turned around— without turning around. One minute she'd been following his ghostly shoulders and the next minute he'd rematerialized facing in her direction, with an expression that indicated she was treading on very thin ice.

She had learned to stay clear of thin ice.

"If you don't fancy my help, that's fine," she assured him hurriedly. "I was just thinking that two heads might be better than one, that's all. Especially if one of the heads were attached to a corporeal body capable of wielding a shovel and things of that nature."

He turned-without-turning again and continued toward town once more. But she heard him.

"You have a point."

She had a point! Ha! She'd help solve his mystery, which was a plus for both of them, and he'd go away forever, which was also a plus for both of them. Now she just needed to know what she was looking for.

"What kind of box is it?" She jogged to catch up. "Pine? Fir?"

"Jewelry."

Jewelry? Another fragment of memory replayed in her head, and she couldn't stop herself from murmuring, "I wonder if it's the same thing."

Dead Mr. Bothwick stopped cold.

Susan jerked to the side at the last minute, barely avoiding dissipating the new ghost right when the substance of his mission was starting to take form.

"You wonder if what's the same thing?" His voice was chilly, his tone suspicious.

"I can't help but notice that we're not the only ones digging for missing items," she explained hesitantly. "Valuable, missing, important . . . things. It's probably just coincidence."

"I don't believe in coincidence." Dead Mr. Bothwick's ghostly arms crossed. "Tell me about this other missing item. Is it a box? What does it look like?"

"I'm not certain. I haven't seen it," she pointed out, "because it's *missing*. All the giant said was—"

"The who?"

"That is to say . . ." What was his real name? The girls had told her yesterday. "Mr. Oliver Hamilton."

The ghost came unhinged.

"What? Ollie knows about the box? Od's blood and damn it. For Christ's—why didn't you say so to start with?" His ghostly form seemed to double in size.

"I didn't know it was the same box," she stammered, suddenly nervous despite the knowledge he couldn't touch her without disappearing himself. "We still don't know for sure. Besides, you didn't want my help with your precious mission!"

"Oh, it's the same box, all right." Dead Mr. Bothwick

zoomed forward far too fast for her to keep up safely. "It's definitely the same box. Damn and triple damn. How did he know? Who could've told him? And—" He stopped again and re-misted toward her. "How do *you* know?"

"He . . . happened to mention it one day?"

"He happened to *mention* it? You're in such confidence with him that Ollie just up and said, 'You know, I'm going to bury this priceless antique jewelry box,' and you said, 'Yes, do, capital idea.'" The ghost's short laugh was chilling. "No, Miss Stanton. You can't help. Go away." He shot forward again.

"No," she called after him. "You've got it wrong. Assuming it's the same box, they've been trying to find it, too. It must be lost."

Dead Mr. Bothwick stopped without turning. "What do you mean?"

"He and the scare—and the butler. They've been searching. I saw the manservant digging in town."

"In town?" He swiveled to face her. "Where in town?"

"In the sand behind the buildings, for one." Susan wracked her brain and had another flash of insight. Of course. There were no missing children—only a missing box. "The grave garden! I mean, the gravesite. In the rock garden. At Moonseed Manor. Someone has definitely been digging there, too. Which means the box could be anywhere."

Dead Mr. Bothwick rose a few inches off the ground in excitement. "You said you know where to get hold of a shovel?"

"Er, actually what I said was, they'd searched themselves and couldn't find whatever it is they're looking for."

"No, no, no." Dead Mr. Bothwick's features blurred with each shake of his head. "They don't want to *find* anything. They want to keep everything *hidden*. I'm running out of time. Without that box . . ." He snapped into focus. "We'll have to dig it up. Tonight."

"We'll what?"

"*You'll* have to, that is." He nodded slowly. "You were right. I can't do this without you. Someone human will need to open it once we've dug it up."

A ball of ice formed in the center of her stomach. "W-where am I digging?"

"The rock garden, of course. At Moonseed Manor."

Dig amongst the graves? Was he barmy? She wasn't stepping foot anywhere near that garden of forgotten bones, tonight or any night. One ghost at a time was bad enough.

"Er, I'm afraid that one's going to be a 'No, thank you.'" She tried for a smile and failed. "But I'm sure there's something else—"

He was already shaking his head. "It's the only way."

"There are *dead people* there! What if I dig up a corpse? An *unhappy* one?"

Dead Mr. Bothwick did not seem to care. After all, he was dead, too. And not particularly happy. What was one more ghost to him? Susan tipped her face to the murky sky and considered screaming. Or tearing her hair out. Or both.

"Without your help," he said softly, "I will never be able to fulfill my mission. I need you."

Argh. That's what she was afraid of. She'd have to find a shovel . . . and pray she didn't get caught digging.

Evan hauled the old rowboat ashore and hid it upside-down in its usual place—right out in the open. Nobody else was fool enough to take a tiny speck of a watercraft like that out on waves as vicious as these. But he'd needed to think, needed to release pent-up energy in some way other than chasing down Miss Stanton and pinning her to a wall. Much as he'd have preferred the latter.

He trudged back toward town with his hands in his pockets. His arms were a pleasant sort of heavy from all the exercise, his back and shoulders just as tired as he was.

Perhaps he'd stop by Sully's before heading up the sheer cliff leading to home. Have some laughs, and a pint of whatever swill was on tap this week.

Wait. What was happening up ahead? Evan paused at the edge of town, far enough away he doubted he'd be noticed, yet close enough to have a reasonably good lay of the land. Gordon Forrester, by all appearances, was angling for a lay of his own.

The holier-than-thou magistrate had one foot in the sand and the other on the second step of the dress shop porch. He had his arms crossed over his bent knee as he leaned forward in conversation with Miss Dinah Devonshire. Whom the magistrate no doubt imagined as pure and self-righteous as himself. They made a pair, all right. Evan hoped Forrester did succeed in winning Miss Devonshire's obsessive attentions.

Invite her to the damn assembly, Evan channeled in Forrester's direction. *For all that's holy, get her out of my hair.*

There was no chance in hell that Evan would be caught dead at that stupid assembly. Bath was just far enough away that they'd be forced to stay the whole weekend. He could barely endure a quarter-hour of such insipid company. Besides, he held no interest in restorative waters that couldn't be distilled into something with a little more punch.

Miss Devonshire's high-pitched jabber assaulted Evan's eardrums, even at this distance. Forrester, apparently deaf to chipmunk frequency, merely inclined his head toward her and smiled.

Perhaps Evan would be better off not walking any farther into view. He could wait to have lukewarm ale another day, if it meant he might finally be wriggling free from Miss Devonshire's talons. The last thing he wished to do was inadvertently catch her eye and ruin everything Forrester was working toward. Although why anyone would want to court a woman—any woman—remained beyond Evan's comprehension.

He dropped to the sand and leaned back on his elbows to wait. And watch. Hopefully Forrester would try to steal a kiss, because then Evan would run forward screaming, "Saw you! Saw you!" and compromise Bournemouth's two most upstanding citizens right then and there.

A figure appeared on the horizon.

What started out as a small dot in the distance was looking more and more like the delectable Miss Stanton. Gesticulating anxiously and deep in discussion with herself, as was her wont. Evan wished he found her quirks alarming instead of intriguing. Perhaps if she'd just froth at the mouth a bit he could finally get her out of his head.

He wasn't the only one to notice her steady, hip-swaying approach. Forrester nearly broke his neck turning to watch her. As it was, the magistrate lost his balance and half-fell, half-leapt from the porch.

Based on the scowl contorting her typically wrinkle-free face, Dinah Devonshire was not amused by this turn of events. Neither was Evan.

Forrester didn't notice, because he was already walking toward Miss Stanton, leaving Miss Devonshire bereft in the open doorway, the last dregs of their conversation still clinging to her tongue. She ran after him, but Forrester apparently hadn't been interested in Miss Devonshire after all. He'd just been biding his time until the real sweetmeat of Bournemouth walked right into his hands.

Evan hauled himself to his feet. He was going to have to make an appearance after all. Just to keep Miss Stanton safe. Not because he was jealous. He could scarce consider that toady Forrester a romantic threat, for Christ's sake. Not that Evan was interested in romance.

As he cut across the sand, the disturbing question he *should* have been asking himself prodded at the back of his mind. What was Mr. Drinking-Is-a-Disgusting-Habit still doing here? Evan hadn't expected the magistrate's high insteps to touch town until it was time for the precious assembly.

Granted, Miss Stanton was certainly alluring enough to turn any red-blooded man's bimonthly visits into biweekly ones. But it wasn't as if the magistrate had known she'd be moving to town. Was it as simple as an upwardly mobile man seeking to make an advantageous match? Or was there an ulterior motive for the unexpected visit?

A motive like . . . investigating the Bothwick brothers?

Evan paused, then shook his head, laughed at himself, and continued forward. Forrester couldn't detect a raindrop in a thunderstorm. The man was too much of a stick to ever actually nab anyone for anything. The day that idiot put two and two together and got an even number would be the day jellyfish fell from the sky.

As further proof, the blank look of confusion that Forrester blinked from his eyes at Evan's approach was all Evan needed to see—his name couldn't have been further from Forrester's flirtatious little brain. Now to get the slug's sights off of Miss Stanton.

Who, upon catching wind of the dashing magistrate in his dry costume and sand-free hair, set off toward him at a dead run.

It was enough to make a man stop in his tracks. And load his pistols.

From the clenched fists on her hips and the upward tilt of her chin, if Miss Dinah Devonshire had artillery of her own, Miss Stanton would already be dead.

"Mr. Forrester! Mr. Forrester!" the latter shouted as she ran. "I am *so pleased* to see you!"

Evan scowled. She had never greeted *him* such.

The dress shop door swung open. Miss Harriet Grey stalked down the steps and to the side of the building. Presumably to watch the proceedings from the open air, instead of the grimy window from whence she usually spied upon the outside world.

Her attention seemed focused on the back of Miss Devonshire's head. Miss Devonshire's attention seemed focused on the back of the magistrate's head. Forrester was facing the sea—or rather, the undulating bounce of Miss Stanton's incoming bosom.

Evan's trigger finger itched.

Miss Devonshire made her move. She sashayed forward, swinging her hips in an almost comical arc until she reached Forrester's elbow. The magistrate didn't appear to notice. His gaze remained on Miss Stanton.

Forrester had never looked so focused. Miss Devonshire had never looked so homicidal.

Evan knew the feeling. From the current angle, he'd have to shoot straight through Miss Devonshire in order to hit any of Forrester's vital organs. While such a trick shot might be eminently satisfying for multiple reasons, Miss Stanton was now within curtsying distance. In a gown far too lovely to splatter with blood.

He stalked closer.

By the looks of the situation, Forrester had completely forgotten Evan watching them from the shadows. The man wasn't qualified to be magistrate of a weevil in a peapod. Miss Devonshire also had yet to notice Evan's approach, largely because she was clutching Forrester's arm and cooing something into his ear so spellbinding that the poor sap's entire face had turned to stone. Miss Grey kept up her role as flying buttress to the dress shop, one stick-straight arm glued to the wall by five splayed, spindly fingers.

Miss Stanton, on the other hand, had no reason not to notice him. She was the only one facing his direction. He wasn't more than ten yards away. Nine. Eight. But she'd apparently gone blind to everything but the angelic magistrate, for she reached forward, clutched the hand opposite Miss Devonshire, and reprised her earlier monologue.

"Oh, Mr. Forrester. How very, very good it is to see you! Can we speak privately? Please?"

Forrester seemed even more entranced by Miss Stanton. Miss Devonshire looked ready to poke her eyes out with sewing needles. Then she registered his approach.

"Evan!" she screeched, in that lovely banshee-at-midnight voice of hers. She started to release Forrester's arm—no doubt to latch herself to Evan's—but then thought better of it, a crafty smile spreading beneath her apple cheeks.

Was she trying to make him jealous? Evan kept walking. Good luck. He'd never suffered a jealous moment before in his life. He almost laughed at the preposterousness of the idea. Then his eyes narrowed. Perhaps he *should* laugh. Loudly. Miss Stanton somehow still hadn't noticed him, although he was now inches from her side.

"Can we go somewhere?" she whispered to the magistrate, his free hand still in her grasp. "Alone? *Now?*"

Everyone present gasped at this over-the-top outrageousness. Except Forrester. Whose eyes lit like Christmas candles as he smiled and said, "Why, I think—"

"—that would be a terrible idea," Evan concluded, his voice booming overloud in the otherwise calm beach.

But at least it earned him a glance from Miss Stanton. A quick, dismissive one. Then a longer, puzzled stare. Then a startled look of recognition. And then she returned her gaze to Forrester.

Evan's jaw set. He could swear that for a moment there, Miss Stanton hadn't recognized him. Two inches from her face. Who the devil had she *thought* he'd been? St. Nicholas? Perhaps it was time for new spectacles. Particularly since she'd failed to notice the bunched fury in his muscles or the cannon blasts firing from his eyes.

"It's something of an emergency," she continued, her voice urgent. At last she turned her gaze to Evan's. "I *must* speak to Mr. Forrester. Alone."

"Without a chaperone?" Evan forced a laugh. Ha, ha, ha. "Out of the question."

"Not a hundred souls live here," Miss Grey put in dryly from her vantage point against the wall. "None of us have chaperones."

"Well, there you go." He tried to look as though she'd somehow helped his cause. "None of you should be alone with him."

Miss Stanton fixed him with an exasperated look. "He's the *magistrate*."

"He's a man," Evan corrected firmly.

A man with an attractive woman clinging to each arm.

Upon reflection, Evan supposed that as long as Miss Devonshire was one of the barnacles, there was no chance in hell of Forrester shaking free long enough to have the smallest second alone with Miss Stanton. But he still didn't like it.

"We were just discussing the assembly." Miss Devonshire's hallmark chipmunk giggle accompanied this announcement. As did a sly look from beneath her pale lashes.

Definitely trying to make him jealous. Ha.

Her statement caused Miss Stanton to break eye contact with the magistrate long enough to glance about doubtfully. "Here?"

"Of course not *here*." More excited-squirrel noises. "*Bath*. It will be a weekend to remember."

"Bath?" Miss Stanton repeated, as if dazed. "They have posting-houses in Bath."

"Er, yes." This observation stole the wind from Miss Devonshire's sails. But only for a moment. "Quite a few stables and beasts, I'm afraid. But we shan't have to see them. For there's to be dancing and champagne and the most cunning little cakes, as well as restorative waters and—"

"When?" Miss Stanton demanded, her grip on the magistrate's hand hard enough to turn a man's fingers blue. "How will we get there?"

This time, Miss Devonshire's smile was pure malice.

"I don't know how *we* will get there," she said acidly.

"But those who are invited will go in the carriages of those who invite them."

"Right." Miss Stanton's face fell, and she dropped the magistrate's arm at last. "That is how it tends to work."

Although he hadn't pegged her for the flighty, let's-drink-weak-punch sort, Evan hated to see Miss Stanton so disappointed at her obvious lack of an invitation. If he weren't already engaged to be smuggling cargo that weekend, he'd have taken her himself just to make her smile again.

"Have *you* an invitation, then, Dinah?" Miss Grey called from behind them. Although the question seemed innocent, the edge underlying her tone indicated it was anything but.

Evan could swear Miss Devonshire's teeth were clenched behind the practiced smile. She turned his way.

"Mr. Bothwick—" she began.

"Ah, so you two have plans already?" Forrester interrupted, neatly extricating himself from Miss Devonshire's physical clutches and preempting the *Mr. Bothwick can't take me, so I just know kind Mr. Forrester will* that had been about to spring from her lips. Perhaps the magistrate wasn't as slow on the uptake as Evan had always thought. "In that case . . . Miss Stanton, may I? If you're not promised elsewhere, of course?"

Evan wasn't sure whose jaw fell open farther—Miss Devonshire's or his.

Date with high treason be damned. He was going to that stupid assembly with Miss Stanton on his arm. Even if it killed him.

He reached for her. "I—"

"I would love to." The right words rushed from her lips. But she beamed at Forrester.

Evan's head exploded.

Forrester, of course, looked thrilled. Charmed, in fact. Why wouldn't he be? Any man could count himself lucky to have Miss Stanton dancing in his arms. *Waltzing.* Evan's throat tightened. Forrester and Miss Stanton, hand in hand, hip to hip. No, no, no. Evan wouldn't stand for it.

Miss Devonshire looked about to have an apoplexy on the spot.

She rounded on Evan. "You're taking me."

"Still busy," he said quickly. Thank God.

Although the idea of dropping in later, alone, just in time to rip Miss Stanton from Forrester's weak clutches and escape with her into the darkness—now, that would be something to come home a little early for.

"Can we *please* speak alone?"

Miss Stanton's murmured plea burned in Evan's blood. Too bad the question had been asked of Forrester, not him.

The magistrate nodded, placing her hand on his elbow.

Evan blocked his path within seconds. "Where the devil are you taking her?"

"To walk along the beach." Forrester's slow smile over the top of Miss Stanton's head indicated he realized the full extent of how he'd just trounced Evan Bothwick. Little slug had a brain between his ears after all. "You may watch us from here, if you would like to play at chaperone, Mother."

Damn it.

The sodding rotter had dismissed him *and* made it unmanly to keep watch, all in the same breath. Miss Devonshire harrumphed. Evan shook with repressed rage. He should've shot through them both when he'd had the chance. If he backed up a few paces, perhaps he still could.

Miss Stanton leaned into the magistrate and strolled with him toward the water's edge without so much as a fare-thee-well. She would no doubt fall head over feet in love with the goody choirboy right before Evan's eyes.

And all he could do was watch.

Chapter 11

He was a dream come true.

A man of the law, possessed of both his faculties and a carriage, offering to get her the hell out of this no-horse town. Susan nearly pranced at this sudden turn of fortune.

"When do we leave?" She bounced on her toes. "It'd be impossible to repack all my valises, so I guess I won't take—well, I won't take anything at all, that's what I'll do. I'll buy a completely new trousseau in London. Father *owes* me. But none of that matters when you still haven't said at what time you prefer to set out. I can be ready in an hour. I can actually be ready, well, *already,* if you care to direct me to the horses right now. Is the carriage close by? Are the chaperones awaiting us?"

She smiled up at him expectantly.

He did the confused, blinking-frowning face typically reserved for octogenarians.

"I'm afraid the assembly isn't until *next* weekend, my dear. And yes, of course we will be properly chaperoned. I've a lovely aunt who's just dying to return to Bath."

Next weekend! Bloody, bloody hell. Who's to say she—and cousin Emeline—would survive that long?

She glanced over his shoulder. Mr. Bothwick, Miss Grey, and Miss Devonshire hadn't moved. Unless one counted the smirk on the latter's china-perfect face, which indicated Susan had not quite walked out of earshot yet.

To quote the recently departed Mr. Timothy Bothwick, damn and triple damn. (It really was an excellent expression, which she would henceforth strive to utilize as much as possible.)

Just as important as her disappointingly postponed escape was the need to rescue Lady Emeline while she was still breathing. Presuming she was still breathing. To her shame, Susan hadn't dared to venture back into the cellar to check on her cousin.

If even half the story about the original Lady Beaune were true, the local residents were the last people she could count upon to see the inhumanity of the situation. If Miss Grey and Miss Devonshire overheard Susan plotting to rid the giant of his captive bride, they'd no doubt run off to tell the "poor man" everything before she or the magistrate could act.

Then Susan would have nothing to show for her efforts except a magistrate who no longer believed her stories (as if anyone could believe such a tale without seeing the horror firsthand) and the knowledge that she'd have to return to Moonseed Manor to face the giant's wrath at her attempted perfidy.

She'd never make it to Bath if the magistrate rescinded his invitation. Or if she were chained to the cellar.

Were they far enough away to speak without being overheard? She cast another glance over the magistrate's shoulder. The two women hadn't moved. But Mr. Bothwick had. He seemed to be strolling after them, keeping an even distance, careful to stay just within earshot. Shameless busybody. She tried to catch his eye, but he tipped his face into the sun and began to whistle a tuneless melody, as if it were just coincidence that he happened to be invading her personal space on an otherwise empty strip of beach stretching along forty miles of shore.

At this rate, her poor cousin would be stuck where she was until after the assembly, when Susan made her break for home. Plenty of people knew the Stanton name in Bath. Getting a carriage on credit would be easy. And then she'd bring the full force of London law down on Moonseed Manor. She hated having to wait another week, but as long as she rescued cousin Emeline in the end, all would be worth it.

"Do you like dancing so very much, then?"

"What?" It was Susan's turn to stare uncomprehendingly.

The magistrate gave a self-conscious smile. "You just seemed so disappointed, is all. I, too, wish the dancing were sooner. In fact, I would like to call on you beforehand, if I may. One week seems terribly long to wait to enjoy the company of a delightful young lady like yourself."

Oh, good Lord. He thought she was pining to be whirled about in his arms? She'd never pined for a man, much less a boring waltz. All the most interesting activities took place *off* the dance floor.

Over the magistrate's shoulder, she spied Mr. Bothwick again. Still watching them. *There* was a man who no doubt knew plenty of interesting activities for which one did not require moving to music. And possibly even more interesting ones that did. Susan tried to tamp down the sudden flash of heat simmering just beneath her flesh.

She needed to get back to Mayfair. Now. Before she did something stupid. But how? Perhaps Mr. Forrester could be of service prior to the assembly.

"When are you leaving?" she asked suddenly. "Where are you going next?"

His brows lifted in feigned (or possibly unfeigned) hurt. "So eager to be rid of me?"

"Not at all," she assured him. Rot. She needed to sound innocently flirtatious, not like she was fishing for escape routes. She hugged his arm a little closer and tried not to feel Mr. Bothwick's gaze carving a hole in the back of her head. "I was just curious about you."

And how she might stow a ride in the magistrate's carriage. Wherever the damn thing was. Assuming he hadn't arrived in a mail coach. Not that she'd seen a single mail coach in the entire time she'd been in Bournemouth. Bloody hell, what if he'd *walked?* No matter. He'd need a proper carriage to take her and his aunt to the assembly. Escape was still on the horizon.

The magistrate smiled uncertainly. "I'm afraid I'm not going home for a while. I've business in the area and various loose ends to tie up. If you'd like, though . . ." He paused, studied her intently, flushed. "I might be able to stop by Bournemouth midweek, before the assembly. May I call on you?"

"Yes," she blurted, then mentally kicked herself when both Mr. Forrester and Mr. Bothwick interpreted her immediate enthusiasm in exactly the wrong way. One beamed. The other glowered.

Unfortunately, she couldn't correct the assumption that she was romantically inclined toward the well-tailored magistrate without offering an alternate explanation. She only hoped that when Mr. Forrester did return midweek, Mr. Bothwick would leave them alone long enough for her to take the magistrate into her confidence.

Or run away, whichever was easier.

They strolled in silence for several long moments. She glanced over the magistrate's shoulder again and started when she realized Mr. Bothwick had disappeared. She scanned the shore until she saw him. Close, but not too close. Skipping rocks into the sea. This was her chance.

"Mr. Forrester, there's something I—"

"Out of earshot, is he?"

She blinked in surprise, then nodded. No sense pretending confusion as to whom he meant.

"Good." The magistrate's voice dropped to a near-whisper. "I need your help."

"You need my—" She stared at him uncomprehendingly. That had been *her* line. "What do you need me to do?"

"I need you to keep an eye on Evan Bothwick."

"You need me to what?"

"Oh, dear. I should have asked first if you find a bit of spying upon others morally reprehensible." He tugged at his cravat worriedly. "And if so, would it change your mind if I assured you all actions were in the name of upholding the law for Mother England?"

Susan shot a suspicious glance at the dress shop but saw no more unfriendly faces. If Miss Grey and Miss Devonshire were watching, they were doing so from inside. Had they told the magistrate their Peeping Tom rumor after all? Was this all a grand joke being played on silly Susan Stanton? Perhaps there was no assembly at all. Just a farce to make a fool of her.

"Will you do it?" Mr. Forrester pressed.

"Why?" she returned with equanimity.

"Because"—for a split second, Susan almost thought he was making up his answer on the spot—"I'm investigating the ladies' dressmaking business."

Susan stared. Well, at least she knew this was no elaborate ploy to humiliate her, orchestrated by the two dressmakers. Her enemies were far too intelligent to come up with something this stupid.

"Investigating them for what? Uneven hems?"

"I've been told," he said, his voice returning to a hushed whisper, "that they've been selling French silk. You are perhaps too genteel to pay attention to such minutiae, but trade with the French is illegal. If they are indeed doing so, I must discover where this silk is coming from. For that, I require your help."

Well, the source was easy enough. French silk came from *France*. There, mystery solved.

"What does Mr. Bothwick have to do with anything?

Wouldn't it make more sense to keep an eye on the dress shop?"

Mr. Forrester shook his head. "Too risky. The girls might catch on. How much business can one woman conceivably have in a dress shop?"

Clearly this man had never been to London. Or past primary school.

Susan had never heard such a ridiculous strategy in her life. To top it all off, his mystery wasn't even a *mystery.* She was dealing with pirates, ghosts, murder, a mysterious jewelry box, and a helpless woman chained in the cellar, and he wanted to know where French silk came from?

"So," she said, trying to rein in his imagination before it ran away with him, "following Mr. Bothwick makes sense because . . ."

"Because he might let something slip. Didn't you hear them back there? He's taking Miss Devonshire to the assembly. From what I've heard, a proposal will be forthcoming at any moment. I'm sure he knows every facet of her life. They're quite serious."

"They're quite—" This time, anger, not lust, boiled Susan's blood. She'd known Mr. Bothwick was a shameless rakehell flitting from flower to flower like an insatiable bee. He'd never pretended to be anything else. But to have kissed her— repeatedly!—when he was the next thing to married . . . No wonder he'd fled through the window when they'd almost been caught. And no wonder Miss Devonshire hated Susan so much!

She glared down the coast at Mr. Bothwick so hard it must've burned his flesh. He dropped the rock he'd been about to throw and turned toward her, puzzled. She maintained eye contact for just a second longer before jerking her gaze back to the magistrate.

Who, as it turned out, was a complete idiot scarcely capable of reasoning his way out of bed in the morning, if he thought such a stupid plan could possibly do any good. He would not be an ally against the giant after all. She'd have to try anyway, of course, but at this rate, she'd be lucky if Mr. Forrester and his questionable brainpower weren't a liability. He couldn't be counted on to help her or her cousin in any capacity more intricate than that of a hired hack.

Besides, who cared about French silk? It was illegal, but so was French brandy, and everyone in town drank the stuff by the bucketful. No wonder they were so open about it. Their local man of the law was a clueless ninnyhammer. Susan kicked at the sand in disgust.

Movement in the distance caught her eye. Mr. Bothwick was approaching. She had little time to finish the conversation in relative privacy.

"Mr. Forrester," she said, "are you aware of the graves in the rock garden behind Moonseed Manor?"

He nodded. "Everyone is. One belongs to Lord Jean-Louis Beaune. And one belongs to his wife."

So he did know. "Why is her gravestone unmarked?"

"Because the priest wouldn't bless the burial. She'd committed suicide, as I recall."

Susan wasn't convinced that being locked up for thirty years and escaping your prison the only way you could, only to be shot dead by your husband as you lay there bleeding, exactly counted as suicide. Or that the gardens of Moonseed Manor constituted anything resembling hallowed ground. But she didn't press the point. Mr. Bothwick was almost upon them. It was time to end the conversation.

After they turned back toward town, however, she realized Mr. Forrester's explanation had been noticeably lacking.

"But what about the third one?"

The magistrate fell into step beside her, with Mr. Bothwick almost on his heels. "The third one what?"

She shivered at the memory of those blank marble slabs. "The third *grave*."

Both men stopped in their tracks and stared at her.

"There's a third one?"

Chapter 12

Dead Mr. Bothwick materialized at Susan's side. "No. Tell them *no.*"

Two large, solid (still-living) men continued staring down at her with something colder than curiosity glittering in their eyes.

"Er," she said brightly.

"Where, exactly, is this third grave?" asked Mr. Forrester.

"When did you first notice it?" asked the still-living Mr. Bothwick.

"Do *not* tell them *anything,*" his dead brother hissed, his entire form rippling in agitation. "Don't mention my death, don't let on you can see me, and for God's sake, take back everything you just said about a third grave in the rock garden!"

"Er," Susan said again, and hesitated. She hadn't been prepared for the *opposite* of Bring-a-Message-to-My-Family day. And she wasn't convinced she should pay more credence to the dead than the living.

The still-living Mr. Bothwick cocked his head and regarded her with something that could only be described as suspicion. "What were you doing looking for new graves?"

"Did the plot appear to be old, or freshly dug?" Mr. Forrester asked, leaning too close. His breath smelled faintly of rosemary and ale. Strange.

"Don't you see what's happening?" Dead Mr. Bothwick cried, whirling around her. "If they find it first, all hope will be lost! I will have died for nothing."

Susan considered the ghost's anguished face. He would haunt her forever, since it would've been her big mouth's fault she'd ruined his mission to find a box of missing jewelry by blabbing the secret location to the townsfolk. She made her decision.

"Three?" she repeated as if confused by the question. "There's only two."

The magistrate frowned, leaned back. "But you said—"

"No, no. There's only two. But two graves are more than enough to discomfit a lady." She pasted on an I-might-swoon-from-fright-at-any-moment expression, which under the circumstances, was not difficult to achieve. These days, she could only hope it differed from her normal appearance. "Might we turn the topic to lighter fare?"

"Oh!" Mr. Forrester appeared everything that was apologetic, the subject easily forgotten. "Of course."

The still-living Mr. Bothwick, however, appeared unconvinced. He stood there, watching her. Silently.

Unaware his ghostly brother was doing the same to him.

"Shall we return?" The magistrate proffered his elbow. When she made no answering move, he reached for Susan's hand.

Mr. Bothwick intercepted the polite gesture in one smooth sidestep, positioning his back to the magistrate and keeping his vigilant gaze on Susan.

"Go on," he said, without bothering to so much as glance at Mr. Forrester—or to ask Susan if that was what she wanted. "Didn't you say you had business to attend to? Far away?"

Mr. Forrester, clueless bumblepot of a magistrate though he might be, looked truly distressed at the thought of leaving

Susan in the very-much-alive Mr. Bothwick's lascivious hands.

Valid as the concern was (because even sprinkled lightly with sand, Mr. Bothwick cut a dangerously tempting figure), the magistrate had proven himself to be possessed of neither sense nor logic, and was therefore of little use until he came back with his carriage.

"Go," she told him as kindly as she could, given she had to bend awkwardly around Mr. Bothwick's frame in order to meet Mr. Forrester's eyes. "I won't keep you. I look forward to our trip to Bath."

"Won't I see you beforehand? You did say I could call on you next week."

Even without glancing up, Susan could feel the displeasure emanating from Mr. Bothwick in waves of black heat. If she didn't get Mr. Forrester on his way soon, Mr. Bothwick would launch himself backward and rip the well-meaning magistrate apart with his bare hands.

"Of course," she assured him. "Call at any time."

Mr. Forrester beamed happily. He bowed and took his leave, casting the occasional doubtful glance over his shoulders at Mr. Bothwick.

Who muttered an unsporting, "Good riddance," and headed toward the cliffside trail without bothering to apologize for his presumptive behavior. Or to see if she followed.

Which she didn't. She needed a moment alone with Dead Mr. Bothwick.

"Now what?" she whispered, turning to face the sea so that no onlookers would witness her apparent discussion with herself.

"Now we dig," the ghost answered, his slender form not quite opaque enough to block a muted view of crashing waves. "Tonight. It's more urgent than ever."

"Where?" The chill rustling the nape of her neck proved she already knew the answer.

The look Dead Mr. Bothwick shot her indicated he knew

she was less than eager to comply . . . and that he didn't much care. "You'll dig up the unmarked graves, of course. It *must* be beneath one of them."

An image of the scarecrow flashed in her mind. "I've no access to a shovel."

"There are several in my house."

"What if someone sees me?" she tried again.

"It's almost a new moon. We'll go after midnight."

"And if—"

"I will keep watch," he interrupted, his voice hard. "Whether you believe it or not, I've even more interest in removing the box from the wrong clutches than you do in getting your beauty sleep."

"I'm not worried about *sleep*," Susan burst out, for a moment forgetting her surroundings. She lowered her voice. "For your information, I haven't slept since I got here. In case you've forgotten, *I see ghosts*." She dragged in a breath. "There are dead bodies in two of three graves. W-what if I dig up the wrong one?"

Rather than reply, Dead Mr. Bothwick's gaze snapped to just over the top of her head.

"What are you doing?" came the still-breathing Mr. Bothwick's voice from not far enough away.

Susan jumped guiltily, and in doing so accidentally brushed against the ghost. Dead Mr. Bothwick sputtered out of sight, leaving the ice-cold wetness seeping into her marrow as the only proof of his presence. Rot. Or rather, excellent. If he didn't reappear until tomorrow, she'd at least have one night's reprieve from digging in gravesites.

She turned away from the horizon.

Mr. Bothwick was two yards away. Then one. Then none.

"Were you speaking to yourself again?"

His tone was curious, not condescending. Nonetheless, she cast about for an excuse less crazy-sounding.

"I . . ." Her imagination failed her. She blurted, "I was talking to the gods of the sea."

To her surprise, his eyes unfocused and his entire body relaxed.

"I do that, too," he confessed, stepping past her so there was nothing between his outstretched arms and the endless span of water and sky. "It makes me feel connected to all this . . . beauty. Savagery. Mother Nature."

Susan's jaw dropped. Mr. Bothwick had regular chats with the gods of the sea? If that were true, he was perhaps the one person on the planet in whom she might confide her own otherworldly peccadillo. In fact, didn't he deserve to know his brother was—well, not alive, of course, and not particularly *well*, either, but at least—

The ghost's dark warning resounded in her ears. *Don't tell.*

She clutched her pelisse tighter as the sun sank into the horizon. Red had been desperate for her to bring the news to his sister. But that was because it *was* news. Miss Grey hadn't known the truth. Mr. Bothwick, on the other glove, was well aware of his brother's passing. Although, come to think of it, no one else seemed to be. If he were the only soul possessed of that knowledge, one might start to wonder . . .

Mr. Bothwick lowered his arms. He turned to face her instead of the sea.

"Childish nonsense," he said, his half-smile self-deprecating. "It's not as if I could really talk to the gods, even if they existed. There's this world . . . and then there's nothing. I just do my best to enjoy it while I'm here."

No. Susan hugged herself, decision made. He was the last person to confide in.

"You're shivering." He stepped closer, put a warm arm about her shoulders, and pulled her to him. "The ocean air does have a bite to it. Are you ready to head back?"

She nodded, torn between jerking free from the man she now suspected to have a bit too much inside knowledge of his late brother's demise, and the wanton desire to hold him closer and let his welcoming arms envelop her in their heat and strength.

Fratricidal tendencies and danger of compromise aside, however, touching him would be tantamount to suicide, what with Miss Devonshire but a stone's throw away in her dress shop.

Mr. Bothwick might not be overly concerned with anti-quated notions of monogamy and fidelity—and, really, what percentage of *ton* gentlemen spent their nights with their wives?—but Miss Devonshire had expressed a clear view to the contrary. Mr. Bothwick was hers, she'd told Susan. Almost married, Mr. Forrester had said. An unapolo-getic rake, by Mr. Bothwick's own admission.

She snuck a glance up at his profile, even more hand-some backlit by the disappearing sun. She tried to imagine him married. Or even almost married.

She failed.

Or perhaps she just didn't wish to think about him spend-ing the rest of his nights with someone else. With china-perfect Miss Devonshire.

Susan shuddered.

Mr. Bothwick snuggled her closer. Looked down at her. His eyes crinkled.

"My arms are nice and warm," he teased, as if they shared a secret joke. As if they were much more than friends. "Shall I carry you home?"

"It's not my home," she told him fiercely. "And it's the last place I wish to be."

If he were taken aback by this outburst, he didn't show it. "Where to, then, my lady? Might I offer my house?" His slow, sensual smile gave voice to wicked promises he had no need to speak aloud.

Her traitorous body thrilled at the thought of surrender.

"No," Susan gasped, more out of self-preservation than desire. She was still in control of herself. For now.

"Name the place," he said gallantly, by all appearances

just as satisfied to stroll about as to—well, all right, perhaps not *just* as satisfied. "I am yours to command."

Susan's skin erupted in gooseflesh that had absolutely nothing to do with the chill night air.

Where could they go that wasn't his lodgings? Or hers? Someplace without a bedchamber of any kind. Better yet, someplace wholly unromantic, so she could tamp down the impossible fantasies galloping rampant through her mind.

She glanced around Bournemouth proper. Cliffs. Sand. A smattering of dilapidated structures. Then she realized what it was she *didn't* see.

"Where's the chicken shed?" she murmured, staring hard at the sparse town.

There was no chicken shed. She'd have noticed a chicken shed.

"What chicken shed?" Mr. Bothwick's brow furrowed in confusion.

"I—" Susan stopped. She what? Had overheard a ghost mention Mr. Bothwick's fiancée had indulged in a midnight rendezvous amongst the poultry? No doubt the shameless rakehell was the very man with whom she had done so. Yet now Susan had to explain her bizarre statement. "I heard Miss Devonshire's cousin raised chickens."

"Yes." His face gave nothing away. "That's true."

He seemed to be waiting for some further explanation. She had none.

"I just . . . wondered where the farm was," she finished lamely. And wished she'd never brought it up.

"Then, come on." He changed course, headed away from town, toward a different trail. A darker one, hidden amongst the shadows. "I'll take you."

You should not be alone with him. You should not be alone with him, the voice in Susan's head chanted. The voice of reason. *If he made love to one woman within those walls, he'll think he can do so with you, too.*

Yet she followed him.

And realized, long before they actually reached the splotch of grass upon which stood a few cows, a pheasant, and yes, a chicken shed: There was no possible way doll-perfect Dinah Devonshire had lifted her skirts in *anything* so messy and rancid and disgusting.

Aside from there scarce being enough room for one person to stand upright, the stench alone kept Susan—and, she was certain, any sane woman—from venturing inside.

But why would Red have lied about what he'd seen? Or *had* he?

Miss Devonshire had threatened Susan's life if she'd dared to breathe so much as a syllable about witnessing her alleged liaison amongst the chickens. The idea now seemed preposterous. But the terror in the porcelain doll's eyes had been real. Which begged the question . . .

What had Miss Devonshire been doing in a chicken shed that could possibly constitute a secret worth killing for?

Chapter 13

Evan considered Miss Stanton's pensive countenance only a moment before making up his mind. He fell back to her side and proffered his arm.

"Come," he commanded.

Miss Stanton's fingers curved around his forearm. It was a testament to her apparent discomfiture that she obeyed without question.

He led her away from the stench of the chickens, away from the cover of trees, closer and closer to the jutting edge of the cliff overlooking the water. Yet with every step taken in tandem, he felt the real danger came not from the possibility of losing his footing to gravity and tumbling to his doom, but of losing a larger and larger part of himself to the woman at his side. Which, to Evan, signified a free fall of an entirely different—but twice as terrifying—nature. He could afford no such fancies.

And yet he led her to his favorite spot in all of Bournemouth.

A half-circle of bleached rocks were all that separated the well-worn patch of dark earth from the endless sky. He loved to come here and lay on his back to listen to the ocean and watch the storm clouds roll in with the setting of the sun. At peace. Just far enough away from humans and animals alike, here it was easy to imagine himself alone in the universe, with nothing but nature to keep him company.

Except, this time, he was not alone. The slender fingers about his forearm would remind him of this fact, if it were somehow possible to have forgotten. Even when she was not present, Miss Stanton was never far from Evan's mind. But he began to doubt the wisdom of bringing her to such a simple place as this.

She would no doubt fail to see the magic he found in every grain of sand and wisp of cloud. It was not at all the thing for proper young ladies to lie in the dirt and while away a lazy afternoon staring at the sky . . . much less grin up at the sun when it ducked from sight and the first cold drops of rain fell from the heavens.

Without a word, Evan turned his back to the precipice, intending to circle back toward Moonseed Manor. It had been a mistake to delay the inevitable. There were any number of more important things they both would be wise to attend to.

Yet Miss Stanton did not budge.

He glanced down. Her lips were slightly parted, her eyes wide. She tried to remove her hand from his arm in order to move closer to the dropoff, but he did not allow her to do so. If she intended to venture to the edge, she would do so with him or not at all. He placed her hand in his and gave a quick squeeze before slowly inching forward. No matter how carefully they tread, dirt and sand and pebbles spit forth from the edge of the cliff and disappeared into the wind and rocks below.

"Thank you." Miss Stanton's grip on his hand tightened, then relaxed. "This is beautiful."

With their fingers still laced, she leaned into his side and rested her cheek against his shoulder. Evan tilted his head slightly so that his own cheek rested atop the softness of her hair. Together, they watched the play of light on the surface of the waves as a sliver of moon came to chase away the last of the sun.

With a jolt, Evan realized he was more content with her, just like this, than he had ever been while alone, in his many visits to this very spot. It was as if the act of sharing the moment, sharing the view, sharing the *peace,* brought even more of the same.

Unfortunately, it also brought a heavy dose of guilt—another emotion with which he was not at all familiar. This incredible woman, with her eyes gently closed behind slightly askew spectacles as she laid her face so trustingly against him . . . He could not return the favor and trust in her as well. He could take no one into his confidences. Not until he'd brought Timothy's killer to justice with the pistol even now tucked into the waistband at the small of Evan's back.

And even then, what would he do? He was a smuggler, a liar, a thief. He carried pistols, and did not fear using them. *Had* used them, when the situation so demanded. He would be sneaking onto the property of a friend this very night, with the macabre goal of unearthing his brother's corpse in order to give Timothy a proper burial. And if that was in fact who lay beneath the third grave in Ollie's rock garden, Evan would be forced to put a bullet right between his friend's eyes.

He turned his head just enough to place his lips against the soft curve of Miss Stanton's forehead. Her skin was cold. Darkness had fallen, and the ocean breeze whipped the air into a wintry frenzy.

"Time to get you home."

"It is not my home," she responded, but the words were without their usual bite. It was as if they left her lips automatically, as if she thought them so often they ached to burst free. "It will never be my home."

Evan told himself he was grateful for the reminder, despite the unwelcome clench to his stomach upon hearing those repeated words. Keeping her hand in his, Evan guided her toward the path leading back toward Moonseed Manor. She was right. Bournemouth was not her home. Would never be her home.

In the future, he would be wise to keep his head from the clouds.

Evan waited until half past midnight before selecting a pick and a shovel and slipping through the night into the shadows behind Moonseed Manor. Under normal circumstances, he might be of the mind that he had no business—or interest—in discovering the identity of whatever corpses might lay in his friend's garden. But these were not normal circumstances.

Evan's brother was dead. And missing. He had to find him.

He also had someone on his tail. No. Not on his tail. He hadn't been detected. But someone else crept through the shadows in a slow, sure crawl, intent on their final destination. No doubt the same destination. The footfalls grew closer. Louder.

Louder? Evan paused, frowned. These footfalls were doing anything but creeping. They were stomping about noisily, as if the owner thought he had every right to be digging up corpses in the moonless night.

Or *she*. A hint of yellow flashed in the distance.

His eyes narrowed. He resumed his approach with the same amount of caution, but a significantly higher amount of ire. If that incomprehensible woman had tried to cover up the truth simply because it seemed a lark to sneak about desecrating graves while on holiday, he had a few choice words to say about the matter.

He burst through the trees—and froze.

Not Miss Stanton. Not a lady at all. Two men, far too intent on their murmured conversation to have registered the leaves rustling angrily at Evan's approach. The flash of yellow belonged to the strawlike shock of hair atop the head of Ollie's rat-eyed butler. The hulking form at the butler's side belonged to none other than Ollie himself.

Both carried shovels. But why? Evan tried and failed to piece together the mismatched evidence before his eyes. These were the only two people who *hadn't* witnessed the earlier misadventure along the shore, much less been close enough to overhear the conversation's content.

Miss Stanton had clearly been less than eager to make her discovery known, once she'd discovered it *was* a discovery. Forrester had left for Wherevershire moments later, so it wasn't as if the brainless magistrate might have gabbed the third grave's existence to Ollie or his lapdog. So how had they known?

A disturbance in the nearby bushes caused Evan to flatten against the side of the Manor. Another flash of blond. Also manly.

So much for the theory that Forrester had left town.

And, by the way he was creeping forward, careful not to step on twigs or dislodge rocks that might advertise his approach—Forrester was about to be just as surprised as Evan had been that they weren't the first to arrive for tea.

The magistrate's sudden stop and muttered curse brought a smile to Evan's face. Ha. Thought so. But Evan remained flattened against Moonseed Manor all the same. This was definitely a night where watching from the shadows might be the better part of valor.

Forrester, it seemed, had the same plan. He neither slunk back into the night nor rushed forward to make some numbskulled arrest citing illegal gardening on one's own property. He stood stock-still, shovel in hand, eyes on the gravesite.

"I told you." The butler's scratchy voice was as low and sinister as wind through autumn leaves. "If it were out here,

I would've found it. I've dug up every square inch that wasn't covered by a rock. See for yourself."

A wet sputter, as his hand moved away from the single candle far enough for the cold breeze to lick at the flame.

Ollie turned away, ignoring the proffered candle, and lumbered through the garden. The butler followed with the flickering candle, spreading more shadow than light. But Evan saw more than enough.

Every inch of the garden *had* been overturned. Recently. But why? There couldn't be *that* many wayward bodies beneath its surface. The soil was too sandy for Ollie to have decided to try his hand at potato farming in a fit of domestic madness. Unless he'd been drunk. Overgrown oaf was well known for making bad decisions after too much whiskey.

Suddenly Ollie stopped. Pointed.

"I said I dug everywhere not covered by rock, didn't I?" The servant's voice managed to sound peevish despite his feral rasp. "What was I to do, dig up graves?"

Hmm. Further proof that, coincidental as it might seem, they weren't all skulking about the grounds for the same reason after all. Evan bit back a frustrated sigh. The thought had reminded him of his brother. Timothy had never believed in coincidences.

"Yes . . . if they're not really graves," Ollie answered cryptically, motioning his butler forward. "What do you see there?"

His lapdog paused, shuffled closer, shrugged. "Graves?"

"Grave*stones,*" Ollie corrected softly. "Which are not at all the same things."

"This is a gravesite," the butler muttered. "Of course there are gravestones."

"And there should be two graves." Ollie jerked the shovel from his lapdog's limp grip. "Not three."

They hadn't known!

Evan looked over at Forrester to see if he was as surprised at this revelation as Evan was, and was startled to discover the magistrate had disappeared. Evan glanced around uneasily. Had he gone for good? Or had he hidden himself better this time, and was even now watching Evan from the shadows? Evan held his breath and waited.

Crunch.

Silence.

Then, "Was that a bone?"

"All the bones in this cemetery are inside caskets, you nancy." Ollie dropped to his knees. "I think I found it. Help me dig."

Metal into dirt. Wet soil splattering against rock. Miniature avalanches of tiny pebbles.

The butler's shocked gasp. "You were right!"

"Help me get it out of here." The shovels dropped to the earth. "We've got to hide it from her."

They had to *hide* it? What the hell was their prize doing buried in the rock garden beneath an unmarked gravestone, if not being well hidden? And from whom? Miss Stanton?

Evan struggled to peer through the darkness at what looked like an ornate gilded box not much bigger than the plain wooden one the captain used to keep his snuff dry while out at sea. A similar-looking bejeweled box graced Ollie's dining room mantle. Or was it the same one?

A crackle off in the darkness reminded Evan of Forrester. And his own presence. He was obviously not meant to know about the events transpiring before his eyes. But why?

True, the gold-filigreed box hadn't been about to remain hidden for much longer. But Ollie obviously hadn't known that. So what had tipped him off? Why would anyone want to bury a jewelry box in the first place? And for God's sake, *where the hell was Timothy?* Evan's muscles bunched in frustration. Then his nostrils flared.

He smelled her, in the wind. Jasmine. Coming closer.

. Leaving his tools on the ground where they were, he slipped from his position against the wall and followed the scent, hoping to intercept her before she made a telltale sound. Or worse, stumbled into direct view.

She gasped when his hand clamped over her mouth. He pulled her backward, into his arms, into the shadows. Now was not the time to explain his presence. Nor was it the time to demand what *she* was doing there. In her nightgown. With Timothy's shovel.

Those questions would come later. As would the answers.

"It's not safe," he murmured into her ear, his mouth brushing against the softness of her hair, the smoothness of her cheek. He plucked the shovel from her hands and rested the scarred wooden handle against the gate. "We'll discuss this tomorrow."

She sagged against his chest. Nodded.

He knew better than to trust that nod, but what choice did he have? He lifted his hand from her lips.

Her mouth opened. But before she could speak whatever ill-advised argument she'd been about to make, her teeth clicked shut. She'd heard it, too.

Footsteps. Coming their way. There was nowhere to hide.

"When I let go," he whispered, gripping her by the shoulders, "I want you to run back to your room as fast as you can. Lock your door. And stay there until morning."

"W-what are you going to do?" she whispered back, eyes wide with terror.

He grimaced. "Provide a distraction."

If anything, her eyes got wider. "Do you think that's a good idea?"

No, no, he didn't. But if he slipped away while he could and let them catch her spying, she'd undoubtedly learn one hell of a lesson. Evan let go of her arms and pushed her toward the open gate. He couldn't put her in danger.

"Go. *Now.*"

With a distressed little cry, she ran.

Evan shouldered the shovel and wished fervently he'd thought to bring his pistols instead.

The inexorable rising of the sun didn't calm the anxiety itching beneath Susan's skin. She sat at her escritoire, scratching a fingernail against the scarred wood. Was Mr. Bothwick all right? Should she have stayed with him? What had he been doing there, anyway?

Although dressed, coiffed, and breakfasted, she couldn't quite work up the nerve to exit her bedchamber to find out. Particularly if this time she really *would* run into Mr. Bothwick's ghost. She shivered.

Had the still-living Mr. Bothwick been hurt? Had he been caught? Had he—Susan's spine snapped up straight—had he been in league with whoever belonged to those footsteps, and simply took advantage of an opportunity to send a frightened young lady back up to her room?

Her forehead thunked forward onto the hard surface of the escritoire. Of course.

She was so slow sometimes. Hadn't she just decided (all right, re-decided) that he wasn't to be trusted? Hadn't she just wondered if he were not in fact responsible for his dead brother's . . . deadness? Mr. Bothwick had just happened to show up in the rock garden, alone, in the middle of the night, directly following her mention of a third grave. Which meant—whether he was in collusion with the others or not—he had definitely not been colluding with *her*.

Next weekend could not come soon enough. She had to get out of this town while she still could.

Susan snatched a sheet of parchment from a yellowed pile and dipped a pen in a clotted inkwell. Although they still hadn't deigned to reply to her previous missive, her first letter was going straight to her parents.

Dear Mother,

    I am desperately unhappy and wholeheartedly repent for all my sins. Please let me come home. I promise to behave.

                            Yours &c,
                            Susan

P.S. If you won't send a carriage, do send money.
P.P.S. Actually . . . please send both.

Her second letter . . . Susan stopped to think. Who else could she send a letter to? Her *ton* acquaintances were quite diverting, but otherwise useless. She didn't *have* any friends unconnected to Society, except—Oh! Wait! At a dinner party she'd been to last Season, one of Lady Wipplegate's unconventional guests had been a Bow Street Runner. Susan couldn't remember his name off the top of her head, but if she sent a note to him inside a letter for Lady W., it should eventually find its mark. If she were lucky, he'd arrive even before her allowance did!

She scribbled off a few lines of twaddle for Lady Wipplegate, and an even more cryptic message regarding Important Matters of Extreme Urgency for the Runner (for Lady W. would no doubt read it aloud at tea before passing it along) and folded both into a neat pile for Janey. Who had hopefully spoken the truth about having some means to secretly post mail and wasn't just tossing all Susan's missives directly into the closest fire.

A Runner would fix everything. He'd solve Dead Mr. Bothwick's murder (assuming Susan hadn't just deduced the villain herself), rescue cousin Emeline (ideally both master and servant would become unfortunate casualties in the ensuing scuffle), and whisk Susan back to London where she belonged. Perfect.

Correspondence thus completed, Susan leaped to her feet—and almost collided with Lady Beaune's ghostly form.

By hopping on one foot and windmilling a bit, Susan somehow managed to steady herself without accidentally brushing against the wraithlike woman with palsied fingers and long white braids.

The ghost fluttered to her fireside vigil, morose, head bowed. She worried at the ornate crucifix about her neck with spotted, trembling hands. And, as before, said nothing. Of course, she *was* a deaf-mute. Which made meaningful conversation difficult—but not impossible. Susan tiptoed to her side, hesitant to startle the ghost, but eager to attempt interaction.

She pointed at her chest. "I'm—"

The ghost was already nodding, although still not meeting Susan's eyes.

"Er . . . you know who I am?"

Another quick, shy nod.

Susan's hand flattened against her chest in shock. Lady Beaune's ghost had just responded (if nonverbally) to spoken communication. Twice. Which made her sense of hearing suspiciously acute for an alleged deaf-mute.

"Can you speak?" she asked softly.

The ghost shook her pale head.

So. At least part of the tale was true.

A horrific gasp sucked from the ghost's lungs and she began to spin, round and round, faster and faster. Susan scrambled out of the way.

Agitated, the ghost ripped the crucifix from her neck, held it aloft. Little by little, her crooked body unraveled as she spun. Ribbons of clothing, of flesh, of essence, trailed out from her disintegrating form and disappeared into the suddenly Arctic air.

Then she was gone.

The crucifix clattered to the floor and winked from sight.

Susan swallowed, allowing her shoulders to slump against the wall. On a scale of one to ten, her communication attempt was perhaps a two. Possibly a negative two. How was she going to grant the ghost's wish if the ghost was incapable of asking for whatever it was she desired?

Then again, if *she* were Lady Beaune—or her barely alive daughter—what she would ask for would be for someone to pull the still-beating heart from the giant's overlarge chest and feed it to the grinning scarecrow before tearing them both to pieces with a pickax. Or something of that nature.

Perhaps she was better off incapable of comprehending the ghost's mission.

Since there was no point hanging about Moonseed Manor if she wasn't going to kill her host in his sleep (and who's to say giants ever slept?), Susan tied her pelisse about her shoulders and headed into town.

Before she'd set foot among the half-ring of tumbledown buildings, it was already clear that Something Was Different.

A motley crowd of locals were milling about the sand, instead of creeping out of sight among the shadows as they normally did during the day. If the fair had come to town, such a turnout might make sense. But Susan saw no signs of revelry.

They all had their faces pointed in the direction of Moonseed Manor, not-so-surreptitiously observing her careful approach. If this had been a matter of a quick glance instead of watching an hourlong tramp down the windy path, such casual attention might make sense. But these were no quick glances.

They backed away as she neared, bending their heads together in excited conversation, letting loose with the occasional titter. If they had just heard a rumor that Miss Susan Stanton got a thrill from spying on trysting couples through dirty windows, such rude behavior might make sense.

Bloody hell. This was not remotely conducive to her plans. But she imagined it was plenty conducive to the evil porcelain doll's. Far be it for anyone to say Miss Devonshire didn't stick to her open threats.

Spread rumors about Susan Stanton, would she? Very well. In return, Susan would investigate Miss Devonshire's treasonous French silk and report her findings to the magistrate the moment he arrived back in town. That'd teach Miss Devonshire a lesson for her crimes against the sovereign.

Or not. What dress shop was without French silk?

Her steps slowed to what one could only describe as a dismal trudge. It wasn't that she was depressed (which, of course, she was) or that she was actively trying to suppress the urge to unleash her inner harpy on Miss Devonshire in a rabid fury (which, of course, she was) but that it was going to be damn near impossible to secretly keep watch on anybody, what with ninety pairs of eyes following her every move. No doubt waiting to see if the Peeping Tom of Mayfair had come to town to spy on someone. Which, as it happened, she had.

Argh.

Susan smiled at the townsfolk as if she were the Queen and they the peasants—er, constituents—who'd come to greet their mistress. She added a little wave of her gloved fingers. Perhaps if she acted normal, if she acted like one of them, they would get bored. They'd return to their usual pastimes and all this would blow over.

Except she didn't know how to act like one of them. She *wasn't* one of them. Thank God.

Dejected, she brushed past the crowd and wandered into the Shark's Tooth. As nonchalantly as possible, she ordered a round for all three patrons too drunk to make it outside to stare at her. Susan couldn't afford the tab anyway, so who cared how expensive it got? She crossed into each establishment one by one, ate a meal on (suspect) credit, and carefully, casually, just-so-happened to end up right outside the Dress Shop of Iniquity.

Rather than go inside and alert the demonic duo to her presence, she collapsed ever so softly against the back of the building, just beneath the open window, and fanned herself as if catching her breath from all that shopping.

(It was a new fan. French, too, by the look of it. Hand-painted and quite lovely.)

Voices floated down from overhead. Boring voices. Voices that discussed this ream or that yard, or what grade of thread was better for such-and-such stitch. *Yawn.* Had she solved the mystery yet? Susan debated just going in and asking. Or buying up all the illegal cloth on her false credit and telling the hapless magistrate, "What silk? I didn't see any French silk. . . ."

She wondered how long she could reasonably stand here, cooling her décolletage with her no doubt treasonous French fan. Perhaps she should come back later. Much later. Like *never.*

Between the disastrous slip of the tongue regarding the chicken shed and the even more disastrous attempt at relaying messages from the dead, the last thing she needed in light of the current social climate was to get caught spying again.

"What the devil do you think you're doing, woman?"

Susan yelped and dropped her new fan in the sand.

Mr. Bothwick. Solid as a rock.

Not dead, then. In league with the Others. Whoever they were.

"Nothing." She snatched her fan back up and recommenced making furious use of the device. "Why aren't you buried in the rock garden?"

"I crawled out." He stared down at her as if tempted to throttle her and toss her in an unmarked grave himself. "Are you eavesdropping on Miss Grey and Miss Devonshire?"

"Nooo," she protested weakly, fanning faster. "Why would you think that?"

He snatched the fan from her fingers, snapped it closed, and tossed it backward over his shoulder. "*Everybody* thinks that."

When she glanced around his wide shoulders, her stomach curdled.

Apparently, whilst she'd been hiding behind her new toy and straining to overhear fascinating statements like, *I don't know, Dinah, perhaps the mauve would be nicer,* the townsfolk had been creeping in. They now surrounded her in a wide, tense circle. Some held . . . rocks?

Chapter 14

The angry mob was edging closer. Tightening rank. Susan had the uneasy feeling a stoning could break out at any moment.

Miss Devonshire's threats were certainly fast-acting.

Mr. Bothwick grabbed Susan's upper arm hard enough to leave a five-fingered manprint. He jerked her out from beneath the window as one might tug forth a rag doll.

"Can you explain what the devil you're doing here?" he demanded, voice low.

She nodded frantically.

His eyes narrowed. "Is there a *good* explanation?"

Susan nodded a bit more frantically.

Mr. Bothwick hesitated, clearly battling inner demons. He scowled at her, displeased with whatever he'd decided. He gave a resigned sigh, pulled her into the wall of his chest, and whispered, "Lesser of two evils."

Then he kissed her.

Not false kisses, or air kisses, or a simple buss to the cheeks. Nor the sort of chaste, closed-mouth kiss, a brief pucker, that one might be able to explain to one's fiancée—however unsuccessfully—had been a mere trick of the light.

No.

This was his strong hands gripping her upper arms in

suspicion and anger, the heat from his muscular frame
melting her core in pure lust, and his warm tongue sweeping
into her welcoming mouth in nothing short of . . . desperation? As if he, too, had never put that first kiss
from his mind. As if he, too, had lain awake every
night, reliving each moment, each taste, each sensation.
As if he, too, had been driven to the brink of madness
with the overpowering desire to have the weight of her
body pressing into his . . . and never stop.

But then he did stop. Briefly.

He tore his lips from hers and tilted his head back just
long enough to say, in a tone deep enough to be intimate yet
loud enough to carry, "I thought I told you to meet me
behind the stables so no one would know I wished to make
you my lover."

Lover. The word careened through her spinning mind.
The entire town had overheard him. A flash of pique. This
was his best attempt at rescue? Although at least he'd had
the sense to imply it hadn't come to fruition—yet—her
reputation amongst the locals had just gone up in smoke.

Then another word crashed into the first, shattering her
vexation: *stables.* What stables? She was really going to
have to start exploring past the town borders.

Then his warm lips were on hers again and the only thing
she wanted to explore was his mouth with her tongue, his
bare chest with her fingertips, his naked body with her
hands and eyes and mouth.

Her back thumped against the dress shop wall. His leg
pressed between her thighs, insistent. His hands now tangled in her hair. She should push him away. Surely this was
too much, going too far. Surely this—this *farce*—had
carried on long enough.

But he didn't stop. And she didn't try to make him. In
fact, one might suppose that the trembling hands tugging
him closer were nothing short of encouraging. One might
further suppose that the rush of unchecked desire drown-

ing her brain (and the delicious pulsing between her legs) indicated a distinct state known as rampant sexual arousal. A respectable lady wouldn't feel such salacious, shocking sensations.

Susan felt them like mad.

This time, she was the one to pull away. Raggedly. Reluctantly. But, at last, successfully. While she still could. She risked a heavy-lidded glance behind him.

Most of the mob had dispersed. Those who remained either wore expressions of shock or disgust, or smirked at her in knowing derision. She hadn't won any friends today. The population still despised her, if for a wholly different reason. *Susan Stanton, village slut.*

But at least they weren't trying to stone her.

"They're gone?" he murmured, his voice husky, raw.

"They've . . . lessened," she whispered back. Startled— but not surprised—to discover her hoarse words as laced with unquenched passion as his had been.

He nodded, twined his fingers with hers, tugged her from the wall.

"Let's go."

She tightened her hold on his hand and allowed him to lead her away from the dress shop, away from the open window, away from the watchful eyes and leering grins of the remaining townspeople. To a desolate strip of empty beach, well out of the line of fire. Yet they kept walking.

"W-where are you taking me?"

"I don't know yet. Out of here." He didn't slacken his pace. "Why were you spying on the dress shop?"

Susan chewed her lip. So he didn't doubt it for a second. Well, he wasn't a fool. The townsfolk might have bought his quick-thinking cover-up, but Mr. Bothwick was waiting on an actual explanation. A good one. Which she did not have.

"The magistrate asked me to." All right, technically he'd asked her to follow Mr. Bothwick. But that made even less sense. So she mumbled, "Sort of." And left it at that.

Mr. Bothwick was not leaving it at that. "Forrester asked you to spy on a dress shop? What the devil for? Is he afraid they're embroidering state secrets into snot rags?"

"Not quite," she muttered. "He thinks they've got French silk."

"He thinks—" Mr. Bothwick came to a sudden stop. His eyes darkened with confusion, then doubt, then wariness. "He does, does he?" He resumed his previous pace. "What do you figure, Miss Stanton? Do the local girls deal in illegal cloth?"

"Of course they do." Susan lifted a shoulder. This, at least, was solid ground. "No dressmaker worth her salt would be without all the latest French fashions. Silk is a mere subset."

Mr. Bothwick watched her, his expression unreadable. "So that's what you're going to report back to Forrester? A simple 'Yes, yes, they do,' and he'll be on his way?"

"Not exactly," she admitted. "He wants to know where it's from."

"Where it's from," Mr. Bothwick repeated. For a moment, they walked in silence. Then he said, "Why, I remember now! As it happens, *I* know where it's from."

For the second time in as many days, Susan had the discomfiting impression that a man was inventing the "truth" with each word he spoke.

"You do?" was all she said aloud, however. "How serendipitous."

"Yes," he said, this time more firmly. "I've just recalled."

Definitely lying.

"Where might that be, if I could be so bold as to inquire?" she asked politely.

He nodded slowly, eyes narrowed at the horizon. "As it happens, Miss Devonshire has a French aunt, who is a famous modiste in Burgundy. I am certain the silk comes from there."

A conveniently French aunt. Who also happened to be a modiste.

Right.

"There you have it," he finished, as if she now had anything at all. "Simple as that."

Utter balderdash.

"No intrigue whatsoever," Susan agreed aloud—and, for the first time, became truly interested in the fabric's origin.

There was definitely more to the story. If that *was* the story. But whom could she ask for the truth? Miss Devonshire herself? Hardly. Not only would that tip her hand—if Mr. Bothwick didn't warn the porcelain doll before Susan had an opportunity to speak to her alone—but what were the chances Miss Devonshire would actually tell Susan the truth? Whatever *that* was?

Mr. Bothwick drew to a halt before a warped old rowboat someone had left to rot amongst the weeds and the sand. What drove Bournemouth folk to leave things—and people—forgotten for years at a stretch?

She didn't realize she'd asked the question aloud until Mr. Bothwick shot her a quizzical glance over his shoulder.

"People?" He bent to pick at a section of peeling paint. "Like who?"

"Like Lady Emeline." She shivered at the thought of that dank cellar. "And her mother. The town abandoned both of them."

Her parents had ignored them as well. Probably because they had the ill taste to live outside Town borders. She hadn't known about either cousin until she'd been ousted from her home and sent to live with "Aunt Beaune." But now that Susan did know, she couldn't help but feel strongly for both women.

"Superstition and fear, I suppose." Mr. Bothwick began to flip the ancient rowboat back upright. "There's those who believed her disease was contagious. Nobody wished to risk catching it. Plus I suppose a bit of 'out of sight, out of mind' was at play, too."

"For thirty years? Shameful, is what that is. Criminal apathy." Susan crossed her arms and glared at him. "And what of Lady Emeline? Why does no one call on her from time to time to see if she's all right? For all they know, she could be dead."

She'd been murderously angry at her parents when they'd confined her to Stanton House after Susan nearly destroyed a marriage by spreading rumors of an illicit tryst she'd had the (mis)fortune of witnessing firsthand. When her mother had tried and failed to pawn her off on the most ineligible bachelor she could find, it was back to the bedchamber for Susan until she'd managed her great escape to the Frost Fair. The friendless weeks of confinement while the bones of her broken arm knitted back together had been an additional torture.

Yet her troubles were nothing compared to what her cousins had been through. What Lady Emeline was *still* going through.

"Folks around here try not to nose about in other people's business." Mr. Bothwick grabbed the pointed front of the boat with both hands and began to move backward, tugging the reluctant rowboat toward the sea. "In case you've forgotten, that's why they don't like *you*."

Susan's mouth dropped open. Of all the rude, hypocritical—

"But we're talking about another human being!" She gestured up at the cliffs behind them. "That's horrible."

"No," he corrected, grunting a little. "That's life."

"How could being deaf-mute possibly be contagious?" she demanded. "That's *ignorant*."

Mr. Bothwick glanced up from the boat. "Her daughter caught it, didn't she?"

Susan gritted her teeth. "Lady Emeline 'caught' being

deaf-mute from her mother? How the bloody hell did she do that?"

He shrugged. "I wasn't there. Supposedly it happened on her wedding night. Shortly after her mother threw herself from a second-floor window."

Susan stopped dead. *Two* rich, landed heiresses. Both with common money-grubbing fiancés. And both came down with an acute case of deaf-mute-itis the very night the contracts were signed and the ceremony performed. This wasn't a case of happenstance. This was the next thing to murder.

The only thing the present mistress had "caught" was a husband with access to the same poison her father had used to incapacitate her mother. Had Jean-Louis Beaune been behind both unfortunate "illnesses"? Or when he'd passed on, had he also passed the family secret on to the new master of the house? Definitely possible. The giant was more than capable of drugging his helpless wife.

"Don't you think there are awfully suspicious similarities between her case and that of her mother?" she asked Mr. Bothwick.

"I don't know." His boots began to splash. "I wasn't here when Lady Beaune disappeared." He rounded the little row-boat and began pushing it into the water. "My brother and I moved here four years ago. We didn't know there *was* a Lady Beaune until there wasn't anymore. And after that, nobody talked about it."

"You weren't born here?" Susan asked in surprise.

Mr. Bothwick shook his head. "Can't imagine such a fate. I was always more for city life, until I fell in love with the sea. Still own property back home, though."

She stepped forward and her shoes squished into wet sand. "Out of nostalgia? Or do you visit often?"

"Out of apathy. I've no plans to return." He swung a buckskin-clad leg into the boat and gripped the thin wooden planks with one hand when a sudden surge of water almost unbalanced him. He reached out a hand. "Come. Get in."

Susan stared at him, then at the raging sea, with its waves crashing so high and so fast she wouldn't have risked being aboard a town-sized cargo ship. Then she looked back at Mr. Bothwick. One of his boots sank into knee-high water. The other pistoned alarmingly in the eminently unstable rowboat. He held out an upturned palm and motioned her forward, impatient.

"Are you *bamming* me?" she burst out, backing up several quick steps.

"Your choices are few, Miss Stanton." Despite the ice-cold sea lapping at his knees, his open hand didn't waver. "You can return to town and take your chances there—or you can come aboard with me."

"In other words," she said with a gulp, "certain death either way."

He inclined his head in apparent agreement.

She placed her palm in his.

He hadn't thought she was going to do it.

Even when Miss Stanton's gloved fingertips brushed his ungloved palm, he was sure reason would intercede and she'd run screaming down the beach.

But then they locked hands, palms-to-wrists, and he pulled her inside the boat. She sat in the center of the wooden cross-plank, feet tucked beneath her, hands twisting in her lap. Terrified. But determined.

Evan fell for her a little more.

The waves were calmer today. To someone unused to the sea, he supposed they would still be unnerving, but when were the waters ever truly motionless? Never. That's why he liked it.

He rowed them away from shore. The ocean sighed, stilled, stretched out around them in a deep blue forever.

The sun glittered in the ripples made by his oars. He let them rest, allowing the boat to float freely. Silence, except for the waves slapping against the side of the rocking boat and the occasional call of a bird.

He loved this. Loved the sun, warming his face and his neck and his hands. Loved the bite to the breeze, ruffling his hair and unknotting his cravat. Loved the salt-fresh scent of the sea, the little fish darting beneath its surface. Loved feeling *alive*. And Miss Stanton—

Seemed to have forgotten her terror entirely.

She wasn't walking a tightrope above her seat, mind you, but she *was* gripping the side of the boat instead of ripping her skirt to shreds, and staring out at the sea in open-mouthed wonder.

"Don't lean too far," he couldn't help but tease. "You might tumble over."

She whipped her head around to face him, eyes overlarge, then smiled despite herself when she saw that he was baiting her. He smiled back. She stuck her tongue out, laughed at his surprise, then returned her gaze to the endless horizon, as if they were but two carefree lovers set adrift for the day with nothing more on their minds than the promise of romance amidst the beauty of the sea.

If only that were true.

Content for a moment to just pretend, he watched her gasp in delight at the tiny fish she'd just discovered a hand's reach from the surface. She stripped off her gloves and braved the icy coldness to try to touch one. They kept swimming, just out of reach.

"First time in the water?"

Her eyes darkened and she returned her shaking hands to her lap. "First time *on* it, anyway." Before he could ask for clarification, she added, "Mother would never let me aboard anything so common as a *boat*."

His back straightened defensively until he realized that her softly mocking laughter was directed at herself, not him.

"And why not?" she demanded. Her direct gaze pierced him as much as the wistfulness in her voice. "How grand would it be to sail to India, see the world, have a little adventure now and then?"

He'd never been to India, but he well understood the allure of adventure. Would die without it. She appeared of the same mind. He felt an odd connection to her deep within his chest.

Evan suddenly wished they weren't in a rowboat after all. He'd very much like to kiss her. But though he'd been teasing earlier about leaning too close toward the fishes, they most likely *would* capsize if he did anything so foolish as join her on her tiny bench and pull her into his arms.

So he picked up the oars and rowed for shore. He would kiss her there, the moment they arrived. Well, he'd get her to dry land first. Maybe take care of his boat. But then he'd smile, hug her tight, and kiss her.

Unfortunately, a lone figure appeared in the distance and ambled ever closer to where Evan had planned to bank the rowboat. Not just any lone figure. That nettlesome magistrate. The man was a plague among plagues. Evan gripped the oars in frustration.

So much for kissing.

Miss Stanton twisted around in her seat to see what he'd been frowning at.

"Look, it's Mr. Forrester!" Her surprised tone turned pensive. "I thought he left. What's he doing out here?"

An excellent question, that.

"Before he's upon us," Evan said, "we need to discuss what happened in town."

Miss Stanton's unblinking gaze met his. "The part when you ruined my reputation beyond all hope and compromised yourself with me in the process?"

He inclined his head and tried not to feel ill. Put that way, what had seemed like the lesser evil at the time now sounded like total folly when phrased so starkly. He had not really been thinking of compounding the situation by kissing her again—had he?

"Luckily for me," she said slowly, "no one here has the ear of anyone in London. The tainting of my reputation is, for now at least, confined to Bournemouth. Unluckily for me . . . so am I."

"I suppose the gentlemanly thing to do would be to offer for you," he somehow managed to say over the currents swirling in his stomach. The impromptu kiss now seemed a death knell. *Marriage.* Much as he still longed to hold her, to possess her, to pleasure her—he had not envisioned a permanent situation.

But she was already shaking her head.

"Thank you for offering, but you needn't bother. I've plans for my future and they don't involve being trapped in this godforsaken town. I'd rather spend the rest of my life imprisoned in my parents' town house than another minute on this beach. Er, no offense meant."

"None taken," he muttered. And couldn't help but feel offended. "So . . . the story is, I asked for you, and you politely declined?"

She had no need to nod her head quite so emphatically.

"You're in no danger of matrimony," she assured him, then narrowed her eyes. "But there can be no more talk of being 'lovers.' And no more kissing. I cannot take the chance that rumor of my misconduct travel all the way into Town. At least, not before *I* get there."

He gave a wry chuckle. "Don't worry on that score. If I so much as look at you lasciviously before the public eye again, we'll find ourselves before the altar no matter how politely we both decline. And I want that even less than you do."

Probably.

"Good." She looked relieved. Too relieved. He might not be a High Society fribble like the fops she apparently preferred, but sharing a future with him couldn't be *that* repellant an idea. Not with the way they had stood together atop the cliff and gazed upon the sea. Or the way the rest of the world fell away every time they kissed.

Used to kiss, rather.

Evan leaped from the boat as soon as the bottom scraped sand, but the goody-goody magistrate had already materialized at the bow to lift Miss Stanton out. Biting back a growl, Evan had no choice but to drag the boat ashore while the magistrate carried Miss Stanton to dry ground. And kept walking. And still hadn't put her down.

Evan abandoned ship and chased them. He snatched Miss Stanton from Forrester's feather grip and hugged her to his chest for a moment before setting her down. On her own two feet. Like a *gentleman* should have done.

Forrester gave him a blank-eyed smile. "Why, good day to you, Bothwick."

Evan fought the urge to knock out his teeth. As if the bounder hadn't just seen Evan rowing the very boat ashore from which he'd plucked the beautiful Miss Stanton! Five gold coins said that her sharp blue eyes and soft little body were the precise reasons the magistrate kept "forgetting" to travel on to the next town.

Before Evan's brain could come up with a viable way to fistfight a man of the law without borrowing too much trouble, Miss Stanton's disingenuousness intervened.

"Oh!" she exclaimed, clapping gloveless hands together. The scraps of silk must be lying soiled and forgotten at the bottom of his boat. "I've solved your mystery."

Forrester's expression went from smug to uneasy as his gaze snapped between her and Evan.

"Have you now," was all he said, despite the edge to his voice. "Already?"

She nudged up her spectacles and nodded. "Miss Devonshire's French aunt sends her the silk. All the way from Burgundy. I imagine it's still wrong, but . . . well, it's family."

"Is that so?" the magistrate drawled, eyebrows raised.

He seemed to be on the verge of disagreeing with the ridiculousness of a French aunt, but in a blink appeared to have changed his mind. "Well, mystery solved, then, I suppose. Good work, Miss Stanton." He gave a little bow. "I do thank you very much for your kind help."

What?! Evan stared at the little toad in disbelief. That was it? *Oh, sure, that explains everything. Guess I'll be on my way?* Now he *knew* the request had been nothing more than a ploy to have ready-made conversation handy for Forrester's next encounter with Miss Stanton.

Whose current expression was likewise lined with incredulity.

"You're welcome, then, I suppose," she said with a too-bright smile. Ha! Evan doubted the magistrate's pea brain recognized that Miss Stanton was actually mocking him. "Delighted to be of assistance."

The ensuing silence stretched out awkwardly.

"Well, good day to you, Miss Stanton." Forrester tipped his beaver, which, in Evan's opinion, was a bit anticlimactic after having just bowed. "It's always a pleasure to see your beautiful smile."

"Thank you, Mr. Forrester." Miss Stanton did not curtsy. "You're most kind."

Another long, pregnant pause. Then:

"Good day, Bothwick." Accompanied by an ingratiating smile.

"Good-*bye,* Forrester." Accompanied by a flash of bared teeth.

At long last, the magistrate turned and headed down the beach. Thank God.

"What a strange man," Miss Stanton muttered.

"Strange?" Evan shook his head. He turned to go rescue his abandoned rowboat. "Forrester's a natural-born idiot."

She snorted. "You don't know the half of it."

Evan paused, glanced back at her. "The half of what?"

"He wanted me to investigate the dress shop . . . by

following *you.*" She shook her head and laughed. "Have you ever heard of anything so absurd?"

No, no, he hadn't. Even from a simpleton like Forrester. Which meant something else was afoot. Something like: The magistrate finally suspected smuggling taking place in his territory and possibly had other, *trained* individuals keeping an eye on Evan.

As the penalty for treason was death, perhaps tomorrow's trip was a suicide mission in more ways than one.

Chapter 15

All evening long, Susan thought about her cousin's current situation, and what—if anything—she could do to improve it.

Mr. Forrester was a pathetic, nonsensical ninnyhammer, but he was magistrate, and more important, *still here* (she hoped), which meant she might have an opportunity to rescue Lady Emeline.

Well, provided the giant didn't catch her disobeying his orders to stay away from the cellar. And provided the scarecrow didn't catch her red-handed, in the act of spiriting away his helpless charge. And provided she *could* extricate Lady Emeline from her prison.

Susan snuck from her bedchamber and made her way through Moonseed Manor to the stairs that went down. She flattened her back against the corner where bone-white corridor met cold grey stone. She didn't move. She didn't breathe. She just listened.

Nothing. No giant, no scarecrow, no maids bustling hither and yon. Thank God. Susan had never been so thrilled to be without servants at her beck and call. Being without keys to the manacle, however, was not such a happy circumstance. But Susan was not without hope. Nor without resources of her own.

After all, she now knew where Dead Mr. Bothwick kept his shovels.

She dashed into the dark stairwell, careful not to let the sharp metal base of the borrowed shovel scrape against the damp stone walls. She crept down each wide, uneven step as silently as possible, straining to hear noises from either direction.

There was no going back now, no explaining how she got "lost" in the cellar again whilst happening to carry about a knife and a shovel. (The ivory-handled knife had just been lying there next to the shovels, right out in the open. Well, "next" meaning inside the house tucked under a mattress, but it wasn't as if the razor-sharp blade was of much use to Dead Mr. Bothwick in his current form.) If she *did* get caught trying to free Lady Emeline from her cage, Susan needed all the protection she could muster.

When she reached the last step, she paused to listen again, but only for a moment. The single candle flickering in the musty stairwell splattered more than enough shadows to have given away her approach.

Susan took a deep breath and rushed into the tiny cell, shovel aloft.

The (thankfully) still-living Lady Emeline shrieked her silent shriek and collapsed to the dirt floor, shuddering in terror.

"No, no, no—" Susan dropped to her knees beside the trembling woman and placed a hand on her bony shoulder. Her cousin recoiled, whimpering in earnest. "I'm here to help," Susan whispered, horrified. "I promise to get you out of here."

She reached for the hem of her cousin's skirts. Susan lifted the soiled fabric high enough to expose a pale, unshod foot and the rusty iron band locked around the skeletal ankle. She tugged, knowing the effort would be useless. The manacle didn't give. The clamp would never open without the key. The chain, however . . . The chain still held possibility. Susan straightened the slender metal rings, felt their weight.

Tears coursed down Lady Emeline's dirty cheeks. She still trembled.

"I'm getting you out of here," Susan informed her firmly. "Tonight."

Her cousin seemed unconvinced.

An insidious thought wormed into Susan's mind. "Do you remember when I came to visit you last time?"

Without looking up, Lady Emeline nodded.

Susan's blood ran to ice. There. Proof. Lady Emeline was equally as *not*-deaf-mute as her mother. There was no mystical contagion infecting the women of Moonseed Manor on their wedding nights. There were only self-serving, fortune-hunting cretins, who were evil enough to steal their wives' tongues. Perhaps literally.

Susan had no wish to check.

She rose to her feet, more determined than ever to free this poor creature before her devoted husband was forced to kill her out of "love."

"This ends now," she told the quivering woman. "Don't move."

Susan raised the shovel as high as she could, both hands wrapped around the wooden pole, the metal base pointing straight down, poised to bisect the cursed chain.

She let loose.

A clang much louder than she'd hoped for echoed in the dark chamber.

Susan staggered backward, shoulders aching from the impact of shovel against chain. Had she done it? Could they leave? She dropped to the ground, inspecting the chain. Still solid.

No! She'd broken half a ring! Not enough to slide the interlocking piece free, but the shovel *had* wreaked damage. Now she had to wreak the same amount of damage again—but to the other half of the ring. Bloody hell. What were the chances she'd hit the exact same ring twice in a row? Susan had never been one for sums, but her best guess on those odds was a whopping zero. The noise had been deafening.

"We have no time," she said in response to her cousin's questioning gaze.

The frail woman had stopped crying. As if she had hope, however small a glimmer. Susan could not fail her.

"We're doing this. Don't worry." She scrambled to her feet with renewed determination. "We're leaving here. Both of us. Tonight."

She poised the shovel. Struck.

Another deafening clang.

She poised the shovel anew. Struck again. And again. And again. Her shoulders screamed with fire and agony, but Susan couldn't stop, had to work faster, had to—Yes! She did it!

Susan dropped the shovel and left it where it lay, no longer worried about keeping silent. Servants in *London* had probably heard, given the racket she'd been making.

"Come. We have to hurry."

She hauled Lady Emeline up by a fragile elbow and, almost as an afterthought, grabbed the fallen shovel as well. She had no experience with knife fights, but she now knew a thing or two about swinging a well-aimed shovel.

With the wooden pole tucked under one arm and the other arm wrapped around her cousin's thin frame, Susan somehow managed to stagger both of them up the stairs, out the door, and into the rock garden.

They did it! They were free!

Elation zinged through Susan's blood, warming her against the chill wind. She dropped the shovel against the vine-covered gate and hauled the sack-of-bones Lady Emeline up into her arms, ignoring her aching shoulders' protest. If Mr. Bothwick could carry damsels in distress up and down this stupid path, so could Susan.

Turned out . . . she couldn't. A mile of winding, twisting

trail was much farther than it seemed. So they developed a pattern. Five minutes in Susan's arms, walking as fast as her aching back—and the treacherous path—would allow. Then five more minutes where both of them did a fair bit of hobbling. And then back in Susan's arms.

Eventually, they reached the bottom. Freedom. Bouncing in place, Susan wanted to clap and shout with glee. She settled for a quick hug to her newly freed cousin.

They still had to find Mr. Forrester. Was he still here? Where could he be?

The last rays of the dying sun withered behind the stormy horizon. The town was enveloped in darkness. Candles flickered in the windows of only two establishments: the tavern and the dress shop.

A drop of icy rain fell on the tip of Susan's nose. Another followed, streaking across one of the lenses of her spectacles. Angry clouds swirled overhead. The sky would open up at any moment.

"Take this." Susan shrugged out of her pelisse and draped it over Lady Emeline's bent shoulders. "Stay here." At her cousin's startled expression, Susan's face broke into her first real smile of the evening. "I'll be back, I promise. This is almost over."

As before, cousin Emeline appeared unconvinced. But she knelt on the sand, shrouded in Susan's best pelisse, and seemed content to wait.

Susan tried the Shark's Tooth first. The tavern had been the place they'd met, even if she'd been in too much shock at the time to register their meeting.

Empty. Mostly empty. Just the town drunks, the priest (who perhaps also fell into the previous category), and Sully.

"A round for everyone?" the barman asked hopefully.

Susan shook her head. "Perhaps another day."

But there wouldn't be another day. She was leaving here. Now. With her cousin at her side. She gave the barman a

little wave before stepping back out the door. He was a good
sort. She'd have her parents send double the tab.

Next stop—the dress shop. The only choice left. If Mr.
Forrester wasn't within those walls . . . No. She wouldn't
think like that. This nightmare would end tonight.

She pushed open the door and stepped inside. Miss Grey.
Miss Devonshire.

And—*thank you, thank you, thank you*—Mr. Forrester.

"I need your help," she blurted. "Please."

The ginger-haired witch didn't bother to glance up from
her sewing, much less rise and ask what the trouble was.

The porcelain doll, however, stalked forward from where
she'd been murmuring with the magistrate (who was no
doubt investigating whether there really was a French aunt
making dresses in Burgundy) and all but spat on Susan in
her fury.

"You've got some nerve coming in here, don't you? And
asking for *help*. I wouldn't help you if you were drowning in
a well and I happened to have a rope in my arms. I'd jump in
the water myself, just to strangle you with it. Then I'd—"

"Not from you," Susan cut in, shouldering past her.
"From Mr. Forrester."

The magistrate glanced up, eyes shining, clearly pleased
to be needed. "Anything at all, Miss Stanton. Name it. I
am now, and always, at your service."

The witch's needle paused. The porcelain doll looked
about to pop.

Susan had no time to waste with either of them. She
grabbed the magistrate's arm and tugged him toward the
open door. "Come with me. Please."

With a shrug of apology at the two seamstresses, Mr. Forrester followed Susan over the threshold and down the
steps. Miss Devonshire slammed the door behind them.

Good. The fewer witnesses to their flight, the better.

The rain picked up, soaking Susan to the bone without her pelisse. Gooseflesh rippled along her icy skin.

No matter. Cousin Emeline needed the pelisse more. She deserved whatever comfort she could get. Susan strode faster, leading Mr. Forrester across the wet night to the foot of the path where a tiny bundle lay trembling.

The magistrate gasped in shock. "Is that . . . Lady Emeline?"

Susan could only nod, relief momentarily robbing her of her voice. They were saved. Thank God. *They were saved.*

"You did the right thing, Miss Stanton."

Susan nodded again, smiling. Of course she did. She couldn't let her helpless cousin fester in that godforsaken stone cage one moment longer. They were escaping, and they were escaping together. But—how did Mr. Forrester recognize Lady Emeline?

"You knew my cousin needed help?" Susan asked, shocked.

"Of course not." Mr. Forrester shook his golden curls and hauled Lady Emeline to her feet. "I had no idea she'd wandered off again. Her husband must be so worried."

Susan's mouth fell open. "What?"

"You were right to come to me," he continued, swinging Lady Emeline up and into his arms as though she weighed no more than a pile of feathers. If he noticed the broken chain swinging loose from beneath her skirts, he gave no mention. "She can be quite a handful, and I'm sure you didn't want to attempt guiding her up this trail in the rain. Gets slippery." He turned and met Susan's eyes. Smiled. "Accidents sometimes happen."

"*What?*" She stared in horror as the magistrate began to march cousin Emeline right back up the very trail that the two women had just fled. Stabbing him with the ivory-handled knife in her pocket suddenly seemed a reasonable idea.

Either the man had less brainpower than the little she'd given him credit for, or he realized quite clearly the atrocities that

took place inside Moonseed Manor but was too frightened—
or, more likely, too well paid—to act as he ought.

"He keeps her locked up," she blurted out, desperate to
try her best while they were still outside the walls of Moonseed Manor. What were the odds she'd be able to free cousin
Emeline twice? Or that the giant wouldn't retaliate for
having done so this once?

Mr. Forrester's brow creased, but his voice could only be
described as kind. "He's her husband, Miss Stanton. While
I hope they are a happy couple, I simply do not have the
power to dictate how a man should treat his wife. My personal belief is that women are to be cherished, but such
beliefs are unenforceable in a court of law." He smiled
gently. "Come, now. You know that to be true."

Yes. Susan did know. She closed her eyes, unable to keep
looking at the disappointment and hopelessness in her
cousin's face. What Mr. Forrester said was absolutely true.
Even Miss Grey had pointed it out when she'd first told
Susan the story. The marriage contract simply served to
transfer ownership from father to husband. The magistrate's
hands were tied.

The assembly in Bath the following weekend was looking more and more like her only possibility of escape—and
therefore her only opportunity to return with an army, and
free Lady Emeline. Because she *would* free her cousin.
Laws be damned.

"Don't worry," Mr. Forrester said over his shoulder, misreading Susan's thoughts entirely. "It's not your fault she got
free. I'll let Ollie know you were the one to find her and
return her home."

Oh, lovely. Susan shivered. The giant was bound to believe *that*.

Chapter 16

The following afternoon, Moonseed Manor was still as a tomb. Susan hadn't seen hide nor hair of her malicious host—a situation for which she was profoundly grateful. She knelt in the grave garden, wrapped in a thick pelisse despite the pale yellow sun overhead. Its weak rays provided little warmth for Susan, and none whatsoever for the owner of the unmarked grave before her.

She reached out to touch the sparse brown grass tangled amongst the dirt and the stones. Most of the brittle blades crumbled at the brush of her fingertips, as if their weakened state could not withstand even that gentle touch.

"I am sorry, cousin," she whispered to the silent patch of earth marking Lady Beaune's grave. "Your daughter will not join you here. I swear it."

Having thus sworn her fealty, she placed her hands atop trembling legs and struggled to her feet. It was difficult to have faith in her ability to make good on such a promise when there was no guarantee she herself would not soon lie at her cousin's side.

If only there was someone to confide in. But there was not. The dressmakers could not bear Susan's presence. Despite his drugging kisses, Mr. Bothwick was a bosom friend of the monstrous master of the manor. And the magistrate . . . the magistrate . . . if even *his* hands were tied thanks to the letter of the law, she could hardly expect a less powerful citizen to hurry to her aid.

She needed someone *more* powerful. Someone who believed him- or herself above the law. She needed, Susan admitted reluctantly, her mother.

One arch of her mother's eyebrow accompanied by the barest breath of the Stanton name and a veritable army would rain upon Moonseed Manor in the blink of an eye. The moment Susan arrived in Bath, she'd rent—or outright steal; she could scarce be bothered with details at this point—the first available carriage and hie directly to Stanton House. She would have to do a fair bit of explaining in order to win Mother to her point of view, but Susan would persevere until her voice cracked and died, if that was what it took.

So resolved, she crossed the small enclosure and shoved open the cold iron gate on the far side. Although no sounds rent the still air save the faint whisper of wind scattering sand over rock, she paused with her hand on the gate and tilted her head toward the thicket of trees teeming in the shadows. She waited, not breathing, irrationally convinced she was better off shuttered inside the grave garden than stepping into the open where whatever animal prowling in the woods could attack and devour her.

The rustle of fallen leaves crackling beneath the unseen beast's great paws seemed overloud to Susan's straining ears. Ominous. If it were not an animal in the strictest sense, it might very well be the villain of Moonseed Manor come home to punish his "guest" for her attempted interference.

She almost turned and fled. Would have, in fact, had her hands not clenched in a palsied grip around the icy bars of iron. Had her booted feet not turned to stone, miring her in place like a sacrificial lamb. Had her heart not been beating so quickly that remembering to breathe became an impossible challenge.

He stepped from the shadows.

Her heart stalled, then exploded double time. Mr. Bothwick. He'd never confessed what he and the giant had uncovered amongst the graves. Or why he had kissed her senseless in front of the townsfolk just to save her. Unless saving her was the farthest objective from his mind. (The thought of danger, in that moment, had likewise vanished from Susan's.) There was far more to Mr. Bothwick than his carefully maintained image of a care-for-naught rake. But while he seemed willing enough to dally with her, he obviously had no intention of sharing any of his secrets.

Nor could she share hers. Last night's crushing disappointment with Mr. Forrester had driven that point home.

Besides, the only thing Mr. Bothwick had ever proven—besides his desire for her—was his utter untrustworthiness. Susan could not risk confiding her cousin's plight to the man who was the best friend of Lady Emeline's captor. Nor could she risk allowing him any more liberties than she already had.

No matter how much her traitorous body might wish to.

He appeared to be heading toward the main entrance. He paused, tilted his head, turned. Almost as if his legs began to carry him to her even before his mind was decided on the matter. He was within arm's reach in moments.

In arm's reach, but not touching her. Not even attempting to. He stood on the other side of the gate, close enough that if she unfurled her fingers from their death grip about the wrought iron, her fingertips would graze against his greatcoat. Even without touching, she could feel his heat. Her entire body warmed. Perhaps too much. She dared not allow her thoughts to show on her face.

Would he never speak?

Perhaps there were no words to be spoken. He had kissed her. She had liked it. That was dangerous enough. She had told him no more kissing. He had agreed. But her fingers gripped the gate because if they did not, they would be around his neck, in his hair, clutching him to her.

Judging by the coiled tension in his stance and the unhidden passion in his eyes, she had only to give the merest indication for him to vault the gate and destroy her with the intoxicating pleasure of forbidden kisses.

She hoped he could not read her internal battle in her eyes.

"I was coming to see you," he said at last, softly, his eyes hooded.

Somehow, her fingers tightened around the gate. Her breath tangled in her throat before she managed, "Why? I thought we agreed we could not . . ."

He stepped closer, closed that final inch, such that her curved fingers were now trapped between the unyielding cold of the wrought iron and the simmering hardness of his body. Perhaps, like her, even that small distance between them had been impossible to bear.

He took a breath. "I'm leaving."

She did not gasp or cry out or any other such ninnyhammered thing. Mostly because she could not process his meaning.

She blinked. Twice. "What?"

"Just for the weekend," he corrected quickly. He stepped back and pulled open the gate.

The unexpected movement sent her pitching forward, right into his arms. Or perhaps the unexpected movement gave her the perfect excuse for allowing her body to tumble straight into his arms. Either way, Susan found his arms about her waist, hugging her close, while her own twined about his neck. At last.

He dipped his head. She turned away, and at the last second his kiss landed against the side of her face. Rather than recoil from this rebuff, he kept his mouth millimeters from her skin, his warm breath searing into her as he dragged his soft lips down to the line of her jaw, to the sensitive hollow beneath her ear.

"I said . . ." she breathed, then gave up. Even she could hear she didn't mean it. "When will you be back?"

"Sunday."

"Where are you going?"

He kept his mouth against her throat, intermingling his responses with kisses. "Can't say."

"May I ride in the carriage?"

"No carriage. Boat." He bit the lobe of her ear. "And no. You can't come."

Boat? Surely he didn't intend to take his little death trap for an extended trip in the ocean. "It's not safe. If you—"

"Shhh." He swallowed her concerns with a kiss.

And for a long, delicious, unguarded moment . . . she let him. She loved the feel of her body against his, of his arms holding her tight, of his mouth hard against hers, then teasing, playing.

Just as she was about to open up for him, to allow the kiss to become as wild and reckless as they both wanted, her rational mind gave its last plea for sense. She had goals. He was not part of them. If she kissed him, touched him, allowed this passion to burn any brighter, she would give lie not only to the words she spoke to him on the boat, but also to the promises she had made to herself.

She untwisted her arms from about his neck, pushed her flattened palms against his chest . . . and warred with her own desires during every second.

Confusion flashed in his eyes, then disappointment, then something more, something else, something she had no wish to analyze. Because he was loosening his embrace. Moving backward. Allowing her to go.

Had she thought breaking the kiss was the hardest thing she could do? More fool, her. Even without his arms around her, stepping away from his warmth, of his need—of her own need—was almost impossible.

But somehow, she did it. And managed to walk away.

She did not look behind her, to see if he watched, to see

if passion still darkened his eyes, to see if perhaps he'd
made a step forward as if to stop her. If she'd done so and
seen any of those things, she might not have been able to
continue her lonesome path back to her bedchamber. She
told herself it was better not to know . . . yet made her way
directly to the closest window to spy upon the rock garden.

But by then, he was gone.

Although he now knew tonight's destination wasn't his
dead brother's final port of call after all, Evan couldn't wait
to step foot on the ship. He brushed past the deckhands who
were milling about telling jokes and climbed aboard.

Usually he loved the excitement. The adventure. The
danger. Tonight, he appreciated the ability to forget his
"real" life, if only for a short time. Whenever Miss Stanton
was within sight, he lost his ability to focus on anything
else. But such an all-consuming fancy was as dangerous to
his neck as to his heart.

Because now Forrester was here. Not *here* here, of
course. Evan glanced down the length of the beloved ship
and smirked. That little nancy would wet his nappies if he
ever came in contact with *real* pirates. Which could happen,
if Forrester was nosing about town in the manner Evan suspected. However, the magistrate didn't have to be the one to
single-handedly bring down the crew in order to ruin—well,
end—all their lives. He simply had to get the right information to the right superiors and the government would take
care of the rest in a heartbeat.

What had tipped Forrester to the idea of smugglers in the
area? Evan crossed to the helm and ran his fingers idly
over the wheel. The idea of visiting the gallows for ladies'
daywear was preposterous. Of all the goods Evan and his
crew had smuggled in over the past six months, the odd
thing was—French fashion wasn't one of them. So if Miss

Devonshire was truly spinning illegal silk in her web . . . where *did* it come from?

He moved into the shadows as a cacophony of footfalls indicated the rest of the crew starting to board. The sight of their ruddy, laughing faces sparked an idea. The other crew might've smuggled the silk. He'd always suspected Poseidon's men—who had once been true pirates—of continuing to deal in something a bit more dastardly than mere cloth. At the least, they'd no doubt taken it by force. Spilled blood over stolen fabric.

Smoking supplies and strong alcohol were more the style of Evan's crew. Snuff boxes, brandy, apparently the occasional hand-painted tea set . . . that sort of thing. They didn't kill, they didn't steal. They were more like illegal businessmen than true pirates. Just a few gents out to help the economy. Evan grinned at this notion. His crew didn't give a fig about the economy. They drank and smoked their half of the spoils. The other half—the nonconsumable half—went to the captain, whose onshore contact made quick work of subtly dispersing the goods along the entire coast, thereby leaving the actual smugglers' hands clean of the merchandising portion of the process.

Could Miss Devonshire have innocently gotten the silk through some such salesman? Was she the last in a series of transactions that could be traced back to the ship—and Evan himself?

Christ, he hoped not. Evan splayed his fingers against the worn wooden column of the main mast. If that shit-for-brains Forrester brought down the entire smuggling operation because he'd followed the breadcrumbs of illegally imported French fabric, Evan was going to be furious.

If that turn of events was remotely possible, he was running out of time.

No, he was *already* running out of time. The coin in Timothy's house had proved that. The crew knew better than to steal the captain's gold. One thoughtless jack had lost his hand just for picking a piece up from the captain's table. It was simply not done. Much like stealing pages from any of the logbooks. The wardroom was Evan's next stop. Quick, before the captain came aboard, or the crew got restless enough to seek out Evan.

The current ledger lay open, with the last page still missing. He hadn't imagined it.

Evan paged backward in time, smiling at a few of the memories and scowling at others. His fingers froze in the act of page-turning. A month had disappeared. How had a month disappeared? He looked closer, seeing the subtle proof in the slight gap between the pages. Another missing sheet. He began to turn the pages more slowly. Ten in all, seemingly at random. But you didn't just happen to accidentally rip out ten nonsequential sheets from the captain's log in careful, perfect strokes that only someone looking for such a thing would have noticed.

What about previous logs? Evan jerked his gaze to the shelf containing the old, dated logbooks.

Empty. Even the dust was missing.

He slammed the current logbook closed and strode for the door before the captain showed up and thought Evan responsible for the thievery. He tried to think of a logical explanation. Without the threat of retribution, the crew wouldn't have stolen any log sheets, simply because they didn't care. What was a jack to do, frame a favorite itinerary in his bedchamber?

Evan headed back to the main deck, his steps as slow and plodding as his brain. He had to be missing something. Well, obviously he was missing something. *Many* somethings, going back well before Evan ever joined the fun. If he could just read what was written on the pages, maybe he'd finally understand what was happening. Of course, he'd have to find them first. Given he hadn't had any luck finding one missing sheet, chances were low he'd happen across all the rest.

Frustrated and discouraged, he rejoined the crew. Their ribald jokes were sure to raise his spirits, if only for the duration of the journey. The sheer joy of smuggling goods across international borders would take over from there.

But the crew was neither ribald nor joking. They were unsettled. Anxious. Worried.

Evan approached with caution, keeping a fair bit of distance as he remembered Ollie's nervous comment that this voyage would be cursed. Ha, ha, ha. Sailors were always a suspicious lot. And setting sail with the worst of them when they were of a mood—particularly with the sea in high dudgeon, as it was tonight—might not be the wisest of choices.

The voices grew louder.

"You really think so, then, do you? I don't know . . . Wouldn't the cap'n have said so if he were?"

"Why would he, ye fool? Right before we hoist anchor? Captain's the last cove as would curse a ship about ter set sail."

Curse. There was that word again.

"Bothwick's brother hasn't been about either, in case you haven't noticed. Supposin' it's not true, then. Supposin' the two of them ran off together."

"Whereabouts, Gretna Green? You're a right cork-brain tonight, Jimmy."

"Look here, both of you—Bothwick's at the foremast, and you know his brother's never more'n eight feet from him. Sure as pudding, he knows what's what."

"Bothwick," one of the hands called. But Evan was already on his way over. "Is it true Red ain't coming back?"

"We heard he was steering the big ship in the sky," said another.

"Dead, rather," put in a third. "As a doornail."

Evan stared at the gaggle of water dogs, suddenly conscious of how a man could be driven to bang his head against the forecastle until he passed out. He hadn't required clarification for "big ship in the sky." What he required, right about now, was a quiet place to go and think. And perhaps a tall glass of whiskey.

He leaned against the mainmast and resigned himself to finishing this conversation sober.

"Red's dead?" he asked. "Says who?"

"His sister."

"She got it from that other girl. Samson, or something."

"Stanford, you numbskull."

Evan snapped up straight. "*Stanton?*"

A chorus of nods. This was making less sense by the second.

"Miss Stanton told Miss Grey that Red wouldn't be coming home, on account of being dead?" he demanded, trying to put the pieces together in a coherent fashion.

"That's right," the jack called Jimmy agreed. "Told her to go forth and carry on without him, she did."

Evan stared at them. "But how would Miss Stanton know he was dead? How would she know Red in the first place?"

"That's what we're asking *you,* mate."

"She even called him by both his names, she did. Looked 'arriet dead in the eye and said, 'Now, yer brother Joshua— well, there's them that call him Red, now, ain't there. Any case, he's a right cold one, he is. Reckon he won't be coming home.' Clear as that."

Evan blinked. He'd forgotten Red's name wasn't really Red—if Evan had ever known the man's given name to begin with. While he doubted he'd just been treated to a precise accounting of the dialogue, if Miss Stanton had been in possession of such an intimate detail as the pirate's Christian name, that would make her . . . well, suspicious. At best.

What if that simpleton Forrester wasn't the one Evan should be worrying about? What if someone far more pernicious— someone actually *clever*—was keeping him under her watchful eye for reasons he couldn't begin to guess?

The captain strode aboard, giving Evan no chance to reason it through.

Time to work.

Up went the anchor and the sails. Out went the booms and the bowsprit. Around spun the tiller. And they were at sea. At last. Waves crashed against the hull. The ship groaned and wheezed as the keel tilted drunkenly with the raging currents. Water splashed aboard. Men cheered.

Eventually the ocean calmed, and the crew relaxed. A few went belowdeck in search of whiskey. Evan chose to stay where he was, portside, staring toward the invisible horizon. A dozen stars braved the blackness of the night. Cold wind tugged at his hair, chapped his lips. The familiar scent of saltwater rose and fell with the waves lapping at the side of the ship.

He *did* believe in the gods of the sea. How could he not?

Purposeful footsteps indicated the captain's approach. Evan turned.

"Captain."

"Bothwick."

A strange silence stretched between them. The captain regarded Evan with his cool blue gaze, drew in on a fat cigar, and seemed well inclined to just let the silence continue.

He wasn't going to mention the missing shipmates, Evan suddenly realized. The crew was right. The captain had to know Timothy was dead—it had happened right on this ship, and *somebody* removed his brother's body. The captain knew, was looking Evan straight in the eye, and wasn't going to say a word.

Which meant Red wasn't "missing," either. He could only be dead.

Nobody'd had the slightest clue . . . except, apparently, Miss Stanton. Come to think of it, all of this—whatever *this* was—started happening the same night she appeared at Ollie's house. Coincidence? Perhaps Timothy was right not to believe in such things.

Who *was* Miss Stanton? She was definitely not the feath-erbrained socialite she'd first seemed. Was she truly Lady Emeline's cousin, as Ollie had claimed? It's not as if Evan could ask Ollie's wife to confirm or deny the familial con-nection. He'd never even met the woman. According to Ollie, his wife was too infirm to leave her sickroom or en-tertain guests.

Come to think of it, every detail Evan had thought he "knew" about Miss Stanton had all been according to Ollie. Who was looking less and less like a reliable source of in-formation.

What if Miss Stanton wasn't working her wiles on Evan on the magistrate's behalf, after all? What if she were doing so on Ollie's bequest? Perhaps the goal had never been to spy on him. After all, Ollie knew just about every detail of Evan's life, seeing as the overgrown brute tended to be pre-sent for most of the law-breaking moments. What if the goal wasn't to watch him, but to distract him? To set him off course enough that he got himself killed?

Evan belatedly realized the captain was talking—and that he should've been paying close attention.

The captain was discussing the last mission. The last *known* mission. The one Timothy and Red went on before striking out on their own and getting killed for their inso-lence. The one whose spoils had appeared and disappeared from Timothy's entryway in a matter of days.

"—an equally fine collection this time," the captain was saying around a curl of cigar smoke. "My contact was quite pleased with the assortment recovered from the last trip. The painted tea sets were particular favorites with his buyers. When we dock, try to load as many of those on board as you can."

Evan nodded slowly, as much to himself as to the captain. The booty hadn't been stolen from Timothy's receiving room, then. It had been recovered from its temporary location and sent on its way. All on schedule and according to plan. *Nothing amiss here, Bothwick. Fetch us some tea sets, there's a good lad.*

Would he be the next to turn up "missing"? Was this his final night aboard ship?

"This may be your last trip," said the captain, by all appearances reading Evan's thoughts.

His fingers twitched in response.

"There have been . . . *difficulties* . . . with the crew as of late." The captain paused to blow a series of smoke rings, as if giving Evan an opportunity to digest those words however he chose.

"Difficulties?" he echoed, attempting an expression of polite interest.

"Among other unfortunate developments, a few important volumes have gone missing from the wardroom bookshelf. You wouldn't know anything about that, would you, Bothwick?"

"No," Evan was able to choke out in all honesty. But more than ever, he wished he *did* know what was happening.

"So be it." The captain's blue gaze turned calculating. "In any case, I have decided to make a few changes."

"What kinds of changes?" Evan asked, hoping he sounded more intrigued than suspicious.

"I'm dismantling this crew. For good. We'll dock in the other cave when we return to Bournemouth."

Evan frowned doubtfully. "We will?"

The captain tapped the ash from his cigar. "And then we won't be docking anywhere. I've decided not to trust my fortune in the hands of landlocked merchants. When the war ends, there won't be much use for those who smuggle goods out of France. The rich will buy their baubles directly."

True enough. Evan had been enjoying the adventure too much to consider how quickly it could all be over.

"So we just say our good-byes and go home?" he asked, unable to keep the disappointment from his voice. The bi-weekly adventures had been a high point in his life the past several months. Until Miss Stanton came into his life. And Timothy left it.

"Not exactly." The captain puffed on his cigar and re-garded Evan thoughtfully. "This here was a pirate ship, you know, before she became a simple smuggling boat."

Evan gave a short nod. The war had changed everything, made sneaking in boxes of nonsense more profitable and less risky than pillaging on the open sea.

Less gunfire involved.

"Well," the captain said, "it's time she returns to her original state. We'll lay low for a fortnight, to give my con-tact a chance to sell this last shipment and pay me my coin, and then those who'll come with me will sail out of here for good."

Pirates. Real pirates. The captain was offering him an op-portunity to live on the high seas. Permanently. No more paying fair prices to transport illegal goods. From here on out, they'd steal whatever they fancied. Most likely from other ships. Leave no survivors.

Never come home.

Much as Evan couldn't imagine himself living in Bourn-mouth indefinitely, the thought of never living *anywhere*—save below the deck of a ship—wasn't as appealing as it first sounded. If it ever had. The thought of killing inno-cents in order to ensure no witnesses remained to tell tales . . . Evan hadn't signed up for that, either. The very thought turned his stomach.

Smuggling was an adventure, a fine joke, a lark. He was never gone more than a weekend, and only twice a month at that. Just enough to keep life interesting. Out-and-out pi-rating, however . . . Despite the romantic allure of being a wenching, ale-swilling, swashbuckling fortune hunter, pirating was for life. And *forever* was a very long time.

Evan hesitated. Perhaps now was not the moment to voice these concerns.

"You don't have to make your choice now," the captain continued, once again eerily close to reading Evan's mind. "I only want those aboard my ship who intend to stay there. I need a crew I can trust. Most of these water rats will join us"—he motioned behind him with a wave of his cigar—"but water rats is all they are and all they'll ever be. You and Ollie, now . . . You're a different breed."

Evan's gaze snapped back to the captain's. *Ollie.*

"I want one of you for my first mate." The captain flicked ash from his cigar. "Poseidon's got that pleasure at the moment . . . but you boys can work that out yourselves."

Meaning "joining for life" would be synonymous with "joining for one night" if he didn't survive hand-to-hand, anything-goes combat with Poseidon, a seasoned pirate, thereby proving his mettle as a single-minded, take-no-prisoners first mate.

Not joining, on the other hand, would mean giving up his chance of ever discovering Timothy's killer. Evan couldn't stand the thought of his brother's murder going forever unavenged. Timothy deserved a proper burial. And justice.

Evan rubbed at his taut neck muscles. "What did Ollie say?"

"Figured you'd ask that next." The captain blew out another round of smoke rings. "Ollie hasn't made his choice known. He's a family man, so he'd have a few loose ends to tie up first. Nonetheless, he's got the same timeframe as you." The smoke cleared. The captain's cold blue gaze hadn't left Evan's face. "Be on board in a fortnight, or miss the boat entirely. We won't be heard from again."

Sunday night fell as fast and as hard as the rain accompanying the twilight.

Evan had never been so happy to reach dry land. Well, if

you could call the briny puddles splattered throughout the cave "dry land." Not to mention the icy water pouring from the black clouds for miles.

He headed straight home to bathe, devilishly glad to be able to do so. This time, he hadn't been certain he'd make it back alive.

The skies had turned stormy within moments of the captain's announcement, and the torrents had continued throughout the weekend. Rough. Cold. Shot through with lightning. Yet it was the atmosphere belowdeck that had kept him uneasy. The men were skittish. Worried. With two dead, they had had every reason to be. The change from occasional smuggling to out-and-out piracy—well, such a turn wouldn't lengthen anyone's life expectancy.

After bathing, Evan dressed for warmth. It didn't work. The thought of never avenging Timothy's death coated his veins with ice.

The loss of his brother left an ache in Evan's heart he was beginning to suspect would never subside. He wished for the hundredth time that he could wear a black armband without being asked questions he couldn't answer. Like whom he was mourning. Nobody knew about Timothy yet. Would perhaps never know, if Evan couldn't find his brother's body. But funeral or no, he would find and dispatch the killer or die trying.

He made his way back downstairs. Forced himself to eat a hot supper. Pushed away his empty plate more slowly than usual. He glanced around his house at all the things he enjoyed taking for granted. No home cooking while the crew was at sea. Not that he'd have much of an appetite if he saw the crew killing innocents in the name of piracy. The thought once again turned his stomach.

Oh, Evan knew why he and Ollie had been "given" a choice. They were the only ones *with* choices. The other water dogs had nowhere else to go. Like it or not, they'd been enlisted the moment the captain had reevaluated his plan of operations. For them, free will was an illusion. For Evan . . . He shoved back his chair and strode out the door. There was *nothing* he valued more than free will.

Even if he seemed not to exercise much of it lately. He told himself he was headed to Moonseed Manor out of ennui. Not because of a magnetic pull he was powerless to deny. He told himself he was headed to Moonseed Manor solely to confront a certain debutante about her alleged associations with dead smugglers. Not because he missed her company. He'd never missed any particular female over any other a day in his life. So he obviously hadn't missed sparring—and trading kisses—with Miss Stanton.

Well . . . not *much*. More like: terribly.

Once at the door, he shouldered past the jaundiced butler and went on the hunt. What had she been doing while Evan was at sea? Had that irritatingly persistent magistrate resumed his pathetic attempts to woo her? Was it possible Forrester had actually succeeded? The little toad was everything Evan was not: polite, respected, boring, pious, interested in escorting marriage-minded young ladies to insipid assemblies. In short, a true gentleman. Whereas Evan . . . Evan . . .

Smelled jasmine. Wafting down from the spiral staircase nearby. He was past the first landing before the thought occurred to him that the only rooms upstairs were bedchambers, which were precisely the sort of illicit location in which a true gentleman would never dream to hunt down a lady.

Thank God he wasn't a gentleman.

He climbed the last stair and headed into the hall. There she was, peering down one narrow corridor after another, trying the occasional door handle and appearing generally lost.

She heard or saw or somehow sensed it was he who closed in on her, because when she whirled around to face him, her eyes were filled not with fear but pleasure. Which she quickly tried to mask. He did not bother to try and hide his own satisfaction at being alone with her once again. Just seeing her made him want to smile. And devour her in kisses.

"You came back," she whispered.

"I couldn't stay away," was all he said in reply. This was not the time to launch into long explanations of cannon fire and high treason.

She stepped forward, then checked her progress. But her gaze was darkening and her breathing rapid, and Evan could no longer withstand this distance between him.

His lips covered hers, and there was no more talking.

He expected resistance. There was none. Her mouth opened beneath his, kissing, biting, tasting. She seemed as desperate for him as he was for her. So he gave her what she wanted. Took what he wanted. And still he burned for more.

"We can't be caught kissing," she breathed against his cheek.

"I know."

But he didn't pull away. Neither did she.

Then: "I meant every word. I can't afford to make another spectacle of myself. I—"

He silenced her with more kisses. Her arms twined around his neck, tightened. Judging by the way she arched into him, Miss Stanton felt about as inclined to stop as he did. He kissed her more deeply, pulling her into his embrace.

His shoulders thumped against something hollow. A door. Vaguely, he realized that they were still in the corridor. Servants might chance upon them. They would be *Ollie's* servants and therefore well used to keeping their mouths sewn shut, but Miss Stanton was right. They could take no more chances.

So Evan slid his hand from her hair and twisted the doorknob behind him. He caught her soft body to him as they tumbled inside. A bedchamber. Not hers, by the still air and general emptiness, but the room contained a bed, which would serve their purposes just fine.

He swung her into his arms, drowning her protests in more kisses. Well, possibly. She seemed to have forgotten to protest. Or perhaps the click of the door closing behind them gave her the same sense of relief and security, and there were no more protests to be made.

He certainly had no complaints. She was perfect. Warm and soft and sweet and eager and matching him kiss for kiss. He carried her to the bed. There was no elegant way to lay her in the center while still kissing—so he didn't try.

Besides, no one had ever begged him for elegance. Passion, yes. And that, he was eager to provide. He backed up to the bed, determined not to remove his mouth from hers a single second longer than necessary. He eased down onto the edge of the mattress with her body in his arms, her fingers gripping his hair. He leaned backward until she was sprawled crisscross atop him. Before she could move, he rolled above her, pinning her to the bed with his gaze and mouth and body.

Her arms tightened around his neck and her breathing changed. "I haven't a clue how that just happened. If you practice that maneuver often, please don't tell me."

Something in her tone was heartfelt enough that he tilted his head back to regard her. But although her words may have been serious, her eyes were smiling, and she didn't tolerate the interrupted kisses for long. She leaned her head up to meet his, her lips parted, her lashes lowering.

He curved his hand beneath her head and kissed her, grateful she didn't expect a response. It was true; he didn't feel like a green boy, fumbling his way through his first sexual encounter. But nor did he feel his usual careless self, taking pleasure for pleasure's sake with this or that wench in a seaside tavern. For one, he wasn't drunk on whiskey and treason. For two, Miss Stanton was the complete opposite of *anyone* he had ever lain with. And for three, he could scarce treat her or the moment carelessly because, well . . . he did care. Immensely.

The horrifying thought might've given him pause had Evan not immediately and forcefully put it from his mind.

The only thought drowning his brain was to keep kissing her. Touching her. He jerked the comb from her hair, ran his fingers through its softness. The blond mass fell to her breasts. Her beautiful, tempting breasts. He ran the palm of his hand along the curve of her neck, her shoulder, her arm, irritated that every inch of her body was covered in layer upon layer of cloth, from her toes to her fingertips.

He could no longer withstand the need to have at least part of her jasmine-scented flesh exposed to his eyes, his mouth, his tongue. He slipped a finger between sleeve and glove and pulled. Neither budged.

She looped her arms around his neck, allowing their desperate kisses to continue as one bit of silk after the other fluttered to the floor beside them. He tugged one of her now-bare hands forward and brought it to his lips. He kissed each fingertip, the lines of her palm, the frantic pulse pounding at her wrist.

He decided he hated long sleeves. Perhaps clothing in general. He wished neither of them were encumbered by winter layers. Particularly those that would require ten minutes unhooking tiny buttons before the bodice would loosen. His heart would expire before he finished.

Assuming she let him try.

Then again, she was returning every kiss, every lick, every nibble. She certainly hadn't been asleep when they'd tumbled into the room, closed the door, and made their way to the bed. She had been the first to start tossing unwanted articles of clothing overboard. In fact, so far she was the only one to have done so. Evan hoped to rectify that immediately. Now that they were alone and abed, he had no wish to remain properly dressed.

He kissed the hollow in her neck, the line of her jaw. His

hand cradled the side of her face as their tongues clashed. Then he slid his palm down to her neck, her collarbone, her bodice. Blood pounded in his ears. He splayed his fingers over one perfect breast. Hidden beneath a thousand maddening layers of cloth.

She gasped beneath his mouth but arched into him as if she, too, resented the obstructions preventing his flesh from touching hers. He imagined he could feel her nipple hardening, rising to greet him through the soft linen of her stays. He stroked the phantom nub gently with the pads of his fingers. No, not imagining. She moaned, arching higher. His cock strained against his breeches.

He dragged his mouth from hers, burning a trail of kisses down the line of her neck, the muslin covering her décolletage, to the round breast cupped in his palm. He opened his mouth over that hard little nipple and laved with his tongue. Damp, the fabric molded to her skin, accentuating the nipple's arousal.

Her fingers gripped his hair, pressing his face into her breast.

Without removing his mouth—he would die first—he reached lower, gathered a handful of skirt in his fist, and pulled. Inch by inch, the rising hem exposed the tops of her boots, the curve of her ankle, her slender legs. He couldn't watch, but his bare palm informed him of every detail. The silken smoothness of her stockings, the heat of her skin, the slight shiver as both cool air and his warm fingers touched the exposed flesh of her thigh.

"I—" she gasped.

He returned his mouth to hers and swallowed whatever she'd been about to say with the passion in his kiss. He stroked her hips, the inside of her thighs, just above the apex between, everywhere but the one place he was dying to touch. He needed her to want it, too.

And she did. The scent of her desire drove him half mad.

Her body writhed beneath him, her hips trying to coax his fingers to quit teasing, to give her release.

With his mouth still mating with hers, he finally lowered his hand, cupping her. Ran the length of his fingers against her slick flesh. She moaned again, bit his lip. He dipped the tip of one finger inside, loving the hot wetness, the contraction of her muscles. He slid his newly moistened finger barely free, just enough to stroke her, to stoke her fire.

Her gasps came louder, faster. She forgot she'd been kissing him. Her head fell back against the mattress and her eyes fluttered closed. He rubbed, teased, dipped the tip of his finger back inside, stroked her in soft circles. Faster. Slower. Deeper inside. Back for more caresses. She was so hot, so wet, so ready, so—

She bucked beneath him, and he sank a finger inside, rubbing simultaneously with the pad of his thumb. She convulsed, gripped his shoulders, sucked in shallow, shuddering breaths.

He kissed her, caressed her until she collapsed boneless beneath him, then finally, finally, allowed his damp and trembling fingers to fumble at the buttons of his fall. His cock strained, pulled, demanded to sink itself to the hilt in all that sweet wetness. There. At last. His cock was free from its restraints, pulsing hot and hard in Evan's palm.

He couldn't wait another moment . . . but he had to do this right. For both of them.

"I want you," he said between kisses. His voice was raw, hoarse. She nipped at his lips. "I need to feel you beneath me, part of me. Every moment I spent away from you, I was haunted by the scent of your skin and the feel of your tongue against mine." She licked him, her eyes slumberous and teasing. He smiled back, a man lost. Helpless. "You've bewitched me. And I am desperate for more." His fingers squeezed his overeager cock, which ached to be inside her. "There is nothing I want more than to make love to you. If you've even the smallest of doubts . . . tell me now, or I won't stop until I'm buried inside you and we're panting in pleasure, again and again." His cock lurched in approval. "Tell me you want that, too."

She blinked. In that second, her amorous gaze went from satisfied to horrified.

She gave a tiny scream and cracked her forehead against his in her desperation to flee his embrace. The pain in his skull was the least of his concerns. She scrambled backward, her expression aghast.

"No." Her face drained of all color. She began to shake her head. "No. Oh, no. No, no, no."

The hard shaft in Evan's hand stopped pulsing.

"I—I—" She rolled away from him with such force she tumbled onto the floor. In seconds she was on her feet, smoothing her hopelessly wrinkled skirts, gripping her silk gloves. She forced them over trembling fingers without meeting his eyes, then backed toward the door. "I can't. I . . . no. I don't know what in the bloody hell I was thinking. Dear Lord, I *wasn't* thinking. We can't do this. *I* can't do this. My—my husband—"

"Your *what?*" Evan stared at her, mouth open, cock in hand.

"Not yet," she rushed to assure him, "but the one I *do* get is going to assume certain things, such as me never having done a single thing that we just did and—" She yanked open the door, then turned her anguished gaze on him. "Believe what you will, I am a lady. I wish to be treated as such. By you, by everyone, by the man whom I will marry. He will expect to bed a virgin on his wedding night. I expect to *be* one."

Evan's fading cock slipped from his slackened grip of its own accord.

"I don't fancy being another one of your conquests," she continued, a creeping blush bringing color back into her deathly pale cheeks. "I have a conquest of my own to make. *London.* And to succeed, I need to guard what few advantages I still have." She backed into the hall. "Please don't kiss me again. Please don't touch me again. Ever."

With that, she was gone. The latch clicked in place behind her with the cold finality of a jailer slamming a prison cell shut.

Chapter 17

Evan rebuttoned his fall. He reasoned that Miss Stanton's inglorious flight from the bedchamber had actually saved both of them from making an exceptionally unwise mistake. He doubted it was just the crack to the head that had made her speak the one word guaranteed to deflate the ardor of a man who'd never tumbled the same woman twice:

Husband.

Luckily, if also a bit insultingly, she clearly had no matrimonial designs on him whatsoever. Unluckily, her desire to remain a virgin until her wedding night—for which he would certainly not be present—precluded them from lovemaking.

He pushed off the bed and glanced about the chamber to make sure he hadn't left any evidence of his presence. A long-instilled habit. Although he had never intended to lay with other men's wives, the women in his past had not always been honest about such details. No, he'd left nothing behind. Except perhaps a bit of his pride.

Miss Stanton's hair comb, however, poked out from the wrinkled folds of the tester. In fact, the entire mattress was awash with wrinkles. He pocketed the tiny comb and idly wondered what the servants would make of the disarray. Perhaps they would assume their master and mistress had tired of their bedchamber and sought excitement in an alternate venue. Evan chuckled. For all he knew, the overgrown oaf made love to his wife everywhere *but* their bedchamber. Perhaps the woman wasn't "too sick for visitors" so much as simply exhausted.

He stepped into the hall. Since he was here, he might as well find Ollie. The servants might be close-lipped to outsiders, but they'd certainly mention Evan's presence to their master. Come to think of it, since the brute wasn't currently breathing down his neck, perhaps now was the opportune moment to search for the ornate box they'd unburied from the garden.

He headed downstairs. First step: Check the dining room mantle to see if the similar-looking ornate box were still present. If it was now missing, then at least he'd have solved that much of the mystery. If not . . . well, then he'd keep searching.

The dining room was empty, but embers still burned in the fireplace. They offered just enough relief from the shadows for Evan to take inventory of the mantle's contents. Brandy. A forgotten cigar. An unlit candelabra. And the same gilded jewelry box that had always sat there.

He plucked a taper from the candelabra and bent the wick to the last of the dying flames. No easy task. He used the thin candle to light the rest of the candelabra and returned the taper to its original location. In the ensuing orange glow, the bejeweled box looked the same as it ever had . . . with two notable exceptions.

First, the jewel-encrusted lid was now closed. Before, it had remained open, the better to exhibit its empty but delicately sculpted interior. Second, the dark clump lodged inside the tiny lock was nothing more than . . . dirt?

It *was* the same jewelry box. He knew it!

He picked up the surprisingly heavy container and gave it a careful shake. Empty. Even without opening the lid to verify, there were no telltale sounds of clinking jewelry or shifting weight as the box's contents slid from one side to the other. Nonetheless, he tugged carefully at the heavy lid. Locked. He'd need a key to open the damn thing. He glanced up to look for one—and found both Ollie and his lapdog standing in the doorway watching him.

Evan froze, his fingertips poised at the crevice between lid and receptacle.

Ollie was the first to step into the room. "Devilish tricky to open without the key, isn't it?"

Evan couldn't very well act as if that weren't precisely what he'd been attempting to do, so he didn't bother to play-act. Instead, he removed his fingertips from the stubborn lock and held out his palm toward Ollie. "Got the key handy?"

Ollie ignored Evan's outstretched hand, returned the heavy jewelry box to the mantle, and set about pouring a glass of brandy. He did not offer any to Evan. Just as well, for this seemed a moment where keeping a clear head would be wise.

"Why is the box closed?" he asked.

Ollie downed his first brandy and poured himself another without responding.

"Because we haven't got the key," rasped the jaundiced servant, crossing the room to stand by his master.

Ollie's jaw tightened, but he simply capped the brandy and lifted his glass to his lips.

Evan turned his gaze to the wiry butler. "Where is the key?"

"Don't know," came the scratchy reply.

"Where did you last see it?"

"Never have."

"Never?" Evan repeated incredulously.

"Don't think there ever was one." The servant shrugged one bony shoulder. "That's why we kept it open."

"Why do you care?" Ollie interrupted at last, his dark gaze focused on Evan.

"Why do *you?*" Evan gestured at the little box. "Damn thing's empty."

"Feels empty," the servant corrected slyly. "Can't know for certain until it's open."

True enough. "If you want inside that badly, a second or two with a hammer ought to do the trick."

Ollie shook his head. "No hammer, no shovel, no ax. Didn't you feel how heavy it was? All that delicate gold filigree and intricate ornamentation hides an iron core. Literally. It's a strongbox, meant to look like a fribble's gewgaw."

Evan turned toward the innocuous-looking jewelry box again, nonplussed. Brilliant, that. How many times had he seen the thing on the mantle and never given it a passing thought? He wondered in which port Ollie had found such a treasure. And why it hadn't come with a key.

"Fair bit of dirt stuck in the keyhole," he commented idly.

The butler's teeth flashed. "That was milady's handiwork, it was. She likes to—"

"—play games," Ollie finished, casting his lapdog a silencing look.

The servant's Adam's apple bobbed in his skinny throat, but he didn't contradict his master's obvious lie.

Why lie? Well, yes, Ollie was a pirate and as such lied on a regular basis, but not typically to Evan, and certainly not about something as silly as whether his wife had buried a trick jewelry box in a fit of matrimonial pique.

He frowned. She couldn't be *that* sick, if she was well enough to traipse downstairs, carry a heavy box and an equally heavy shovel out to the rock garden, and bury the former in the dirt. And add a gravestone.

Perhaps she was socially . . . awkward. Or painfully shy. Or simply reclusive. Given her parents' history, she would not have had what could be termed a typical childhood.

He picked up the box again, hefting its weight. There had to be some way to open it. "Can I take it home for a few days?"

"No."

Not even a breath had passed before the refusal came.

Evan replaced the box on the mantle, unsurprised at Ollie's answer. No matter if it were nothing more precious than ordinary snuff inside an ordinary snuff box, Ollie wasn't one to share what was his when he didn't wish to. Perhaps it was time to turn the topic.

"Are you going to join the captain's crew?"

Ollie's dark brows lifted. He gestured with his now-empty glass. "Leave all this?"

Evan inclined his head and wondered whether there was any truth to the captain's promise to leave them behind alive and well, if they decided not to enlist.

Normally, he would've shared such concerns with Ollie. But Evan still wasn't 100 percent certain whose side Ollie was on—if on anyone's side but his own. He *was* certain he had overstayed his welcome. Particularly since they were all aware of his unannounced arrival and subsequent ignominious discovery in the dining room.

"I'm for home, then."

He took a step toward the doorway. The butler stepped aside, his tiny eyes watchful.

With his broad back facing Evan, Ollie refilled his brandy glass without turning around.

"Do that."

Right. Evan had definitely overstayed his nonexistent welcome.

He quit the dining room. He eased the door shut behind him and made his way toward the rear exit. Partly because the back door led more directly to the trail going toward Evan's house. And partly because he wouldn't mind having another look at the rock garden, now that he knew a woman too frail to leave her bed had supposedly decided to do a bit of nontraditional gardening.

At the time, he had thought Timothy might've been buried in that third grave, but what had everyone else been thinking? They couldn't all have been after an empty jewelry box.

Evan could scarce ask Forrester what he'd been doing there without admitting to his own presence. Miss Stanton, however . . . Evan cursed himself as he realized he'd missed several good opportunities to ask her just what exactly she'd thought had been buried beneath that unmarked gravestone. Next time he saw her, he'd—

Jasmine. There she was. Right by the rear door.

Not facing the exit, however. She stared in the opposite direction, down a darkened stairwell Evan assumed led to a larder. Miss Stanton had her back to him, her outstretched hands splayed against each stone wall, a booted foot hovering over the first step.

He approached with caution. "What are you—"

She jumped, spun around, pushed him.

He didn't budge.

She put a finger to her lips, eyes wide. "Shhh."

Evan stayed quiet, more out of perplexity than any desire to be obedient. The woman made absolutely no sense.

She turned back toward the blackness, dismissing him.

He considered leaving as planned.

Galling as it was, she seemed to have forgotten their aborted lovemaking in her obsession with—with what? She was neither descending the staircase nor returning fully to the hallway. She was doing precisely nothing.

He was wasting his time. She wanted a husband; he wanted to run off screaming. Why he continued standing next to her instead of running, he wasn't entirely sure. She was a marriage-minded woman. He was a bachelor-minded man. Expectations of commitment accompanied any relationship she entered. Consequence-free encounters were the only variety he ever had. So it wasn't as if there was anything left to discuss.

He had almost turned to leave when he remembered they still did have plenty left unsaid, once he dropped his sexual frustration and wounded pride from the picture. He hated the idea that this woman who'd fled from him seconds after finding release would eagerly bed some insipid *ton* fop, simply because he had something other than "Mister" before his name.

With such an image in his head, no wonder he'd almost forgotten why he'd come here in the first place. It wasn't because he'd missed her. Not at all. It was because he didn't trust her.

"Did you tell Harriet Grey her brother was dead?" he demanded.

"Shhh!" She flapped a hand at him as if shushing a recalcitrant child and then whispered, "Not my finest moment, I admit. Do be quiet and let me listen."

He stared at the back of her blond head.

Not her finest moment? What the devil did that mean? He'd expected her to deny the accusation. She had not. Which meant it was true. How, he couldn't begin to fathom. He had no guesses as to where she'd met an unsavory like Red in the first place—particularly since such a meeting would've had to occur prior to her arrival in Bournemouth—much less who would have informed her of his death.

"How did you know he—"

"*Shhh.*" She tugged him closer. "Help me listen."

Irritably realizing he wouldn't get anywhere with her until he'd indulged whatever fantasy had gripped her nonsensical mind, he cocked his head to the side and listened. Hard. For several long moments. Then he gave up.

"I hear nothing."

"Me neither." She turned to him, her eyes almost as wide as the lenses of her spectacles. "I wonder what it means."

It meant she was utterly off her hooks, by the look of it. What kind of noises *would* come from a larder? Pheasants, rising from the dead?

"I have to see," she whispered. "Come with me. I don't want to go by myself."

She took three or four steps into the darkness. She stopped, glanced up at him, and gestured for him to hurry.

Evan sighed. If Ollie caught them spying on neat little rows of tins and jars, Evan would never hear the end of it. The crew had taunted Evan and Timothy for their alleged "fancy" tastes ever since they'd both balked at the slop they'd been served in dusty bowls their first night aboard ship. Evan felt no shame for liking good food. But he didn't particularly want to set himself up for another round of ribbing when now more than ever it seemed wise to stay out of the captain's eye. And out of Ollie's house.

Miss Stanton, however, had not stopped staring up at him and making furious "Come *on!*" motions with her hands.

All right, fine. But she'd better hurry.

He descended quickly, brushing past her and continuing on. He snagged a candle from the sole candelabrum halfway down the stairs and moved faster. The sooner he got to the bottom, the sooner he could head back to the top. It wasn't as though there were any reason for her to act as if something frightening lurked just around the corner. It was a *larder,* for Christ's—

Evan stopped so suddenly, candle wax dripped on his ungloved fingers. He scarcely noticed. All he could see were the high stone walls, damp with age and mold. A thick iron chain led from a clamp in the wall to an ankle the width of a child's. The terrified owner of said ankle rocked in the far corner with her hands wrapped tightly about her knees and a dirty handkerchief tied around her head in a gag.

"Oh no," Miss Stanton cried out, running past him to kneel before the emaciated young lady with long blond plaits and pale skin. "Cousin Emeline, what have they done to you?"

Evan almost dropped the candle.

This was Lady *Emeline?!*

He'd thought—he'd thought—well, he wasn't sure his brain had been firing fast enough to think much of anything, but he certainly hadn't thought this poor creature was Ollie's *wife*. He ran his fingers in the cracks between the stones, searching for a key to unlock her.

"Don't bother." With her eyes focused on the trembling young lady before her, Miss Stanton began to carefully untie the soiled handkerchief. "The scarecrow keeps the keys with him."

He blinked. "Scarecrow?"

"I'm forced to keep hold of the keys with *you* nosing about," scratched a voice from the stairwell.

Although he'd recognized the speaker immediately, Evan had half-expected an actual scarecrow to appear in the doorway. Why not? His evening had lost all sense of reality hours ago.

But no, it was the butler standing between them and the stairwell.

And Ollie.

"Why do you have your wife chained to a wall in the cellar?" Evan challenged, unable to hide the shock in his tone.

Ollie made no response.

The lapdog, however, grinned. "You know a better place to chain her?"

Evan's hands clenched. His fists ached to plant themselves right in the center of the servant's smug face. He warred with temptation. But this was Ollie's lackey. And Ollie's house. So Evan kept his focus on the master.

"Unlock her."

"No."

As before, the response was swift, monosyllabic, and final.

Worse than anything, there was nothing Evan could do about it. Well, short of breaking the captive free and abducting her from her home. Then *he'd* be the one in violation of the law. With him in gaol, the woman would be returned right back to her husband.

Miss Stanton rose to her feet, handkerchief clenched in her fist.

"Why did you gag her?" she demanded, eyes flashing with fear and outrage.

Evan couldn't help but admire her in that moment. She was clearly terrified, yet willing to stand up to an oversize brute despite being powerless to stop him from doing whatever he fancied. With a backbone like that, she wouldn't make a half-bad pirate.

"Why *did* you gag her?" Evan repeated, when it seemed the twosome would ignore Miss Stanton's question indefinitely.

Ollie raised his brows and said nothing. He didn't have to answer to anyone. He owned Lady Emeline. Period. No matter what Evan or Miss Stanton thought about his conduct. Ollie was reminding them of that fact without saying a word.

"Why?" Miss Stanton choked out again. "She already— she doesn't have—"

"Turns out," the servant said with a malicious glance at his mistress, "milady's a screamer."

Evan's blood froze.

"Doesn't like her punishments much." The servant smirked at the cowering woman. "Do you, milady?"

"She—She—" Miss Stanton gasped, clutching the handkerchief to her chest. "It wasn't her fault! I made her go! I'm the one who—the one who—"

Ollie crossed the room and plucked the dirty cloth from her fingers. He turned to his wife. "You weren't making noises again, were you, love?"

Lady Emeline shook her head and shrank farther into the corner.

"No? In that case . . ." He straightened and turned toward Miss Stanton.

Almost as a reflex, Evan reached out and latched on to her wrist, tugging her close. He released his grip once he realized what he'd done. But she remained at his side, pale and trembling.

Ollie seemed to double in size. "If you didn't hear anything that required investigation, Miss Stanton, I have to assume you came down here entirely on your own. In direct violation of my . . . suggestion . . . to the contrary. Have you changed your mind as to where you preferred to have your own living quarters?"

It was Miss Stanton's turn to shake her head frantically.

Evan's jaw dropped.

"In that case," Ollie continued as if nothing were amiss, "I suggest you retake your quarters immediately. Or I will provide you with alternate accommodation."

She swayed, and for a second Evan thought she would slump against him in a dead faint. But then she gasped for air, gave a final anguished glance at the woman in the corner, and fled up the stairs.

"And now Bothwick," Ollie drawled. The blackness of his full beard couldn't hide the fury of his expression. "Shouldn't you be on your way, too?"

Yes, yes, of course he should. He had no pistols handy, no legal recourse, and no way of winning no matter which moment he chose to fight this battle. Yet the thought of inaction nauseated him.

"Do not terrorize Miss Stanton."

"Terrorize?" Ollie repeated mildly, toying with the chain that led down to his wife's ankle. "I merely suggested she not spend her time so far below stairs, that's all."

Evan cast another frustrated glance at the trembling young lady in the corner.

"Repugnant as it is, I can't prevent you from treating your wife as you wish," he bit out at last. "But no matter what incomprehensible motives drive you to cage your wife in the cellar, surely the occasional visit from a friendly face cannot hurt."

"Don't misunderstand me." Ollie's black eyes glittered in

the candlelight. "I couldn't agree more. In fact, I informed Miss Stanton I'd be more than happy to let her stay with Emeline. Indefinitely."

The pointed arch to Ollie's thick black brows left no doubt as to what, precisely, he was threatening. *Both* women were in danger. From a man who could do whatever he damn well pleased with either one.

Lady Emeline let out a whimper, then clapped both hands over her mouth as if to trap the tiny noise from escaping. A twitch of Ollie's brow indicated the sound had not gone unnoticed. Nor would the infraction go unpunished. His lapdog's self-satisfied grin hinted he got just as much pleasure from the power to bedevil his mistress as he did from Evan's powerlessness to stop him.

Damn it all. There was absolutely nothing Evan could do to protect Lady Emeline *or* Miss Stanton.

Nothing.

Even with Timothy's ivory-handled knife in her pocket, Susan was afraid to unlock the bedchamber door the next morning.

She glared at her self-imposed cage and swore beneath her breath. For a sociable young lady who'd been (unfairly) confined to her room for the better part of a year as punishment for spreading a devastating piece of (verifiably true) gossip, one might think the last thing she would voluntarily do was remain locked in her bedroom.

Particularly in a place like Moonseed Manor.

However, she had no wish to step out into the corridor, only to find herself shackled next to cousin Emeline in the cellar. Poor cousin Emeline. Susan dropped her face into her hands and tried not to imagine what she'd suffered as a result of Susan's unsuccessful attempt to free them both from the monster of the Manor.

Heartsick, she dallied in the relative safety of her bedchamber. Breakfast came and went. Janey came and went as well. Bearing no tidings—or money—from home.

Again.

Leaving Susan with the disheartening realization that no one was coming to her rescue. *If* her family had received her pleas in the first place. Whether her letters ever got posted remained a matter of speculation.

She eyed the locked door. Could the giant knock it from its hinges by brute force? Possibly. She cleaned her spectacles and peered closer at said hinges. Make that *probably*. The latch was old. He was big. And she was an unarmed Town miss with no one to turn to.

Her cheeks heated at this lie.

But she didn't know what to think about Mr. Bothwick. They'd gotten off on the wrong foot perhaps, what with him trying to shoot his pistols at the master of the house (which turned out to be an excellent character assessment on Mr. Bothwick's part) and her erasing the footpath with her derrière (which turned out to be yet another directional misstep on her part). Then there was last night.

She hadn't meant to kiss him. Well, maybe she'd hoped he'd steal a kiss. Or two. But she certainly hadn't intended for things to escalate any further. His mouth and his fingers made an excellent case for giving up on "purity." Unfortunately, she didn't have that luxury.

Mr. Bothwick, however, had been nothing short of offended when she'd deemed him not the sort of man one married. Not to hurt his feelings, but he was certainly not husband material. He was the sort of shameless rakehell who lifted women's skirts in strange bedchambers. (She'd consider her own complicity in the matter at another time.)

She shoved open the bedchamber door and stepped out into the corridor, wishing she could have the best of both worlds but recognizing the impossibility. One of them had to keep a clear head.

The irony of the situation, Susan decided as she carefully

crept through the Manor and out the front door, was that the man she'd thought would be her ally was not. She'd been certain Mr. Forrester would be shocked and horrified and wish to rescue both women immediately. Yet he'd patted her on the head and immediately returned Lady Emeline to her prison.

Whereas the man she'd labeled a villain from the first, who carried pistols and lost his brother's corpse and never let a second pass without an attempt at divesting her from her (thus far continuing) virginity—*that* man had stared the giant down, demanded Lady Emeline's prompt release, been so furious at the giant's refusal Susan had been certain only one of them would leave the cellar alive.

All of which boiled down to one surprising truth: There was the law, and then there was the law unto oneself. And sometimes the latter was more effective.

She pondered this conclusion as she headed down the sandy path toward town. True, they hadn't managed to rescue Lady Emeline last night. But Mr. Bothwick had been so outraged on cousin Emeline's behalf, Susan was certain his aid could be enlisted in the future. Perhaps he could rescue them both.

That still didn't make him husband material, of course. In fact, his very usefulness lay in the fact that he was the *opposite* of eligible. She'd seen what an honorable, proper, law-abiding gentleman would accomplish: absolutely nothing. Mr. Bothwick, on the other glove, was the sort who made things happen.

Before she could ruminate more on the topic, his dead brother chose that moment to materialize at her side.

"I don't know what happened to the box," she announced preemptively. If she was a bit defensive about the topic, it was because she'd barely left her bedchamber all weekend. She presumed the ghost's absence indicated he'd been watching over his brother.

"I found it," Dead Mr. Bothwick said, keeping an arm's

length between them as he accompanied her by floating backward down the trail. "It's in Ollie's dining room."

She pushed up her spectacles. After last night, no way was she stepping foot in the giant's domain. "And?"

"And now," he replied, "you steal it."

Susan stumbled on the rocky path. "Are you bamming me? You have *no idea* how displeased with me that monster is at the moment. If he catches me trying to steal that jewelry box, he'll cut off my arms."

"Unlikely."

"Or my tongue."

Dead Mr. Bothwick winced. "Perhaps."

She stopped walking. Even the wind seemed to cease for a moment. "What do you mean, 'perhaps'?"

He flickered. "Nothing. I meant nothing. Go steal the box."

"I think you did mean something. I think you meant, 'Perhaps he will, Miss Stanton. Oh well.' Which means you have reason to believe it could happen."

"Can we please talk about the box?"

"No." Susan narrowed her eyes at the shimmering ghost. Not for the first time, she felt Dead Mr. Bothwick was not telling the whole truth. Nor was he overly concerned about her mortality. In short, she didn't trust him. The odd thing was, he didn't seem to trust her either. And the black cloud for them both? They were stuck with each other.

"Please pay attention." His ghostly form rippled. "It is of utmost urgency that you hide that box somewhere neither Ollie nor his servants will ever find it."

"Why? What's in it?"

He flashed her a look of pure exasperation. "It doesn't matter what's in it!"

"Why should I risk my life for something that doesn't matter?" she asked in her most reasonable tone, knowing the twisted logic would drive him mad. He deserved some consternation. His half-truths and dangerous missions were more than she could handle right now. She stormed forward.

All Red had wanted was for her to pass a simple message, and look where that had gotten her. That business in the rock garden? She was lucky the still-living Mr. Bothwick had intercepted her. If the giant and the scarecrow had found her trespassing . . .

Susan shivered. She didn't want to imagine the lengths to which they might have retaliated. She didn't want to go back to Moonseed Manor at all.

Ignoring Dead Mr. Bothwick, she stood at the base of the path and glanced around the town. Nobody had come out to stone her today. Nor were there balloons and a parade. Instead, she was studiously ignored, as she had been the last time she dared show her face. A stupid woman, for not accepting Mr. Bothwick's supposed proposal. A fallen woman, for having kissed him passionately.

A madwoman, for talking to ghosts. But at least she'd kept that much to herself.

"What do you think?" Dead Mr. Bothwick had apparently concluded his monologue. "Will you do it?"

"No," she replied without bothering to ask for a summary of the speech she'd blessedly fallen deaf to. "I won't. What I need to do is find a friend. Preferably a living one. Someone I could 'visit' until next weekend, when the magistrate comes to take me to Bath."

Dead Mr. Bothwick stared at her doubtfully. "A friend? Nobody in town likes you."

"Thank you," she said icily. "I hadn't noticed."

They stared at the dilapidated buildings in awkward silence.

"Your brother likes me well enough." Susan bit her tongue as soon as the words were out. She'd meant to trivialize that fact, not draw further attention to their relationship. Whatever their relationship was.

Suspicion returned to Dead Mr. Bothwick's face. "Don't trust him."

She rolled her eyes and stomped away from him, away from town. He didn't immediately follow, but kept watch from a distance. She ignored him, choosing to focus on the sea stretching before her. She continued down the beach, as wary of its savage beauty as of the black clouds threatening the horizon.

The dark water looked like she felt. Restless. Turbulent. Uncertain. The incoming waves crashed ashore, then retreated just as quickly, as if ashamed of crossing an invisible line in the sand. But seconds later, the pressure would build, and the dark froth would tumble inland before scrambling once again to the sea. Susan glanced down. The tips of her boots were wet. Had the indecisive ocean sneaked too far ashore, or had she been the one to throw caution to the wind? Either way, she ought to start minding her steps.

Of course she didn't trust Mr. Bothwick. Worse, she couldn't trust herself when she was around him. Asking him to shelter her for the night would be tantamount to agreeing to let him deflower her. That's what the already-disapproving townsfolk would think, anyway. She did *not* need anyone carrying rumors to Bath. Not when her familial connections still seemed a strong enough motivator for the giant to keep her alive. If barely.

What she did need was a female friend. Someone respectable. With a clean guest room.

Susan couldn't think of a single soul matching that description. She cast a despairing glance over her shoulder at the distant town and then returned her gaze to the sea. She'd gladly lower her standards to a common inn, if only there were one to be had. Well, and if she had money. The arrival of which was looking less and less likely by the hour.

Almost time for the assembly, she reminded herself. Once she made it to Bath, the Stanton name would get her back home. Five days of purgatory, then freedom for her and a rescue for cousin Emeline. Susan could survive five more days. She had no other choice.

She backed up until she reached the line where wet sand met dry. She turned and headed in the direction of Mr. Bothwick's boat. Not because she was going to touch the thing, of course. Once was enough. But she could feel the weight of the villagers' stares burning into her back. She had to get out of the townsfolk's collective eye before their judging glances and general air of virtuous superiority made her nauseous.

Perhaps Dead Mr. Bothwick still floated somewhere around her and perhaps he didn't. She didn't know and didn't care. Because she saw a familiar face up ahead. The open, honest face of the charming Bow Street Runner from Lady Wipplegate's dinner party. Yet Susan's leaden feet were anchored to the sand.

The good news: Janey was somehow secretly posting Susan's letters to Town after all. Otherwise, the handsome Runner would not have come to rescue her before more disaster struck.

The bad news: He was dead.

Chapter 18

Despite being encased in long gloves, Susan's fingers were ice-cold.

She edged closer. He lay in the sand, one arm flung out toward the sea, the other crossed over his chest as if he'd died attempting to staunch the still-seeping flow of blood from the knife protruding from his chest.

She forced her feet to approach the dead man. Prepared herself for the sight of the Bow Street Runner rising from his body in spirit form to castigate her for sending him on this death mission.

No such ghost appeared.

Wait . . . he was still bleeding? Perhaps he was alive! Filled with a mixture of hope and horror, she dropped to her knees beside him. She laid her gloved hand over his pale, ungloved one and pressed her ear to his parted lips. No. He was irrevocably dead.

He had come to save her, and she was too late to save *him*. She sat back on her heels and tried to think what to do. The magistrate wouldn't be back until midweek sometime. And the killer . . . Susan leapt to her feet, breath hitching. The killer was still here. Somewhere.

"Murder," came a faint male voice at her shoulder.

She bit back a shriek and spun around. Dead Mr. Bothwick. Just what she needed to make a bad situation worse.

"Go away." She swiped at him and missed.

He floated above the body to peer into the Runner's face. "I don't recognize him."

"I should think not. He's from Town."

Dead Mr. Bothwick cast her a withering glance. "You aren't the only one who's ever been to London. Who is this chap, then, Miss Society? An ex-paramour?"

Susan's teeth clenched. "If you must know, he's a Bow Street Runner."

"Was," Dead Mr. Bothwick corrected drolly. "Whoever he was."

"Insufferable plebian," she muttered, irritated at herself for allowing him to goad her. "Have some respect. Can't you see he's dead?" She dropped back to her knees. "I never dreamed . . ."

Dead Mr. Bothwick dropped to face level, frowning at her curiously. "You mean . . . he truly is a Runner?"

She glared at him. "That's what I said."

"Quick! Search his pockets!"

"Why?"

"To see why he's here, of course. We need clues."

"I know why he's here." Shame clawed at her stomach. "I summoned him."

"You *summoned* him?"

She stared guiltily at the lifeless form and nodded. "For all the good it did either of us."

Dead Mr. Bothwick hovered over the corpse. "Search his pockets anyway."

"There aren't any clues to find," she burst out in frustration. "My letter was purposefully vague. I meant to explain everything once he arrived."

"Explain everything about what?"

"A family matter."

"Now you *have* to search his pockets."

She tried to ignore him, but her cursed curiosity won out. "Why?"

Dead Mr. Bothwick stared at her. "I can't speak to how special you are back in London, Miss Stanton, but do you really think a Runner would come all the way to Bournemouth after receiving a 'vague' note from a young girl with 'family matters'?"

Susan matched his stare. Put that way . . . No. It didn't seem likely. In fact, after the experiences of the past week, the Runner would've been of little help with regard to the imprisoned Lady Emeline even if he had witnessed the wretchedness of the situation firsthand.

Then why *was* he here?

She cast a considering glance at the ghost fluttering on the other side of the body. How many people knew that Dead Mr. Bothwick was no longer among the living? His brother, for one. And her. But she'd heard no other mention. Was the Runner investigating the ghost's murder? Or Red's? Perhaps the Runner's visit had nothing to do with murder at all. (Until his own, of course.) Perhaps he wasn't investigating some*one,* but some*ones.* Her mind flashed back to the coin she'd found in Dead Mr. Bothwick's living room.

Pirates.

She returned her gaze to the prone lawman without speaking her thoughts aloud. She didn't know how involved Dead Mr. Bothwick might be with whatever schemes were afoot. But he was right about one thing: She needed to know more. She touched the blood-soaked waistcoat, then yanked her gloved hand back as if his chest were made of hot coals.

"What happened?" Dead Mr. Bothwick jerked backward. "What is it?"

"I . . ." She closed her eyes and swallowed hard. "I can't do it."

"Why not?"

"He's *dead.*"

"That's right," the ghost agreed, his tone harsh. "Because someone killed him. Possibly in a fit of rage. People in the midst of a rage are not in their best form. They forget things, like removing evidence from dead bodies. But when they calm down, they remember, and they come back. Often to remove the body itself. Do you want to be here when that happens?"

Susan started. Dead Mr. Bothwick was no doubt an expert on that particular situation. "I don't want to be here at all, if you're saying the madman could return at any moment and kill me, too."

He shimmered in repressed fury. "For God's sake, woman, just—"

"Fine!"

Susan held her breath and plunged her shaking hand into the Runner's wet pockets. A ruined handkerchief, assorted candies, a few coins. She hesitated. Could she steal from a dead man? A sovereign or two meant nothing to him now. She wavered, then shoved the coins back into his pocket. No. She hadn't sunk that low. She was five days from Bath anyway, and it wasn't as if she could hire a hack to get her there any faster.

At last, her trembling fingers brushed against a damp scrap of folded parchment. She tugged it slowly forth, half expecting to find a treasure map or a pirate's likeness sketched in ink.

Instead, she unwrapped her own missive.

"What is it?" Dead Mr. Bothwick demanded. "What does it say?"

"It says," she replied, unable to hide the disappointment in her voice, "'Dear Sir. I'm dreadfully sorry to address you thusly, but although I have misremembered your name, I have not forgotten your Intelligence and your Kindness, and I therefore must make a desperate plea for your immediate assistance regarding Important Matters of Extreme Urgency—'"

"Your letter." Bizarrely, Dead Mr. Bothwick's disappointment seemed to eclipse her own.

She nodded and began to refold the bloodstained missive. "We have now proved he did come to Bournemouth on my behalf. I told you I was important back in . . ." She couldn't finish the thought.

The ghost hovered closer. "What? What is it?"

She stared. There, half-hidden in a crease on the reverse side of the paper, was a hurried note jotted by a male hand. (Women, and Susan specifically, had far superior penmanship.)

"There's something written on the back," she admitted. Dead Mr. Bothwick exploded—literally—in excitement, then rematerialized at her side. She pointed at a faint smudge. "See? Right there. It says, 'T.B. has proof.'"

"They came for me," he breathed.

She could swear the ghostly whisper slid across her cheek. "You're 'T.B.'?"

He nodded slowly, his form rippling. "You're not the only one who summoned Runners. Perhaps it's not too late after all."

"For whom, exactly?" She gestured with the folded missive. "You're dead. He's dead. Both villains have escaped."

"I'm not sure there are two villains." He stared at the corpse lying in the sand. "And yes, this state of reduced animation is highly limiting, but that note proves I'm being taken seriously. The Runner came to check my facts. Someone will become suspicious of his continued absence. We need to be ready. We need that jewelry box."

Enough with the impossible mission. "Why do we need the stupid jewelry box?"

Dead Mr. Bothwick's pointed a translucent finger. "Read the paper again, Miss Stanton. 'T.B. has *proof*.'"

"Proof of what?" The answer flashed and she blurted the word without thinking. "Pirates?"

The ghost stared at her for a long moment before he responded quietly. "You'd be wise not to speak that word aloud."

She gulped. "Then it's true?"

He inclined his head.

In that case, they did need all the evidence they could get. She tried to think of a way to steal the box without the giant noticing its absence or suspecting the theft. She failed. "Why put the proof in a jewelry box, of all things? Was it a hide-in-plain-sight trick?"

He sighed. "As you might suspect, my contingency plan went grossly awry. I never intended the jewelry box to be buried in the rock garden, but at least its contents were safe. For a while. Now they're not. You *must* get that box away from Ollie before he finds a way to open it."

Susan blinked as the puzzle pieces fell into place. "Because he's a . . ."

This time she didn't finish the sentence.

"Yes." A flicker of worry crossed the ghost's face. "And you can't trust anyone."

Her brain roared louder than the sea.

What chance did she have against *pirates?* Outwitting the giant had already proven impossible. Now that she knew the extent of his crimes, finding herself chained to the cellar might well be the least of her concerns. She'd be just as likely to walk the plank. Or wind up on the beach with a knife sticking out of her chest. Or—

She glanced up. "How did you die?"

"Shot between the eyes."

Spectacular. Her lenses weren't thick enough to deflect bullets, that much was certain. She could scarce help the ghost shimmering beside her. She couldn't even manage to help herself.

No matter what Dead Mr. Bothwick thought, that had been *her* letter in the Runner's inside pocket. Perhaps they'd also been looking into claims of piracy. Hard to say. But this Runner, this man lying dead in the sand, was murdered because of a letter she had written requesting his aid. Susan shuddered. She now had blood on her hands.

She glanced down in her lap and choked back a sob when she saw the state of her gloves. She *did* have blood on her hands. The white silk was soaked with crimson. Susan struggled to her feet. She, in a fit of self-importance, had summoned an innocent Runner to his death. Compounding matters, she'd rifled through his corpse. And was now loitering about covered in blood, as if just waiting for the villain to return, when it was obvious she was no match for the situation at all—

She ran.

"Wait!" Dead Mr. Bothwick stayed glued to her side. "Where are you going now?"

She swiped at him with a scarlet hand.

Direct hit. He disappeared from sight.

She pulled off the wet gloves. Should she throw them into the ocean? No. They'd only wash ashore and she had no wish to explain their appearance. She'd burn them to ash in her bedchamber. Susan shoved the sticky gloves into her inner pocket, next to the ivory-handled knife. Now she knew she could never use the blade. She couldn't stand to touch blood. Get it off. Get it off *now.*

She ran to the water's edge and washed the crimson from her fingers in the frigid ocean. As she rose to her feet at last, she dried her trembling fingers on her skirts. No more blood. But she didn't feel clean. The Runner . . . Susan started to run again, then slowed.

Where was she going?

She needed a friend. She needed a living, breathing person, someone to hold her and comfort her and make her forget, if only for a moment, what a complete and utter mess she'd made of her life—and the lives of others. Someone who might be able to help. She needed . . . Mr. Bothwick.

It was a sign from the heavens that she managed to find his house without becoming hopelessly lost on the way there. In a further stroke of luck, Mr. Bothwick wasn't merely at home. He answered the door himself.

And pulled her inside.

Chapter 19

Susan launched herself into Mr. Bothwick's arms. They were warm, strong, safe. Attached to a living, breathing man. She wrapped her arms about his neck and held on as tight as she could. He returned the embrace, pressing his lips to her forehead.

"It's going to be all right," he whispered.

She shook her head. It would never be all right.

"Yes, it will, sweetling." He held her close. "I don't know how, but I'll make it stop. I promise."

She clung to her knight errant. How could he stop anything? Pirates were here. The body count was already up to three. And—oh. Susan closed her eyes.

Mr. Bothwick had no idea any of those things were happening. He probably thought her distress was about Lady Emeline, whom he'd just met. While Susan was still frantic to do whatever she could to help her poor cousin, she'd just been handed a completely new nightmare. Her brain felt as sluggish as her limbs. She held on to him tighter, breathed in his scent.

She should correct his misconception. And she would. She needed somebody on her side. But right now she didn't want to discuss the dead investigator whose blood now stained the pale sand. Or the girlish note that had summoned the doomed man to the sea. Or the even greater dangers afoot.

Right now, she wanted to forget. Just for a few moments. She wanted . . . *release* from all this anxiety, all this horror, all this fear. Mr. Bothwick could provide her at least that much.

"Kiss me," she whispered, and pressed her lips to his before he could say no.

He kissed her back, sweetly, tenderly. She was having none of that.

She bit his lip, hard. Swept her tongue inside when his mouth parted in surprise. Forced him to taste her, to feel her desperation, her passion.

His hands tightened on her hips, but not to set her down. He pulled her closer.

"Don't go back there," he whispered. "Stay here. With me."

Susan didn't want to think about Moonseed Manor, about the dead Runner, about the giant's threats. She pressed closer to Mr. Bothwick's warm body. She felt his hard length trapped between them and remembered what it looked like, swollen with desire. She wished for the chance to touch him as he'd touched her. She'd dreamt of closing her hand around him, stroking him, watching his face contort with pleasure. This time, perhaps they could bring release to each other.

He lifted her in his arms. She let him. Until he passed the staircase.

"Where are we going?" she asked against the side of his neck.

"Receiving room?" he guessed.

"No." She shook her head, looking him in the eyes. "Bedchamber."

He stopped, hesitated. His gaze sparked with the war between obeying what she said now, and complying with what she'd told him only last night.

"Are you certain?" he asked softly.

She kissed him, thrusting her breasts against his chest. "*Bedchamber.*"

He gave no argument.

With his mouth on hers and his arms wrapped tight around her, he turned and somehow made it up the stairs. The room he entered was awash in blues and greens. Colors of the sea. How very like him. The presence of pine furniture only augmented the feel of the ocean, by bringing in touches of brown and beige the color of sand, both wet and dry.

He laid her in the center of a large, night-blue bed and cupped her face to kiss her. His were not the soft hands of an idle *ton* lordling with nothing more taxing to do than play deuces and bet on ponies. His were the rough hands of a man who toiled at hard labor, who'd done so recently, and with pleasure. He was not the Society gentleman she'd been waiting for, but she couldn't make herself care. For now, she was his. And would make him hers. If only for this moment.

She licked at his lips. "Touch me."

At last, he slid one of his palms from her cheek to her neck, to her collarbone, to her breast. He cupped her as best he could through all the layers separating them, pinched the budding nipple. The sensation was heavenly . . . but it wasn't enough. She arched into him, lifting her back from the mattress.

"Unbutton me."

He paused. "Miss Stanton . . ."

"I believe I'm Susan, at this point," she corrected, unsure whether she felt like laughing or crying. She kissed him so he wouldn't detect either emotion. She needed to feel real, to feel *alive*. "Unbutton me."

He paused only for a second. "Turn around."

She tried to kiss him. He gripped her shoulders, turning her himself. Yes. That was what she wanted. She didn't wish to think. She only wished to feel. He kissed along her neck as his fingers traced her spine. Perfect.

After he made deft work of the buttons, the ties, the hooks-and-eyes, and everything else that had caged her in layer upon layer of cotton, he seemed to hesitate.

She did not.

She shrugged her gown off of her shoulders, wriggled it over her hips, kicked the heavy mass off the bed. The knife in her pocket thunked when it hit the floor. Her stays were the next to go—bloody busk made it impossible to do half the things she'd dreamed of doing. Now all that covered her trembling body were her gartered stockings and her thin shift.

She lifted her gaze to the fully clothed man watching her. His hazel eyes darkened with passion, but he made no move to disrobe. Very well. She would do it for him. She sat on her heels and considered him. This was a good task. Something positive to concentrate on. She would empty her mind of everything but the man lounging next to her on the mattress.

She began with his coat. Why was he wearing a coat? Had he intended to go out-of-doors? No matter. She was here now. The gold buttons easily slipped free of the dark blue fabric. He sat up a little when she pulled at the sleeves, helping her work his arms free. She pushed the coat to the floor. It landed with a soft whoosh against the thick carpet.

Mr. Bothwick looked just as handsome unencumbered by a jacket. If anything, it was easier to see that the width of his shoulders had not been exaggerated by padding, that the muscular arms still encased by billowing lawn were as hard and strong as they'd always seemed. If twice as warm. Still on her knees before him, she ran her fingertips down the front of his waistcoat. His entire body radiated heat.

She drew in a deep breath and focused on his cravat. It was perfectly white, perfectly starched, perfectly styled. In a house of this size, he certainly had a few servants. But where had he found a man able to tie a cravat as beautifully as this? Had he done so himself?

The fleeting thought returned that Mr. Bothwick would not look out of place in a ballroom. He was striking, even

without his smartly tailored coat. She reached for him. He
obligingly leaned forward. A few careful tugs loosened the
knot at his throat. She crumpled the cravat and tossed it
aside. There. Now he didn't look like a gentleman. Now he
looked rakish. Dangerous.

She shivered in anticipation, and decided it had been too
long between kisses. Shameful, really, because with him
propped up on his elbows and her perched on her heels, all
she had to do was swoop down and kiss him.

So she did.

What was meant to be a simple kiss quickly turned raw,
then hungry, then carnal. She fed the flames, let them burn.
She needed it to be this way. Needed him to be as desperate
to be lost in her as she was to be lost in him. They could
forget the outside world together.

Mouth still locked with his, she fumbled with the buttons of his waistcoat. Too many. Far too many. But at last, the
final button popped free. He broke the kiss in order to shuck
the irritating garment. She took the opportunity to hike the
hem of her shift high enough to allow her legs to straddle
him. Mmm. This was a much better position from which to
remove his shirt. In seconds, the fine lawn had joined the
growing pile of abandoned vestments on the carpet.

The soft buckskin of his breeches was now the only
fabric remaining between them. She smiled. With her thighs
spread atop his, her lips were no longer in line with his.

Her breasts were.

He took one in his mouth. The nipple hardened and
reached for him through the damp fabric. He suckled. She
latched onto his hair. Her back arched as she pressed his
face into her breasts. The movement caused her to slide de-
liciously against the hard shaft pulsing between her legs.
His fingers dug into her hips. Was he trying to make her
stop? He gave her bottom an impatient slap. No. He was
telling her to do it again.

Gripping his shoulders, she began to rock against him.

Slowly. Tentatively. Then again with more pressure, more confidence, more *need* as the whirlpool of desire began to swirl between her legs.

He reached between them and unbuttoned his fall, releasing the hard proof of his arousal. This time, she wasn't staring from across the room. This time she was stroking that hot naked flesh with her own wet heat. Could he—could she—like this? Simply by rubbing herself against him? His teeth closed gently on her nipple, laved, then nibbled again. Her eyes fluttered in pleasure. Yes, yes, she could. Just like this. Was about to, in fact.

His hand slid up her thigh, squeezed, then dipped between them. Now she was riding the edge of his hand as well as his shaft. She gasped as he slid a finger inside of her. The pad of his thumb caressed her, stroked her, until the threads of her self-control began to unravel.

"M-Mr. Bothwick . . ."

"Evan," he corrected, the syllables muffled by her aching breast. His thumb continued its lazy assault, his finger its delicious in-and-out movement.

"Evan," she repeated blindly, her own words breathless and ragged. "I'm going to . . . You're going to make me . . ."

And then she did, her entire body jerking as her muscles contracted around his finger. She fell forward, panting into his hair. His finger disappeared. He shifted her hips. Something else was pressing against her, something longer, something harder, something infinitely bigger. *This* was what he felt like. Slick with her desire, his shaft stretched her, filled her. She moaned, clutched him to her.

His left hand splayed against the curve of her bottom, coaxing her to continue rocking against him as his shaft pulsed and slid within her. His right hand slipped between them, his knuckles rubbing against her sensitized flesh in the most delicious of patterns.

Her nails dug into his shoulders, but not because she wished for him to stop. She would die if he stopped. She wanted to keep him there, hold him to her, deep inside of her, forever. His thighs flexed beneath her as his shaft filled her again and again. Her legs clenched around his hips as the intoxicating pressure began to build once more. He suckled her. Squeezed her. Stroked her.

She cried out as his thumb's inexorable caresses coalesced with the heady fusion of their bodies. Her muscles spasmed. Joyfully, desperately. He didn't stop rubbing with his thumb or driving his shaft into her until the last of the contractions.

He rolled them over as one, their bodies still locked together. She twined her arms about his neck, wrapped her legs around his hips. He captured her mouth with his. His body tensed and flexed as he slid in and out, faster, harder.

Susan's body thrummed. *This* was life. This was love.

Her hips rose and fell in rhythm with his. She hugged him with her arms. Clutched him with her legs. He never stopped kissing her, never stopped the delicious thrusting that was even now building the tension in her womb. His breathing came faster, as if he sensed she was about to crest again. As if the knowledge brought him to the edge of the same precipice.

Her head fell backward as her body contracted around him. He waited until the last of her contractions, then jerked to the side, dousing her hip with hot liquid. He collapsed half on top of her and pressed a kiss to her cheek. His eyes fluttered shut. He cuddled her a little closer.

Despite his weight, she smiled to herself as she hugged him to her. He felt good. Warm. Strong. A little sticky.

She frowned. Why had he—and then it hit her. Of course. He'd withdrawn at the last second so as not to fill her with his seed. To make sure no bastard children would result from their illicit liaison.

Bloody hell, she'd just had an illicit liaison.

Chapter 20

To say Miss Stanton didn't take the aftermath well would be an understatement.

Susan, rather. Or not. She'd bade him address her by her first name in the heat of passion, but if the horrified expression draining the blue from her eyes was any indication, Evan was about to have that privilege revoked.

"What have I done?" she said, her voice nearly wheezing with horror.

He rolled aside to let her breathe. *Lovemaking* didn't seem the response she was looking for, so he tried for a bit of levity. "Some call it the featherbed jig."

She disemboweled him with her glare.

Not in a humorous mood, then. Fair enough.

"I didn't force you to do anything you didn't wish to do," he said, as much for his benefit as for hers. Truly, he hadn't even left the house. She'd come to his door, attacked him with kisses, issued commands like *Bedchamber*. He could've sworn they both wanted the same thing.

To his relief, she answered simply, "I know."

And looked nauseous.

"You seemed to . . . enjoy it?" he tried again, starting to worry he was completely misreading the source of her displeasure.

She slammed her head backward into the pillow. "I *know.*"

"At the risk of starting a conversation I almost certainly have no wish to partake in . . . May I ask what's wrong?"

"I won't marry you."

Right. They'd covered this ground. And, as before, this statement simultaneously relieved and offended. Playing the part of temporary lover should not have bothered him. Yet, this time, it did. Was he nothing but a guttersnipe work-horse, meant to satisfy her baser longings while she searched for the titled fop who would satisfy her High Society standards?

"Technically, I still haven't asked," he replied crossly. He propped himself up on one elbow and tried not to show his wounded pride.

She closed her eyes as if in pain.

Perhaps she was. She *had* been a virgin. Evan was immediately contrite. He'd tried not to be rough. Her body had seemed more than ready to accommodate him. But what did he know about such things? He'd never tumbled a virgin. Until today.

"Did I hurt you?" he asked softly, brushing her cheek with his knuckle.

She jerked away from his touch. "It's not you. It's me. What seemed like a good idea turned out to be a very, very bad one." She scrambled off the bed and stared down at the pile of crumpled clothing. "Damn and triple damn."

Evan sat up straight, his bare skin suddenly ice cold. "What did you just say?"

"I said it's my fault." She kicked at her wrinkled gown. "Don't worry. Don't marry me. Things will be fine."

"No." He swung his legs over the side of the bed. He leaned forward, gripping his knees so as not to throttle her. "You said, 'Damn and triple damn.'"

"I—" Her mouth remained open, but no further sound escaped. Something flickered in her eyes. Wariness. Guilt.

"Where did you hear that phrase?" he demanded. He knew he sounded like a wild man. He felt like one. When she shook her head mutely, he grabbed her shoulders through her thin shift. "*Where?*"

"If you know, then why ask me?" she burst out.

He yanked his hands from his shoulders before he did end up shaking her.

"Where," he asked, pronouncing each word carefully and distinctly, "did you meet Timothy?"

"Here in Bournemouth."

"Liar."

Lips pressed tightly together, she lifted her chin and said nothing.

Evan crossed his arms over his chest and tried to think over the blood rushing in his ears. "Timothy was dead before you arrived."

She raised a slender brow, but did not otherwise respond.

Cursed woman. What the devil did she mean to say? That she'd met him beforehand? Impossible. Timothy hadn't stepped foot out of Bournemouth in years, except for when he traveled by sea. Evan was willing to bet this was Miss Stanton's first visit to their charming beachside home. There was something else, too. Something he'd meant to discuss further.

"Red had also gone missing before you arrived," he said slowly.

She glanced away. It was quick, but he saw it. She was hiding something. Well, obviously she was hiding something; he didn't need shifty eye movement to tell him that.

But there was a connection here that he wasn't making. A connection she feared he *might* make, solely given what little evidence he had. *Think logically, Bothwick.* Miss Stanton knew Red well enough to know his given name. She knew Timothy well enough to cop one of his pet phrases as her own. Both men had presumably been killed before her arrival. Which meant . . .

"You never met either of them, and you've just been play-acting?"

She let out a frustrated breath. "I met them after they *died*."

"You what?" he asked incredulously, not for a moment believing her words. He had no better hypothesis, but her explanation was absurd. What kind of fool did she take him for?

Her eyes widened with the same two emotions as before. Wariness. And guilt.

"Nothing. Forget it."

Uneasiness coated his stomach. "How would that be possible?"

"I don't know," she snapped. "I didn't plan it."

Evan laughed. He couldn't help it. "You expect me to believe you can see *spirits?*"

"Apparently not all of them," she muttered.

Not all of them? He leaned back and looked her in the eyes. She truly believed he'd swallow this cockamamie tale. He'd play along, try to gauge whether she believed it herself. "Which ghost are you missing?"

Mute again. Defiant. Frightened.

"You met Timothy," he started over, careful to keep the skepticism from his voice, "after he was dead."

She hesitated, then nodded once.

Liar. Evan shook with repressed rage. At her, for dragging his brother into her Banbury tales. At poor misguided Timothy, for being such a lackluster jack-tar that he'd been killed by a rogue pirate. At said soulless blackguard for being cowardly enough to shoot an unarmed seaman. At whoever had stolen Timothy's body, robbing him of both a proper burial and the chance for his loved ones to say good-bye.

What he wouldn't give to speak to Timothy himself, to apologize for not being there, to tell his brother how much he missed him. But he would never have that chance. Evan didn't believe in spirits. Much less that his brother would return home as one, and then choose to have tea with Miss Stanton.

And yet, uneasiness continued to congeal in his belly.

"What did Timothy say?" That look again. Guilt. Mistrust. "God damn it, Susan, if you expect me to believe—"

"He asked me not to tell anyone. Including you."

Evan stared at the woman before him, still damp and flushed from his lovemaking, and couldn't believe his ears. "Your loyalty is greater to my *dead brother* than to me?"

Again with the deafening silence.

His couldn't keep the sarcasm from his voice. "Is he here right now, watching us?"

She blushed. Then shook her head rapidly.

That was a plus, at least. He didn't want Timothy witnessing the brother he'd always considered an indomitable lothario being utterly destroyed by a debutante in her shift and stockings. Wait. Evan rubbed his face, frowning. Was he starting to believe this rot? If Miss Stanton saw spirits, that would mean there *were* spirits. And that Timothy had chosen to reveal himself to a complete stranger rather than his own brother.

Unless . . . he'd had no choice.

Evan did his best to keep his voice calm, reasonable. "Have you always spoken to dead people?"

She shook her head. "Just since I died."

Thunderclouds gathered in Evan's head. "For the love of all that's holy, woman, if you don't start making sense, I can't be responsible for my actions."

She thrust out a pale arm, palm up. A wicked scar zigzagged from just above her wrist to very nearly her elbow. She offered no explanation. Evan began to suspect this was because she was *barmy* and all indication to the contrary mere coincidence.

"Ghosts speak to you through your . . . magic scar?"

"No!" Her hands fisted and she tucked them beneath

crossed arms. "I broke my arm when I fell into the Thames earlier this year. I drowned. Before that, I was an ordinary young lady. Afterward . . ." She bit at her lower lip for a moment. "At first I thought Moonseed Manor was haunted. Then I realized it was me."

"Does Ollie suspect that you—"

Her small hand latched around his wrist like an iron manacle. "Don't tell him."

"I didn't say I was going to."

"Do not trust him, Evan. Whatever you do."

He considered the seriousness of this directive. "Because of last night?"

"Because . . ." She took a deep breath, as if to rally courage. "He's a pirate."

Evan's mouth fell open. "He's a what?"

"You can't breathe a word," she said quickly, her hand still preventing blood flow to his fingers. "There's already been at least one death because of it. Two, I suppose, counting your brother."

Evan's skin turned clammy. "Timothy told you Ollie was a pirate?"

She nodded. "He was investigating them."

"Timothy was investigating . . . pirates?" He felt like a deuced fool repeating everything she said, but his brain was boiling in his skull.

She nodded again. "I imagine they're all going to prison. Then they're going to hang." She looked particularly pleased by the thought of Ollie dangling from a noose.

Evan, however, was not as delighted by this news.

At what point had Timothy decided to go turncoat and ferret information to the law? He would've had to realize that although he might save his own neck from the morning drop, there would be no pardoning the rest, Evan included. The entire crew would hang. Some of the jacks were conscienceless knaves, yes, but . . . to pretend to be complicit, solely to ensure a trip to the gallows, when to do so would condemn your own brother to go down with the ship?

Oblivious to his inner turmoil, Miss Stanton began pulling on clothing. First her stays, then her gown. She turned and gave Evan her back. He did his best to button and lace her without snapping any strings. His hold on sanity seemed equally frayed.

She knew about Ollie. She even knew things about Timothy that Evan himself hadn't known. Which meant it was all true. There truly were spirits. Who spoke to her. One of which was the late Timothy Bothwick.

Brother. Smuggler. Traitor.

The giant wasn't the only pirate in Bournemouth.

Susan had turned her back toward Mr. Bothwick the moment his expression had changed from gobsmacked to furious. She'd left immediately after he'd slipped the last button into place and hadn't looked back. She couldn't face him without giving away what she'd seen darken his hazel eyes: betrayal. Incredible as her previous obtuseness now seemed, Mr. Bothwick was one of the soon-to-be-condemned pirates.

And she'd *lain* with him.

She pushed blindly through the trees, scarce able to keep her feet on the trail. Between the dark clouds and the thick branches converging overhead, it felt more like nightfall than late afternoon. A wet drop slipped through the sparse leaves and streaked across one of her lenses. The skies were about to open up, and she wasn't 100 percent certain this was the footpath that led from Mr. Bothwick's cliff back to Moonseed Manor.

But the trampled dirt was *a* path leading *somewhere*. With the cold rain falling faster by the second—and the house she'd just escaped from home to a bloody pirate—she would seek whatever shelter she could find.

She should continue to be safe from Mr. Bothwick as long as he didn't realize she knew the truth. The giant should continue to spare her life because of her parents. The Stantons knew in whose company they'd entrusted their daughter and their connections were considerable. Crossing the baron and his wife would be begging to visit the gallows.

Nonetheless, the idea of immediately returning to Moonseed Manor held little pull.

Her hands were freezing. She longed for the relative warmth of gloves. Perhaps she should wear her soiled ones, despite the blood staining the once-white silk. She reached numb fingers into her pocket, pulled out the dark crumple, and gave it a good shake.

Now the cloth was brown and damp . . . and consisted of a single glove. Spectacular. Where had the other one flown off to? She hesitated, her clothes and hair and skin getting wetter by the moment, and debated just leaving the other glove where it lay. But no. She'd had sound reasons for not tossing them aside before, and those reasons still stood. With a sigh, she retraced her steps to the point where she thought she'd shaken out the wrinkled silk.

Nothing but dirt, mud, and fallen leaves. Most of which clung to the remaining glove and her now-ruined gown. Perhaps she hadn't retraced her steps correctly. Perhaps she'd wandered down a *different* footpath. Typical. Susan gave up on the missing glove—it had to be buried under a foot of mud anyway—and headed back down the trail. At least, she hoped she did. She would go mad if she broke through the trees only to discover herself once again at Mr. Bothwick's door.

A bloody pirate!

No wonder he had that aura of danger and arrogance, that unapologetic delight in doing whatever he wished. Such as threaten another pirate with pistols. What if he'd done more than threaten? Hadn't she already wondered at the connection between Mr. Bothwick and the death of his brother? He'd apparently accepted the fact of Red's death without any physical proof. Perhaps there was a reason for that, as well. And the Runner—oh, Lord, the Runner—mightn't the poor man have gone to his informant's brother for information and help? Hadn't she found his corpse a mere shell's toss from Mr. Bothwick's rowboat?

She stumbled, gripped the slippery bark of the closest tree, and dry heaved. She'd thought herself a better judge of character. She'd fancied the man lowbred but well-meaning, rakish but misunderstood, hot-tempered but overall harmless. How wrong she had been.

The rain let up a little, and she forged forward along the trail. The path was beginning to widen, the trees to disperse, the leaves more scarce. She stepped free at last—and there, up ahead, like a beacon of light, like a mirage on the desert, like the Holy Grail itself, were:

Stables.

Half-laughing, half-crying, she ran toward them. She slipped and fell in the mud, but picked herself up without stopping and flew to the structure as if her life depended on reaching the horses inside. It very likely did.

A gaggle of unsavory-looking liverymen loitered by the open door. No matter. She would win them (and use of a horse, please, God) with charm and aplomb in a matter of seconds. She slowed to a walk, soaking wet and out of breath, but filled with hope for the first time in ages.

"Good afternoon," she called out.

As one, their fingertips went to pistols strapped to their hips, then fell casually to their sides as they judged her no threat. Susan stumbled. The liverymen were *armed?* She started to have a very bad feeling about the grounds on which she trespassed.

"Er . . . Whose stables are these?" she called out, deciding to stop where she was, rather than close the last couple yards between them.

One of the men spat a bit of leaf onto the ground before replying, "Mr. Bothwick's."

Spectacular. Susan briefly considered stabbing herself with the ivory-handled blade right then and there, thereby saving everyone else the hassle of killing her.

"Timothy Bothwick's?" she asked anyway, despite the sick feeling in her stomach indicating she already knew that not to be the case.

The liveryman shook his head. "His brother."

Of course. She'd finally found the only stables in a twenty-mile radius and they belonged to Mr. Bothwick. The *pirate*. To whom she'd mistakenly given her virginity and her trust. She'd never again possess the former, but at least now she had the faculty to be more judicious in the latter. The man did not deserve trust. And, most likely, neither did his liverymen.

"M-may I see the horses?" she asked, despite her better judgment.

Once again, they all touched their fingertips to their hips. But this time, they kept their hands at the ready.

"No," came the flat reply.

There was no room for argument.

Bloody, bloody hell. Damn and triple damn. Susan cast her gaze up to the still-rumbling sky and blinked when a raindrop splattered against the lens of her spectacles. She simply did not know enough swear words to properly convey the level of frustration burning through her blood.

The liverymen waited, silent, watching her.

She wanted to cry. She stood before them, miserable, pathetic. A woman with matted hair clinging to her frozen face. Clad in a mud-splattered dress with torn sleeves and a battered hem. One bare hand clenched her soiled skirts for warmth, the other encased in ruined silk stained brown with a dead man's blood. Not an inch of her body had escaped the onslaught of the rain. And, to top it all off, she was lost.

"Could one of you please tell me how to get to Moonseed Manor?'"

She hated how much her voice shook. She wasn't sure whether her body trembled because of the cold, because she was afraid the liverymen would just as soon shoot her as help her, or because she was even more afraid they wouldn't know how to get there either and she'd wander around this wet hellhole until she died of cold and starvation.

But one of the liverymen began to gesture. Not the one who'd spit—a different one. A nicer one. Still armed, of course, but at least willing to tell her how to get out of there.

"Not too far up that way," he was saying, "you'll see what's another trail. Can't miss it. Just keep straight on. There's no forks and the like. You'll come out by the gate with all the roses."

"You mean the rock garden?" she asked hopefully. "Just behind Moonseed Manor?"

He nodded. "That's the one."

"Thank you so much."

She gave him a smile—no need to make more enemies—and headed in the direction he'd pointed. Eventually, she did come across another footpath. A wider one. With fewer branches. She made her way down the very center, so as to ensure she didn't accidentally wander to the left or to the right. After what seemed like weeks to her exhausted legs and blistered feet, she clapped eyes on the gate behind Moonseed Manor.

Who knew the day would come when she'd be relieved to step foot in the grave garden?

She wasn't thrilled to be anywhere near the giant and his henchman, but at least she was reasonably assured of survival until Mr. Forrester came to spirit her away to the assembly. So long as she kept her big mouth shut and did her best to stay out of sight. Perhaps the best plan was to lock her chamber door until the magistrate arrived.

She went straight upstairs, where she immediately rang

for a bath. If only she'd been able to leave Mr. Bothwick's house with the same warm glow of happiness and optimism she'd had while in his arms. But she could no longer suppress the horror she'd been trying to deny. Although the Runner's blood was gone from her fingertips, the sensation of bone-deep uncleanliness had returned. She shoved the knife into a drawer before throwing her clothes and soiled glove into the fire.

While waiting for the hot water to arrive, she collapsed onto the antique chair before the escritoire. She had been doubtful when Janey had admitted she could frank mail without her master's knowledge, and ensure clandestine missives would be taken by foot to the nearest town with capabilities of posting mail. Susan had certainly hoped such a feat were possible, but hadn't allowed herself to believe it true until she'd laid eyes on the corpse at the beach. But Janey was a godsend. Fully convinced of the maid's resourcefulness and secrecy, Susan penned a new letter. This time, to the headquarters of the Bow Street Runners.

She said there were pirates in town, one of whom was master of Moonseed Manor. She said they had started to turn on each other, leaving at least two dead. She informed them the emissary they'd sent had suffered a fatal knife wound for his troubles. She begged them to send an army.

At last the bath arrived, and Susan was able to sink into a tub of scented soap and hot water. A few moments later, a faint but recognizable sound came from outside. Horses! She jerked up so quickly froth and bathwater splashed over the sides of the tub, and then she realized to whom the horses must belong.

Mr. Bothwick. Here to share the details of a shocking turn of events with his best mate and fellow pirate. And to forbid her from ever stepping foot near his stables again. No doubt that was why he arrived on horseback instead of on foot.

She sank back into the tub, but the warm water had ceased to relax her tense muscles. Nonetheless, she stayed buried in jasmine-scented bubbles until the horses outside whinnied their impatience. Ten minutes. Fifteen, at most, had passed. Well, she supposed it didn't take that long to say, "Miss Stanton knows we're pirates," and "Are you certain her parents will notice if we kill her?"

After the last of the bubbles died, she called for the lady's maid.

Janey eased into the room with a wooden box clutched in her too-thin fingers. She set the small object atop a dresser as if it were a miracle straight from God.

"What is that?" Susan stammered, barely resisting the urge to leap from the lukewarm tub and fetch the box dripping wet.

"For you. From your parents."

"My what?" She grabbed at the closest towel.

The maid helped Susan to dry, then took what felt like an impossible amount of time layering her in shift and stays and a fresh gown. When Janey went to fetch dry boots, Susan half-ran, half-slid across the slick wooden floor in her bare stockings and grabbed up the box, which bore a very familiar crest. She opened the lid and blinked. Money. Heaps of it. Coins, bills, signed bank notes. And a small scrap of parchment reading only, *You'll feel better after shopping.*

"M-my parents sent this?" she asked stupidly. "In a . . . in a mail coach?"

Janey shook her head. "In their carriage."

Susan's heart stopped for a second too long, then exploded into double time. "My parents came for me!"

Again, the maid shook her head. "Servants. I got this from a groomsman while my master was talking to the driver. Don't suppose he'd be too happy to know you had it."

Susan returned her gaze to the pile of coin and nodded slowly. No, she didn't suppose they'd be too happy to know she'd just been handed the very means to escape from Bath in a legally hired hack. But with the carriage here—she wouldn't *have* to. She could simply travel right back to Town with the servants! She forced a small handful of coin into Janey's spidery hands for all her efforts.

Still in her stocking feet, Susan shoved the box into the drawer with the knife and dashed for the bedchamber door. It was the height of impropriety to appear in public without proper footwear, but the most important objective at this moment was ensuring the servants waited for her before departing. She jerked open the bedchamber door and bit back a scream.

The scarecrow stood on the other side. Grinning his terrible grin.

"There you are," he rasped, his tiny black eyes glittering with satisfaction. "Your family sent round a carriage."

"Thank you." She shouldered past him. "I'm going to speak with the driver immediately."

"Are you, now? Well, that's going to be a mite tricky." His scratchy voice clawed at her through the oppressive air. "Since they're gone."

No.

Muscles twitching in fury, she turned on him. "Why didn't you send for me?"

His face split into his awful smile and he gestured at her stockinged feet with a jaundiced hand. "You were busy."

Chapter 21

Punching the wall—twice—did not improve Evan's disposition. The strong surface remained as stubbornly unyielding as his dead brother's thick head. He'd known from the first Timothy would make a terrible smuggler. The ridiculous lists. The cleaning schedules. The pathological aversion to breaking laws. But Timothy had said *yes,* damn it. Yes meant *yes.*

"Yes" did not mean "I will feign complicity temporarily whilst plotting to bring about my brother's imprisonment and subsequent public hanging."

Evan punched the wall again, this time with the other hand, and swore. Now he had two sets of bruised knuckles, a perfectly solid wall, and the same maddening lot of problems as before.

Damn it.

He had to compose himself. To think. To plan. He crossed his arms against the temptation to keep throwing punches, and propped his bare shoulders against the irritatingly immobile wall.

Calm down. Think of something pleasant. Think of . . . *Susan.*

No matter how gobsmacked he felt about his brother, Evan shouldn't have let her run off. She'd come to him out of fear and worry and he'd likely only added to both, rather than bring her the comfort she'd needed. He couldn't blame her for being upset over Lady Emeline. His own muscles had jumped with fury when he'd seen the tiny woman treated like an animal. There had to be something he could do, short of killing Ollie. Although that didn't seem a half-bad plan.

If Timothy had his way, Ollie would swing soon enough. They all would.

Stop thinking like that.

Evan couldn't believe that his little brother was still managing to complicate life from the grave. Or that he was able to talk to Susan about it. And that she hadn't breathed a word. No, that wasn't fair. If Evan saw spirits, he doubted he'd write a column about it for the *Tatler.* It must be lonely to have an ability like that and be unable to mention it. He supposed he could have schooled his own reaction a bit better.

He pushed away from the wall, crossed to a small drawer, and pulled out the pearl-encrusted hair comb that had tumbled from her hair before she'd fled from his arms in Moonseed Manor. Sometimes it seemed as if she was always running from him. Or perhaps it was he who kept chasing her away.

He pocketed the comb and gazed unblinking at his rumpled bed. Today marked the first time he'd made love in it. Amazing. During the four years he'd lived at Bournemouth most of his interaction with women had taken place in other locales. Happenstance. Convenience. He'd cherished the ability to ride or sail back home with the knowledge no complications would ensue from the liaison because he'd never lay eyes on the woman again.

And now look at him. Standing alone in his room, a stolen memento in his pocket, the smell of lovemaking still rich in the air. Thinking of Susan.

Longing to see her again.

He gritted his teeth at the irony. The one time in his life

he found himself interested in a woman as more than a means to pleasure, and he could do nothing about it, thanks to his Janus-faced brother. Or could he?

Evan paused halfway to the bed, beside which his shirt and waistcoat still lay crumpled on the floor. What, precisely, had Susan said? Timothy had been investigating pirates, yes. But for whom? Perhaps he'd been doing so on his own, for whatever incomprehensible reason. Perhaps he fancied himself a novelist. Timothy had always preferred the company of his mind to that of living people.

She'd said she imagined they would all hang. Yet she hadn't given any reason for this eventuality to transpire. If Timothy had died before setting his plans into motion—whatever those plans might be—perhaps there *was* no imminent threat.

Not that Evan shouldn't continue to be cautious. He often took risks, but always weighed the odds first.

He slid his hand into his pocket. The pads of his fingertips traced the teeth of the small comb. It wouldn't be the first time he'd left town more or less overnight. But it would be the first time he'd regretted it.

He wouldn't consign himself to the captain's new adventures. But that wouldn't be enough. He also had to make sure there was no evidence tying him to the crew's previous activities. Otherwise, the only option would be to leave Bournemouth. Now. Before undesirable outcomes like *prison* or *death* came to pass.

He lifted his waistcoat from atop the crumpled cravat and shirt, then dropped it back onto the pile. Better to ring for new clothes. He'd never learn to tie a cravat as fine as his valet anyway.

Fifteen minutes later, Evan emerged from his bedchamber freshly dressed. He strode downstairs and came to a surprised stop when he discovered one of his liverymen pacing just inside the front door. The servant looked . . . not nervous, precisely, but undeniably . . . unsettled. Unsettled might not be as alarming a state as nervous, but in Evan's current frame of mind, anything out of the ordinary was cause for concern.

"Yes?" he asked cautiously.

"It might be nothing," the liveryman began, instantly snapping Evan to high alert, "but there was someone come nosing about the stables, just a moment ago, and as ye said to inform ye immediately if we seen any strangers poking their heads where they oughtn't . . . well, sir, that's why I'm meant to interrupt yer day."

The humidity in the room increased tenfold. For a moment Evan couldn't breathe. Escaping in the dead of night was going to be a problem if they were already here for him *now*. But who were "they"? The constabulary? And why start with the stables without sending a man to subdue him at the same time? *Stay calm. Concentrate.*

"Did you get a good look at him?" he asked. "What exactly was he doing?"

The liveryman shook his head. "He'd be a she, sir. Wanted to see the horses, she did."

Evan blinked. "A . . . she?"

"Little blond thing, about so high, as I recall." The liveryman gestured just above his shoulder. "Pair of spectacles, now that I think about it. Didn't say her name, but she came out of the path leading from the house. Maybe ye saw her hereabout?"

Yes, yes, he undoubtedly had. Evan ran a hand through his hair and tried to think. Susan had been nosing around his horses? But why do so clandestinely rather than just ask to see them? Hell, he hadn't realized she'd known he *had* horses. He kept his stables well hidden.

Belatedly, he recalled her odd reaction to news of the assembly in Bath. She hadn't asked about the food or the fashion or the guests or the entertainment. Her first priority had been to ascertain the presence of posting-houses. Doubt wriggled beneath his skin. She couldn't possibly have intended to steal one of his mounts and ride to Bath . . . could she? If she no longer wished to stay in Moonseed Manor—and, truly, who could blame her?—why hadn't she trusted him enough to ask for his help? She could've stayed here. Or left *with* him. She didn't realize it, but she wasn't the only one interested in leaving town. Lingering overlong in Bournemouth could be hazardous to Evan's neck.

He had better set his servants to packing. Just in case. He lurched over to the closest bell pulls, his feet leaden. A few words from him, and a timely departure would be set into motion. A matter of days, if he took everything. Tomorrow night, if he left all but the essentials behind.

What few servants Evan employed had been with him for over a decade. The instruction to begin packing was dispatched quickly, and incurred neither questions nor raised brows. They were, for better or worse, loyal to a fault.

His manservant, however, lingered behind.

"Yes, Croxley?"

The man hesitated before stepping forward. That alone was all Evan required to make his heart start pounding anew. Croxley never hesitated.

"I found a glove beneath your soiled linen," the manservant said at last. "I would have thrown it in the fire, but since you hadn't done so yourself . . . I wondered if you knew it was there."

"A glove," Evan repeated stupidly. "Why would I throw a glove into the fire?"

Rather than respond with words, the manservant held out his hand. His fingers uncurled to reveal a lady's silk glove. The crusted-brown cloth stuck to itself in clumps, dampened with what could only be blood.

Silently—more because words failed him than out of any desire to hold his tongue—Evan took the soiled object from his manservant. The hair comb in his pocket now seemed a ridiculous keepsake. He could scarce believe he of all people had suffered a romantic moment over the duplicitous woman who'd left behind this mass of ruined silk.

He brought the glove to his nose and sniffed. Definitely blood. The scent brought too many memories. The glove held far too much blood for a mere scratch. And Susan had been uninjured.

The cloth was still damp in some areas. Evan transferred it to his other hand and stared in disbelief at his rust-stained palm.

Someone nearby was severely wounded. And Susan had said nothing.

He made a fist to hide the blood from view, but he could still smell its coppery odor, feel the tackiness stick to his fingers and palm.

Why *had* she come here? He now doubted her panic had anything to do with the caged Lady Emeline. Upon whose bleeding body had she attempted to staunch the flow of blood? Or had she been the one to cause the injury? And why had she not confided in him?

Once again, he would have to hunt for clues. But this time, he didn't know the identity of the victim. Or if said person was alive or dead. Whatever was going on, Miss Susan Stanton was involved up to her eyeballs. Evan had no way to know whose side she was on.

But he doubted it was his.

Susan forced her shaky limbs back to the escritoire and sat down to compose a response to her parents. She endeavored to keep the missive free from swear words, but doubted her darling progenitors would fail to perceive her ire.

Send the carriage back, she wrote, then underlined the final word a half dozen times. *My life is in danger. Others have died. I must return home.*

After Janey left with the newest letter, Susan locked the door behind her and planned to stay put until one of her missives actually summoned help. But after a lonely tray of tea, an equally lonely supper, and a long, sleepless night, she could scarce stand to remain cooped up in the bedchamber any longer.

A full day might have been enough time for her pleas to reach London, and for a rider to return—if a rider had been going to do so. The fact that breakfast came and went on its little tray and brought no word from Stanton House or Bow Street Runner headquarters . . . well, Susan didn't want to think overmuch about that.

If they'd taken her seriously, they would have arrived by now. And if they dismissed her words as the ravings of a madwoman, then she was simply back where she started. She'd have to save herself.

The promise of Bath loomed larger and larger until she could think of nothing else but escape. The presence of the money box only served to underscore her cursed powerlessness that much more. The necessity of waiting until the assembly was more untenable than ever, now that she had enough coin to rent a coach yet still no immediate course of doing so.

After the breakfast tray had been fetched, Susan rose to her feet. She couldn't remain in this house. Not with the scarecrow belowstairs, grinning his slash-faced smile because he'd managed to deflect her first (and, thus far, *only*) opportunity for escape whilst she'd been upstairs in a tub of tepid water.

For now, perhaps she could pay her debts. She stuffed her pocket full of coin, then frowned. The heavy pouch no longer had room for the little blade. Her debts weren't overmuch. Given a Bow Street Runner had been brutally murdered—with a letter bearing *her* signature in his pocket—perhaps she ought to keep the weapon with her at all times. Thus resolved, she dumped a portion of the coin back into the money box.

Toying with the knife, she crossed toward the door. As

she passed the fireplace where Lady Beaune's ghost always disappeared, a cold breeze slithered down Susan's neck, causing the slim ivory handle to slip from her fingers. The knife thunked hollowly to the wooden floor.

Susan jumped backward (thankfully with her toes intact) and looked about the room for the ghost. No Lady Beaune. Had she accidentally walked into the poor woman, just as she was beginning to materialize? Bloody hell. If it weren't for bad luck . . . Susan knelt to pick up the fallen knife, frustrated at having missed an opportunity to attempt communication. At this rate, she'd never decipher the dead woman's mission, much less complete it.

No sooner had Susan's fingers lifted the knife mere inches from the wooden floor, the ghostly breeze returned. Gooseflesh rippled down her arms. This time, the current was strong enough to ruffle Susan's hair. The handle once again clunked hollowly against the floor.

Wait . . . hollowly?

Susan rapped at the wooden panel against which the knife had fallen. Definitely hollow. She rapped against the adjacent panels. Markedly solid. She sat back on her heels, frowning, then eased the blade from the ivory handle. She slipped the tip into the crack between the first floorboard and its neighbors, and levered gentle pressure on the handle until the stubborn board began to creak open. As soon as the corner rose high enough for a fingertip to slip beneath, Susan did so, wrenching it all the way open.

Dust. Spiderwebs. And Lady Beaune's antique crucifix.

Susan lifted the latter by its thin golden chain. The necklace was in want of polish, but overall unbroken and in decent condition. The crucifix itself was as bejeweled and ornate as she remembered, if much heavier than expected. No wonder the ghost was always dropping it. Susan cleaned both cross and chain with the underside of her skirts and fastened the clasp around her neck. She fingered the intricate loops and whirls of the crucifix for a long moment before tucking it out of sight in her bodice.

"I will keep it with me always," she whispered aloud, just in case cousin Emeline's much-wronged mother could hear her. "It will be a symbol of my commitment to do whatever it takes to rescue your daughter."

She stood. Perhaps she couldn't legally take Lady Emeline from her husband . . . but she *could* do her damnedest to take the husband from cousin Emeline. The giant would torture his wife no more, once he swung from a noose for treason against the Crown. Susan just had to ensure that took place.

As she twisted open the handle to her bedchamber door, the magistrate's cherubic face flashed into her mind. Perhaps Mr. Forrester would be of use after all. He'd single-handedly botched her prior escape attempt but, although Susan still felt him a cad for not having at least *tried* to intervene on Lady Emeline's behalf, he was right when he said the law had not been on their side. In the case of piracy, however, it certainly was.

For the first time, Susan looked forward to the magistrate's upcoming visit. In fact, she began to wonder if her suspicion that Mr. Forrester had never been interested in the origin of French silk had been correct all along. What if he suspected piracy afoot but had no means by which to prove it? Confirming a connection to smuggled silk could provide that link.

She, with her much-honed gossip skills, was the perfect person to undertake such a mission. In giving the magistrate firm evidence of smuggling, she would not only save her cousin (and herself), but also simultaneously set both Lady Beaune's and Dead Mr. Bothwick's minds—and spirits—to rest.

Within an hour, Susan had found her way out the door and into town. She stepped inside one establishment after another to settle her debts, hyper-aware she was showing her face for the first time since Evan had finally divested her of her virginity. She was now the common slut they believed her to be.

Mr. Bothwick, not Evan, she corrected herself. They were not friends, had never been friends. And they would never again be lovers.

She ignored the pang in her heart and the acid twist in her stomach. Instead, she focused on charming the townsfolk, who seemed equally determined to remain uncharmed. Their antipathy reversed the moment she began spending her coins. Ah, the power of money. Until she began seeing ghosts, Susan had believed gold the last true magic remaining in the world.

She saved the tavern for last (and skipped the dress shop altogether—there were some cold hearts even gold could not warm) and over-tipped Sully. She bought the occupants a round for old times' sake. Everyone but herself, rather. Now more than ever, she needed to keep a clear head.

As she'd done in the other establishments, she felt out the crowd for gossip pertaining to the dead Runner. And as before: nothing. No mention of blood or knife fights or strange corpses lying on the beach. Perhaps the Runner had yet to be discovered. Or perhaps, as Timothy had intimated, the killer had already collected the body.

She propped an elbow against the bar and considered her options. If the killer hadn't returned and the Runner was still lying in the sand, perhaps she ought to "accidentally" stumble across him. She could start screaming. *Somebody* was bound to come running. Then the poor man could have a proper burial. She'd pay for it herself, if necessary.

The Runner wasn't the only one who deserved to be properly recognized. Susan touched her palm to the heavy crucifix lying between her breasts. Lady Beaune deserved much more than a blank gravestone. Susan waved over the barman.

"Who carves headstones in town?"

If Sully found this question odd, he made no mention.

"Nobody," he answered distractedly, more intent on inventorying his brandy than on focusing on Susan. "Got to order special for that. Bath, maybe. London if you fancy a nice one."

London. Ever the crock of gold.

She thanked the barman and headed back outside in the direction of the Bow Street Runner. She'd order the finest gravestones London had to offer, the moment she arrived back in Town. She'd commission the calligraphy to read—

Gone. Good Lord. *Gone.*

She turned in a slow circle, peering down both sides of the empty beach. No blood. No body. Had she walked too far or, perhaps, not far enough? No, impossible. There was the rowboat, still covered in dried seaweed. The waves had washed any tracks away and erased the last of the spilled blood.

Now what? Susan stared at the ocean, then the rowboat, then the wet sand where the Runner had lain the day before. Was this how Mr. Bothwick had felt when he couldn't find his brother's body? Helpless and frustrated and angry? He'd felt much worse, she imagined. He'd lost family. She bit her lip. Perhaps he'd had nothing to do with his brother's death after all.

She squeezed her eyes shut and recognized this train of thought for what it was. An attempt to justify the unjustifiable. He was a pirate. Innocence of his brother's murder, if that were indeed the case, did not make Mr. Bothwick an innocent man. He was not to be trusted. The fact that she *had* trusted him . . . Well, all that proved was that love made one stupid.

No. She'd only thought she was in love. A *tendre.* A passing fancy. That was the only explanation for seeking him out time and again, for throwing herself in his arms at the first sign of trouble, for willfully relinquishing her virginity. But it wasn't real love. It couldn't be. He was a pirate.

Besides, even if she was ninnyhammered enough to fall in love with an adventure-seeking criminal, it hardly signified. She'd been taught since birth that something so fleeting as a mere emotion should never become a decision-making factor in one's life. One set goals for oneself, and one reached those goals through logic, determination, and a fair bit of planning.

Returning safely to London was her number-one goal, now more than ever. The fantasy of marrying an inattentive old title for his pocketbook and laissez-faire had paled significantly, now that she had a better idea of what she would have to endure to produce his heirs. No wonder Mother had always stood by the trope of closing one's eyes and thinking of Mother England. Without passion, the act would lose all of its magic.

Not that she wished to worsen matters by indulging a stupid girlish fancy like being in *love*. Besides, it wasn't as if the feeling was returned. Whether or not Mr. Bothwick had any plans to fulfill Miss Devonshire's suspect matrimonial predictions, he had been clear from the start that any interest he showed in Susan—or any woman—was that of the carnal variety. She had known that. She had willfully exploited that fact to alleviate her own anxiety. And now she would have to live with the repercussions. Somewhere far, far away.

She inhaled deeply. The scent of the ocean and salty taste of the breeze reminded her it was perhaps best not to wander alone too far past town borders whilst a murderer still roamed free. She opened her eyes.

Mr. Bothwick was striding toward her. No one else was in sight.

Susan's traitorous heart gave up on calming down. She told herself it was fear, not misplaced lovesickness. Luckily, he did not yet realize she knew the truth of his involvement with treason. She would have to act as if nothing had changed. She would have to act as if she . . . cared.

A distressingly easy charade.

"You ran from me." A brief wince indicated this was not the statement he'd meant to open with.

"Good afternoon," she answered inanely, her twisting hands incapable of portraying casual indifference.

Silence stretched between them.

He had changed clothes. He looked a perfect gentleman about to pay a call to a *ton* soiree, not a conscienceless rogue equally at home aboard a pirate ship. He brushed idly at his waistcoat. Probably to keep his hands close to his pistols.

If the situation were different, she might never have guessed the truth. Part of her longed for her previous innocence.

"Have you spoken to Timothy today?" he asked at last.

She hesitated before answering. Eventually, she decided to take the question at face value. It might be a non sequitur, but at least they weren't discussing piracy or her wanton behavior in his bedroom. Speaking to spirits was reasonably safe ground. Susan wished his acceptance of her dubious talent didn't bring such a strong sense of relief. She didn't need his approval or his understanding. She didn't need him at all.

"No," she said aloud, and shook her head slightly. Where *was* Dead Mr. Bothwick? Had he borne witness to whomever had removed the Runner?

The still-living, still heart-stoppingly handsome Mr. Bothwick shifted his weight as if uncomfortable in his boots. He remained just outside of touching distance and turned his gaze to the sea.

"I wish he would've come to me."

Harrumph. Of course he did. What pirate wouldn't have wanted advance notice that his non-pirate brother was about to turn him over to the Crown for a hanging? But since she didn't dare ask such a question, Susan hoped the cynicism didn't show on her face.

She forced a one-shoulder shrug. "It's not your fault. I didn't ask for this ability, remember? The accident—"

"I mean before," Mr. Bothwick interrupted, shifting his gaze from the sea to her face. "I wish Timothy would've come to me while he was still alive. I wish . . . I wish we could've *talked.*"

"Yes, well . . ." Susan faltered uncertainly. What could she possibly say in response to that? "Perhaps he had reason to keep his thoughts to himself."

"Oh?" Mr. Bothwick's brows lifted, his expression overly bland. "And is it your opinion that it's fine to keep something like 'investigating pirates' a secret?"

"Yes," she answered honestly. She certainly wouldn't have told him, if she'd been Timothy. The man had still ended up dead. She imagined he would've been murdered all the quicker if he hadn't kept his mouth shut.

"Would *you* keep secrets from me?" Mr. Bothwick asked, entirely too casually. "*Are* you, even now?"

She stepped back a half-step, caught herself, and forced her feet to stand ground. He knew nothing about the missing body. Nothing about her complicity in the Runner's arrival or her further missives to their headquarters. He also had no reason to believe she knew a single thing about his involvement with pirates. She had to keep it that way. Stay calm. Look innocent and trusting.

"I—"

"What are you doing out here?" he interrupted. Something in his tone made her believe he'd waited for her delayed response just so he *could* interrupt. His fist rose slowly, face up, something small clutched inside. "Have you . . . lost something?"

Susan froze.

The glove. He must have found the glove. His questions had nothing to do with piracy and everything to do with the man who'd bled to death on the sand beneath her feet. Perhaps by Mr. Bothwick's own hand.

He didn't take his gaze from her face. She couldn't tear hers from his closed fingers.

"I believe," he drawled, "you may have dropped this."

She couldn't force her lungs to breathe.

He smiled and opened his hand.

Chapter 22

Susan stared at the object in Mr. Bothwick's palm for far too long before it finally swam into focus.

"My hair comb." Her voice was weak, a mere whisper. Her heart thundered.

He raised a brow. "Have you lost something else?"

She lifted her gaze to his too-innocent face.

So he *did* have the glove. He wanted her to know, but he wasn't yet willing to show his cards. But why play mum? Because he was guilty of the crime? Or for some other heinous reason? Unfortunately, she could scarce ask questions without being required to answer some of her own. And he knew it.

"Thank you," she said crisply.

She plucked the comb from his hand with still-trembling fingers and deposited it in her pocket, where it clinked against the knife and coins. After having paid out a considerable sum in the sundry shops, there was just enough room for the comb. She'd have to take care it didn't fall from her pocket. As she was now convinced her cursed glove had done.

"My pleasure," he responded, looking self-satisfied.

Insufferable blackguard. She'd let him feel like he had the upper hand for now. He wouldn't be wearing his Cheshire grin when he and the rest of his pirate friends were led to the gallows.

As before, this thought brought a devilish cramp to her insides. And as before, she staunchly ignored said cramp. She hadn't forced him to go about pillaging and plundering and whatever else pirates got up to. So she certainly wouldn't feel guilty about him being caught. Particularly if he'd been personally involved in murder.

"How did you find me out here?" she asked, hoping she didn't sound suspicious. Or disillusioned.

He nodded at the overturned rowboat. "Find you? I was just about to take a turn about the ocean. Care to join me?"

Not on her life. "Perhaps another time."

Possibly the day after hell froze over.

The dark sky was turning blacker by the minute. Apparently the recent rain had just been the beginning. Inclement weather aside, she'd have to be the veriest fool to go anywhere alone with him. Especially somewhere so prone to easily explainable "accidents" as the sea.

He inclined his head, but made no move toward the boat. Probably because he well knew to row in such conditions would be tantamount to asking the gods to strike him down. Then why bother with the bluff?

Deciding that trying to understand him would be the quickest path to madness, she turned her back without saying farewell. She headed toward Bournemouth proper with one hand pressed against her overstuffed pocket and the other cupped above her spectacles. The falling rain found her lenses anyway.

She made it almost to the town border before glancing back over her shoulder. Despite her blurred lenses, the overturned rowboat was just visible in the distance.

Mr. Bothwick was not. It was as if he'd been smudged from sight.

Discomfited, she turned back toward town and focused

on returning to the dry warmth of her bedchamber before catching her death of cold.

After a change of clothes and a hot meal, the last of Susan's energy drained from her exhausted body and she longed for nothing more than to go to bed. Unfortunately, someone was already in it. Hovering a few inches above the covers, rather.

Dead Mr. Bothwick.

"Good evening," he said cautiously. Apparently her disposition showed on her face.

She declined to answer. The only thing good about the evening thus far was that it meant the day was finally over. Well, almost over. First she had to get rid of a ghost.

"The Runner is gone," she informed him.

"I know."

She *knew* he'd been watching!

"Who took the body?" she asked eagerly.

His face contorted in frustration. "I don't know."

"How don't you know?" She stared at him with incredulity. "Weren't you there?"

He shook his head. "I was watching over something more important."

"What could be more important than a murdered Runner?"

"The box he came here to find."

That cursed box. Susan's tired hands fisted briefly at her sides. Hadn't she risked her life enough for one day?

"You must take it tonight. We're running out of time. *They're* running out of time." He floated away from the bed, toward the door. "And they know it."

"How would—Oh. Right."

Somebody had recognized the Runner for what he was, and eliminated the immediate threat with a sharp blade to the ribs. The Runner's presence at all, however, indicated that there were others who suspected, who knew of his visit, and would be coming to investigate and take permanent legal action against the pirates. They would not be content to sit and wait.

"No doubt the scarecrow did it," she muttered angrily. She wouldn't have been half surprised to see a shovel rising from the Runner's chest instead of a mere knife.

"Who?" Dead Mr. Bothwick blinked, then laughed. "You think the butler did it? Unlikely. Murder is one of Ollie's favorite treats. He would never delegate such a task to an underling."

"Perhaps you don't know him as well as I do," Susan began, then paused. His statement had been off-the-cuff and perfectly matter-of-fact. Perhaps Dead Mr. Bothwick *did* know the giant's mind much better than she. Which could only mean . . .

"You're a pirate?" Incredulity was quickly replaced by a sense of betrayal. No wonder he'd been able to "investigate" the others. "You *are* a pirate!"

"Was," he corrected reluctantly. "And I never enjoyed it."

"Oh, as long as you didn't enjoy it. That makes it all right." She swiped at him angrily.

He flashed backward, out of arm's reach. "I tried to do the right thing at the end, didn't I?"

"I don't know." She crossed her arms and added uncharitably, "I don't see that you did much of anything."

Dead Mr. Bothwick swirled above her head. "I gathered evidence, which I need for you to *please go retrieve.* Now, before they take the box somewhere inaccessible."

She glared up at him. "Like where?"

"Like the ship! Like the bottom of the ocean! It doesn't matter where, so long as we get it first."

"Why wouldn't they just destroy the evidence?"

"They can't. It's locked inside the jewelry box."

"Why wouldn't they just destroy the box?"

"They *can't.* It's forged from iron." He floated through the door, then poked his head back in through the wood frame. "Listen to me. The strongbox is indestructible, not unsinkable, so if we could please move this conversation from your bedchamber to the dining room—"

"Why the dining room?"

He sighed dramatically. "If you would take your meals somewhere other than your room once in a while, perhaps you would have noticed the box in plain sight on the mantle."

Her hands clenched into fists. "If you would take your head out of your arse once in a while, perhaps you would notice nobody in this house has offered to dine with me."

"Miss Stanton, could we please—"

"I can't believe you lied about being one of the pirates!" she burst out, equally angry at herself for not having guessed.

"If we must hash over the details, I was actually a smuggler, not a pirate."

"What's the difference?"

"We *paid* for the goods we took from France."

"Paid, as in 'giving aid or comfort to an enemy of the Sovereign,' thereby committing high treason punishable by death?"

He paused. "Yes."

"You thought your involvement wasn't an important detail?"

"I *thought* you would go get the damn box instead of sitting around asking questions about it all day. They can hardly hang me, since I'm already dead. If you're so concerned about crimes against the Sovereign, here's your chance to make a difference to the living."

"Fine. Lead the way." Susan wrenched open the door and stalked into the corridor behind the ghost. At least the jewelry box was in a common area. If she got caught inside the dining room, she could say she was looking for biscuits and tea. If the giant didn't kill her on sight.

She glared through the back of the ghost's semitransparent head as they made their way down the darkened hallways. He hadn't been honest with her. But then, would she have helped him if he'd introduced himself as a smuggler? She had to admit, he was nothing if not eager to correct his wrongs. Which meant not all pirates were irredeemable. This one, at least, had turned rogue and gone *good*. If only his brother had made a similar transformation.

"Evan would like to speak with you," she blurted.

Dead Mr. Bothwick halted, then rematerialized facing her direction. "Regarding?"

"I know you said not to let him know we'd been speaking, but he deduced the truth on his own," she said quickly, then hesitated. "He said he wished you had come to him . . . before. And that he wished you could come to him now."

"If wishes were horses, then beggars would ride." He gave a casual shrug, but something in the ghost's eyes hinted he was not as indifferent as he strove to appear.

"We could, you know," she said slowly. "All three of us. It would be awkward, but possible. If you wanted to try."

Well, presuming she got both men together in the same room fairly soon. Once she helped the ghost complete his mission, he'd disappear forever and the chance would be lost.

Dead Mr. Bothwick turned and continued through the maze of corridors without responding.

At least he hadn't said no.

She hurried to catch up. "How did your proof get into the strongbox if you're not the one who put it there?"

Dead Mr. Bothwick closed his semitransparent eyelids. "I was getting ready to secretly set sail. I knew if I were caught, I would be killed, and every inch of my property searched. I needed to entrust the evidence to someone who knew what was going on, yet could be depended upon not to breathe a word."

She cast him a doubtful glance. "It could just be me, but a fellow pirate doesn't seem—"

"Not *Ollie*. His wife."

Susan stumbled. Lady Emeline had been helping?

"I knew about the jewelry box," the ghost continued as he floated from one corridor to the next. "Everyone who'd ever been in the dining room had seen it on the mantle, open and empty. But since there was no key, it served no higher purpose than decoration. To me, it was my contingency plan. If I didn't return by midnight, she was to shut the papers inside and hide the box until someone trustworthy came looking for answers."

"And she did," Susan marveled. "Cousin Emeline escaped the cellar, and—"

"No. To my shame, her assistance is why she's now trapped *in* the cellar. She was the only one who could've taken the box and the cellar is her punishment for having done so. Ollie was furious."

"He knows what's inside?"

"He has a fair idea. Compounded by the fact that Lady Emeline isn't stupid. She would never have crossed him without strong motivation."

Such as seeing her evil husband drawn and quartered. Susan couldn't blame her. She, too, would have done whatever it took to protect the proof from the pirates. Lady Emeline, like her mother, was willing to risk both life and freedom. Susan could not remain passive.

"Let's get that box." Squaring her shoulders, she marched past the ghost.

"Wait," he murmured, hovering so close to an unassuming door that one of his arms was no longer visible. "I hear Ollie talking."

"Good. That means he's not in the dining room." She waved him to follow. "This is our chance."

"Shhh. I want to listen." With that, he disappeared inside.

Spectacular. What was she to do now? Wait for him? Or fetch the box alone?

Sighing, Susan pressed her ear to the wall and decided to

give the ghost thirty seconds before she left in search of the dining room.

"You shouldn't be here," sounded a deep voice. Dead Mr. Bothwick was right. That was definitely the giant.

"Don't be so skittish," came the calm rejoinder, the voice gentlemanly with a touch of country. Mr. Forrester?! "After that near-debacle with your houseguest, at least I have a story to spin. If she asks, I can always say I've called to check on your wife. I assume you've purchased thicker chains?"

Susan gasped, then belatedly clapped both hands over her gaping mouth.

"Watch what you say," the giant growled. "The walls have ears."

Trembling, she pushed away. She had heard enough. Whatever was going on between the giant and the magistrate, Mr. Forrester knew about Lady Emeline—had known the truth all along—and deliberately chose to do nothing. He was a hypocritical cad, at best. Another man not to be trusted. What else might he be turning a blind eye to?

She could no longer trust him. With anything. She needed a real man of the law. Would find one, the moment she arrived in Bath. She had to arm herself with as much proof as possible. Frantic, she raced down the corridor. She had to steal the strongbox.

It was her only hope.

The moment Miss Stanton had turned her back to him on the beach, Evan had resumed his march toward Poseidon's cave.

With no outbound journey scheduled for over a week—and that voyage being of the one-way variety—this could be Evan's last opportunity to sneak aboard the ship. Having decided that saving his own neck now took precedence over determining his brother's killer, he desperately wanted another look at the captain's logbook. In fact, he planned to destroy it. With any luck, the previous diaries were also back on their shelves. He'd destroy those, too.

Or, since those dated back to long before he joined the crew, perhaps he would be wise to keep hold of them for leverage.

Like the glove.

His blood simmered as he recalled the panicked expression on Miss Stanton's face when he'd first held out his hand. She *had* been out looking for her glove. Not that he blamed her. Misplacing easily identifiable blood-soaked garments was never a good idea.

What the glove's presence meant, however, he had no clue. He'd asked around as carefully as he could. He'd looked around even more carefully. Yet there was no gossip of any altercations involving Miss Stanton. No signs of struggle. No injured man or woman. Certainly no dead body.

Just a single glove with a hell of a lot of blood.

Evan slipped into the mouth of the cave, flattened against the wall, and listened. The cave should be empty. With no cargo to guard—and the threat of discovery thick in the air—the last thing the sea dogs would want to do was get caught aboard a notorious smuggling ship. They'd been sighted enough times that their mere presence on board might be enough to connect them to the crimes.

With no time to lose and daylight fading fast, Evan crept into the darkness.

Damn his brother's nettlesome sense of honor rearing its ugly head. He had no wish to sneak off in the dead of night because of Timothy. If Evan could obliterate all evidence linking himself to the smuggling, he might not have to run. But he needed every scrap of proof to be in his possession. Now. Tonight.

He paused before leaving the safety of shadows to approach the ship. He heard no noises, saw no activity, felt no eyes upon him, but there was a hint of . . . smoke. The faint odor hung in the air. Soft, but bitter and insistent. The scent was old enough that he needn't fear anyone still bent over open flames, but recent enough that he couldn't waste another second dallying.

He boarded the deck.

The ship, as he'd hoped, was empty of life. Unfortunately, the captain's quarters not only still lacked the older leather-bound diaries but the current one had also gone missing. *Damn* it. He was never going to erase all references tying him to the crew if every time he looked for something, somebody else had already stolen it.

He lifted his chin and gave the air another sniff. Perhaps he wasn't the only jack-tar on a mission to seek and destroy incriminating evidence. He disembarked and followed the scent of smoke through the cave until he came upon a round pile of ash.

He knelt and sifted through the fragile cinders. His fingers came across no conveniently unscathed parchment explaining precisely what had been burned and why. If paper had been incinerated, no indication remained. He shifted position and kept sifting gently.

Then he saw it. A charred scrap of leather no larger than a farthing. The color and thickness matched the spine of the captain's logbook. Evan rose to his feet, the crusty piece of leather feather-light in his palm. Poseidon's crew must have been burning the older diaries last week when Evan had invaded their camp. Now he would never have an opportunity to peruse the pages to see what incriminating evidence remained. Then again, no inquisitive magistrate would be able to connect Evan to any of the ship's journeys, rightly or wrongly. How it would've rankled to be found guilty for missions in which he hadn't participated.

When he shoved the tiny fragment into his pocket, his fingers brushed against Miss Stanton's glove. Was it possible he was judging *her* unfairly? He doubted she'd been out in silk and lace to slaughter chickens, but he'd certainly seen no sign of foul play. Perhaps the panic in her eyes had been because she feared he would leap to conclusions rather than listen to explanations. And wasn't that precisely what he had done?

Contemplative, he strode from the cave. If he had been rash in his judgment, he would have to make amends. Just as soon as he procured that jewelry box and destroyed whatever evidence lurked inside. Only then he would be free. Free of worry, free from under the captain's thumb, free to pursue Miss Stanton as an eligible gentleman. Not a dead man walking.

Evan jerked to a stop at the foot of the trail leading to Moonseed Manor. He wanted to pursue Miss Stanton? As in . . . to love and to cherish, now and forevermore? He shook the not unpleasant image from his head and forced his ash-smudged boots up the steep cliff. Now was not the time to entertain such thoughts. Without the contents of that strongbox in his possession, he wouldn't be able to risk spending another day in Bournemouth, much less spend his remaining hours courting a woman.

First things first: destroy the last of the evidence.

Moonseed Manor was silent when Evan let himself in through the servant's entrance. Too silent. It was just past suppertime and he'd yet to catch sight of a footman or a maid, much less the master of the house and his lapdog. Which meant the latter two had to be up to no good in some dark corner of the Manor—if they were home at all. As to the servants, Evan had no idea where they might be. Unless they'd been given the same instructions he'd given his: *Pack. We leave soon.*

With any luck, however, he wouldn't have to quit Bournemouth. At least, outside of his own free will. With the logbooks gone, all he needed was the contents of Ollie's deceptively decorative strongbox and Evan's life would once again be fully his.

He headed straight for the dining room. Dark. Empty. Perfect. He crossed to the still-warm fireplace and lifted the heavy jewelry box from the mantle. He could scarce believe his good fortune.

A creaking footfall in the open doorway demolished the premature sense of relief.

Cradling the box to his chest as a father might hold his firstborn son, Evan turned slowly, willing to use the iron box to bash in Ollie's head if necessary. He hadn't come this far, gotten this close, to risk the gallows now.

Ollie, however, was not in the doorway. Miss Stanton was.

She looked at the jewelry box clutched in his arms, then looked him dead in the eyes. The expression in hers could only be described as . . . disappointment. As if she'd finally begun to think better of him, and he'd gone and proven her worst suspicions correct.

Pain slashed against his ribs. He could see the truth in her gaze: Even with the evidence duly destroyed, he could never be good enough in her estimation, never redeem himself from the lows to which he'd sunk. But he couldn't back down now. Not with the last link tying his neck to the noose finally in his hands.

"I know what's in the box," she said, and took a small step into the darkened room. "And I know why you want it."

Evan blinked and gripped his prize tighter. If she knew what was in the box, she was several steps ahead of him. Although by now he had a reasonable guess. If she knew why he needed the box's contents . . . well, then that meant she knew just about everything. And his dreams of someday playing the eligible gentleman in complement to her role as marriageable young lady were just that: dreams.

"You may be used to taking whatever you want, whenever you want," she continued softly, inexorably. "But it stops now." She paused, touched a chain at her throat. "I had hoped . . ."

She trailed off, her expression both rueful and sad.

He didn't speak, was incapable of formulating a believable explanation to justify any of his actions. She was a lady. He was a water rat. A libertine. A thief. He longed to say, *It's not what you think.* He ached to be able to tell her, *I'm not who you think I am.*

But he couldn't. Because she was right.

He had always been beneath her. Likely would always be beneath her. She had simply never realized just how far. Somehow, she'd imagined him a better man than he was, forgiven him when she should not have done, given him chances he didn't deserve. And was now realizing the extent of her folly.

He yearned to toss the box aside and take her into his arms, promising to be the man she'd hoped he was. But he didn't have that choice. As much as he wanted her, as much as it pained him to see her look at him with such regret and disappointment, saving his neck had to come first. At all costs. Even at the risk of whatever small thread of hope still bonded the two of them together.

Tucking the box beneath one arm, he strode forward, intending to shoulder past her without attempting to explain or mitigate his actions.

She widened her stance, hands fisted on her hips. A waif half his size, she did her best to block the doorway. Her attempt was valiant, if laughable in its chances for success.

As always, he could not help but admire her. Determination stiffened her posture, but a tiny sliver of hope still shone in her face. His heart twisted a little more. She still wanted to believe in him. Hoped he would prove her wrong. And he was going to fail her.

"Step aside, Susan." He kept his voice soft, but knew she heard the steel beneath.

She swallowed, shook her head, appeared to be thinking furiously. Then she took a deep breath and slipped a hand into the folds of her skirts. Her fingers emerged, shaking. And holding a knife. She looked pale, her skin pasty white. But she opened the blade and gripped the handle so the sharpened tip pointed directly at him.

"I'm sorry," she said then, her voice wobbly but determined. "But I can't let you have it."

Evan hated himself in that moment. He couldn't help but wish he were anywhere else, in anyone's shoes but his own. He certainly hadn't wanted what little relationship he still had with Miss Stanton to end like *this*. But he had no choice. His death by hanging would benefit neither of them.

"I'm sorry," he answered truthfully. Achingly. Then used his free hand to retrieve the loaded pistol from his waistband. "But I can't let you stop me."

Fear flashed in her eyes. Her back thumped against the doorjamb. She truly believed he would kill her without another thought or moment's regret. The last thread of his humanity died at her feet.

He'd *had* to bluff with the pistol. He could've wrested the knife from her with brute force, but he couldn't risk hurting her in the process. He wanted to explain himself, to justify his actions, to see trust replace the agonizing expression of terror in her eyes. But despite the war raging in his heart, Evan could not chance loitering in Moonseed Manor a moment longer. He took the opportunity to finally escape with the strongbox in his arms. The thrill of victory no longer raced through his blood.

Instead, he felt the pain of loss.

No matter what Mr. Bothwick might think, Susan was *not* going to let him get away with that box. Too many people were counting on her. Some of them still alive.

She dashed upstairs for her pelisse (having been caught in the rain enough for one week), then swore when she realized the round trip back to the front door had sucked a quarter hour from her evening. She was going to have to seriously consider trailing biscuit crumbs behind her.

At least she had no doubt as to her destination. Mr. Bothwick must be taking the strongbox back to his lodgings.

Nor did she doubt he would prevent her from reclaiming it by any means necessary. Which meant she would have to proceed at her very stealthiest. And hide the jewelry box somewhere so clever, he would never be able to guess the location.

She headed into the darkness, moving toward the trails connecting his property to Moonseed Manor. She wished she'd brought a lantern, then chided herself for the silly thought. A lantern wasn't stealthy. A lantern was stupid. If Mr. Bothwick could find his way to and from the two houses in the dead of night, so could she.

All she had to do was stay on the footpath.

"Just stay on the footpath," she repeated under her breath what felt like more than an hour later. "Those noises do not belong to feral animals. Keep moving."

It was no longer raining, but the ground was slippery with wet leaves. The sandy soil shifted beneath her boots with every step, keeping her off-balance and her gait uneven. The visibility had gone from poor to nonexistent when a mass of black clouds had swallowed the thin slice of moon. The only reason she knew she was on a path at all was that she had yet to crash face-first into a tree.

The branches, however, ripped at her pelisse, tugged at her hair, tore her bonnet off completely. She didn't wish to admit it, but the very narrowness of the trail meant she was no longer on the one she'd taken to Moonseed Manor from the stables. If she ever had been. She briefly considered turning around, but she'd walked for so long that surely there would be a break in the trees at any moment.

Besides, this might be her only chance. Susan's cold fingers closed around the gold chain hanging about her neck and tugged the antique crucifix from beneath her bodice. She held the cross tight in her hands, pressed it to her chest. She *would* get that strongbox. The smugglers would be captured, Lady Emeline would be freed, and the spirits of both Lady Beaune and Dead Mr. Bothwick would finally be at peace. It was all up to her. She had to succeed.

Her already-slow steps slowed even further when she heard distant noises up ahead. Footsteps cracked across fallen twigs. Mr. Bothwick? Perhaps she'd found her way to the stables after all!

She crept as close as she dared before peering through the trees, then recoiled in shock.

Chapter 23

Not the stables. The chicken shed. Not Mr. Bothwick, but Mr. Forrester. With a lantern half-hidden beneath his great-coat. By all appearances, the magistrate had only just emerged from the selfsame path on which she still stood. Good Lord. Susan gripped the closest tree for support and tried to remain dead silent.

She almost failed to breathe when she saw the person he'd come to meet.

Dinah Devonshire.

Surely they didn't intend to rendezvous in the chicken shed! Susan had been so certain Miss Devonshire would die before stepping foot inside the dirty little hut. Then again, Susan would've thought the same about Mr. Forrester just a few hours prior. But the man she'd considered good-intentioned but naive had turned out to be the opposite on both counts. Perhaps Miss Devonshire, too, was not the hollow-headed doll she appeared to be.

"Go." Miss Devonshire waved him back, casting furtive glances over her small, round shoulders. "We'll meet another night."

The magistrate did not halt his approach. "No. I need to speak with you."

"It's unsafe," she insisted, but preened as if delighted to

discover her charming company held more sway than whatever danger lurked outside the little shed.

"Unsafe how?" Mr. Forrester gestured at the lone cow, asleep where it stood. "The animals are the only ones listening."

Miss Devonshire touched his arm, blinked up at him with huge eyes. "But Miss Stanton saw us here last time. What if she comes back?"

"She cannot. I had Ollie Hamilton's manservant lock her chamber door."

Susan resisted the urge to bash her head against the closest tree. Not only had she gotten utterly lost en route to Mr. Bothwick's stables, she wouldn't be able to reenter her own bedchamber when she returned to Moonseed Manor. Assuming she could retrace her steps at all.

"You . . ." Miss Devonshire's voice wobbled. Dark lines creased her beautiful forehead, as if she just realized her tattle might've engendered consequences more serious than she'd anticipated. Her fingers no longer grazed the magistrate's arm, nor were her wide eyes focused flirtatiously on his face. Her hands were now twisting together beneath her bosom. "I don't think she means ill. She's simply too . . . *curious.*"

"Don't worry." The magistrate gave a kick to the hind leg of the sleeping cow. The animal jerked awake and lumbered away. Susan clutched the tree and fumed.

Miss Devonshire's shocked gasp did not earn the slightest flicker of acknowledgment from the magistrate.

"I'll take care of Miss Stanton's curiosity." Mr. Forrester's cherubic smile looked more demonic than angelic.

Susan hoped she was overestimating the level of finality in his tone.

Miss Devonshire recoiled from the magistrate. However, the scant inches between her shoulders and the shed did not allow for much distance, and her shoulders banged against the closed door. She cast about nervous glances again at the unexpected noise, but this time her eyes hinted she more than half-hoped someone *would* overhear.

"I need the money you owe me." Mr. Forrester's bald statement neatly changed topic without affording Miss Devonshire the opportunity to ask further questions about Susan's fate.

Miss Devonshire frowned, her nervous fingers clenching together. "How much?"

His expression was ruthless. "All of it."

Her jaw dropped. "But I haven't sold even a third! I'd been hoping Miss Stanton would spend some of her city money. She flashed coin today in every shop but mine. Perhaps when the next shipment comes in, things will be different. Didn't you say you might procure new fashion plates for me? With the right look as incentive, the local ladies will—"

"There will be no more shipments."

"What?" Miss Devonshire's voice rose a few notches higher. "But the French imports are the only reason *anybody* comes to the shop. If you stop providing them, Harriet and I will be destitute in a matter of weeks!"

"I hardly care," the magistrate replied coldly, "about you or Miss Grey. I expect you to pay your debts by midnight tomorrow."

"That would take every penny we own! Most of which we've been saving for months, and some of which wasn't even earned on silks." She sagged against the wall of the shed, then gazed up at him with desperate eyes. "I could return the fabric. . . ."

"I don't want *fabric*," Mr. Forrester spat, "or pathetic excuses. I want money."

"But—"

"Midnight, Miss Devonshire. And not a moment later."

Head spinning, Susan tightened her grip around the tree she used as cover. She'd suspected the magistrate's French silk mystery was a sham, but she'd never have guessed he acted as intermediary between the pirates and the purchasers. What a perfect scheme the lot had devised! She touched the crucifix hanging from her throat and swore Mr. Forrester's little blond ringlets would be the first to flutter in the wind.

Miss Devonshire's porcelain face looked ready to crack. "Where will—"

"Don't worry about me." His malicious smile didn't mask the underlying threat. "No matter where you are, I'll find you."

He turned and cut around the shed toward a (blessedly) different path leading God-knew-where. At least he wasn't returning to Moonseed Manor tonight.

"Wait," Miss Devonshire called out.

Mr. Forrester glanced over his shoulder, one eyebrow raised in cold condescension.

She swallowed visibly. "W-what are your plans for Miss Stanton?"

"Why, Miss Devonshire. You know my plans. I'm taking her to the assembly." He widened his eyes in a parody of his hapless-magistrate act. "Assuming she survives the long journey, that is. Country roads can be so treacherous. Especially with these cliffs. If one doesn't have the door latched just so, it would be easy to tumble right out of the carriage and fall to one's death on the rocks below. I shudder to think how I would ever get over such a loss." His cherubic smile returned, be-dimpled and perfidious.

Susan's stomach dropped. There went the last of her hopes for escape.

"What the deuce do you think you're doing?"

Susan jerked upright as the masculine voice invaded her restless dreams. She squinted in confusion as light streamed through the face of her visitor. She shook the bits

of dried leaves and tree bark from her hair and fumbled for
her spectacles.

Dead Mr. Bothwick hovered between her sleep-creased
face and the morning sun. He made a poor parasol, but was
overall a welcome sight.

"I fell asleep."

He stared at her dubiously. "Against a tree?"

"So it would seem." She pulled herself to her feet and
wondered if it were safe to step outside the path.

"I've been looking for you all night. You took the strongbox, I assume. Did you hide it already? Why didn't you
come back?"

She shook her head. No box. And she didn't want to
admit that in her attempt to find her way back to Moonseed
Manor, she'd somehow ended up outside the still-living Mr.
Bothwick's stables completely by accident. Mr. Bothwick's
extremely busy, bustling, overcrowded stables. There had
been no chance of approaching unnoticed. She'd stayed
hidden in the surrounding woods and sat with her back to
a tree to wait.

She might've overdone the waiting.

"Your brother has the jewelry box," she explained. She
shook out her skirts, averting her eyes so she wouldn't have
to see Dead Mr. Bothwick's reaction to that bit of news. "I
tried to detain him, but he had a pistol."

"My brother pointed a weapon at a woman?" the ghost
asked doubtfully.

"To be fair," she admitted, "I threatened him with a
knife."

She'd even been prepared to use it. Until he'd flashed a
pistol. That's when she'd realized some things could hurt
worse than bullets. Like discovering the man she loved
would rather end her life than help her to fix it. Susan
forced the memory to the back of her mind.

When she lifted her head, Dead Mr. Bothwick was staring at her as if she'd grown an extra eye.

"I meant to steal the jewelry box back, but when I finally arrived at the stables, servants were everywhere. Loading carriages. Why does a country man need multiple carriages?" She tried to clean the lenses of her spectacles but only succeeded in smearing them further. "I think he's going to leave. For good."

"Not with my evidence, he isn't. Did you see what happened to the box?"

"No. But I did see the magistrate discussing smuggled goods with Miss Devonshire as if extorting payment for illegally obtained fabric was an everyday occurrence." She started walking in what she hoped was the direction of Mr. Bothwick's house, then paused to glance at the ghost. "Er . . . is it this way?"

He nodded absently and flashed ahead of her.

She quashed her joy at having actually chosen the correct trail and hurried after him. "Why didn't you tell me Mr. Forrester was involved?"

"Because I didn't know," Dead Mr. Bothwick answered grimly. "Until last night when I heard him talking to Ollie. That's why I had to watch and listen. Forrester wanted to see what Ollie had dug up from the gravesite. Ollie claimed it was nothing, a box of fripperies Lady Emeline had hidden. But Forrester didn't believe him. He suspects the end of his game is nigh. He's frightened, and there's nothing deadlier than a man backed into a corner."

Susan shuddered. She'd overheard more than enough about the magistrate's penchant for convenient "accidents."

Dead Mr. Bothwick floated down a fork in the path. "They went to the dining room to fetch the strongbox, but it was gone." Dead Mr. Bothwick bobbed in place. "I've been looking for you ever since."

"How did the magistrate get involved in piracy?"

"How would I know?" The ghost darted forward amongst the trees. "I can't ask many questions these days. But since Ollie's been with the captain longer than he's been with

Lady Emeline, I'd have to assume the smuggling crew has been together since long before Forrester weaseled his way into the plot. He's always been one to manipulate others for his own profit. The sort who scored good marks at university by any means other than academic effort. Some people mistook him as stupid. I never made that mistake."

Susan hurried to catch up. "You knew him before he became magistrate?"

"I've known him since Eton. My brother had already completed his levels but Forrester and I were of an age."

"You went to *Eton?*"

"Head boy every year, I might add."

Susan narrowed her eyes at him. "Where exactly did you say you were from before you moved to Bournemouth?"

"I didn't." He floated ahead. "But if you're curious, London. Although I suspect Evan has always preferred his cottage in Bath."

"He has a cottage in—did you just say *London?*"

"His cottage is in Bath, the town house is in London. He always kept a room for my use whenever I was in Town because I spent most of my time on Father's estate in Surrey."

Mr. Bothwick's current lodgings were finally in sight, but Susan couldn't take another step. She stumbled against the closest tree.

Vertigo assailed her from each of the ghost's carelessly thrown words. No wonder Dead Mr. Bothwick had seemed offended and disdainful when she'd presumed superiority for being a member of Society. He had moved in those same circles.

And no wonder the still-living Mr. Bothwick had so many times evoked the image of a Society gentleman as easily at home in Almack's or Jackson's as racing along Hyde Park or playing whist at a dinner soiree. He *was* such a gentleman, had likely done all those things and more when not taking holiday elsewhere. A cottage in Bath. An estate in Surrey. And she'd had no idea.

She had gone to him, made love to him, because she'd believed that despite his many and varied flaws, she had fallen hard for the goodness he possessed deep inside. And now, to her utter humiliation, she discovered she'd as much as given herself to a ghost, for all the substance between them.

"Enough tittle-tattle." Dead Mr. Bothwick bobbed across the sandy soil, floating away from the footpath in the direction of his brother's house. "Let's fetch that strongbox."

Susan trudged along behind him. At least Mr. Bothwick had not patronized her with romantic lies. Had he spoken words of love, and had she foolishly permitted herself to believe such fancies . . . Susan doubted her broken heart would ever have healed. Particularly when she'd discovered he planned on leaving and hadn't bothered with so much as a good-bye. Unless she counted the pistol he'd pointed at her chest.

Dead Mr. Bothwick glanced back at her over his semi-transparent shoulder, his ghostly face lined with impatience. This was a man who had died for his strong faith in right and wrong. She had been less than exemplary. This was her chance to prove her character and set things to rights.

"Ready?" He motioned her forward. "If his carriages are full, we haven't much time."

"You're right. Let's have done." She touched her fingertips to the crucifix hidden beneath her bodice. *Someone* had to fight for those who could not.

Shoulders squared, she marched away from the trees.

Chapter 24

Evan placed the ornate strongbox inside a secret, specially built enclosure behind his stables, engaged the locking mechanism, and covered the access point with dung-scented soil. Once his horses trampled atop the location a few times, the hay-strewn area would look no different from any other. The perfect hiding place. They could rip up every floorboard of his house, tear apart the very walls, and never find the jewelry box.

He'd considered taking the damn thing with him, but determined such a measure an unnecessary risk. If he were stopped at any point, it would be far too easy to discover something of that size in a mere carriage.

The real question, at this point, was: Where to now?

Although there was no more physical evidence linking him to any crimes against the Crown—save whatever was buried beneath the area where one of his mares currently relieved herself—remaining in Bournemouth was no longer wise. Though generally close-lipped, too many of the town's inhabitants traded in smuggled French goods. Were they to be questioned by anyone intelligent as to the origin of such items, Evan's name might be mentioned. He preferred not to be present should that come to pass. There might be suspicion forever, but without proof, he could at least *attempt* a normal life. Somewhere.

Perhaps Bath. The cottage there was far enough from the town center that he wouldn't have to see or speak to anyone if he didn't wish to.

And he definitely would not be attending the stupid assembly.

A wry quirk lifted the corner of Evan's lips, then died. Now that he was no longer engaged in piratical pursuits, his weekend had become free of commitments. Had the situation unfolded differently, he could've escorted Miss Stanton to the festivities after all. Fetched her dry biscuits and warm punch to her heart's content. Held her to him as they swayed and swirled with the music.

Disgusted with his inability to stop fantasizing over the impossible, he strode into the stable and hung his shovel on the wall. He might as well face the truth. He was in love.

He might reminisce about his escapades aboard the captain's ship, but he wouldn't feel as if he'd been robbed of an important part of his life.

Miss Stanton, however, would be missed something fierce.

He could be content enough, he supposed, without illegal adventures bringing drama and excitement to his life. But he would never be truly happy without Susan at his side.

This realization should have had him trembling in his boots. And, to be honest, it did. For the first time, however, his fear was not due to the heretofore heretical thought of a man needing a woman to be happy. The erratic beating in his heart was due to the terrifying thought of not being able to have her.

Evan quit the stables and headed toward his house. His problem, he realized clearly, was that he was hopelessly lovesick, and there was nothing to be done to cure it. He'd alienated her so thoroughly—at the point of a pistol, no less—that she would undoubtedly prefer to press her knife to his throat than grant him a moment's audience.

He pushed open his front door and came to an abrupt halt to find the object of his desires trapped against the far wall by two footmen.

"Release her," he said softly.

They did.

She yanked her hands up and lashed out at them with closed fists. They'd apparently anticipated this move, for they'd already hurried out of range. She crossed her arms over her chest and glared at Evan defiantly, her chin held high.

Such bravado might've had greater impact, were she not garbed in a much-mistreated version of yesterday's costume, every fiber of which was frayed or spackled with sand and dirt. Her hair was a tangled blond mess of fallen curls and bits of leaf. What was hopefully just a bit of mud streaked across the dull lenses of her spectacles.

Yet she was the most beautiful woman he had ever seen.

"Why are you here?" he asked, unable to keep the wonder from his voice. Perhaps he'd been wrong not to believe in Fate.

The look she cast him was withering at best.

Ah, right. The strongbox. Well, she couldn't have it. She was just going to have to trust him.

He stepped forward and tried to take her hands.

She pulled away.

"I'm leaving," he began, then paused when she let out what sounded suspiciously like a snort. He raised his brows in question.

"Really?" she asked sarcastically, gesturing at what he belatedly realized was his completely vacant anteroom. *All* the rooms were empty.

"I won't be coming back," he started again. He gazed at her earnestly, determined to make her understand. "And I want—"

What *did* he want? Did he dare verbalize his desires?

"Come with me," he said in a rush. "I know I'm not as well-heeled or well-behaved as the upstanding Society gentlemen who pursue you back home, but their staid little hearts cannot possibly feel the passion for you that I do. I know I can't offer the precise life you had in mind, but we would at least have each other. Perhaps someday, we could—"

She laughed. *Laughed.* With patent incredulity etched across her face.

The insidious sludge of defeat smothered his last strand of hope. He had expected her to refuse because she thought him beneath her, not because she didn't believe his love was real.

"I mean it," he said, no longer caring if she heard the bleak desperation in his voice. "Let me fetch the priest from the tavern, and I'll swear upon his Bible that I want you by my side. And more. Can't you tell that I—"

"Don't say it," she interrupted, placing a palm to his chest as if to stop him from speaking further. Just as his body warmed to the contact, she realized what she'd done and jerked her hand back to her side. "Even if I thought you capable of true emotion, what exactly are you offering? The life of a fugitive, forever consigned to backwater village after backwater village so you won't have to bother with such things as morality and consequences and the law? I would resent you before the end of the first week. In fact, I'm already insulted you think me stupid enough to take such trope as truth. There is no 'we,' Mr. Bothwick. There never was. Now tell me what you've done with that box."

She didn't care about him. Not even enough to let him unburden his soul. All she wanted was the evidence necessary to destroy him. Little did she know her dismissal of his feelings had already destroyed him in a way the gallows never could.

Despite the cold seeping through his pores, Evan rallied what remained of his pride.

"No."

She bristled. "Without that box—"

"Why do you suppose I'm so determined no one else have it? Besides," he threw out carelessly, "I destroyed it."

Her eyelashes fluttered heavenward. "I *am* aware that it's indestructible."

"Nothing," he said softly, "is indestructible."

Like the heart he hadn't known he still possessed. The one he'd given up on when he'd taken to the sea in search of adventure. He'd had nothing to lose.

Until now.

And he'd already lost her. Which, as she'd pointed out so eloquently, was his own bloody fault. Never to be forgiven. And never to be reversed.

"Balderdash." She stared up at him in exasperation.

Not because she saw the internal battle, the frustration, the despair of Evan the man who would prostrate himself before her if he thought it would make a difference. But because he stood in the way of her retrieving a jewelry box that could severely shorten his life. If there was love in the equation, it was only on his side.

Her gaze unfocused somewhere over his left shoulder, then narrowed at nothing. Her left shoulder twitched. Someone who wasn't watching might have thought it nothing, a twitch in the muscle. He knew it for what it was: a shrug. She was communicating with someone. And it wasn't him.

"Are you talking to my damn brother instead of listening to me?" he demanded.

Her eyes refocused on his. "He's the one doing the talking. He wants to know why I don't shove my knife hilt-deep in your belly and have done with you already."

"Truly?" Evan frowned. That didn't sound like Timothy.

She sighed, her shoulders slumping against the wall. "No, he just said that arguing with you has never gotten anyone anywhere. I added the bit about the knife because it seemed as good a solution as any."

That much sounded like *her*. He remained convinced she'd make an excellent pirate. Much more so than Timothy.

Timothy, who had either betrayed him from the start, or simply hadn't thought to inform his brother after suffering a severe change of heart with regard to smuggling. Evan wasn't certain which was worse. Nor was he sure how he felt about having an unexpected opportunity to find out.

"Can you . . . ask him something for me?"

She raised a brow. "He's invisible, not deaf. He can see and hear splendidly."

"Oh. All right." He turned to face the direction she'd last looked, then realized Timothy may or may not still be there. He glanced at her for help.

Compassion filled her eyes, and she reached out to touch him before remembering herself and letting her hand fall with the act uncompleted. "Don't worry about trying to face him. He understands the impossibility. Just ask your question."

Evan nodded, feeling more awkward and uncomfortable by the second. He was about to converse with his dead brother. His *invisible* dead brother. Via the one woman with whom he'd wanted their failed romance to last . . . forever.

"Timothy," he said aloud, the back of his neck warming uncomfortably when he heard his voice crack. He cut his gaze to Susan's to see if she noticed his discomfort. This time, she did brush the tips of her fingers against the back of his hand. With that simple touch came strength. "Why—" He cleared his throat. "Why did you take Red instead of me?"

He shifted uncomfortably. He hadn't had any questions prepared for a moment such as this, but he hoped it was as good a start as any. He opened his mouth to clarify what he meant, but Susan was already responding.

"He says, 'Because Red doesn't ask questions.'"

That *did* sound like Timothy.

"Of course I ask questions," Evan said, irritated at how quickly his brother could put him on the defensive, even after death. "I still have plenty more." Susan's steady fingers twined with his. Evan took a calming breath and started anew. "You went on a secret mission without breathing a single word. Why didn't you confide in me?"

She glanced somewhere above his head. "He says, 'Because I had no way of knowing which side you'd take. I don't even know where you stand now.'"

Evan's heart twisted. "But you're my brother!"

Her grip on his hand loosened. "He says, 'And you're an excellent actor. I'm not sure I've ever known what you were thinking, or if you meant the words you were saying.' Harrumph. That's certainly true enough. *What?*" She frowned at the air. "Fine, no personal asides." She paused, as if listening intently. Her fingers tightened around his again. "Right now he's saying, 'Sometimes you stood aboard ship with the wind in your face and an expression of such pure pleasure, it was as if you were born to the seas. Other times, when you thought no one was looking, I could swear you wished you'd never stepped off dry land.'" Her head angled slightly, and her gaze met Evan's curiously. "'You loved it . . . and yet you didn't. I had no reason to believe you didn't feel the same about me.'" She lifted a brow with a wry smile. "You have no idea how much I long to voice my opinion on *that* statement. Respond quickly, or I won't be able to help myself."

But he couldn't respond quickly. He couldn't respond at all. Timothy had seen what Evan had never admitted even to himself. He *hadn't* been happy with his choices. Although every risk he took brought a rush of adventure, the losses he suffered invariably outweighed the gains. To acknowledge that, however, was to admit being wrong. Since he'd burned every bridge he'd passed, there was no going back—and no point indulging maudlin hypothesizing over what might have been.

"I doubt it," she whispered sotto voce to an area just to the left of her shoulder. "All right, I'll ask." She straightened and turned her gaze to Evan as if he hadn't just overheard her speaking to thin air. She kept her hand in his, as if willing him to have strength for the next question. The sensation of being supported was starting to seem . . . normal. "Your brother would like to know," she said, her expression carefully blank, "what role you played in his death."

"What?" he sputtered, his skin turning cold. "None at all! I didn't know he was *on* a secret mission. How could I have murdered him while it was in progress? I swore to kill the villain myself the moment I discovered his identity, and I still plan to put a bullet or two between the blackguard's eyes."

Evan cut himself off as he realized a simple "no" might have been better than openly admitting to premeditated homicide to a woman whose faith in him was tentative at best.

"He says, 'Just checking.'" She paused, then added softly, "and that he believes you."

"Timothy doubted me? Even for a second?" The realization his own brother thought him capable of such a heinous act sliced through Evan's heart, rendering him unable to keep the hurt from his voice. Both the people he loved had believed him completely heartless.

Susan shook her head. "He says, 'Not anymore.'"

"What about him?" he demanded, then remembered he could address his brother directly. "What about you, Timothy? You see no wrong in turning traitor on your fellow jacks, on your family, on *me*. You were perfectly willing for your own brother to ride backward up Holborn Hill. You know good and well I'd be unlikely to slip-gibbet once you ratted over the crew."

Susan blinked, then shook her head as if to clear it. "He says he never once intended you to climb the . . . Deadly Nevergreen?" She cast an exasperated gaze over Evan's shoulder. "Would you two please speak English?"

"Ha. If that were true, he wouldn't be so keen to get the contents of that box into the hands of the law." Oh how he wished he could see his brother's expression, to look into Timothy's eyes and see what he was truly thinking. "If whatever's in that box is enough evidence to bring down a smuggling crew, how could I possibly not go down with the ship?"

"He says—" She broke off, eyes wide.

Evan froze.

Horses.

If a carriage was close enough to hear, it couldn't be more than half a mile away. With no other town for miles, it wasn't hard to guess where the visitors must be heading. Why now, why already? Had that insufferable toady Forrester actually gotten someone of import to listen to his talk of smugglers in Bournemouth?

Susan ran to the open door, poking her head outside to listen.

"The Runners are back." She clapped her hands to her chest. "It must be!"

"The Runners," Evan choked out, "are *back?*"

She turned slowly, guiltily, but kept her shoulders squared and her nose high. She removed a folded piece of parchment from a pocket hidden in her skirts and handed him the small square.

He read it silently, then tossed it to the floor.

"Bow Street Runners come on your summons?" he asked incredulously. "Then how did you get this letter back?"

"I found it," she admitted, not meeting his eyes. "On the first one's dead body."

The bloody glove.

He struggled for calm. "Who killed him?"

She bent to retrieve the parchment. "One of your mates, I'm sure."

"So you sent . . . another missive?" he asked. *After we made love and knowing you were consigning me to death?*

She flinched as if she'd heard every word of the unspoken accusation. Then she nodded. "I believe I said, 'Bring an army.' It's not about you," she added hurriedly, as if any justification could possibly mitigate his connection. "It's for cousin Emeline, and her mother, and your brother, and—"

"Oh, it's about me, all right," he muttered, staring at the open door. How much time did he have, if they were coming straight here? Ten minutes? Five? His carriages were ready, but there was only one road leading on and off the cliff. He was well and truly stuck. And the cause of his current predicament had just moments prior been holding his hand, earnestly supporting him through what might well be the last conversation he would ever have with his younger brother.

Apparently oblivious to the conflict she incited in his soul, Susan stepped out onto his front walkway and turned into the wind.

The hoofbeats kept coming closer, each striking the ground with enough force to rattle the foundation. Or perhaps that was the pounding of his heart, thumping against his ribs. Evan's fists clenched.

"Never mind the bit about running away with me," he said beneath his breath. "Doubt you much want to go where I'll be headed."

But she was already gone. Most likely to help his brother find more nails to drive into his coffin.

Chapter 25

Susan ran all the way to Moonseed Manor.

She hadn't been certain that's where she was headed, of course—she'd just been doing her best to follow Dead Mr. Bothwick, who could be devilish tricky to keep in sight. He was as eager to see the Runners as she was. Perhaps more so. Despite her excitement at finally being able to rescue Lady Emeline from her prison, sending Evan to an even deadlier one held no attraction.

She hated that there was no compromise.

Either she directed the Runners to the proof hidden in the strongbox, thereby freeing cousin Emeline and condemning both Evan and her captors . . . or she allowed the evidence to remain "lost," thus saving Evan—and all the pirates—from the gallows, as well as dooming Lady Emeline to suffer the rest of her undoubtedly short life at the hands of her husband.

Susan held no wish to see Evan captured, much less tried, convicted, and hanged. She loved him, despite all valiant efforts to deny the truth.

However, she was forced to admit, he was guilty of his crimes. Cousin Emeline was not. If the only way to free her cousin was to bring the pirates to justice—*all* the pirates—Susan's loyalty to the innocent woman who had been tortured for so long had to take precedence over the desolation ripping apart her heart.

She slowed as the bone-white Manor loomed into view. People walked the grounds, all of them looking about as if searching for something.

Ollie Hamilton. His butler. Some two dozen townspeople. Even Miss Devonshire and Miss Grey, for heaven's sake. What the dickens was going on? The giant caught sight of her at the same time as Sully, the barman from the Shark's Tooth. Only the latter, however, jogged up to greet her.

"Miss Stanton!" he shouted. A few heads turned to stare. "We thought you'd been abducted!"

Why the bloody hell would she have been—ah. Yes. Her gaze met the giant's, and she allowed her eyes to smile. Thought he'd locked her in her bedchamber, didn't he. What a surprise he must've gotten this morning, to find her not inside. She would've feared his retribution, were it not for the arrival of the Bow Street Runners and her impending escape from Bournemouth altogether.

Right on cue, the first of the carriages rattled around the corner and into view. Make that the only carriage. Nor did it belong to the Runners. Susan gaped. The crest on the side belonged to . . .

Her parents.

After a moment's shock, she sprinted past the still-babbling-incoherently barman and cut off the incoming carriage at the pass. What incredibly terrible timing. If she managed to talk them into letting her return, she'd save her own skin—but no one would be here to champion Lady Emeline. Her cousin's evil husband and the worthless magistrate would escape scot-free, along with the rest of the pirates.

She let out a mirthless laugh at the irony. Last week, she'd have sold her soul to the devil for an opportunity to convince her parents to allow her back home. Now that they'd arrived—and she was able to speak to them directly—it was no longer what she wished.

Well, not *yet*. She had a few other things to take care of first.

The driver leaped from the carriage. He was not one she recognized, but this was scarce surprising. Despite the money paid to their servants, her parents' personalities were not conducive to instilling long-term commitment in their employees.

She waited for him to open the carriage door and hand her mother down.

He did not.

"Aren't you going to hand them out?" she asked, once it became clear he was not going to do so without a nudge.

"Hand who out?" he asked in confusion, then had the effrontery to wrinkle his nose at her as if she were the veriest peasant and he a member of Parliament.

She'd forgotten she wasn't exactly looking her finest.

"Lord and Lady Stanton," she bit out icily, gesturing at the closed door. "They're in there, are they not?"

The driver looked down at her. "Indeed, they are not. But they have sent for their daughter. She is to return to Stanton House immediately. Would you be so kind as to relay the message to Miss Stanton?"

Susan stared in disbelief.

Not only did the new driver not recognize her for who she was (although, truth be told, she doubted she'd recognize herself if she caught sight of her reflection in a looking glass) but her parents had obviously received her last missive and *still* didn't feel compelled to check on their daughter firsthand. How utterly like them.

"Well?" the driver prompted.

"Just a moment," she muttered.

She had some thinking to do, and she obviously had to do it quickly. If she sent him away empty-handed, she well knew her parents would never again pay heed to a request to return. Or welcome her home if she arrived on her own. Susan certainly had no wish to be exiled in Bournemouth for the rest of her life. Yet her conscience wouldn't let her abandon her cousin, just to appease her own comfort.

The driver coughed. "Miss?"

"Just a *moment.*"

Think, think, think. She'd sent her plea to her parents a few hours after she'd sent her emergency missive to the Bow Street Runners' headquarters. The Runners had taken her—and Dead Mr. Bothwick—seriously enough to send one investigator, who had never returned or reported back. Which meant they would take her follow-up letter doubly serious. And would be arriving at any moment.

"If you don't know who she is," the driver began, "allow me to find someone who—"

"I know her personally," Susan interrupted, a plan taking form at last. "But she won't be ready until at least nightfall. Do you give your word to remain until then?"

He gazed at her haughtily. "I gave my master my word that I wouldn't wait a moment past twilight. He gave me leave to tell her so."

Susan forced a brittle smile and glanced up at the cloud-covered sky. Noon, at the earliest. She had a maximum of eight hours to find the strongbox and pray the Runners arrived. If not, her choices would be severely limited. Leaving with the driver risked her cousin's life (and ensured the freedom of the pirates) even if Susan's first stop in Town was to the Runners' front door. Letting the driver go home without her, on the other glove, risked no one coming back for her at all. *Ever.*

"She'll be here," Susan promised. "No matter what."

When the horses continued past without stopping, Evan realized they must not belong to the Runners after all. Relief coursed through his veins. Briefly. Then a sense of foreboding returned. Just because carriage wheels hadn't rolled onto his property this time didn't mean they would not do so soon.

He strode out to his carriages. Having both a phaeton and a coach might seem a bit excessive in a town where bare feet often passed as an acceptable mode of transportation, but the phaeton was an oversize frippery left over from his Town days, and the coach was stuffed to the gills with his most cherished worldly belongings.

But now . . . The truth was, for perhaps the first time in Evan's life, he didn't long for escape, whether literal or figurative. He didn't want to adventure-seek as a ruthless pirate sailing the high seas in search of treasure and pleasure. He just wanted to be Evan Bothwick.

So long as he had Susan Stanton.

Which was why he was standing uncertainly outside of his empty house, staring at his still-waiting horses, and trying to decide what the devil he was going to do.

He'd asked her to go with him. She'd said no. And he couldn't blame her. Asking her to give up the life she wanted just because he'd made a muck of his was hardly fair.

What if he stayed here? Bah, nonsensical. Neither of them held any love for this town. The constant trepidation would cast a dark cloud over their potential happiness. Could he return to London? His fingers twitched. The very thought of that falsely gay town gave Evan hives. Besides, rumors of having a former smuggler for a husband would not be conducive to regaining the life Susan wished to live.

Husband. That was the real point, wasn't it? One of the words he wouldn't let himself think in the privacy and secrecy of his own mind, much less escape his lips when he'd asked her to give up everything to be with him. But those were the stakes.

Marriage. Commitment. Forever. The biggest risk of all.

He glared at his pawing horses. The groomsman he most often employed as a driver cast inquisitive glances toward his master but asked no questions, despite having had both carriages and horses at the ready for several hours.

Evan swore under his breath. He couldn't stay. And he couldn't go. Rather than his usual circumstance of being overwhelmed by possibilities for adventure, he found himself mired in a horrible limbo between two undesirable choices. Stay, and face the law. Leave, and lose Susan.

Branches cracked from the footpath up ahead. The woman of his dreams burst from the trees and blinked in shocked pleasure at his stables as if she hadn't expected them to still be there. She turned a little more, caught sight of him watching her, and starting running toward him. She looked deadly focused.

He didn't *see* a knife in her hands. Although one never knew.

What he preferred to see on her hand was a wedding band, marking her as his. But he couldn't ask her yet. Not so close on the heels of his previous failed proposition. She wouldn't see that anything of significance had changed. And really, had it? *He* felt different, inside. As though he'd reached a turning point in his life—or was, at least, attempting to. But he would have to prove himself before she would believe such a thing.

"I need the box," she panted by way of greeting. "I'm out of time."

If she was out of time, so was he.

"The carriage?" he asked.

"My parents. Well, not my *parents*." A self-deprecating smile flashed at her lips. "Father would never do anything so vulgar as step outside London with the Season under way, and Mother swore off travel altogether after our last misadventure. I had hoped—ah, but that doesn't signify. The point is, the arrival of their carriage means the help I requested cannot be far behind. If my parents heeded my words enough to send for me, they undoubtedly also put their not insignificant influence toward an exhaustive investigation."

She nudged up her spectacles with a dirt-stained knuckle. "I expect nothing short of Town judiciaries and full militia. Very soon."

She glanced over her shoulder, as if by *soon* what she really meant was *now.*

"The smuggling crew isn't likely to still be here," Evan said. "This weekend's mission has been canceled, and I have no idea where any of them go when they're not aboard ship."

"To be honest, I'm not overly concerned about your pirate friends, largely because I enjoy French fashion as much as any young lady." She paused to reflect, then added, "And apparently French brandy." Her shoulders straightened. "But there are bigger crimes being committed than those against the Sovereign, and I cannot stand back and let the perpetrators of true evil live free."

He did not pretend to misunderstand. "Lady Emeline?"

She nodded. "There are three men who have conspired against her and her whole family. To an inhuman level. They deserve nothing less than their heads on a gibbet. If I must risk myself for the chance to save an innocent like her, then so be it. If you would not do the same . . ." The breath she drew in was shaky, but her blue gaze never wavered from his. "Then you are not the man I hoped—*believed*—you to be."

Evan looked into her eyes for a long moment without responding.

An excellent point. What kind of man *was* he? A bacchanal adventure-seeker and wastrel, who cared naught for others, who took idle entertainment wherever it could be found, and left for greener pastures at the first sign of clouds?

No. That was the man he *had* been. That was why she had refused him. The old Evan was not worthy of anyone's love. His only thought had been for himself. If the new Evan, the man he *could* be, the man he believed he'd become, was no longer the self-centered bastard of before—this was the time to prove it.

"I need the evidence," she said softly.

He shoved a hand through his hair. "There's no getting that box open."

"Nothing is indestructible." She arched a brow as she tossed his words back to him.

Evan snorted. He'd better be right about that.

He turned toward the stables. He needed to see—and, perhaps, filter—whatever proof the strongbox contained before he found himself up Newman's lift alongside Ollie and the rest. But he would do his part to help Lady Emeline. He had to. Because Susan was right—some men deserved to die for their crimes.

With her at his heels, he plucked a shovel from the stable wall and cut straight to the strongbox. Well, almost straight. It was a damn good hiding spot. Even knowing the location, it still took a couple tries before he finally cleared the dirt from atop the locking mechanism.

He lifted the heavy jewelry box from the chasm and placed it gently on solid ground. He turned it on its side so that the crease between lid and receptacle faced skyward. He grabbed the shovel like a spear and drove the blade into the box with all his might. Jewels and gold filigree sprayed across the muck-covered dirt.

Evan very nearly took out his shoulder.

"Nothing is indestructible," Susan called out from behind him, with a bit less conviction than she'd had just a few moments before.

He smiled grimly and let the box have it one more time.

As the shovel blade hit the strongbox, more jewels and tiny gold roses went flying. Evan's spine jumped as though it were about to do the same. Yet he couldn't give up. He slammed the blade into the box again and again, destroying its beautiful exterior until only the iron core remained. He went for his pick, his ax, his hammers, and kept trying.

Nothing worked. Perhaps the damn thing *was* indestructible.

Which would be splendid insofar as the safety of his neck, but a terrible blow for Lady Emeline. Damn it. Even if he handed the box over as-is to the first lawman to appear, that man would be equally incapable of opening it on the spot. Perhaps back in London, there were better tools, savvier locksmiths. But by that time, it would be too late.

He turned to Susan, planning to apologize, to swear he'd tried his best. But she was on all fours on the dirty ground, picking up handfuls of jewels and broken filigree with a shocked expression on her face. Evan frowned. She could not possibly be concerned about the loss of antique craftsmanship at a time like this.

"It appears," he said tentatively, "I may have damaged Ollie's box."

Susan's head jerked up. Instead of anger or censure, her face was alive with hope and laughter. Between her thumb and forefinger, she held up an intricate whorl of sparkles and gold, no less beautiful for being broken.

"It's not his jewelry box." She pulled herself to her feet, one fist closed around the scrap of bejeweled gold and the other hand splayed against her chest. "It belonged to Lady Beaune."

Evan blinked at her in confusion. "How do you know? And why would the original owner make a difference?"

"Because I now believe," she said, pulling at a thin chain about her throat, "I've had the key all along."

Chapter 26

Susan tugged Lady Beaune's crucifix free from her bodice and compared the artistry to the shard from the strongbox. The same fine-spun gold, the same tiny swirls, the same choice in jewels. If only she *had* found the box before the others! Upon studying its workmanship, she might've made the connection between the ornate crucifix at her neck and the erstwhile splendor of the intricate jewelry box. Now all that remained intact was the gold-encrusted cross. It was a shame to ruin such artistic genius, but there was no other choice. She tried to carefully lift the crucifix up over her head, but jerked it free when the chain caught in her hair.

They would finally know the truth.

Thus resolved, she held the talisman out toward Evan. "Destroy it."

"Destroy a *crucifix?*" He recoiled, staring at her as if she'd gone mad.

"Feel it yourself, and tell me if it's an ordinary crucifix." She forced the heavy charm into his palm, noting his surprise as he registered the unexpected weight. "It's got an iron core, doesn't it?"

He answered by placing it atop the now-flat iron lid of the strongbox and picking up the closest hammer. He hesitated again, but only briefly this time, then brought the hammer down onto the center of the crucifix.

As with the strongbox, bits of delicate gold and precious stones splintered everywhere. Also like the strongbox, a dull iron core peeked through. He gazed up at her, eyes shining. Then he set back to work with the hammer until all that remained was an ordinary metal key, once hidden beneath the baroque beauty.

Susan glanced around the otherwise empty clearing behind the stables, unable to believe Timothy was going to miss this crucial moment. Then she remembered she hadn't seen Lady Beaune since the night she'd found the key. Timothy had probably gone on, too. She and Evan were on their own.

He picked up the key and held it out to her.

She shook her head. "You do it."

She owed him that much, at least. He had just as much at stake, if not more. Although she did believe him a good man at heart and knew his outrage over cousin Emeline was very real, part of Susan couldn't deny the knowledge that Evan was making many of his current decisions for her.

He loved her.

She'd stopped him from saying so because she'd thought it a falsehood, a trite line an accomplished rake delivered to manipulate the emotions of his target. But that wasn't true. He was on his knees in dirt and muck, unlocking a box that would seal the fate of several men who deserved to hang for what they'd done. And quite possibly consigning himself to the same gruesome end.

He did this willingly. For Lady Emeline. For himself. And for Susan.

She dropped to her knees and pressed a quick kiss to his cheek, shamed by the fleeting traitorous thought that perhaps she should have run away with him when he'd first asked. But she'd been right—he was a better man than that. And she was a better woman. Had *become* a better woman, sometime over the course of the past few weeks. Together, they would get through this. Somehow. And then she'd gladly go with him to the very ends of the earth.

Evan twisted the key in the lock. It made several clicks as it triggered a gear mechanism inside, then came to a stop. He removed the key, tossing it onto hay and dirt. He reached for her hand.

She twined her fingers with his. He lifted the lid with his free hand. They both stared at what was inside.

Parchment. How would they convict anyone of anything with *parchment?*

Spectacular.

"The missing pages." Evan reached inside and began to unfold one of the sheets. "Looks like all of them."

Susan flipped through the folded stack. "Missing pages of what?"

"The ship's logbooks. Cross-referencing these details with any of our schedules is probably enough to find us all guilty." He sat back on his heels. "The log doesn't list individual hands by name, of course, but the captain keeps records of each journey, where we dropped anchor and when, weather conditions, as well as who we—"

"What?"

"Not 'we,'" he said with wonder, snatching up sheet after sheet and scanning the contents. "That's what Timothy was trying to tell me. He stole the listings that *don't* correspond to voyages I went on. These diary pages link everyone to the ship's itineraries but me."

"*Almost* everyone," Susan said bitterly. "I'd wager there's nothing in there about Gordon Forrester."

In her opinion, that man deserved to be hanged twice.

Evan stared at her blankly. "Forrester?"

She arched a disgusted brow. "You know, the evil, lying, manipulative cad who's been strongarming innocent people into selling your smuggled goods while he sits back, looks pious, and collects a tidy profit?"

His mouth fell open. "*Forrester?*"

She nudged up her spectacles. "You didn't know?"

He shook his head, still speechless.

"Well, there you go. I told you there'd be nothing in there about him. I hate that he's going to walk free."

"Nothing about him by *name,*" Evan corrected, and placed a sheet of parchment on her lap.

This page was different from the rest. It had clearly come from loose-leaf, as opposed to having been ripped from a bound book. Unlike the barely decipherable scribbles slanting across the captain's log, this sheet had been outlined with carefully delineated rows and columns in neat boxes.

The top read simply, "Unknown Intermediary."

The first column was a list of dates the ship had docked in Bournemouth. The second column was a list of the booty they'd brought ashore. The third was the payment extorted by the local contact in exchange for his silence and protection from the law.

"Charts and figures." The corner of Evan's mouth quirked as he shook his head. "My brother is a piece of work."

Susan grinned at him. "I'd wager an examination of these dates against when our friendly magistrate strolled into town would make for a shocking comparison. And perhaps the owners of a certain dress shop would be more than willing to provide corroboration, in exchange for impunity."

"Here." Evan pointed at the bottom entry. "Look at the last row. Only the date is filled in. That's the night Timothy went on his secret mission."

She stared at the otherwise empty row. Evan was right. "I guess Forrester discovered Timothy's duplicity before Timothy had a chance to reveal Forrester's."

"And the self-righteous cretin murdered my brother on the spot. Red, too." Evan rose to his feet, his hands going straight to the pair of pistols tucked in his waistband. "Now he'll pay."

A distant thunder coalesced into the distinct sound of

incoming hoofbeats. More horses. Lots of them. Coming quickly.

This wasn't a single carriage. This was the army she'd been hoping for.

"Put your pistols away." She repacked the strongbox and pocketed the key. "We ought to let the law take it from here."

He was already racing for the trees, weapons in hand.

Susan tore after him.

Evan had only had a moment's head start, but keeping up with his breakneck pace was next to impossible whilst clutching a heavy iron box to her chest. Her lungs would explode at any moment. When she flew from the trail to the rock garden, the townsfolk loitering about Moonseed Manor were now crowded amongst the graves with their gazes riveted on the back door.

It was off its hinges. Unsurprising. Given the cockeyed appearance of Timothy's house after his death, Susan now suspected that the man she loved had a propensity for using any means but a door handle when entering a room in a rage.

Evan had both giant and scarecrow backed up against the wall, just inside the battered doorjamb. He had a pistol aimed at each man's stomach. Susan approached carefully.

"Where is he?" he demanded. "That toad has to be around here somewhere."

Both scarecrow and giant glared at him without responding.

The crowd was equally silent, although whether they were afraid any intervention on their part would spur the cornered men into action or cease the spectacle altogether was anyone's guess.

Susan rested the battered strongbox on her hip and listened for horse hooves. Faint, but increasing. She doubted the townsfolk had registered the significance yet. The Runners were still at least ten minutes away. Which could be good or bad, depending on one's viewpoint. She shifted the box to the other hip and made her decision.

"Hold them there," she called out, and marched through the crowded grave garden. People fell aside to let her pass. When she reached Evan, she flashed him a smile to let him know they were in this together, then turned her gaze back toward the slash-faced scarecrow.

"Give me the key."

He glanced down at the iron box on her hip, but didn't seem to recognize it for what it was. His tiny black eyes smirked at her.

"Not my box," he rasped.

"Not that lock," she returned, wishing she had a pistol to shove in his stick-thin belly, too. "I want the key to release my cousin's shackles."

The scarecrow's black eyes glimmered. "Tell your lover to put his pistols down and I'll think about it."

Susan turned to Evan with a sigh. "Shoot him."

Keys jangled, seeming to appear in the scarecrow's jaundiced palm from thin air. She plucked them from his fingers and made her way down the cellar steps.

"Follow," Evan barked at his hostages.

Twin clicks of pistols ratcheting to the ready echoed in the still chamber, and then three pairs of boots slapped against the stone steps behind her. It was going to be a full house.

When she reached the bottom of the stairwell, she set the strongbox in the dirt. She went straight to her cousin and unlocked the iron shackle fettered around her thin ankle.

Emeline's terrified gaze went from Susan to her former captors to the manacle lying open and harmless at her bare feet. She touched Susan's cheek with cold, trembling fingers, then put her face in her hands and cried.

"You're free," Susan swore, enveloping her shaking cousin in a strong hug. "I promise you. Nobody's going to hurt you again." She hugged Lady Emeline tighter, stroking her hair as she sobbed heartwrenchingly silent cries on

Susan's shoulder. "You can live with me, and be safe. I swear on my life."

It was all Susan could do to keep her own tears from doing more than stinging at the corners of her burning eyes. But she had to be strong, for cousin Emeline's sake. She couldn't let her believe for the tiniest second there was any risk of being chained again, all by herself, in the dark.

"You'll never be alone again," Susan promised her fiercely. "You have me now. Forever."

Lady Emeline kissed Susan's cheek. She leaned back long enough to scrub at her dirt- and tear-streaked face, then linked arms with Susan and stared up at her with an expression Susan had never seen on her cousin's tormented face.

Hope . . . and trust.

Susan smiled and squeezed her arm. Cousin Emeline *believed* in her. This time, she would be worthy of it.

"I've got to find Forrester," Evan said, without averting his gaze from his two captives. "Before the knave gets away clean."

"Go find him, then," came the scarecrow's scratchy taunt. "We'll wait for ye."

Evan growled and shoved the barrels of his pistols deeper into their stomachs.

The men began to argue.

Susan lifted the open manacle from the floor and caught cousin Emeline's eye. Both scarecrow and giant were too focused on the pistols aimed at their midsections to pay attention to two mere women kneeling upon the dirt floor. Susan handed the fetter to Emeline, who nodded in understanding. Susan reached out, caught hold of another manacle, fumbled with the keys. At last, it fell open.

They edged closer to the men's feet, Susan toward the giant, and Emeline toward the scarecrow. The chains just barely allowed the distance—but it would be enough.

"Now!" Susan cried, and snapped the iron band closed around the giant's thick ankle.

Emeline did the same to the scarecrow, but her wasted limbs couldn't move backward fast enough to avoid the scarecrow kicking her directly in the face with his manacled boot. Evan smashed his fist in the scarecrow's belly, and followed that impact with an elbow to his nose.

Susan scrambled to Emeline's side, terrified what she'd find when she lifted her cousin's bowed head.

Despite a rapidly forming bruise across her cheek, Emeline was grinning in victory. She gave Susan a joyous hug.

Horse hooves clomped overhead. Susan's army had arrived at last.

She helped Emeline to her feet, then tugged at Evan's sleeve. "Leave them. Let's tell the Runners about Forrester."

Evan hesitated as if the thought of putting a bullet in their ribs was too delicious to ignore (and, truly, Susan was of the same opinion) but turned and shoved his pistols back into his waistband.

"Get the strongbox," he said, swinging Emeline into his arms. "I'll carry your cousin outside. She's been down here long enough."

Susan grabbed the iron box and raced up the stairs after them. The number of people outside had doubled. The Bow Street Runners had in fact sent a militia to Bournemouth. Susan was convinced every inhabitant was also present in the garden.

Including Gordon Forrester.

"What's that, now?" he was saying with a little laugh. "Pirates? Not in a quiet beach town like this." The magistrate flashed the newcomers his hallmark dimples.

They were patently unimpressed.

One raised his voice. "For the last time, where is Miss Stanton?"

"Here!" Susan stepped forward, then turned and held out a hand for cousin Emeline. When Evan set her gingerly to the ground, she immediately latched on to Susan's arm. Susan smiled and squeezed back.

The horror was finally over.

At least, that's what she thought until the now-familiar click of a pistol sounded from just behind her shoulder. *Evan.* With the barrel aimed straight at the magistrate's cherubic face.

"You lying, traitorous, murdering—"

"Why, it's Evan Bothwick," Forrester interrupted smoothly, as if this were just another example of Evan's typical erratic behavior. The magistrate gave a what-can-you-do shrug at the lawmen. "If you want to know about smuggling, I suppose there's the one to ask."

When Evan's pistol didn't waver, Susan realized he really meant to shoot Forrester right here and now—and didn't give a damn if he consigned himself to prison in the process.

"Why not ask you instead?" she said loudly, striding toward the militia with the iron box on one hip and Lady Emeline still strong at her side. "You're the one who's been facilitating the transport of goods from the ship to the local merchants."

Only a slight widening of the magistrate's eyes gave away his fear. "Those are some strong accusations, Miss Stanton. I don't know how High Society does things, but we small-town commoners don't like to cast aspersions on a man without proof."

Susan smiled. "Then you'll be happy to know I brought plenty with me."

Forrester's dimples disappeared. With trepidation lining his features, he no longer looked angelic and self-assured. He looked guilty. And scared.

Good.

Susan handed both box and key to the closest constable, then walked back toward Evan.

His pistol was still trained at the magistrate's head.

She crossed to him quickly and laid a worried palm on the hard muscle of his arm. He didn't move.

"Put the pistol down," she whispered urgently. "It's over. Let the militia take him away."

"I—I can't," he answered, his voice bleak. "He killed my brother."

Susan swallowed her compassion. "I know."

"He killed *Timothy*."

"I know. But as horrible as that is, it can't be reversed. Forrester's going to hang." She stared up at Evan beseechingly, but the dark light of vengeance was in his eyes. "You found the evidence that's going to convict him. What else can we do?"

"Kill him," Evan spat without hesitation, tightening his grip on the pistols. "He murdered my *brother*. A pirate would take revenge."

"Yes," she agreed softly. "A pirate would."

Chapter 27

It wasn't until the last of the militia's coaches rolled away that Susan realized her parents' carriage was missing. She had no fob, but the sun's cloudy presence indicated it was by no means nightfall. Yet the driver had left without so much as a fare-thee-well!

She scanned the remaining crowd. Ollie Hamilton and his erstwhile butler could have nothing to do with the carriage's untimely departure. They'd been marched from the cellar to the back of a coach, which the Runner had promised was headed straight to the prison where the men would await trial.

Dinah Devonshire and Harriet Grey were the next most likely culprits. Miss Devonshire, however, was nowhere to be seen, and Miss Grey was even now plodding down the path toward the beach, as if the call of hems and stitches was far more fascinating than smugglers being arrested at Moonseed Manor.

A warm arm drew Susan into a possessive embrace. With her cheek pressed against Evan's chest, Susan squeezed him tight. For the first time, her muscles began to let go of the tension they'd carried since her arrival.

He kissed the top of her head. "What are you looking for?"

"You," she answered automatically, and smiled up at him.

He hugged her close, then placed her hand in the crook of

his elbow so they wouldn't make such a public spectacle of themselves. Susan was tempted to throw herself back in his arms and overwhelm him with kisses, the remains of her tattered reputation be damned.

"That's all?" he asked, his eyes toward the sea.

"And my parents' carriage," she admitted. "I can scarce believe the driver left without me."

Evan's gaze snapped to hers and he pulled her to him fiercely. "I would *not* have let you go."

"No?" she asked breathlessly. The idea of launching herself at him and attacking him with kisses was sounding better and better. Before she could do so, however, he loosened her fingers from his elbow. He dropped to his knees in the rocky sand and took her hands in his.

"I love you," he said, and the stark emotion in his face nearly brought Susan to her knees as well. "I cannot imagine life without you. I swear I will do everything in my power to make you the happiest woman alive, from this moment until the end of our days, if only you will agree to marry me." His strong voice cracked, and his grip on her hands tightened. "Please."

Susan pulled him to his feet. *Now* was the moment for the scandalous kissing.

"I've been waiting for you to ask," she told him in the brief seconds when her mouth was not open against his. She twined her fingers in his hair and pressed herself to him. "I love you, Evan. You've already made me the happiest woman alive."

His lips trailed kisses along her jawline to the lobe of her ear. "That's a yes?"

"Absolutely."

He swung her into his arms and covered her with kisses. Whether they were the object of scandalous attention, she had no idea. In that moment, her world consisted of only Evan and her.

Which was as it should be.

Epilogue

He went to the stupid assembly after all.

It had been one of the many conditions set down by his wife after their wedding breakfast. Along with providing for Miss Grey and ordering beautiful headstones for Lady Beaune, the Runner, Red, and Timothy. His condition was for every one of them to receive a proper funeral ceremony, whether their bodies had been recovered or not. She'd stared at him as if that much was obvious, kissed him, and said, "Of course."

Wife. Just thinking the word still made Evan's head spin. As did the fact he'd get to keep her forever.

Bath, Susan had agreed, was a compromise for them both. She would give up London—where, apparently, things hadn't been at their finest anyhow—so long as he gave up Bournemouth. Scarcely a hardship. He'd move to the farthest corner of the globe so long as it meant he could be with her.

Which was why he was piling bland sandwiches onto a tiny plate and juggling two cups of the worst punch he'd ever tasted in his life. Laughing at himself, he made his way back to her side.

She accepted both the punch and the sandwiches with a grateful smile, and sipped a fair bit of the insipid liquid without spitting any of it onto the dance floor. How she could look as though she actually enjoyed the stuff, Evan had no idea. He had half a mind to upend a bottle of brandy into the mix, just to give it some flavor.

He restrained himself. His wife would probably frown upon such behavior. And he was trying to be a good husband. Well, depending on how you defined "good." He'd danced two waltzes with her, and even managed to sneak her into the gardens during the boring country sets. He should probably let her know bits of leaf still clung to the back of her chignon . . . but he didn't. He got a wicked sense of satisfaction from knowing how it got there.

He was damn glad he hadn't shot Forrester after all. Going to Canterbury to fetch a special license had worked out much better than going to Newgate for murdering a magistrate in front of witnesses. Evan still hadn't decided if he wanted to be present when Forrester hung, but he kept an eye on the papers for news. His wife might wish to attend Ollie's drop with her companion.

Even now, Susan and Lady Emeline were engaged in one of their odd conversations, wherein Susan did all of the talking and Lady Emeline mostly just nodded. It seemed to suit them both just fine.

Apparently able to feel the heat of his gaze on her neck, his wife turned and raised her brows at him from over the tops of her spectacles. Then she winked. Evan got the distinct feeling she well knew there were leaf bits in her hair and was keeping them there on purpose, just so he wouldn't be able to stop thinking about her. As if he ever could. She was perfect.

Susan whispered something to Lady Emeline and both women toasted him with their matching cups of pink water. He toasted back with a flask from his waistcoat pocket. Susan affected a scandalized expression, but his partner in crime laughed her infectious silent laugh and held her pink punch out for another dollop of French brandy. Susan held out her cup, as well. When he took her cup, she plucked the flask from his hands and downed a healthy swallow. Was it any wonder he was absolutely mad for this woman?

Evan pulled her into his embrace and swung her in a circle. Still smiling, he covered her mouth with his. She nipped at his lower lip, then pulled him closer. Her kisses tasted like warm brandy.

She would've made an excellent pirate.

GREAT BOOKS, GREAT SAVINGS!

When You Visit Our Website:
www.kensingtonbooks.com
You Can Save Money Off The Retail Price
Of Any Book You Purchase!

- **All Your Favorite Kensington Authors**
- **New Releases & Timeless Classics**
- **Overnight Shipping Available**
- **eBooks Available For Many Titles**
- **All Major Credit Cards Accepted**

Visit Us Today To Start Saving!
www.kensingtonbooks.com

All Orders Are Subject To Availability.
Shipping and Handling Charges Apply.
Offers and Prices Subject To Change Without Notice.

Books by Bestselling Author
Fern Michaels

___The Jury	0-8217-7878-1	$6.99US/$9.99CAN
___Sweet Revenge	0-8217-7879-X	$6.99US/$9.99CAN
___Lethal Justice	0-8217-7880-3	$6.99US/$9.99CAN
___Free Fall	0-8217-7881-1	$6.99US/$9.99CAN
___Fool Me Once	0-8217-8071-9	$7.99US/$10.99CAN
___Vegas Rich	0-8217-8112-X	$7.99US/$10.99CAN
___Hide and Seek	1-4201-0184-6	$6.99US/$9.99CAN
___Hokus Pokus	1-4201-0185-4	$6.99US/$9.99CAN
___Fast Track	1-4201-0186-2	$6.99US/$9.99CAN
___Collateral Damage	1-4201-0187-0	$6.99US/$9.99CAN
___Final Justice	1-4201-0188-9	$6.99US/$9.99CAN
___Up Close and Personal	0-8217-7956-7	$7.99US/$9.99CAN
___Under the Radar	1-4201-0683-X	$6.99US/$9.99CAN
___Razor Sharp	1-4201-0684-8	$7.99US/$10.99CAN
___Yesterday	1-4201-1494-8	$5.99US/$6.99CAN
___Vanishing Act	1-4201-0685-6	$7.99US/$10.99CAN
___Sara's Song	1-4201-1493-X	$5.99US/$6.99CAN
___Deadly Deals	1-4201-0686-4	$7.99US/$10.99CAN
___Game Over	1-4201-0687-2	$7.99US/$10.99CAN
___Sins of Omission	1-4201-1153-1	$7.99US/$10.99CAN
___Sins of the Flesh	1-4201-1154-X	$7.99US/$10.99CAN
___Cross Roads	1-4201-1192-2	$7.99US/$10.99CAN

Available Wherever Books Are Sold!
Check out our website at **www.kensingtonbooks.com**